THESE
GOOD
HANDS

THESE
GOOD
HANDS

Carol Bruneau

Canada Council for the Arts   Conseil des Arts du Canada    ONTARIO ARTS COUNCIL CONSEIL DES ARTS DE L'ONTARIO an Ontario government agency un organisme du gouvernement de l'Ontario

 Canadian Heritage   Patrimoine canadien    Canadä

The publisher gratefully acknowledges the support of the Canada Council for the Arts and the Ontario Arts Council for its publishing program. We acknowledge the financial support of the Government of Canada through the Canada Book Fund (CBF) for our publishing activities, and the Government of Ontario through the Ontario Media Development Corporation, an agency of the Ontario Ministry of Culture, and the Ontario Book Publishing Tax Credit Program.

LIBRARY AND ARCHIVES CANADA CATALOGUING IN PUBLICATION

Bruneau, Carol, 1956–, author
These good hands / Carol Bruneau.

Issued in print and electronic formats.
ISBN 978-1-77086-427-6 (pbk.).— ISBN 978-1-77086-426-9 (html)

1. Claudel, Camille, 1864–1943—Fiction. I. Title.

PS8553.R854T44 2015   C813'.54   C2014-907691-6
C2014-907692-4

This is a work of fiction. Though inspired by historical events and individuals, the story and its characters are products of the author's imagination. Their resemblance to persons dead is figurative, as is the novel's institutional setting. Any resemblance to persons living is coincidental.

Cover photo and design: angeljohnguerra.com
Interior text design: Tannice Goddard, Soul Oasis Networking
Printer: Friesens

Printed and bound in Canada.

 MIX Paper from responsible sources FSC www.fsc.org FSC® C016245

The interior of this book is printed on 100% post-consumer waste recycled paper.

CORMORANT BOOKS INC.
10 ST. MARY STREET, SUITE 615, TORONTO, ONTARIO, M4Y 1P9
www.cormorantbooks.com

For Joan, Helen, Sara and Elizabeth

Only in our doing can we grasp you.
Only with our hands can we illumine you.
The mind is but a visitor:
it thinks us out of our world.

— RAINER MARIA RILKE

I

I SOLEMNLY PLEDGE MYSELF ...

MONTFAVET, VAUCLUSE
21 AUGUST 1943
21H00

No journey's end could've looked better, I must say. Rattletrap nerves — mine and those of other travellers, especially those wearing yellow stars — all the way here from Lyon. Might as well have been a freight train, cars no better than boxcars really, jam-packed with hordes heading south — hordes. Grumbling oldsters, crying babies, the gamut. And just what I needed: a couple and theirs sharing my compartment, the poor little thing screeching its head off each time we stopped and soldiers boarded to check us all over.

It felt like we were a herd of cows being sent to market, even those of us with everything in order — which my papers were, thank you, thanks to the nuns. So sweet in their gloomy way they'd been, huddled on the platform seeing me off, the sisters and their chilly kisses. The steamy swoosh of trains tugging at their wimples. Not to say I wasn't grateful, especially for their lunch — stale baguette, some questionable *jambon* — to tide me over. Sustenance for my "mission," as they called it, this move after nursing under their watch, their guise, ten years more or less inside their "cocoon." My training under them completed so long ago it mightn't have even happened: making beds, washing linens, peeling potatoes; a month at the san, another at the fever, another at the mental. By some fluke I'd been spared any longer than that in maternity, obstetrics just not for me. Getting capped was like getting crowned, though our coronation hardly eases the workload!

The child's wailing gave me pause at each bump and sway. *Spare me*, I thought more than once, fending off nerves that had little to do with the purpose at hand: professional development, this new phase. After the nuns' prodding — "Time to flex your wings, broaden your horizons, Mademoiselle Solange" — I was more than ready for it, out of passion for the profession, of course, not personal gain or advancement.

Amen to that as the train pulled in, the station a blink-and-you'll-miss-it siding in the woods. The evening was wet and dark by the time we disembarked — a partial relief if not a full one. Shouldering guns, two Nazi officers herded people onto a waiting train, an express bound for Marseille. Herded, I say. A woman and her idiot daughter, an old couple, and a fellow carrying what looked to be a newborn. After a scuffle and a get-a-move-on, they were loaded lickety-split. I watched the cars lurch away, and soon enough was alone — the only arrival?

As I hoisted my suitcase, something rustled underfoot: money, a Yankee dollar bill. But when I grabbed and unfolded it, sweet Mother, there it was, printed on the back: *Ce Dollar a Payé La Guerre Juive. L'Argent n'a pas d'odeur ... MAIS LE JUIF EN A UNE.* Talk about mistaking *chocolat* for feces! Worse than finding a severed foot left in the OR drapes, I thought, ripping it up and watching the pieces flutter away.

I decided I was home free, until a *gendarme* demanded my identification, taking his time to scour my credentials, check my photo, and eventually give a nod. France is hardly ours anymore, it seems. I lugged my bag into the station and asked for directions from the stationmaster, who scowled up — "Can't miss the place" — from under a fresh poster of Maréchal Pétain in his bright blue uniform. A bit of colour at least, the place as drab as any in the middle of a war.

The station's light was the only one for miles, it appeared, when I started walking. So much for Provence, lovely Provence. Rain whizzed down as I headed up the road and turned left as instructed. The only shelter to be found was beneath the overpass. A newly painted swastika glowing from its concrete made me think of the nuns — fools for Christ sheltering "Catholic" Jews, devotion the one thing the enemy can't confiscate, I guess. Without devotion the less saintly of us would wither at our first bedpan.

The winding road ahead, the only road in sight, was quite deserted. I hoped it was the way, cursing my suitcase. Along the ditch gurgled a walled stream choked with runoff, a miniature canal — bringing water to farmers, or for the pleasure of children sailing sticks? All I knew of this place and these parts was that absinthe had been invented here, imagine; and the church, the sisters had happily briefed me, was dedicated to Our Lady of *Bon Repos*. Tranquility, rest. A lovely start so far, hair plastered to my head, travelling clothes all but pasted to me, soaked to the skin and chilled to the bone.

Finally, by a tall stone wall the road forked. Could this possibly be it?

Montdevergues, the hospital was called — Mount of Virgins — though there was no mountain in sight, none that could be seen for the wall, and the trees, and the darkness. As good a place as one: white-haired Marguerite, stern and mannish in all her pictures, unlike Florence the sylph walking the wards with her famous lamp, so genteel and pretty, and who, for all of her action, managed to write up a storm. In other words, do as I say, not as I ...

And which would one rather be? Wasp-waisted and tending cholera victims and amputees when not wielding her pen, or the patron saint of epileptics, hysterics and worse, who never ever took a day off? Hmm. Let me see. I'm not in this for the sainthood, merely to do a job and do it well.

Just then, I have to say, the idea of writing anything rankled. Still, finding a pen and jotting down all this blather on the day's adventures calmed me. Not that I'm in the habit of this sort of thing, for goodness' sake. But, it struck me, it strikes me — the seeds that weariness plants in the mind! — such nightly note-taking could serve as a record, a reflection, of professional progress. "A Record of My Path to Martyrdom." God, I hope not. Sincerely. Because right now all I'm aiming and longing for is a decent sleep.

2

ASYLUM FOR LUNATICS
AUGUST? SEPTEMBER? 19–?

LINES ARE WALLS and walls are lines and what are days but boxes of air? Pen and ink, pencil on paper pin down the hours: squiggles separating something from nothing. My life a study of squiggles, lines. Lines on paper equal lines cut in marble? You tell me. Though writing sets you free, they say — my brother says, or used to say. So long since I've heard his voice, I dream it? Its sound and the scratching down of sentences as he wrote and wrote and wrote. His lines straight but mine crooked, crooked as the streets ... the streets of —? Le Marais? Montmartre, because meandering and steep! Unlike this room. Slanting shadows, corners: bars of sunlight thrown across the floor. So much kinder are the curves of a body, a face, a river.

The only comfort, my only comfort, is that he's there, somewhere. Cracks in the clouds whisper it, their blue the colour of my eyes. The colour of the Mediterranean. Darker than sapphires, he would say — *magnifique* leaking from his pen, a word that turns my heart to a *boulette,* cold and hard, with no pockets of air. Could the warmth of hands soften it? Palms shape it, fingers score it, in order to lay every last feeling down?

Better just to write, as I have by the hour, by the year. Letters, letters — so many letters, unanswered. Walls, because of walls. People are walls. Yet I take up my pen. By the hour it pokes and scratches a peephole to see out of. A small one. A one-way view, alas. Though when I speak to you, you listen. *Let us begin with walls,* I tell the paper. Moving a pen much neater than shaping mud, or *merde,* as the case may be.

Yet they come, my jailers, as they always do, to wrench the sword from my hand. *Time to rest,* they say, and bolt the window — as if this prisoner had Rapunzel's hair! The only rescuers the clouds out there tearing themselves apart.

Enough for one day, Mademoiselle. You know the rules. Lights out.

And blue becomes purple, and purple black. More lines tomorrow, if tomorrow must be. Shaped into letters, the bond between paper and ink. More work, always more work, for the one who would not rest, the one who would send you a kiss. For there it is: the task to capture what outruns rocks and clay.

3

... BEFORE GOD AND THE PRESENCE OF
THIS ASSEMBLY ...

MONTDEVERGUES ASYLUM
22 AUGUST 1943
22H15

Somehow, who knows how, I overslept. The dorm was practically empty by the time I woke, famished, twenty minutes before shift. All was quiet on the grounds too, despite what I knew of hospital routine. At least the rain had stopped, giving way to steamy dawn — a dawn rowdy with chirping birds — and Pavilion 10 wasn't all that hard to find.

"It's that way," the one person I encountered pointed out, while asking what day it was.

On a knoll behind the church, a pair of lofty whitewashed buildings backed onto the wall and the treed slope behind it, cypresses barely stirring in the faint breeze. Set apart from its lookalike, Pavilion 10 appeared a bit formidable, though hardly daunting.

Still, after climbing the path and pressing the bell, I was nearly three minutes late.

The nurse who let me in introduced herself as Head, her voice mildly sarcastic as she made allowances for my first shift: "Ah, Mademoiselle Poitier, good of you to come. Let's not waste any time getting acquainted." I'd never been late a day in my life, of course.

The corridor I soon found myself in featured none of the usual ladies' auxiliary efforts to brighten things, no pictures of flowers or fruit. It smelled — not medicinal but stale: notes of excrement and ammonia, to be precise, not unexpected. But, oh, Mother, the noise was unexpected, especially following the stillness outdoors. Cackling laughter, bellowing, wails and sobs — the way hell might sound if one believed in it.

My new Head was a big, soft-looking woman with eyes that looked as tired as the woodwork. Evidently pleased to have me, she soon displayed Monsieur Directeur's good cheer. "Pavilion 10 is all female, even the doctor," she said, rummaging through papers in the nursing station — a desk behind thick glass with a photo of Maréchal Pétain in all his grandfatherly glory beaming above it. "Not a soul here in trousers," she reiterated. "It's a good place to begin your stay, among the easy ones. There are three of us to care for sixty, who are mainly either epileptic or imbecile and quite manageable."

She ran over the schedule. At 06H00, doors unlock. We spongebathe and dress the guests, comb their hair, and examine them for cuts, infections, bite marks, etc. In some cases, we inspect their evacuations. *De rigueur*, more or less. At 06H30, the ones who work in the laundry have to be taken there, my new superior adding — surprise, surprise — that it helps to work quickly. Full baths on Fridays. Every day but Monday, patients have chapel at 07H45, and breakfast at 08H15. The same as what I'd been generally used to in Lyon, except she emphasized the curative air, as if our charges are tubercular.

Then she inspected me, giving my nails, hair and cap the once-over before finally fixing on my apron, which was slightly less than crisp after its night in a suitcase. Ignoring the screams from farther up the hallway, she repeated the need for neatness, but added I'd find the rules somewhat relaxed. *Odd*, I thought, since the place was steely-bright as a gun factory, all hard edges and light — sterile enough, but not even a nun's idea of a spa. "You'll find the basics apply," she promised, in case I'd misunderstood. "Sometimes the work takes different turns. But keen observations count most."

Jingling the thick ring of keys at her waist, she gave me a cursory tour. First stop, she unlocked a utility room, a cubbyhole where a teakettle and a hotplate — for our personal use — shared a shelf with syringes, stacked bedpans, and kidney basins. A decent supply of greyish linens adjoined a cabinet filled with leather cuffs and anklets, and hanging from a rack, like freshly laundered shirts only a little yellowed with use, were straitjackets — *camisoles de force* — dangling buckles and straps. Next to these stood the medicine chest, which had a special key and was stocked, I was shown, with the very best of drugs, Veronal and Aspirin.

More screaming and loud sobbing issued from nearby. "Nothing urgent," my supervisor said, showing me into a dim room filled with Utica cribs, five in all. Fitted with lids of metal and wooden strips, they reminded me of baskets, the type men might take fishing, only a little larger. I'd read about them, of course, though seeing them was something else. "You're familiar with the cot? Invented by one of our own, a Frenchman," Head seemed happy to point out, "before the Yanks laid claim to it."

"Ah, yes, the great Dr. Anabanel," I nodded. The beds resembled instruments used to martyr subjects in the sisters' illustrated biographies of saints. "Of course. The crazy crib."

My superior seemed a little bemused. "The Bedlam bunk. Indeed." So she has some sense of humour, despite the initial curtness. "A saving grace, you'll find, Poitier, for some." She then said that when the crib didn't work, there was always the Wyman's bed strap, an added restraint.

"And failing that," — I was keen to impart my brilliance — "the Freeman-Watts procedure, of course. The new method of leucotomy, going through the eye sockets instead of through the skull. I do wonder about its precision, don't you? Not to question the doctors —"

She picked a speck of dried blood from one of the cribs' lids, lids that swung back on hinges, and raised a brow. "At least with the crib and fetters keeping limbs and torso in place, Nurse, we see how it works."

"Of course — but is it more humane?"

Though I hadn't spoken hastily, she just about took my head off. "What could be inhumane about preventing someone's scratching herself to death? The trick is tightening cuffs sufficiently without causing undue bruising. Though injury is often unavoidable. Novice could use some practice." She fanned herself with one hand, as if the topic made her warm.

Head locked the room behind us as a string of women in civvies shuffled past, escorted by an orderly and a gap-toothed nurse in blue who looked barely old enough to be finished training. The patients, a drooling, nail-biting crew, displayed various and sundry tics and automatisms; their eyes appeared to look right through us. One stood out on account of the bright green blouse she was wearing, a cheery note amidst drabness.

Their mutterings echoed as they slouched off — out of our hair, joked Head Nurse, unlocking a ward. The room was narrow as a railcar and just as bare, with yellowish walls scrubbed to a dull sheen, and not a shred of curtain, the better to not strangle themselves with. There was a solid row of beds along each wall which were hastily made, not unlike the one in my cell, their wrinkled white blankets yanked into place. So much for the sisters' perfect corners. It was airless and stuffy, yet I felt a chill. This ward was designated for the better ones, I was told, *les aliénées* able to work. To think what "better" meant might've made some girls shiver, despite the sun creeping through shuttered windows, everything shellacked in a somewhat unforgiving light.

"The cribs," I asked, as mildly as could be, "is there much need for them?"

"It depends. If shackles and Veronal don't help — care must be taken not to give too much. So some appreciate the crib, Poitier. Those at risk of harming themselves."

—✺—

I WAS LED to the next ward and put in charge of washing and dressing. The little nurse brought hot water, which apparently has to be brought from the Men's Pavilion. A temporary inconvenience due to shortages, I wondered, though my question went unanswered.

"They don't bite — not all of them anyway," Head Nurse joked, hinting that most of our guests are quite docile — an advantage, certainly, though my mettle of a decade's experience flagged ever so slightly when she added, "at least until after breakfast."

Two dozen patients wearing threadbare gowns lolled on their beds, some moaning. One sang at the top of her lungs, *Sur le pont d'Avignon, on y danse, on y danse.* I tried humming along as I started at the first bed, checking the patient over for sores, lice, etc. She made no fuss at having face and hands wiped, pulse taken. If only the rest had been so easy. The next, her hands curled and useless, wailed and turned to the wall. Another tried to lick me.

Have mercy, a voice inside me coaxed, a carry-over from Lyon that clashed somewhat with *Sur le pont d'Avignon, on y danse, tous en rond.*

The songstress I left till last. She clawed at my cap and managed to overturn the basin — a small ordeal given the rigmarole of fetching hot water. But once I got her calmed down enough to bathe, she went soft as putty and even asked to kiss me before launching back in: *Sur le pont d'Avignon ... les filles font comme ci ... les garçons font comme ca ...*

I managed a peek at the watch pinned to my apron bib. 07H40. It was Sister Ursula's parting gift, the days of her supervision suddenly more remote than I could have imagined. Despite the day's promise to be sweltering I felt a bit clammy. So much for looking crisp.

Head Nurse said to hurry so those able and well enough to attend wouldn't miss chapel; as if to hammer this home, some-where a bell tolled. The little nurse — Novice — and two orderlies rounded up the freshly toileted and herded them out. Head wanted their beds straightened but told me not to strip them. What ailed our guests generally wasn't communicable, she said, her gums showing when she smiled. Oh, she had a sense of humour all right. Only badly soiled bedding, and that of patients with unwanted company — *pediculosis corporis,* the lousy — was to be changed.

The instant the task was accomplished, my supervisor thought of something else, someone we'd missed: a "mademoiselle" who was something of a special case. "The poor thing," she said with a snort, her expression impatient. "Almost famous, once. If you can believe it."

I glanced at the crucifix above the doorway. A relic from the nuns? The ward's sole decoration, it was well out of reach of anyone inclined or determined to stab or puncture herself, even a tall person perched on a chair. Since it posed no threat, no one had bothered taking it down.

"You'll find some of them stubborn — they generally are, at first. This one dislikes being bathed." Despite the number of patients earlier dispatched, Head Nurse needed to shout to be heard. "But if she's approached properly, where there's a will there's a way. Like our Maréchal dealing with *les fritz,*" she said, quite seriously.

—ᚷ—

ON THE UPPERMOST floor, we followed another corridor, our footsteps absorbed by the shrieking around us. The light splintered rather than glowed, showing fresh repairs in the plaster.

Head stopped before a closed door and rattled the knob. "Mental's different from general, I'm sure I don't need to tell you. It often requires a different tact. The summer's been hard on this one, and the spring. Do your best." With that she hurried off, hefting her keys to unlock the heavy doors barring the stairwell.

Not a bite to eat since the directeur's croissant, I have to say my throat filled with a sourness. Ignoring the wailing from across the hall, I knocked, then tried the knob. It refused to turn: some mechanical problem? I tried again, no luck. Good heavens, could it be locked? What kind of place allowed a lunatic to bolt herself in? Just a little mortified, I was reduced to peering through the keyhole.

What filled it would've made someone with less experience reel back: an eye, large, unwavering and blue, a November blue, blue as a winter sea. The taste in my mouth went bitter, harder to ignore than the taste of hunger. Perspiration beaded my lip, the feeling in my abdomen not all that different, perhaps, from the first time I'd watched a scalpel split skin — a queasiness that was quickly overcome, though I resisted the urge to bless myself, a hangover certainly from the Hôtel-Dieu.

"Madame? I'm here to bathe you," I was forced to call out, my voice of composure met by a cough, not, mercy me, by cackling.

"Mademoiselle. In your dreams." The voice correcting mine was imperious if frail. "Never satisfied, are you. Go away! If you weren't under that rat-scum's thrall, you'd know I've nothing left to steal!"

I rattled the knob, feeling slightly silly. For someone infirm, the *aliénée's* grip was tenacious. "Mademoiselle?" My tone was full of resolve. "Let me in, please." A nunnish voice inside me, not unlike Sister Ursula's, chided, *Feel the fire of your vocation,*

Solange, the duty to help those who cannot help themselves. Yes, yes, yes. *You have the upper hand,* I reminded myself.

The eye's feeble-minded owner was surely gloating, however, having wangled a private room and exemption from Mass! So much for Principle One, our profession's foundation, about treating the sick equally and disavowing favouritism. Very likely this patient was dangerous, blaming others for what might be her own degenerate, even criminal acts. That pupil with its blue, blue iris blazed steadily through the keyhole.

So much for easy.

"Open up!" I was reduced to ordering, grateful no one was nearby to hear. "Let me introduce myself." A *gendarme* without a stick was what I felt like, pushed to abandon Principles Two and Three, which Sister Ursula so emphatically advocated: *Be gentle, practise humility.* Though I've faced similar resistance — convincing people with kidney stones, burst appendixes, gangrenous feet, and so on, to lie still — this was different. Unlike the sick in body with the will and reason to live, such patients as this require protection from themselves. It boiled down to trust, and routine.

A blessing and a comfort, routine — hadn't I said so to Head not ten minutes earlier? Especially with the war on, the bombings and *rafles,* our own government aiding the Boche. "You don't know who to trust," our supervisor had agreed, perhaps a little too hastily.

Just then, Novice appeared with a steaming basin. "Don't take any guff off anyone. Don't hold your breath, either." She quickly trotted off.

Balancing the basin on one arm, I tried the knob again, succeeding only in sloshing water on tiles in need of buffing. I began to fidget. If the patient didn't open up by the count of ten, I'd call an orderly. "Don't be alarmed, I'm not here to upset you — I won't hurt you, I promise — just a nice little sponge-bath, then I'll take your pulse —"

"You can drink your bathwater," the voice replied. "May the lunatics have pissed in it!"

Foot poised to tap *nine*, I felt my voice rise. "No need to get excited. I'll simply be a second." I looked for a buzzer — there must be a way to call someone. "Please?" I finally begged, to a sobering degree of chagrin.

Only then, rather miraculously, there was a click, of the lock being tripped or a bolt sliding back. Hinges creaking, the door inched inwards by a crack. However, something made me pause and wait. I listened to the patient getting into bed and, straightening my cap, entered.

The room was no larger than mine, its furnishings a straw chair and small table heaped with papers. Sunlight straggled in between the bars, or attempted to. A gnarled little thing wearing a seedy woolen hat and coat with, of all things, a skeleton key pinned to one lapel, was lying atop the covers, stretched out on her back.

As I set down the basin, something brushed my shin. I all but leapt out of my skin — *mon Dieu*, it was a cat! A ginger tabby worming out from under the bed.

The old lady struggled to sit, dangling her feet — swollen, from what I could see of them in their worn-out shoes — over the bedside. Ignoring me, she held out her arms, and the cat leapt into them. The patient kissed it, crooning, "Wise little soul, don't you hate water!" I glimpsed her teeth when she spoke. The state of her dentition was appalling, not that she seemed troubled by it. She studied me suspiciously as she cradled the cat, her piercing blue eyes peering over its head. "You like cats? If not, you had better get out."

I said I needed to check her pulse, among other things.

"Who do you think you are? An angel?" The patient laughed quietly and scratched the cat's chin, cooing to it. Leaping to the table, it swung a leg up and licked itself. I tried to take the patient's hand, but she wrenched it away with surprising strength.

Even bundled up — under her coat was a shabby blue woolen dress — she looked to be all skin and bones.

"I need to check for lesions — sores, dear." Picturing Sister Ursula, I thought of her raising up Jesus as a model of patience. Jesus tending lepers.

The patient gave me a sour look and held out palms lined with dirt. "There! Not a scratch, you see?" She batted me away when I went to remove the coat. "Are you stupid — can't you see how busy I am?" Again I noted her teeth, or what remained of them, some blackened stumps. The poor creature narrowed her eyes that once, long ago, in her youth perhaps, her very distant youth, would have been pretty. Her voice was a snarl. "Surely you have more pressing business? The lunatics need you far more than I do."

"Time for some freshening-up." I spoke more loudly than necessary, unfortunately remembering too late that geriatrics and dementia do not automatically indicate deafness. Head Nurse's comment about the patient's dislike for bathing reasserted itself. "I just want to give you a little wipe-down, dear."

"And who are you?" She sounded half amused. Rose, shrinking from my reach, and with a tottering exactitude lowered herself onto the chair. A trembling hand flicked a wisp of hair under a hat that might've been fashionable during the last war. She picked up a stub of a pencil from the table and began scribbling away on a paper scrap. Other items strewn there included a leaky-looking pen and some broken nibs.

Weren't writing implements dangerous in such hands? No telling the injury such objects could inflict. Should they be confiscated?

In a strip of sunlight, the patient bent over her efforts — enraptured, suddenly, as though I weren't there. Symptoms of schizophrenia. I ran through a mental list: lack of insight, unwillingness to co-operate, flatness of affect, suspiciousness, apathy, delusions of persecution, emotional withdrawal, restricted speech, hypochondrial/neurasthenic complaints, hallucinations, collecting and hoarding, incessant letter-writing.

By now Novice's water was cold. Must someone be called each time you need hot? I took the opportunity to peep out into the corridor. There was no aid in sight, so I dampened the face rag.

She dropped the pencil — "No!" — and almost overturned the basin.

"Now, now — just a lick and a promise." Sister's term. "It'll make you feel better." It wasn't exactly easy, keeping an even tone.

"If it was true, you'd give your name. Unless you use an alias."

I flushed, I admit, enunciating, "Solange Poitier, RN" — heavens, almost the way I had done addressing the *Milice* on the train.

"And I should believe you?"

"I'd lie?" I couldn't restrain a tiny laugh. The spill had wet the bedding, hardly the end of the world. Better laugh than swear — it was important to maintain a sense of humour. "Enough cat hair here to cause an asthma attack," I let slip, on the lookout not just for flea bites but wheals and any other signs of allergic reaction. None were in plain view, oddly enough, but that was hardly reassuring. "For extra warmth, is that it?"

I took advantage of her blinking to dab at her mouth. Exasperated, she shoved the cloth away. Her eyes darkened — with a mixture of fear and rage, the one barely distinguishable from the other. Cause to hesitate, anyway.

The poor thing raved, "Trying to gag me! Smother me! As if I won't soon enough be silent! I knew you were up to no good, breaking in! And here I thought the worst of my enemies had died off!" Then as sharply as it flared, her hysteria flickered and went out. The patient's face brightened, her ravaged look dissolving. Her voice was triumphant if weak. "But you have no power over me, Soitier Polange, none whatsoever. You're to be pitied, that's it. One of that rat-face's minions, that's who you are, charmed like the rest, then sent to torment me."

Ignoring the thudding in my chest, I began to strip the bed. "Leave it!" She withered then and turned to her papers. With her looking so pitiful in her coat, the stray sunlit threads no doubt picked and pulled by the cat, it was all I could do not to seize the pencil, likewise that ridiculous key. Perhaps the patient sensed my frustration — one must never forget, patients can. "Don't touch anything," she shouted, "and don't come back till you have news for me — good news."

—⁓—

BUSY IN HER station, Head Nurse was too preoccupied with filling in charts to see me coming. The blue of the eyes in her portrait of Maréchal was almost welcoming, set against so much faded green and yellow. It was louder here than on the upper floor, which housed mainly guests in isolation. The lights' hum threaded together all the shrieking and moaning until their blended drone grew almost comforting. It wasn't so very different from Lyon, where patients cried out before and after diagnoses and procedures. Silence would've been alarming.

"So you and Mademoiselle are acquainted," Head remarked without looking up. "I should've warned you. Seeing a new face, some think we've been invaded." She was drinking tea, and smiled grimly into her cup. The room with the kettle was close by; difficult, though, to imagine wangling a break, and I happened to say so. "Be grateful you have the lambs, then," she reminded me. "Speaking of which, you'll meet the doctor in charge on her rounds."

"About the hot water, the inconvenience —" I managed to blurt out.

"Oh — but a little cold never hurts to revive them." Was she being funny? *Show pity, never scorn,* the voice inside me piped up. If I appeared a mite distracted, Head picked up on it, frowning. "A daydreamer, are we?"

She sent me back to the first ward to unlock and clean the

windows, get things aired out before breakfast. The task, which meant locating a stepladder, was a chance to enjoy the view, though the sound of praying — someone's loud, feverish cries for deliverance — kept me grounded, thank you. From such a height, a slash of purple could be seen beyond the chapel and the sprawling pavilions' tiled roofs, bordering a distant field: a lavender crop?

As I squeegeed, dusted and wiped, my eyes on the fields and some faint, snow-capped mountains in the farthest beyond, I began thinking of the cribs, and the remarks Head had made earlier about the savagely deranged. I tried summoning the fullness of an article I'd crammed on the train — not that I'd absorbed its entirety — and when I completed the chore, once again sought Head out at the desk, eager to carry on our discussion. It was important to demonstrate that I was knowledgeable.

"Bed straps, *camisoles*, concomitant bleeding — all the more reason, surely, to trust in new treatments," I began. "Sine-wave therapy, electroconvulsive shock —"

"*Bien sûr*," she cut me off. "Those you'll find in the building behind the Men's. You'll find too that, largely, our guests don't merit them. The tried-and-true works equally well. Dr. Cadieu prefers it, in fact. Fever and coma when necessary, fresh air, exercise." She eyed my watch. Admiring it?

"And work, Poitier. Never underestimate the therapeutic value of good, honest work. Speaking of which, you're to escort those exempted from chapel to Laundry. Then Mademoiselle's breakfast must be seen to — you might take her to the refectory if she's up to it." She saw my confusion. "Yes, yes, special treatment isn't condoned. But she's been with us so long she's unlike the rest. You're to make her as comfortable as possible, Cadieu's orders. The poor thing's failing." Her eyes met mine, benignly. "You were able to bathe her?"

It was the perfect moment to raise something I shouldn't have had to. "About that cat — isn't vermin a worry?"

She pointed to the patients huddling farther up the corridor.
"If you don't mind, they're due in Laundry."

—⁓—

OUTSIDE, THE SUN was already blazing. Armed with vague directions, I led the little troop through a maze of buildings to one
tucked behind Admin, not far from the directeur's villa. By now I
was ravenous, it's fair to say weak with hunger.

The laundry was a concrete bunker as grey and echoey as a
gym, filled with steaming vats, boilers, mangles and washboards.
Workers moved about like jerky machines as a burly, red-faced
gentleman oversaw them. He waved my charges toward a huge
pressing machine flanked on either side by women feeding in, catching, and folding linens.

One of them, the woman in green I'd noticed earlier, pointed
to my apron. I was flushing when I unbuttoned and gave it over,
the steamy heat enough to cause a faint. It was soon returned,
slightly scalded but perfectly smooth, by a guest who had the face
of a saint on one of Sister's holy cards, never mind her wild hair.

"Feed them in nicely, girls," their supervisor barked. "Many
hands make light work." *Indeed,* said the nunnish voice lodged
inside me.

I hastened back to the Pavilion and hurried to the second floor.
When I entered Mademoiselle's room — unimpeded, as luck
would have it — the patient swept whatever she'd been scribbling
on into the table's little drawer, all but a sheet or two. She was
still dressed for winter despite the rising heat. At her elbow was a
cup of tea; on the floor was a saucer, from which that abominable
creature, the cat, was licking eggshells.

When she decided to look up at me, the sight of her face was
a shock. It was pasty white — had she powdered it with talcum?
Only, I detected a floury scent.

"Goodness! We have a ghost?" *If you could see yourself,* I

had the sense to withhold — particularly since the room lacked a mirror, which could be put to horrific use if shattered. I made my voice loud and convivial. "I'm here to take you to breakfast, Mademoiselle."

"You're too late." The poor thing uncapped a little vial of bluish milk and, bending creakily, emptied it into the saucer. "Puss-puss," she murmured, ignoring the bits of eggshell floating there.

"That animal needs that far less than you do, dear. You need it to keep up your strength."

"Who are you, my mother? Cruel, you think, using a cat as a canary?" she erupted. "Try minding your own business, Soitier Polange. If you haven't noticed, the food here is unfit."

"My business, love, dictates that you need to eat. I'll help you to the dining room if you like — the common room," I corrected myself. "Some company will do you good."

"The common room," she spat, "for common lunatics. Where do you come from?"

This I chose to ignore. "You have a special diet, then?"

"Whatever they can't touch, the creatures in the kitchen. Not to be trusted."

Pointless to debate the irrational, I'd discovered some years before during the briefest possible stint in pediatrics, a week there the most I could bear. Biting my tongue, I gripped the *aliénée's* elbow to help her from the chair. She shook me off so violently I almost stumbled. Remembering Head Nurse's instructions, I tried a different approach. "If you show me where the kitchen is, I'll see to it that —"

"Their excuse for a cook adds enough poison? I've been, thank you, and outsmarted them," she said, smug as could be. "Quite easily, too. Imbeciles never learn." Her grin made cracks in her cakey mask.

I found myself counting again, imagining Sister's adage, *Refrain from showing undue emotion.* "Imbeciles, Mademoiselle?"

"The imbeciles in charge, of course! The ones who do the rat's bidding — as bad if not worse than the lunatics themselves. Why, Soitier Polange, are they so cruel as to keep me here?"

Over her tweedy shoulder, I glimpsed a stray paper, on which was an address in Paris and, in a similar scrawl, the words *When may I see you?* I gripped the patient's arm more firmly and tried once more to raise her, intending to guide her to the hallway.

"Unhand me! Please! If you have any mercy — if you know what's good for you!" Her shriek was enough to send the cat scuttling. Collapsing there, she pressed her cheek to the page.

"Good enough, then," I conceded.

—∞—

IT WASN'T TILL I'd found the common room, and found myself enlisted with feeding the others, that I realized how shaken I was. A pencil, a broken pen, a plate, possibly dashed against a wall: all weapons in the hands of the sick, and in Mademoiselle's case they ought to have been removed.

But there wasn't a moment to nip back upstairs between helping Novice coax porridge into drooling mouths, retrieving dropped spoons, and wiping up spills. Though I had no illusions about table manners, it wasn't pleasant watching those who could feed themselves tuck into their food, watching their grinding jaws. Novice offered an untouched serving and, kindly, to cover for me while I ate it, but though my stomach growled, I could barely get it down. To think that most of these guests were fortunate to be here, housed and fed, while to the north and across the border, *les fritz* wouldn't have treated them half as well. *Treat the ill with equal compassion regardless of affliction*: thank you, Sister Ursula, for instilling that cardinal rule!

When the feeding was accomplished, we checked sleeves and pockets for cutlery, counting everything twice before the kitchen girls came to trundle away their carts, and a bit of a lull followed.

Some guests rocked in their chairs, jabbering, while others slouched and slumped, speechless.

Head Nurse appeared out of nowhere, accompanied by a grey-haired woman whose presence was announced by a clean but threadbare white coat. Dr. Cadieu greeted me with a bright if weary smile, her pouched eyes hawkish but not unkind, the lines around her eyes and mouth perhaps the toll of patience. "So you've met our Mademoiselle — and how do you find her?" she asked me.

Head cut in to confer about a fever treatment; I, perhaps overly eager and forgetting myself, asked, "A treatment for Mademoiselle?"

"If you don't mind, Poitier, the doctor and I have other patients to discuss."

Cadieu, however, shrugged this off. "Poor Mademoiselle, she's excitable all right. But her age and her condition — her heart, you see — make fever risky, alas." Head Nurse gave an impatient little nod, tapping her fingertips together, but the doctor seemed in no hurry. "The patient wasn't always so, Nurse Poitier. On more than one occasion I'd have released her, let her go in a heartbeat, had it been my choice. Little can be done for her now, I'm sorry to say."

"Poitier. If you'll excuse us," Head said, before speaking quietly with Cadieu — too quietly for me to hear. When the doctor retreated, my supervisor explained, "Poor Cadieu has been here as long as Mademoiselle." She winced at the shuffling squeak of Cadieu's soles, raising her brows — their thinness less the result of over-plucking than of low thyroid, I surmised. Or menopause. Head would be that age; her moodiness suggests it.

Without warning, she brightened. An orderly was approaching, juggling my stepladder and something flat and square wrapped in paper. A painting to perk things up? Very nice. There must have been volunteers somewhere eager to contribute their handiwork.

But when the orderly unveiled the object, Maréchal Pétain's smile beamed from the frame.

Looking positively dewy-eyed, Head gave a salute, and recited the maréchal's slogan, "'Work, Family, Country.'" She peered at me, looking a little peeved, and sighed. "So that's it, Poitier. Your job's cut out for you. Rest assured, Cadieu's logic isn't mine. But Mademoiselle's all yours. As if we have the bodies to spare. You're to make her as comfortable as possible: doctor's orders."

4

OF HAPPIER TIMES I'm happy to write, lest you've forgotten them. I won't let you forget. Shysters in white coats say, go back as far as you can remember. So many years between us, I've lost count. If you could see me now — this moment — if I could see myself! Whiteface. A geisha's makeup, all the rage in Paris, where under the shadow of Eiffel's *grande asperge* we hankered after *japonisme*. All because of Hokusai's wave swamping tiny boats, a village. And studies drawn from life — no *École des Beaux-Arts* for people with tits! But. Bodies, freedom: the shape of vastness? Like God, some might say. Or Paris. A wisteria-tangled *joie de vivre*, a well-pruned riot — heaven; and you its debutante, at what age, forty? That show they gave us near La Madeleine: a coming out?

But before the tormenters return I must get to the point ... the point before the troubles began, when the world was fresh, that other time: April in Paris, what finer place to start?

ASYLUM FOR LUNATICS
DAY? MONTH? YEAR?

MY DEAREST C,
In the grey-green thrall of another life, this earlier time (what's to
erase memory's greenness?) the only bounds we knew were in
Montparnasse. Maman's, and the walls of our flat. Flocked paper,
Papa's pipe smoke. A holding pen, a corral and its starting gate
bolted by rules, rules, rules. In those unbroken days — correct me
if I'm wrong, it was 1884? — you were as headstrong as any horse.

Released, we raced along the boulevard at gunshot speed.
As fast as they would take us, our feet skimmed cobblestones,
fish-scale shiny after the rain. Moisture breathed up from everywhere — sidewalks, sewers, budded lilacs. Coffee smells, butter
smells. Gutted fish, orange peels and piss in the gutters — the
muse of all these scents enough to hold us, hold us up.

We were with a friend, of course; it didn't do to be alone, girls
flying arm in arm past shopkeepers sweeping shop-fronts, setting out fruit. Equally eager to escape Maman's badgering, our
friend behaved as one of us, though she was merely a boarder.
We could not move fast enough with Maman's voice in our ears.
Who had time to waste taming a wild mane or properly lacing a
corset? The dandruff dotting my hair was marble dust and dried
clay, and my middle was bound, but by yesterday's smock stiffened with plaster and not whalebone. When it bunched over my
skirt and rode up, I peeled my jacket off and tied it around me
by its sleeves, barely stopping.

"A target for pigeons, you look like. You might've been shat
on!" our friend jeered, as if she too wasn't splotched and splat-
tered, a compliment paid out of mouth-full-of-marbles English
decency. But, then, she wasn't so different from us. Cutting through
the Luxembourg Gardens, politely holding the gold-tipped gate,
she paused to light a cigarette, took a puff, passed it. Its taste

cut the perfume of freshly pruned trees.

Forgetting Maman's well-pruned urbanity, we didn't bother hiking our hems to jump puddles. Down chestnut-bordered *allées* we raced, past fountains and old men reading newspapers. We barely ogled the statuary, far too rushed to speculate about man-bits under fig leaves. Sprinting round the perfectly circular pond, even you hardly noticed the little toy boats drifting there.

Not soon enough we swung out into the streets again, past windows dressed with finery: hats, gloves, parasols, soaps, tarts, rainbow spreads of *macarons* and chocolates shaped like roses, fruit, birds, rabbits and any other form of flora and fauna imaginable. Vanities now, they were treats we would buy for ourselves when we were rich and famous, with the wealth caked in the creases of our knuckles and beneath our nails — dried clay, from which we made our treasures. Seduced by marzipan pigs and *tartes citrons*, my friend pressed her nose to the glass.

"Today of all days" — I stamped my foot, wrested her away — "how dare you think of your stomach?"

"Yes, Maman. No, Maman," she mimicked my accent pathetically. "Because I can't buy doesn't mean I can't look. If I could I'd window-shop down every bloody street here."

"No time to be a *flâneur*! You said yourself, this is the chance we've been slaving for!"

"I as much as you." Such presumption in one so falsely humble.

"Can we not speak for each other? Though perhaps one can't and mustn't gauge another's mind. But one can try."

I had awaited this day all eighteen years of my life, as far back as I could remember. Long before we'd made the city our home, I'd delved with both hands into muck and murk, shaping faces out of mud, to Maman's great disgust. All I had thought of was the chance, ooh-la-la, to study with a great artist, even persuading Papa to move our family — Maman, our brother, sister and me — to Paris.

Alas, studying here was to sketch statues, drawing from death, not life. How could we hope to show true anatomy, movement? To students like us, blessed with breasts, not penises, real bodies, living, naked ones, were off-limits. Most would give their eye teeth for the opportunity which had landed in our laps. Some would have given eyes and teeth.

As we wound our way up rue Jacob, and rue Jacob broadened and straightened into rue de l'Université, my friend's babbling overran the river's sounds — such a torrent that I quit listening. My belly was a bundle of nerves, and a brassy wonder took such hold that my bad foot dragged.

My foolish friend teased, "You're not getting cold feet — you're not *afraid* of him, are you?" I suppose that you remember this? My friend had acquired a habit of baiting me, finding a warped delight in it, perhaps, ever since our old teacher had brought the Master to our atelier and said Monsieur would instruct us in his absence.

"Cold feet! Don't be stupid. Afraid of that runt of a man? Talking to him will be like talking to Papa, he must be that old." I believe you put those words in my mouth. They shut her up, momentarily. Still her round eyes swooped over me.

"I've heard about him, from the other English girls — the ones studying too. He's got a reputation for getting inside people's knickers."

I let out a snort. "And we're lambs for the killing? I can't speak for you, of course. But I care only about his work. The work of his hands, our own Michelangelo's." And I waved my own grandly, for we stood before the Dépôt des Marbres.

It was a gloomy building, arched windows glaring behind the lofty planes and their seedpods' fuzzy, dangling bursts of green.

"Since you're so sure, missy, you go first."

A tenacious joy, climbing like wisteria, choked out any trepidation. The light inside, barely interrupted by the leafy branches beyond, was so harsh that we squinted. Pouring in, it showed a dusty purity — an oxymoron like our brother, who, after getting religion, could be sharp and dull.

Men worked silently in the clammy brightness, barely looking up, the air charged with its cellar-smell. Despite their bustling industry, their hammering and chiselling, we seemed the only breathing ones. It was a morgue of sorts: statues making a company of ghosts frozen into position.

Is it vivid to you, still? Everywhere, stacked and scattered over worktables and shelves, were body parts shaped from clay or plaster-cast. Torsos, heads, arms, legs. A limbo of fragments, as if plucked from a battlefield. My friend was agog. In this purgatory of white lay paradise.

Only then did I notice one of the workers breezing past, a wraith-like fellow with a vaguely familiar face, who half nodded. I couldn't think of his name. Perhaps he had been at our old school, was now privileged to be among the legion of Monsieur's *praticiens*?

My friend, entranced, put out her hand, stroked a rigid ankle. Someone coughed a gruff *Bonjour*, and we were no longer so alone. Trapping her hand in her pocket, my friend struck the pose — do you remember? — so useful in currying Maman's favour.

"Mesdemoiselles ...?" Monsieur said vaguely. He was short, with threads of grey in his reddish beard and itchy-looking eyes. Exactly level with mine, his gaze was neither masterly nor instructive but just shy of being rude, lingering with a blunt curiosity, his blue eyes roving under pinkish lids. In one arm he held a sketchbook, in his hand a stub of chalk. He ran his other hand over his bristling grey hair, rubbed his big fleshy nose, and clapped his hands.

A girl appeared, with translucent skin set off by the dark triangle between her legs. With feline grace she stepped onto a platform and crouched. Neither you nor my friend looked at her. Then a man slipped from behind a curtain, naked as *David*. His face might've been raw canvas; my friend's too, only hers was filled with such dismay it might have been her posing, undressed, stripped, by his hands. Not that it would've been torture. The muscles of his torso rippled like those of a Michelangelo, his penis a fat snail curled against his thigh.

It would be lying to say only my friend gaped. Not that we hadn't seen a penis before, each of us lucky enough to have a brother. You were silent. But my friend elbowed me, choking back a giggle, a cough. *Stop*, I nudged her back, hoping our new master hadn't noticed. Affecting the indifference fools take for wilfulness, I tried not to imagine Maman's chiding: Your attitude will be the death of us all, my girl!

Fears of Monsieur seeing our display lifted when we saw that he had set down the sketchbook, seized a *boulette*, and was busily shaping it into a pointy lemon tart topped with a raspberry — a much too perfect boob.

Around us fell such quiet you could hear dust settle. A taller girl, naked as day, strutted past, muscles yielding to some inner current, while another (her twin?) moved as through a dream stripped of thou-shalt-nots. Circling, they slipped past, the soft flexing of limbs vibrations you could almost feel. Just when I felt dumb and peeled my eyes away, another man appeared, supple-arsed as a Marly horse. Around and around he strutted in a silent rhythm with the others — a soundless ballet, each perfecting a *pas de seul*. A dance of flexion, a musical of the imagination, it evidenced a heaven our brother — our dear Paul, for all his prudishness-to-come — would gladly have died to enter.

When it ended Monsieur drew me aside. Hand at my waist, he whisked me to where the woman squatted. Guileless, sharp-kneed, thighs spread wide, kohl-rimmed eyes blazing, she might've been a cancan girl from Pigalle or the seediest stretch of rue Saint-Denis.

"Look closely — pay attention." His voice had a banker's rasp. Stroking her thigh, he placed my palm there. The cool of her skin gave me chills. Was I choosing a cut of well-marbled meat for Maman at the butcher's? Monsieur's hand guided mine. I saw through my fingertips: skin rougher than it looked, a firmness that was hungrily pliant.

"Perfection?" he breathed into my ear, then strode off to reposition the others and prod the man into a half-kneeling crouch.

The rosy, canine hang of testicles is what we saw.

Forgetting us, Monsieur returned to his posing woman. Gave her a slap, forcing her into a deeper squat, flaying her open. Her hips were a walnut's lobes, thighs etched with a dishwater-blue light, reminding me of our cook whose bust I'd done in plaster, of our maid's nimble fingers. It piqued an urge to fly back to our apartment — not to see our bookworm brother or spoiled sister, and certainly not our dear Maman, but to observe the help at their chores, hands like birds.

My friend huddled beside the cold stove and observed Monsieur's man from across the room, as if he were an explosive device she mustn't get close to. Busily she inspected a plaster shin, her hand falling away when Monsieur rushed to nudge the man's elbow to his thigh.

"Hopeless, hopeless — I pay you to sleep? Try looking like there's a brain in your head!"

The Master began pinching and pummelling a lump of clay, spitting on it as he worked to keep it moist. Faded from his sight, my friend was as wan as the fellow from school who'd gone off to do Monsieur's labour, chiselling, spruing, casting, pouring plaster — the domain of anyone lucky enough to apprentice here.

Job description: *Praticien/Praticienne:* Practitioner, one who enables. From *pratique:* method, practice; clientèle. Related to *practical:* businesslike, convenient. Expedient, advantageous, profitable. A sibling of *pratiquer:* to exercise; to frequent; to open; to build; to cut. To practise not all that different from being a church-goer, our brother might say.

Was being a model also required?

Once more Monsieur was beside me. Shyly, it seemed, he stroked his beard. "You're good with marble, I hear. Have you the patience to pose, too, Mademoiselle?" Out of the blue it sounded playful, like the things Papa said to thwart Maman.

We'd discussed this, over pots of tea and an asphyxiating number of cigarettes. How we would not model to foot the rent for our studio, tiny as it was and just steps from home. We would refuse distractions from our work, would starve before we'd take off our clothes!

My friend stood. "I can tell you right now, sir," she spoke for me, "Mademoiselle does not."

"*C'est impossible*," I declared, glancing at her. I hope you know I meant it, too, that I'd have sooner licked the pavement than bare myself and have some old goat finger me with his eyes.

Except, except — until then, no one had shown me the gift of sight. True sight. What it was, what it is to see through one's fin-gertips. Nor had I felt towards anyone before that the slimmest debt of gratitude.

Can you blame me?

Like our Paul, I write for the certainty of writing, and send you a kiss.

— Mademoiselle

5

TO PASS MY LIFE IN PURITY ...

MONTDEVERGUES ASYLUM
25 AUGUST 1943
23H15

So much for a daily examination, of conscience or activity! There's no end to the troubles our guests suffer from: pernicious anemia, phlebitis, pinworm, pink eye, palpitations, etc., in addition to psychoneurosis, paresis, neurasthenia, schizophrenia. At times one might as well be an IV drip on a pole being pulled in a hundred directions. The treatable physical ailments provide a lull, a normalcy, to be valued given the workload — our efforts being of less therapeutic value than custodial, I suspect. Three full shifts passed before the chance arose, with the pair of us working elbow to elbow on charts, for me to put it to my supervisor: "So Dr. Cadieu wants privacy for the patient — fine. But, allowing her a key?"

Head's response was swift — "So she can come and go as she pleases, of course" — as if I were brainless to ask. "Cadieu has her way of doing things. Our dear doctor would retire if there were someone to replace her — so difficult, with the war."

"France is hardly ... well, yes, thanks be to Vichy —"

The way she eyed me, I instantly wished to retract it. But if the Maréchal and his friends weren't so eager to accommodate *les fritz*, things wouldn't be so bad. So the clergy in Lyon says, those above the sisters, some of them, anyway.

"We'll let the politicians run the country, shall we? They wouldn't presume to run things here — nor would we want them to." Giving me a pitying look, Head chuckled, her sternness stemming the possibility of further chit-chat. The thought of doddering old Pétain wiping a guest's face, or worse, brought a smile to mine. "As long as Cadieu's in charge, see that Mademoiselle gets her exercise," she instructed. "As long as she's capable of getting up and around, she must be encouraged to do so."

"And the rules for her?" Of course I respected protocol, thanks to the sisters; I only sought clarity.

Forcing a smile, Head rhymed the rules off. "Mademoiselle is to have no contact with the outside world. No visitors, no correspondence of any kind."

It was difficult to mask my surprise. "But what possible harm —?"

"Family orders. What does 'sequestration' mean to you, Poitier? Too much for you to absorb?"

I truly hadn't meant to be chippy. Though it wasn't easy, I ignored Head's tone. "No time whatsoever with family or friends? At her age she can't have many left."

"As you know, undue excitement leaves patients unnecessarily agitated. Buffering them has always been the logical course. The most anyone can hope for our guests is a measure of peace. One way or another, by now we expect Mademoiselle has found a little."

I was well versed in the *Essentials of Medicine*'s tip that the psychoneurotic be shielded from as much of the world and its obligations as possible, protected from all that irritated or depressed her. "But, various therapies — surely —"

"For our benefit, Poitier. To let us think we're helping." She was awfully abrupt. "As I told you, the rainy spring set Mademoiselle back. Her confusion's returned."

"Her diagnosis — the original prognosis, I mean?"

"Persecution mania — perhaps. It was so long ago. But you can appreciate the family's wishes." She chose her words carefully. "Anything the guest expresses stays contained. I can't stress enough, any letters she writes mustn't under any circumstances leave these grounds — unless in some rare, unusual instance, and the directeur approves it. Any she receives are to be screened by him as well." She quickly consulted her watch. "Above all, we respect the families' instructions. Do I make myself clear?"

—⁓—

IT WAS FRIDAY, day of days, the one slated for baths, top to tail. The washroom was on the first floor, with two porcelain tubs, both grainy with use, to do the entire pavilion. Novice and I took the guests fifteen at a time, managing to strip and scrub one and all. The orderlies had their work cut out keeping the tubs filled, ensuring the water — what we managed to keep off the floor, that is, trying to conserve as much as possible — wasn't too cold or too hot. The poor things shivered despite the heat.

"Cleanliness matters, as Nightingale is our guide," I quipped to Novice, who, with an orderly's help, wrestled a flailing guest into her greyish bath. I coaxed those who resisted but could respond to reason: "Now now, how can you expect to feel better smelling like that?"

Given the numbers, it was impossible to do everyone before breakfast. Head Nurse urged us to aim to finish before lunch or, at the latest, Quiet Time, so once each group was washed and dried, it was a scramble getting them dressed, buttoning buttons, snapping snaps, et cetera. I got the orderlies to replenish the hot water while I went to rally Mademoiselle and the second-floor guests, having left them till last.

Mademoiselle was sitting on her bedside, bundled as usual, the cat at her feet washing its nether parts. It had gotten used to my interruptions. Not so the patient, who clamped her mouth shut while I took her pulse and gave her hands an inspection. The day before, I'd asked to see her feet; as expected, they were yellow and swollen, the toes of the left quite gnarled.

"Bath time!" I announced, offering my arm for support. The patient didn't budge. "Come, please. We'll have you smelling like a rose," I said. "You'll feel better for it."

Holding on to her hat as if it were bejewelled, she gave an indignant hoot. "You think I mind my stink, Polange Soitier?" But she rose — mystery of mysteries — and with my aid tottered into the hall. *Count my lucky stars*, I thought. She moved at a pace so doggedly compliant, who knew what was in her head?

She'd been writing again, that much I guessed. Likely seated at her little table since breakfast, tossing more word salad onto paper she'd wangled from somewhere.

Novice had already corralled the rest of the second-floor group, who huddled waiting to be undressed. Steamy light bounced from the tiles. The taps' dripping, a fluty metronome, added a brightness to the whimpering and keening. Orderlies bustled in and out, the steaming water they added suspiciously grimy against the gritty porcelain.

Head Nurse helped us strip the guests, fortunately for me, because Mademoiselle dug her heels in and hung back. With her noggin held high and her foolish hat sliding down, she cried, "Don't hurt me!"

"Wouldn't dream of it." Gently but firmly I drew her in among the others. An urchin off some wintry, northern street is how she appeared against their nakedness. Except for their lively vocals, most were cadaver-like, that pale and wasted. The effects of time and gravity on the female body, the wizening of certain parts, never cease to amaze me — not to mention the ravages of illness, the mind's decline hastening the body's. At one point I had to look away. To think a normal, healthy female had at least some of this to look forward to, parts going south.

I reached for the buttons on Mademoiselle's coat.

"I've been baptized, Poitier Solange, if you care to check. I'm sure the scoundrels holding me have records!" In the greenish light the patient's face resembled chamois-cloth, her jaw sagging. "You needn't worry about my salvation!"

I tightened my grip on her wrist. Always the real and present danger of a geriatric falling and breaking a hip, the floor slick after all their thrashing. I succeeded in peeling off the coat, to the amusement of a calmer guest who risked a smile. A few bellowed with laughter, including a girl who I tried not to notice was smeared with feces and was better left to Novice. Sniffling, another folded herself into a ball and rocked herself until Head arrived, with an off-putting ease, to help us coax her into a tub.

An orderly came with fresh, steaming water. As I directed him, my grip on Mademoiselle loosened slightly and she lurched backwards. The soles of her shoes slid out from under her, a dull clang rising as she collided with the tub. Luckily Novice broke her fall, but not sufficiently to prevent an outcry. "How much more must I suffer to prove your cruelty?" the patient gasped with breathless satisfaction. "I forbid you to rummage under my clothes!"

"Nurse Poitier!" Head's shrillness cut above the din of the others joining in to mimic Mademoiselle's outburst. "There's no point forcing her. I would expect better judgment; you know she's better left alone."

"Yes, but —"

Plucking at her coat, Mademoiselle hobbled out, leaving the rest to be quieted.

"Well?" Head said, exasperated, in the midst of dunking a thrasher. Despite water everywhere, drenching her apron, she had the wherewithal to bark, "Go after her, for goodness' sake. See that she's all right. Novice and I will finish up."

For one so frail, Mademoiselle was quick on her feet. She'd almost made it to the stairwell before I could apprehend her. "Who are you, my mother?" She shook me off.

It took every effort, every ounce of patience not to scold. "Goodness, no. Do I remind you of her, your mother?" Instantly I thought better of saying it.

"Goodness, no," Mademoiselle mimicked. In the stairwell's dimness she looked hungry-eyed, the set-to having sapped her strength. "But since you seem to mistake me for a child ..." She clutched the railing.

"If you say so." *Keep the upper hand*, I told myself.

To my surprise, my relief, she let me escort her upstairs. She sighed, "Make it quick, then. I'm very busy. I have no time for your nonsense. But if you must." Once rested in bed, still wearing those gamey clothes, she didn't object when I went to check for injuries. She lay quite still, in fact, eyes screwed shut as I lifted her hem and, one after the other, rolled down laddered stockings gartered to equally ragged drawers. Socks would've been much easier, but everyone must be allowed her little vanity. A bit of a marvel, the guest managing these herself. A welt on her thigh already showed signs of bruising, the skin unbroken at least. While I was at it, I took the liberty of turning the patient sideways, the bedsprings chiming in protest. There was something else. As suspected, there was an ulcerated spot in the lumbar region, the beginning of what all too easily could become a bedsore.

"Well, Mademoiselle — at least your legs work. As long as

they do, exercise is important. Too much lying down — you know. Use it or lose it," I said, then wished I hadn't. It was how I'd spoken to wounded soldiers sent to Lyon for rehab.

The old woman gave me a look. Bitter approval? "Like any gift — unless you use it, it will eat you alive?" She sucked what remained of her teeth, smiling her pitiful smile.

"I suppose. Now that you've been up — I don't know what you have against water — and since Quiet Time is any time you like, apparently, we should see to a walk."

The cat leapt up and stretched out on her papers. "But I have my writing," the patient huffed. "And I have nothing against water, Miss Soitier. It's being around lunatics that I can't bear. Would you mind very much, Soitier Polange, being stripped naked before a bunch of raving imbeciles? I doubt that you'd enjoy it. Perhaps you have no such experience?"

Forcing a practical smile, I bit my tongue. Of course I do not, and trust that I never will, though perhaps I had come close to it once, lying on an examining table, feet in stirrups. Just thinking it was enough to make me flush — though more precisely, it was the room's swelter that caused the blood to rush to my face. Not even noon and each of the floors hot as Hades.

Her eyes pierced mine. "You have a family, Poitier Solange? People who care for you?"

Patience, I told myself. "Please. The name is Solange Poitier — Nurse to you."

"Do you?"

"Let's get you outside, shall we? The air will do you good." I braced for resistance, but Mademoiselle had turned pensive.

"All those creatures with their hanging dugs, like overbred bitches. Do you know, Nurse Solange — once, I paid a model who looked like that?"

Disassociation, a textbook case. When was the last time she'd seen herself? No point in stirring her up, of course.

"Never mind, now. Let's see how far we can get before it's too hot."

—⟋⟍—

THE RIBBON FROM which Mademoiselle's key dangled was just long enough to not require unpinning. Sure enough, it worked not only on the second but on the first and ground floors as well. Outside, the air barely stirred the ivy spilling over the wall. Even the birds seemed stymied by the heat. Guests relegated as gardeners weeded flowerbeds and pruned hedges, the cat-pee scent of box wafting up. They moved as if they had forever to finish their chores, which in a way they did.

Already high, the sun was blinding. Pushing at her hat, Mademoiselle squinted even in the shade, taking snail steps as I led her past the chapel. A short but steep flight of concrete steps led to the roadway which linked buildings arranged more or less like spokes around it. Helping the infirm negotiate stairs was old hat, and I happily shared tips physiotherapists provide to crutch-users: *Lead with the left foot going down: right foot heavenward, left goes to hell.*

"You make me laugh, Miss Solange. As if I've never done stairs."

The sprawl of stucco and clay roofs shimmered in the heat, summoning an eerie languor. The grounds were deserted, save for the gardeners. Mademoiselle seemed to know her way, trudging through the maze of pavilions, past Admin and the directeur's blue-shuttered villa, and along the paved *allée* of well-trimmed planes that led to the gate. A large black car festooned with little Vichy flags crept towards, then slowly past us. Taking a little rest, we watched it stop outside the directeur's, the only building whose windows looked welcoming.

"A picnic day," the patient murmured, and shut her eyes, savouring something, it was hard to imagine what. The scent of fresh-cut lavender perhaps, from beyond the hospital's fields where, just visible to us, work gangs of able-bodied guests gathered some sort of harvest. "There. You see it, Miss Solange" — the old woman pointed upwards at nothing, or the cloudless sky — "as pure and good to me as to you a sheet without a wrinkle?"

Far above, swallows darted and swooped.

"You must be melting in that coat."

"Why would you care?" Mademoiselle snorted, any earlier gumption faded and disappearing now that we'd reached the grounds' limits.

In his small gatehouse the guard glanced up from whatever he was reading. *What harm, what possible harm, if we stepped out just for a moment?* I thought, dazzled by the distant purple, lured even. The tiniest taste of freedom, however delusional, worked wonders. Even Head Nurse said so.

"When did you last...?" Escape, I could hardly say.

"To see the dentist. In Avignon." A faraway, almost bored look filled her eyes.

"A while, then." I sniffed, squeezing the patient's hand. Waving to the guard, I called out, "We won't be but a minute," fully expecting to be asked for a pass. Instead, he simply buzzed us through. "Hold on to my arm," I instructed. "The last thing either of us needs is you breaking a hip, dear."

But beyond the wall Mademoiselle refused to venture farther. She was content to peer out into the roadway and across the pavement at the tiny canal running past some dusty trees. Walled with concrete, it was no wider than a brook, its current as swift as it had been the evening of my arrival, offering me its vague direction. Not too far off, silhouetted by lavender, women dug potatoes, turning earth dark as a freshly let-out hem. Mademoiselle bent to inspect a rose bush in the wall's shade, more thorns than blooms. Before I could stop her, she sagged to her knees with terrific effort and traced a circle in the dirt with a small stone.

Oh well, what harm? I supposed, before she picked up a clod of earth, the way a baby would, and squeezed it in her fist. She let the dirt sift through her fingers — not quickly enough, considering my worry that she might try to eat it. "Mind now, or I'll have to call the guard to help get you on your feet." I bent to assist the patient.

Tears glazed her eyes. "Gold — fool's gold! Give me chalky silt, I'll fill my boots with it!" Mademoiselle fretted, her voice rising. "If I'd never left the country, you see, none of these horrors would've happened."

Better not to listen and not to argue. Besides, something had caught my attention, something snagged in the tufted grass. A banknote. *Finders, keepers.* I held on to Mademoiselle's sleeve and went to grab it. My stomach rose even as I picked it up. Once again, it was a crisp dollar bill with that vile message on the back: *L'Argent n'a pas d'odeur ... MAIS LE JUIF...* The enemy's propaganda, and to think our own government was in cahoots! *Worth how many francs*, I thought, disgusted, *if such filth could be exchanged?* Repulsed, I crumpled it up — but not quickly enough.

Mademoiselle's eyes widened. "The Americans! The scoundrel's friends!" the poor woman wailed. "Trying to lure me, don't you see? A bribe! Now they say he's dead, his friends act in his place!"

Stay calm, be agreeable: no point debating sick thoughts. To the insane, such reasoning is true, no matter how irrational and — thankfully, in Mademoiselle's case — its excitability short-lived.

"Even from the grave he pursues me! You see for yourself, Nurse — you won't deny it," she continued to rant. Passion, or fear, had at least got her to her feet. "Leaving their petty cash to butter me up. That's how they operate, the rodent and his gang. Next they'll be at the shutters, forcing their way in."

By now the guard was watching through his little window.

Mademoiselle leaned heavily on me. "Have mercy, Soitier Polange — hide me from them."

"Of course, dear. No need to worry. I will." How stupid I'd been, profligate, assuming I could manage her outside on my own. Annoyed with myself, I waved to the guard; best to keep on his good side, and hope I wouldn't be questioned. *The new girl in Number 10, is she qualified to escort patients off grounds? By whose authorization?*

Wordlessly he buzzed us back inside.

—⁂—

NOT TILL I'D settled Mademoiselle for her personal Quiet Time did I remember what I'd so hastily pocketed. Beyond troubling, it was. I locked myself in the staff WC, tore the "dollar" into tiny pieces, and flushed them.

Lunchtime loomed. With fifty-nine mouths to feed, there was not another moment to fret about the enemy or any other presence. One of the epileptics chose just then to take a fit, body jerking and chattering over the linoleum, Novice needing help to depress the tongue. Next I was called to administer Veronal by suppository to a patient after two injections had no effect; following that, a fever treatment to manage, which Novice had to commence without me because several guests were tearing off their clothes in the heat and required restraints. Head Nurse took the time to mutter "Good work" — less a compliment perhaps than a nudge to remind me about Mademoiselle's meal.

Housed in a separate building, the refectory was a virtual steam bath of boiling pots. Mercifully for all but the priest, guests had chapel again before the evening meal, allowing workers to wash up from lunch and prep supper. The red-faced cook eyed me. "Oh yes — you're here for Herself, the artiste," she snorted. "Mind, last time she was here, the mess! Both hands in the bin, flour everywhere, till we shooed her out."

A girl plopped down a potato — or was it a knob of petrified wood? "She wants the usual?"

I swear, Miss Solange. You see," her voice fell to a whisper, "fighting fire with fire is my only hope — the only way to deal with the devils holding me here." With the eyes of a hawk, she watched the envelope's uneasy progress into my pocket.

—⁂—

EASILY ENOUGH DISPOSED *of*, I assured myself, bound for Head's desk and the folder marked ADMIN, *Attn: Directeur* — but in the stairwell, my professionalism made it impossible to resist peeking inside the envelope. It was purely in the patient's interests. Not only was writing therapeutic, it could offer insights into illness itself.

Mon cher petit, the note began and ended simply enough, *I send you a kiss, your sister.* Perfectly benign, perfectly disappointing. It was an old woman sending her brother fond wishes. What could be more harmless, or welcome, than that? I tucked it carefully into my apron's bib.

Before I could reach the nurses' station, Dr. Cadieu flagged me down. "I hear that you're interested in new treatments." She sounded slightly bemused, almost shy. "If Head Nurse is in agreement, if just once she can spare you, perhaps we'll send you to Number Five to observe?"

"I would like that very much," I said.

When I got to the desk, I looked for the folder. It wasn't there.

"Never mind that now," said Head, waving me off. "Make sure the guest on Ward One gets food and lots of fluids into her. And Cadieu wants you to see to a fever on Ward Two. That business of yours — of Mademoiselle's? — whatever it is will have to wait."

6

DEAREST C,

Life would've been grand if we'd never had to go home, if my friend and I could've lived in our atelier around the corner from Maman's, that tiny hole-in-the-wall on Notre-Dame-des-Champs. Oh, Paris! But you remember my friend, her taste for a cozy featherbed and good table. Our bellies and lack of a cook-stove drove us to the flat and Maman's finery — finery, if your taste ran to Samaritaine's quick-sale bric-a-brac, finds laid out to impress our boarder and Papa home from his week at work. (Do you suppose he worked in the suburbs to escape Maman's badgering, his job taking up all but those precious weekends he visited?)

"Look who it is," Maman greeted us, my friend and me. With her black dress and hair scraped into a bun she resembled a widow weaned of grief on vinegar! Papa kissed our cheeks, and Maman offered hers to be air-kissed, the rosy scent of talcum prickling our noses till the smell of food blessed it. She'd had Cook prepare Papa's favourite, *coq au vin* and *pommes purée*, a nod to our country roots. But the bickering at table made a farce of family bonds. Maman nattered at me to wash my hands, to allow our guest to be served first; at our brother to pull his nose from his book; at our sister to stop treating her place as an octave, her fingers skittering over the fresh cloth, executing scales.

Afterwards Maman invited my friend to the parlour to watch her sew while our sister and I helped the maid clear the table. "Yes, Madame, no Madame," we heard her saying, as our brother — trying to study — coughed. For all her ingratiating sweetness, my friend soon excused herself to take refuge down the street, working all hours till we were due at the Master's next morning.

"How many times must she play that?" Papa groused of our sister's practising.

"Can you guess what piece she's playing?" our brother sneered, and even the maid rolled her eyes when our sister threw her sheet music, pages everywhere.

Maman's harangue: "Fathersonandholyghost! What have I done to deserve such children?" Perturbed at the state of my fingernails, she lamented that I would forever be her burden. "Who'll marry a girl with fishwife hands?"

Why a fishwife, who knows? A farm-wife would've made more sense.

"Has she told you about the goings-on, where they spend their time?" our brother chimed in, too young to know the dangers of his question. Of course my friend wasn't there to defend us. He wouldn't have said such things in her presence. "It's no place a decent girl would go, from what friends tell me. No chaperones. Last week I heard about a girl, very loose, petitioning the government to let her wear pants — petitioning, imagine! — the friend of a friend who —"

"*Cher Enfant!* Infant heart of Jesus! My son, you don't mean to say —"

Plink-aaaa-plink-a-plinnk went our sister's piano, pot lid cymbals clashing from the kitchen. Papa whacked the table with the stem of his pipe, so hard it snapped off. But he beamed at me, pride in us children tempering impatience. Protective of my gift, our gifts, he was pleased by my arrangement with the Master. In a few short months, with head-spinning ease, I'd gained an apprenticeship. Papa saw the value of my studies, though his taste, like Maman's, ran to tabletop cherubs and urns sold by the lot. It tickled him to have his offspring's talents praised, even our sister's, doomed to be amateur.

Yet always, always the arguing.

"It's your fault, if there's anything untoward — you spoil her so!" said Maman.

"If not for your high-horse tone, your battleaxe tongue ... what's a man to do for a second's peace?"

"Peace?!"

The ceaseless game of cat-and-mouse forced me to the balcony for more than one calming cigarette. No escape from their quarrelling and from our sister's Chopin, played as if she were typing. Drawn by the smoke, Maman soon appeared and cuffed my ear. A hairpin flew out over the railing that might've jabbed a passerby below.

"Smoking! God knows what you'll get up to next. Get inside before the neighbours see." A fish out of water, our Maman in Paris.

I used flattery to reach her softer spot, certain it was there, only buried. Reaching out, I tucked behind her ear a free strand of hair. "You're pretty when you're angry! Sit for me. Will you, Maman? Let me do your portrait. Will you? Please? For me." Even if her

side of the family. His eyes moving to my blouse, I could almost feel them turn back my collar. His breath whistled. He smelled earthy, less of clay than of poorly digested meat.

A voice whispered, a voice rather like yours. It was the passing *praticien*, the wispy young man from our school, breaking from his task. "Monsieur loves his women, in all shapes and sizes."

The Master himself rambled, "Ah, Mademoiselle, what are we but muscle and bone — what, if not our bodies? More to us than that, you think?"

"Ask my brother." And I laughed.

"What does he know?" Monsieur pressed my hand, playful as Papa. He clumsily capped my shoulder and gestured to his work. "You see? You mustn't worry about shadows. They take care of themselves. It's how things look in profile that concerns us — surface variations. Think of the river reflecting sunlight: the inward transposing itself outward."

A voice more pressuring than his fingers whispered, *the inward what?*

"Beauty," murmured Monsieur, pleased with himself, his indulgent tone like Papa's.

His lingering hand compelled me to see things better unacknowledged. No longer Michelangelo instructing me, but a middle-aged goat with a river of beard and wearing a coat that might've been the target of many pigeons. My ears played tricks, surely, when he said I must know how lovely I was — that a girl like me would know beauty beyond the kind blinking from a mirror.

"If you don't mind my saying it," — his voice was gruff — "you're a pupil anyone would be glad of." His grip lightened. "Have I offended you?"

I tell you this, believing that it will help you to know.

Monsieur moved toward a statue so lifelike the model could have been cast in plaster. "Pay attention," said the *praticien's* voice, distant but clear.

"My *Age of Bronze*: true perfection," the Master flattered himself. "It can't be helped, with the Greeks and Florentines preceding us. What's to be done?" He cursed the Salon, the monocle-wearing dinosaurs for whom I had no love either, who'd accused him of casting his piece from life. "But people want what looks real. The government has bought a copy of it, after all, for its collection at the Luxembourg!"

"So things turned out in the end," I said, refusing, unlike my friend, to flaunt my awe. Though his achievement was, apparently, hard won.

"If one persists," he said, shrugging, and invited me to walk some time with him through the Gardens and to the Musée. But then he was off on a tangent. "You know Nietzsche?" Our brother would. "'The awakened and knowing say: body am I entirely, and nothing else.' 'Soul is just a word for something about the body,'" he recited. "True, would you say, Mademoiselle?"

Abandoned, the Italian snorted. Monsieur clapped his hands and the model stepped down, winding himself in his sheet, eyes slithering over my dress.

"Montmartre teems with people like you, Giganti," grunted Monsieur. And to me? "To work, Mademoiselle. We can't afford to have you languish, can we."

—⚹—

A KIND OF graveyard, the Dépôt des Marbres, as crowded with chunks of marble as the Cimetière du Montparnasse with tombs.

But for me it was a place of conception.

We modelled busts of the Italian, my friend and I. Hers replicated a wholesomeness that didn't exist; I captured youth and a rude bravado, as if a lewd remark was on the tip of his tongue. *Head of a Bandit*, I called it. My friend was dismayed. "But why make him ugly?"

Monsieur defended me. "What is art if not honesty?" He mocked her English fascination with toenails and nose hairs, details one didn't need replicated to know they existed. "Less is more. Why include what adds nothing? Aren't I right, Mademoiselle?"

He ordered me back to work on the heads I was doing, maquettes for a series of characters for his commission — not just any commission, of course, but one to seal his fame. He trusted me to help.

By then I'd had a wealth of practice, toiling away nights in our own petite, cramped atelier, modelling busts of our brother and, yes, the one of our sister who would only sit if my friend and I let her bring a piano. (How could we object with Papa footing the rent?) You can imagine: little Louise tickling the ivories while our brother yawned and stretched, and my friend worked her safe, pretty portraits. The warmth of my hands softening clay hard as iron, making it as malleable as Paul's future. He talked about his plans. Mused about them. To be France's world-travelling Shakespeare was his dream; what I dreamed was to capture the glittering ambition coiled inside him. Never mind the dimness around us, the shadows — for there were shadows — or his impatience, as bad as a child's needing to pee. Forget Papa's conviction that he'd make a great statesman. I stifled his whining by labouring over a cowlick.

—⟋⟍—

ONE NIGHT AFTER these sittings, I was alone casting the bust in plaster — God knows where you were — when who appeared at the door but the fellow from Monsieur's, Criteur, with whom I'd become a bit more acquainted. He generously helped prepare the mould; when I went to thank him, he'd already disappeared into the dawn lighting the street.

"Brava!" said my friend, there to watch me tap and loosen the mould and, expert as a midwife catching a baby, lift the final product free. It had our brother's gaze exactly, even in profile. Sightless eyes fixed on godly visions, not earthly ones.

When Paul came to view it I blindfolded him. His arm, when I gripped it, felt scrawny as Criteur's, who stayed away. A pity, since he might've enjoyed watching our game of blind man's buff. "Try to see yourself through your fingers!" I teased.

Taking his Lord's name in vain, our brother tore the scarf from his eyes. Paul — who suited the priesthood but loved the world, who would travel to China when anybody who was anybody favoured Japan, land of Hokusai, style, inspiration, the destination on art's spice road — had the nerve to question how I made him look: "A smart young stud teetering on the cliff above an adventure — aren't I right?"

Difficult not to jeer a little, though our day-to-day lives paralleled each other as closely as the rue de Babylone and the rue de Sèvres. As he lived and breathed poetry, so did I live and breathe sculpture, the wriggling joy inside me emerging in one creation after another.

"If you believe in yourself you can't fail," our brother preached to the converted.

—⁕—

OF COURSE FAME was our due, no reason or room to think otherwise. With the right connections, the right teacher — Monsieur was a patient guide to the texture of a model's skin, the tensing of hidden parts — the only way for me to go was upwards.

Monsieur's hand was as rough as pumice on mine. "Take time to feel. Don't be shy."

He was as hungry to teach as I was to learn — I would be stupid to deny him the pleasure, my only fear being that of running out of time. The making of work plays tricks with calendars and clocks, coupling urgency with a stillness that mimics inertia. In your childishness, would you know about this?

"Your little friend," he said, "perhaps she lacks your passion?"

What besides passion enabled me to go on day and night,

pressing, pounding, pummelling, scraping, spruing, chiselling, polishing?

—๛—

"IT'S HARDLY LADY'S work," Maman observed. We'd run into each other on the sidewalk, Maman and I, my friend (for once) waylaid. She ogled the *putti* above the entrance to our building which someone, undoubtedly someone with a penis, had been paid to sculpt.

"Praise the god of necessity, Maman — and the city's love of decoration."

"That god you work for," she started in, riding the creaky little elevator to our floor. "I hope he's proper. Never mind how famous he is. A decent girl has no business being there, *if* I'm allowed an opinion."

"No business?"

She removed her hat in the hallway. "I wasn't born yesterday. I've heard what goes on. Your brother —" she said as Paul, just home from school, skulked to his room.

"Piss on you both," I murmured into my glove. Neither were supposed to hear but Maman had the ears of an owl.

"Not only have you a fishwife's nails, but you've got the mouth of one, missy!"

Curtseying (how would my friend have behaved?) I went to kiss Maman's cheek. She pushed me away, calling out to our sister to cheer her with a melody.

"How can I, with nothing decent to play on?" *petite* Louise wailed. The piano they'd bought to replace the studio's refused to stay in tune.

—๛—

PERHAPS, DEAR C, what follows might not surprise you.
One dim afternoon, Monsieur ushered me into his cubbyhole of

an office. A torn green blind covered the door's windowpane, a dim light illuminating the clutter. Sketches strewn over the desktop showed women's parts: breasts, rumps, and places more private rendered with painstaking grace. The nub between a pair of thighs was a tulip bud, shy of opening. Like a doctor, he sat facing me. "How old are you?" he asked, running his fingers over the little sculpture I'd brought for his approval. "You see how the light plays with it — draws out the feeling as if it's there inside." He repeated his question.

"Old enough," I said. Nineteen.

Running his hand over his bristly hair, he reminded me of a hedgehog or a pot-bellied pig or, more aptly, a boar. He sat gazing at me, his patient with no complaints. "There's nothing more beautiful than the female body, you must agree, Mademoiselle?" Reaching out, he stroked my cheek. "Good structure, the planes of your face. A pity such beauty ages. A tragedy, really."

I pushed his fingers away. Silly old man.

Still he praised me. "What you have is gold, Mademoiselle. I'm only here to help you mine it — of course, inspiration is a two-way street. Pose for me."

"Why," I said, "when you have the Italians?"

That answer would have made you laugh.

—⁊⊗⊱—

MONSIEUR'S ADORATION OF the dark-eyed sisters, Anna and Adèle, was no secret, no mystery, reciprocated in how they gave themselves to him. They did it for art, those girls.

The haughtiness of Adèle's expression, captured in my maquette, pleased him as much as it pleased me. The bust showed a woman spurned, eyes closed, lips parted to receive a kiss forever withheld. Lingering over my study, Monsieur admired the jut of its chin, the curl of its hair. The model, adorned only by wavy black hair and giving off a healthy whiff of kerosene — poverty's perfume —

barely blinked at her half-finished portrait. She stalked off when he told her to get dressed and not return till he needed her.

"But, Monsieur — I need more time with her," I objected. Warmed to my gouging and slapping, the clay was no longer material resembling the model's profile but a shape to be filled with her spirit, a cup waiting for milk yet to be poured.

He found another girl to pose for him, and made Adèle mine to use as I pleased. Such kindness came with a price, as you might expect. "Mademoiselle. Have you considered my request?" he persisted. But hours posing would disrupt my schedule, be a terrific waste of time. I was frantic to complete *Buste de jeune femme aux yeux clos*, fresh ideas all the while kicking and screaming for attention.

Criteur marvelled at Adèle's completed terracotta. "So true to life, she looks about to speak!" he said. I suspect you'd have thought the same. One compliment whetted my appetite for more.

Monsieur gave my subject a playful slap and made her squat so all of her showed. Indecent, Maman would've said, and her voice in my head made me blush, no matter how I pushed it out. Yet in my mind's eye, the girl's butterflied backside turned to marble.

Flitting about the periphery, my new friend Criteur chanted *stones bones crones drones thrones*, or something equally insensible, as could be his wont. Understandable though, for the *praticien*'s lot grew tedious, chiselling not his own but the Master's grand ideas out of stone, scaling his rough little maquettes into larger-than-life plasters, making the moulds to cast the plasters in bronze. Chasing, dressing, and spruing copies; making and testing ceramic shells; polishing, patinating, replicating every dimple to win acclaim, not for himself, but for Monsieur!

Sighing, my model folded herself into a gentle *contrapposto*, bending one shoulder and arm forward to half-conceal a breast.

"Give her your best, Mademoiselle. Show me what you can do with her!" coached Monsieur in a choked voice. Too soon, he impatiently pulled Adèle from her platform and took her behind the curtain. No need to explain what went on.

I blissfully devoted myself to modelling the torso and thighs caught in my imagination, was at it still when Adéle emerged in her shabby cape and, leaving, gave me a diffident look. In defiance, or defeat?

Monsieur reappeared in the blush of late afternoon, a tired little man in his dusty suit. "Pose for me," he begged, "or is there someone else you sit for? I'll pay you — whatever you wish." He muttered inanely about men who'd happily eat out of my hand, how Adèle's beauty couldn't hold a candle to mine. Posing would show me how inner feelings could be brought to the surface and made eternal, he seemed to plead, forgetting the piece on my worktable. Headless, it would be my own *Torso of a Crouching Woman*. If he could do one, why couldn't I?

"Your father needn't know," he said, and that "any arrangement" would be "in the strictest confidence."

Barely listening, too busy to, I imagined Adèle's hands, compliant and pale, hatching into doves that I would free — I was thinking, of course, of you.

Monsieur breathed through his nose and smelled of cigars, like Papa after riding the train. Tenderly, awkwardly, he touched the curve of my jaw. When he kissed me his tongue felt chalky, and his mouth tasted of tobacco. "With talent such as yours, Mademoiselle, you'd best spare no effort."

—⁓—

TO LANGUISH OR not to languish? *Anguish* with an *l* is all. A word for waiting while already captive. Like a girl on the seashore given up to the surf, drowning or riding the tide to freedom?

I leave it to you to decide, C.

7

... AND TO PRACTISE
MY PROFESSION FAITHFULLY ...

MONTDEVERGUES ASYLUM
4 SEPTEMBER 1943
23H45

On a break, the first possible chance, I took it upon myself to hand-deliver, hand-surrender, Mademoiselle's letter, hoping to catch the directeur before his day ended.

Admin was all gunmetal-green filing cabinets and pebbled glass — notwithstanding the odd effort to make it welcoming, the secretary being one of them, tapping away at her typewriter in her scarlet dress and matching heels, and yes, a bunch of poppies wilting on her desk. Contrived, I imagine, to reassure those forced to place loved ones.

Unpleasant-sounding voices spilled from the directeur's inner office — a bit of a shock, given his demeanour my first evening here, one not unappealing if one likes reedy, balding men in suits.

It was a dispute, apparently. A grilling by some unsuspecting family member? Unsuspecting, I say, because if most had a clue what our work entails they might think twice about complaining. Thank heavens it's his job and not ours to field requests and complaints.

I was on pins and needles, anxious to return before Head noted my absence. Waving the envelope, I mouthed "bonjour." Expressionless, the secretary — a girl who evidently fancies herself more glamorous than she is, not to be unkind — rose and tottered over. *Where do you get your lipstick?* I would've liked to ask.

"The directeur's occupied," she said, between grabbing a quick puff of the cigarette in the ashtray perched on her desk, and adjusting her belt. She gave the envelope in my hand a perfunctory look.

Though the angry voices dropped by a decibel or two, I heard enough to know it couldn't be a meeting between Admin and a relative. "You're obliged by law, Monsieur," one of them said. "Work, you say yourself, is of the utmost value. All patients of that persuasion are required to contribute, under order."

A thankless job, the directeur's — no argument here — ensuring all are kept happy, from doctor to patient and family, and each and every one of us in between. He'd been sufficiently patient explaining to me the hospital's probation period, three months for new employees, a formality. His job was frying much larger fish, of course: seeing that fees were paid, payees apprised of guests' conditions, and expenses held in check — all the more difficult with Vichy forcing France to go hungry while handing over food to *les fritz.*

"You'll have to come back later," the secretary said, speaking above what sounded like his protests.

Where does Miss Scarlet buy her makeup? I dearly wanted to know, but didn't want to appear rude or overly familiar. She was more dolled up than anyone had a right to be, squeezed as we were by the Maréchal's austerity measures.

"The directeur's busy," she repeated, as if I were mentally

deficient. "I can book a spot with him tomorrow. For yourself?"

This threw me, slightly. "If necessary," I hedged, because a curiosity had seized me, if seized wasn't too strong a term. On a whim, I wondered if I might take a peek at Mademoiselle's file, though I had only minutes to spare before evening chapel — my turn to play escort.

"Excuse me?" The secretary seemed surprised, but also relieved by a request easily handled. She rooted for a key, then clomped in her heels to a cabinet hemmed in by a number of cardboard boxes, which she gracelessly dragged aside.

The dispute in the office, meanwhile, had hit a lull; in the quiet I pictured my chapel-goers lining up, Head Nurse already miffed. I checked my watch. Hôtel-Dieu and the nuns were so distant, Mass felt as specious as a lesson on bandaging, something to be sat through — which was how it had felt for a fair part of my life.

"You have to be patient," the secretary warned, her tone almost noxious. Soon she extracted a folder and, sighing, set it on the counter. I grabbed it, still clutching Mademoiselle's letter. "It stays here, sorry. Files aren't to be removed." She glanced toward Monsieur Directeur's door, where the argument had given way to what sounded like cheerful banter.

Fortunately the file was thin, containing only a few old letters and notes. The patient had begun exhibiting symptoms as early as her twenties: paranoia, *marked feelings of persecution*. A vague diagnosis, early on, of Kraepelin's dementia praecox or Bleuler's schizophrenia; no mention of treatment protocol besides the standard ones, physical labour and fresh air — though surely fever or coma therapy had been tried? Some lofty, unspecified references to her "talent" were noted, as well as periods of near-recovery, with carbon copies of several doctors' recommendations for her release.

Accompanying these, a letter caught my eye — from a relative, the mother, I gathered — refusing responsibility *under any circumstances* for the patient's freedom. *She's hurt us enough*, it said. Date of committal: March 10, 1913, to an asylum north of Paris; the following year, a switch to another institution; and not long after, the transfer here. Mount of Virgins, Pavilion 10. The Mount of Venus, the orderlies called it.

"Thirty years — she's been here ever since?"

The secretary blew a smoke ring and stubbed out her cigarette. Perhaps it was her eyebrows that made her look slightly scared.

The door opened and the directeur appeared. Behind him was a man, obviously some kind of official, in Vichy blue. The fellow jammed on his officer's cap and bustled past, jostling my arm enough to knock the letter from my hand and most of Mademoiselle's file to the floor. The directeur stooped to help retrieve her papers, his faded blue eyes meeting mine.

"So you've met 'the sculptor,'" he said, his smile jocular but distracted, one could even say skittish. "And how was your first week — Miss Poitou, is it?"

The secretary cleared her throat. *Best not to correct him*, I took this to mean, the poor man befuddled by whatever he had on his plate. Never mind that I'd put in nearly two weeks.

By then I'd almost forgotten my purpose. "Sir, there's something that needs your vetting."

"Oh dear — as you've noticed, surely, I'm afraid I have business slightly more pressing." He waved off Mademoiselle's letter. "Miss Poirier, I'm sure you can take care of it."

—⚭—

MAKING CERTAIN ALL were decent — a few persisted in trying to strip to their birthday suits in the sweltering heat — I managed, just, to get everyone queued in time. During the head count, who limped up but Mademoiselle, haggardly resplendent in her hat? Just the ticket, a special case to deal with, never mind that one needed six pairs of eyes to monitor the rest.

Head promised, as she took her supper break, that the priest who served as chaplain would help out. *Fat chance*, I couldn't help thinking, if there was a God and he implemented what the Church said I deserved. Absurd to think that before nursing I'd almost chosen the cloister. *But, for you, wouldn't this be like refusing to cook after burning yourself*, Sister of all people had said to dissuade me, even after waiving the requirement for permission my father refused to give. To think I was that green. *Vows are made out of passion, not fear. Are you so ready to give up on the world, because of what happened?* Of an accident really, though in Sister's view there's no such thing as an accident, only providence. The answer was fairly obvious: No.

Ever since, I'd missed more holy days of obligation than an epileptic could shake ten fingers at. If only the *aliénées'* outbursts could be as predictable — not that anticipating disturbances made attending Mass easier. Marching my guests in single file down the walkway, I felt my abdomen contract in dread.

The chapel, with its slender, grimy steeple and keyhole slits for windows, was as far as one could get from Lyon's cathedral. There, hard to imagine, I'd knelt for more than my share of Sundays, a business finally put to an end by a doddering priest who, instead of hearing and absolving me of my sin, blamed me for it. Well and good.

My charges filed inside like obedient cattle — all but Mademoiselle, who hung back, seemingly engrossed in some distant activity. The faintest breeze stirring the palms outside the directeur's villa and an ambulance slowly wending its way past Admin.

"Coming?" I held the door and she slowly caught up, gaze fixed on the flagstones.

Enclosed in the tomb-like stillness ahead of us, the witless blessed themselves, fervently bobbing and curtseying. *Be a healthy example*, Head's constant reminder dogged me, as if I needed it. Happy to dip my fingers in the font's cool water, I thought of Sister

Ursula's faith, her encouraging nudges. *Expect the best — E.T.B., Solange. Not that one acts with rewards in mind. But with God's help no sacrifice is too dear. And no door is permanently shut.*

I took a seat next to Mademoiselle, the rearmost pew offering the best vantage point for watching the others. Loud humming and Tourette's-like swearing had erupted; headbanging, rocking, and a full range of catatonic tics and automatisms were sure to ensue. Expect the unexpected; adjust and adapt. Being an example, I knelt. *Is it too much to ask, a half-hour without violence,* I prayed.

Accustomed to the congregation's quirks, the chaplain welcomed us. Easy for him — tending souls has nothing on tending bodies and minds. Sit down, stand up, kneel. Despite everything, Mademoiselle had the routine, if not its execution, down pat. A guest two pews ahead prostrated herself. Another swayed to some lively inner music. My mind was set adrift by the snuffling, hawking and cawing, the chaplain's mild drone, the smells of candle wax, incense and ammonia. Heavens, if I'd joined the convent, received a new name — *Sister Marie Charles,* perhaps — to purge me of my former self, I'd have become service personified. The moniker safe as a number, stripping away the foolishness of the sixteen-year-old girl I'd been.

Momentarily, I confess, I nodded off, awakened by Mademoiselle's sharp nudge. *Don't let the candles' flickering trigger any fits,* I thought. Mademoiselle coughed and I patted her back, the clammy heat of her coming through that fetid tweed. Guests rocked noisily to their feet and, not soon enough, were trooping up for Communion. Frowning, Mademoiselle peered straight ahead, lips moving slightly. Despite my lack of faith, I felt a twinge sitting things out to keep an eye on everyone. The nuns' words kept coming back: *The gift of believing comes through the Holy Ghost.* As the *aliénées* loped forward, it seemed to me that if the Ghost were here, and had a sense of humour, He might be amused.

When Mademoiselle stayed put, I patted her arm. "You're not

receiving?"

"A sin," she said, "to take the Sacrament without confessing —
my brother insists." Her laugh broke the uneasy stillness, that hat
of hers drooping over one eye. "The sinners are those who keep
me here. No fault of mine."

When in doubt summon dear Nightingale. *Encourage your
patients in all goodness, in any way that can relieve their suffering.*
Yet another voice stirred. *The sacraments comfort the disconso-
late.* Swallowing my hypocrisy, I suggested that she might find
some consolation — in Communion, I meant.

"And when was your last confession, Soitier Polange? You
sound like Paul," she began to rant. "What have I done worse
than anyone else? The priest nastiest of all telling me to 'repent.'"
Her tone caused two guests ahead of us to turn. "Before I die, he
says, or face damnation. God would be so cruel. Hell could be
worse than this?" Smiling smugly, she gritted what remained of
her teeth. *I've made my peace,* her look said.

What could one do but nod?

"If I've done anything wrong, which I haven't," she sniffed,
"I've paid through the nose!"

"Of course you have, dear." *Who hasn't?* I wanted to say.

Not soon enough the chaplain gave the final blessing, "Go in
peace." I shepherded the group as quickly as possible through the
stifling dusk. With the bombings not far away — in Marseille,
the orderlies keep reporting, probably just to scare us — and
most of the patients already terrified of the dark, night can be
slightly nerve-racking. Though welcome, the pavilion's lights were
piercingly bright, reviving those in a stupor with a near-Pavlov-
ian promise of supper — boiled cabbage on this occasion. While
I rushed to get them settled, the notion of a sharp instrument probing the frontal lobe stayed in mind.

Mademoiselle refused supper to scribble away in the lamplight.
When I returned to collect her plate, she pushed it away untouched.

"Did you mail it?" she demanded, barely looking up.

"It makes you feel better, not eating? Poison, my eye." It was an effort at levity, about all I could muster after the long day, bedtime yet to be gotten through.

She didn't so much as turn her head. "Hunger brings peace. If you knew a thing about the world, you'd see." The only sounds — immediate ones, anyway — were her breathing and her pencil's scratching. "But I wouldn't turn up my nose at warm milk."

Warm milk, St. John's wort, other old wives' remedies: if only they were curative! I remembered Head's remark, made while straightening the pins in her cap, that at a certain stage in life some guests feel an urge to make peace. *Yes, Dr. Freud*, I'd felt like laughing, mostly out of tiredness. "Peace with themselves, peace with loved ones, with God," she had said — almost something our dear Pétain would say — even as she chided, "We aren't their confessors, Poitier. It's not for us, whether we believe or not, to act as proxy. The chaplain should hear Mademoiselle's confession. Whenever she's ready to give it. In case the end is sudden and quick."

A fine can of worms *that* would open! Mademoiselle's baring her soul as helpful now, I would imagine, as treating cerebral hemorrhage with Mercurochrome.

Looking over her shoulder, I saw that it wasn't words filling the page but drawings. A scribbled likeness of the guest herself, and that of a mousy girl in a cap — a stiff, starched one, a nurse's. Something about her features was all too familiar, and it was not a bit flattering.

"Do I really look like that?" I said, managing a laugh. I recalled Dr. Cadieu's remark, or Monsieur Directeur's, that Mademoiselle's talent had been artistic. "I always wanted to draw."

Her smile was sugared paraldehyde: sweetly, burningly unpleasant. "And, like you, I always wanted to poke needles into arms and wipe arses. Go ahead," she taunted, rolling the pencil toward me.

Remembering the mountain of chores yet to be done before
night nurse came on — utensils to be counted and sealed away,
teeth brushed, faces washed, guests toileted then put to bed, the
wards locked down — I drew a daisy, a leaf and stem.

"Brava!" she brayed. Now her look was sugar with a tincture
of paraldehyde, burningly sweet. She began rooting through her
drawer, produced a hatpin — a good-sized one! — and, struggling
up, stuck the picture to the wall. "So you're not completely useless,
Solange Poitier, after all."

"You ... liked making pictures, then? You used to paint,
or draw?" I had been to Paris, once, had seen beret-wearers at
their easels along the Seine and in the Louvre, which I'd visited
at Sister Ursula's insistence. *Don't miss the Raphaels.* The raffles,
I'd thought she said.

Mademoiselle peered at me oddly. "Don't be stupid. Anyone
can make a picture. Think of the *belle époque*! A renaissance?" she
crowed in a pinched, mocking way that, if not for her hat, teeth
and the fusty odour rising from her, would've been comical. "I
was to sculpture what Gentileschi was to painting! I made men
and women as beautiful and as ugly as the gods, do you hear — as
only God himself, my brother's God, could."

"Well, that must've kept you out of trouble." I couldn't resist
a wink. Out of the mouths of lunatics, each word was to be taken
with a serving of salt well sifted.

Our guest gave me a haughty look. "And they say I should
repent, that I'm so full of sin I'll be shut out of glory." Smirking,
she welcomed the cat onto her lap; in the dim light its fur appeared
lank. "Do you believe in such things, Miss Solange? Being of a
pure and simple heart, perhaps you'll be my confessor-saint?
'Bless me, Nurse, for I have sinned.'" Chortling, she bowed her
head. Sister would've been rightfully offended.

But who knew, really, what to make of it? Despite my being

quite new and rather green, I was wise enough to realize that knowing too much can sometimes bite you, or force you to bite someone else — all the more trying for those who know better. Best, always, to keep things light.

"Tell me about your statues. Maybe you'll draw one for me. You did ... make statues?"

The old woman flapped her hands. "Do you know what it is to have a child, Miss Poitier? Each and every creation is just that. No more, no less."

The edge in her voice was wearying. I checked my watch.

"You live by that thing, your hands by its hands," Mademoiselle remarked. Her gaze narrowing, I could see the tiny blue veins in her eyelids. "So did I, once. Life according to the hands of a timepiece, the hands of a scoundrel — what difference?" The old woman shrugged morosely. "Did you post my letter?"

A change of subject was needed, badly. "What sorts of statues did you make?" An idea struck me, bright but hopelessly obvious. "Maybe if I brought you something to ... work with," — *sculpt* was the word, but it hardly seemed appropriate — "you could make something to jolly things up? The place could use some decorations, couldn't it."

The possibilities, I thought. Flowers and storybook animals, domesticated yet free. Numerous guests were enjoying second childhoods, and anything of a cuddly nature an antidote to the Maréchal's portraits. Given his official love of children, his upholding of motherhood and procreation as our country's salvation, it would hardly be contradictory.

"You haven't answered my question, Miss Poitier. My letter?"

I chose my words carefully as I lifted the cat from Mademoiselle's lap and shooed it under the bed, out of sight, out of mind. "Perhaps, if you agree to make us something, I can arrange with the directeur —"

"A pox on the directeur, and the rest! I'd be careful if I were you, Solange Poitier. Yes, even you, working for them while acting as my friend" — *Friend?* I almost said — "you'll see the dangers of playing one off against the other."

Don't take their ravings personally. Novice's frequent advice. "Is there something I can get you, anything you'd like before lights out?" I said.

"Only to be home, lying in Maman's garden." Turning to the wall, the old woman hugged the cat so tightly its eyes bulged, yet it purred. "Have you any clue, Nurse, what it's like longing for something that is everything and nothing?"

Suffice to say: "yes," sleep being it. Thus ends this entry.

8

MY DEAREST C,

Perhaps, in the smallest way, you take after Maman? She remained steadfast, you'll recall, in refusing to let me sculpt her. Was it 1884, '85? You watched me follow her from room to room, asking, "What are you afraid of?" Was it some secret the clay would reveal? Or was she a primitive, scared the white man's camera would steal her soul? I don't suppose you know any better than I do.

"Don't be ridiculous," she would brush me off. "Pictures are nicer, something to hang on the wall. This apartment, the clutter — look around. Is there an inch of space for yet another bust? Unless you wish to contribute to renting a larger place."

Surely she saw that I needed practice? I insisted, persistence being the key. Eventually my attempts to sway her were partly paid off when, in our father's presence, she agreed to let me draw her. "But only if you'll leave me in peace." I promised she wouldn't be sorry, finally winning her confidence.

The portrait I did in pastels showed her at her needlework, the only way she consented to sitting idle. Still she quibbled. "But I look so stern, my eyes too far apart. It's not how I appear, is it?" she demanded of Papa.

Our brother snickered. "Of course not, Maman."

Louise, always one to suck up, put an arm around her shoulders. "You're beautiful to me, Maman!"

And my friend, our boarder, whose prissy English lifted everything into a question? "Oh, Madame — it makes you look like there's something troubling you?"

My friend was bold if foolish to raise it, and not long after, was asked politely to find "more suitable" lodgings. It was awkward sharing a table with a stranger, Maman decreed, the expense raising the price for room and board. You weren't there the day my friend moved out. It wouldn't affect our friendship, she said. If a rift grew between us, it was Maman's fault.

For a time Maman's portrait hung above the vanity in her bedroom. "So this is how I look to you, my girl?" she said one night as she was brushing out her hair, its darkness barely threaded with grey. "And I thought a daughter loved her mother."

"Of course we love you, with all of our hearts, Maman," we each piped up, ready as ever with what she wanted to hear. Our brother having fetched her nightly cup of tea, each of us bid her goodnight.

"Do you know? A son loves his mother, but a daughter will always be there. It's what I decided when your brother was born. Not you," she said, to Paul's dismay, "the brother who came before any of you. A perfect baby boy whom you, missy, might have replaced. The one I lost."

"And this is the pain you wear on your face?" I meant in no way to upset her.

You went awfully quiet at that.

"Can't you see it's my bedtime?" was her swift, sad reply.

That same spring she and Papa found a more spacious flat a few boulevards over. Wouldn't you know, during the shift from one dwelling to the other, her portrait went amiss, not to be displayed again. "The movers, they lost it," both our parents claimed. Too true, alas: the world full of thieves, though I was not yet fully aware of it.

No matter — Maman's drawing led to studies, inspiring me to capture age (we won't say ugliness) in ways useful to Monsieur's employ. I continued to work on his characters, little figures representing the tortured and damned in his overwrought *Gate to Hell.* But the studies in Maman's likeness aided the piece taking shape in my mind. The only problem was finding the time to begin it while facing other demands.

"I show you where to find the gold," he insisted, "but the gold you find is all yours, Mademoiselle." What else to call his flattery but artful manipulation, its intent clearly to spur me into giving him my best work, an indirectly brazen request?

Of his more brazenly direct one, I wondered: what harm, posing? What harm, if it placated him enough to give me more time with Adèle, whose fees I couldn't afford? What could be wrong with letting him do my face? Working strictly, as he promised, from the neck up? At the end of one long day I said yes. A logical barter, expeditious for us both, he agreed, beside himself with delight — and fear? A master chameleon even then, I was only beginning to see.

I have to ask you. To what end, your silence? Why? You might've spoken up!

His palms were cold and rough, but masterful enough. He turned me every which way. Fingers like calipers. He stood so close his beard tickled me. He pressed on my neck, cradling my skull. He tugged and tilted my head this way and that, like a dummy's. Grunting, dissatisfied, he instructed, "Don't smile. Close your eyes, if you would be so kind — no, open them, but relax. Try to look as if you're daydreaming — that's it! No, no, you're much too stiff. Are you choking for air inside that blouse?"

Mademoiselle this, *Mademoiselle* that.

My God, C, if you'd been there! But maybe you were too young to understand.

His fingers pushed against my collarbones, his breath swarming my ears, his eyelashes brushing my cheek. The man was terribly myopic.

"If you undid a button or two, Mademoiselle, you'd find it easier to breathe."

To hasten things I obeyed. Opened my blouse, but only to the lacy edge of my chemise.

"Better," he breathed, and then I was in his hands again. One palm cupped the back of my head, the other my ear. "This way, so the light strikes your brow. No, a little to the left. It's not a corpse I wish to sculpt!" Such an actor — he trembled, even his hands, his gaze so intent.

The entire atelier was watching. It was hard not to laugh and shout at them all to mind their business. My friend, though, did not once glance up from her chiselling.

Finally, he worked the clay. His fingers rolled, pinched, fondled: the flying parts of a machine. A head grew from nothing. A face with my likeness, right down to the pout that bowing to Maman perfected — you know it. Wilful, she called it. Here, it appeared less wilful than meek.

Young Girl in a Bonnet, Monsieur named the piece, which showed my eyes downcast, a gloomy meditation. I detested the weakness of its chin, its sulkiness.

"It's heavenly — you must be thrilled," my old friend gushed.

"If the work is fine, it's only because I've shown what's there," said Monsieur. Such unusual modesty. Monsieur thought little of words, I had come to realize, their clumsiness stacked against the certainty of touch.

—⁂—

LACK OF TRUST in words made sense to me, then. But not to our brother, who loves words because they don't dirty the hands.

"And what besides a clear head and heart is more important than clean hands?" I'd tease him at the supper table, picturing Adèle's oval ones, works of art of a divinity Monsieur was only too glad to have me create. Adèle enjoyed having only to flex her fingers, spared shivering naked. While I modelled the wrists, my former friend watched, unimpressed: what possible meaning could they have, hands detached from the body? Calling herself an artist, she should've been more open. Value fragments for what fragments say, the beauty of less being more. The Master treasured fragments. His huge inventory enabled rapid groupings, his larger-than-life statues an endless repurposing of copied parts, effects tried and true. Commissions rolled in as proof that he excelled at made-to-order art.

Monsieur, having just returned from a day's jaunt visiting the cathedral in Chartres, unveiled my hands himself, as he did many of my creations, pulling the wet rags (rumpled cuffs?) from their wrists. The first glimpse of them startled even me, so graceful, their gesture. He was all agog. "You did these yourself, Mademoiselle? Bourdelle —" Bourdelle, a favourite among his *praticiens,* maker of things oppressively massive! "— must have helped. While the cat's away the mice will play."

Only the feline reference lessened its offence, since, like you, I've always been partial to cats. Still, anger simmered as he inspected each digit. I wish you could've seen them. Fingers fluid as coral, the hands splendidly offered themselves, my work a gift of perfect

form reaching upwards and out! His look resembled that of
Papa's when, in a rare fit of temper, he won an argument, and
Maman was forced to place her hand on his. A similar satisfaction
lit Monsieur's eyes. His cheeks flushed above his beard and, with
a galling lassitude, he gripped the pieces by the base, held them
high.

"Look closely," he shouted for everyone's attention, "here's
what you aspire to." He started clapping, applause echoing when
the others joined in — all but my friends, one busy with her work,
the other nowhere in sight.

Louder than anything was the sound of my pride swinging
open, my heart telling my head to forget Maman's petty, proper
ways. Yet a voice more humble, and cannier by far than hers, leapt
from me: "If I've managed anything, it's thanks to your instruc-
tion, Monsieur." It was a voice that Maman would approve of,
nonetheless, stickler for form that she was, or could be.

It bears repeating that the benefits of Monsieur's acquaintance
were many. His work was often interrupted by visits from the
cream of society, arriving to take him to lunch, dinner; soirées
with men in the government, men writing for the papers. All of
Paris wished to rub shoulders with him by then. Why wouldn't I?

You do see my point, my darling C?

—⟋⟍—

BUT I WAS also greedy for time. Things with Maman only chafed.
At night, while "sleeping," I perused my sketches of her, searching
for erstwhile recollections — sweet ones — of you, safe in her lap.
Imagined her attention poured out on you in her arms, though
the details of such memories are fuzzy. But you know how things
escape us. Our child's memories so selective, I've heard, that the
saddest times, not the happiest, push forward. I dwelt on this,
not the grudging snores drifting from her room, knowing that
every woman loves her child. It's the way we are made, most of us.

So I would redeem our Maman, working from these studies. I would create a *maman* in marble. A mother with a child, showing a tenderness to make the academics spit in their wine: *So sentimental, so gauche!* A cardinal sin to sculpt such homely feelings, pompous old men would dictate. As if I cared.

"Let them laugh," said Monsieur, all for it when, alone with him in the atelier, I divulged my idea. Stupid, stupid.

"It's just between you and me," I emphasized, withholding more. Talk only jinxes things before they can thrive. The last thing I needed was our brother hearing through his writer friends (that gnarly grapevine) and telling Maman of the statue I would make to win her over; she mustn't know a thing till it was done.

I thought Monsieur was only teasing when he asked, "What do I get in return for keeping quiet?" Gliding his thick fingers over my sculpted ones, he started: "My dear. Don't you see what you'd gain, my muse? I can't be happy knowing just your face." Eyes lingering on a group of figures, their gestures those of people in a dream, he waxed philosophical. So much more to the body than even the eyes conveyed, the eyes the window to the psyche, and on and on. "The way the spine curves; isn't that a clue to the life within, Mademoiselle?"

"You speak in curves." I laughed, to test his patience. "Please, make your point."

"I want to sculpt you, all of you. One isn't lovely forever, my dear."

You might well have gagged, if you'd been there.

"You would know," I said.

"I can help you," he repeated — feigning weakness? Something more than disquieting about his tone, alarming. A puppet's, it was, one looking to be danced and jigged. Just as disquieting was the cramp in my belly, the sudden, scratchy feel of lace at my chest.

Monsieur asked if I was religious.

"What stupid question —?"

"No, no. You misunderstand. To see as you do, so knowingly, you must ... imagine the Creator making us, his little clay pots." Wheezing a little, he mocked me! "Am I pompous to suggest that what the world takes for arrogance in you is humility?" His remark found a waiting nest in me. Would Maman have made this allowance? Given me the benefit of her doubt?

Monsieur was reaching for my waist when we were interrupted by my old friend, returning to drape a terracotta perilously close to drying out. "I saw nothing. Not a thing. I promise," she said with an embarrassing stammer, hurrying out into the street.

—⚬—

IT'S NOTHING MONSIEUR hasn't seen a thousand times before, I told myself. Nothing his eyes haven't already caressed. As a courtesy, he gave me privacy to undress, to lament, briefly, my slightly turned foot, and our family's righteousness. I wound myself in the sheet; otherwise, in such a draft, I'd have kept on my clothes.

Monsieur is the doctor; you have a fever. So reason spoke, as did the need to feel for myself the movement behind our creed. To sculpt it one must know it. To know it one must break rules, certainly the kind of rules that ruled Maman. I was young but not naïve. I was curious but not foolhardy.

At his knock, the twinges inside me — similar but less certain, less consoling than menstrual ones — grew urgent. He smiled, his a bumbling warmth, a modest charm. For a man his age he wasn't completely unattractive.

Good things come to those who wait, Maman always said; focusing on Monsieur, I perceived how it could be true. The sheet fell away, and it seemed a curtain rose, a curtain as grand and sweeping as Opéra Garnier's, rich red velvet, storeys tall. Except Monsieur's eyes were blue. Light blue unlike mine. My nakedness reflected there. His silent approval. Boisterous applause.

I might've bowed, but our inner Maman made me slouch and

hug myself. "Imagine, Mademoiselle," he said, "that a beam of light links you to heaven."

His finger pressed the crown of my head. He tugged my shoulders back, bringing me into perfect alignment.

"Look at you, my dear. You're nothing but grace."

Stroking my skin.

Yet once again he sculpted only my face, framed this time by a bonnet. My disembodied head emerged from a marble block like a guillotined one on a plate, as if my body did not exist. *Thought,* Monsieur titled the work. "Think Medusa," he said, "all that power in her head."

At least his wealthy patrons would know my face.

But as you might imagine, things did not stop there. Posing meant working twice as hard to keep up in the studio. Not enough to have me doing faces for his little vision of hell, I became his chief provider of hands and feet. No one could render them more finely.

Nothing like praise to win admiration, and admiration, devotion.

—◈—

HOW DIFFERENT IT would've been if things had remained from the neck up. Our arrangement, and what, alas, became mutual admiration. Late evenings. Our workplace emptying ... Do I need to tell you, this was impossible?

He'd chosen me, above all others. His favoured model and *praticien* and more than just a muse: he said not in words but by touch.

His lips, his thumbs pressed my nakedness. A different manipulation. His beard brushed my collarbones, my breastbone, my ribs. Too soon, or not soon enough, he was touching me all over. Parts of my body were doors being opened, as though with notes tucked inside. Reminders to keep my eyes on the star, my rising one shining down from everywhere. In reaching for it I reached for him, weak with determination.

I suppose you think I make excuses. But in my reeling imagination (what endures like the imagination?) a muscularity, quite statuesque, had led me past the curtain, laid me down on its mouldy divan, unbuttoned itself. Behind my eyes a dancer — smooth-skinned, tall, erect — flitted. It was a dancer who pushed his way inside, not this gnome grunting with exertion. A live version of his *Crouching Man* had entered me, a transaction sealed with a brief stinging warmth, then softness.

Afterwards, kneeling, Monsieur thanked me. His ear was to my chest while he railed against God for the "tyranny" of loving an idol. He spoke as if I wasn't there, but, touching my face, said, "Mademoiselle, you feel it too." A statement, not a question.

I had no idea, really, what he was talking about.

—◊—

SO IT WAS in our artist's universe. Life arched its back and curled its toes, straining towards a climax. Some elusive timelessness, a fleeting immortality.

Weeks, months, passed before my English friend spoke to me, her silence borne of self-interested caution? Then, out of the blue, she offered cigarettes, chocolate. "Your smile is more frustrating than *La Joconde*'s," she said slyly. Eyes bright with envy, she blushed the blush of a transparent rose. She found a use now for our friendship. "He's in love with you, isn't he."

"Not in my dreams or yours." I suggested she take up with one of the Salon's whitebeards if she hoped to get ahead. Not being rude, simply speaking the truth.

"No need to get owly," she huffed, when I was the one offended by her prying.

Good reasons for keeping things with Monsieur mum. Maman's finding out would've set off a war not of words but arrows and knives. But then the papers ran a little note about one of my statues, which made Maman smile. Knowing nothing about art, she took as much pride in my creation as she would've in her own, a crewel-work cushion, a pillowslip daisy. She ordered Cook to make a celebratory meal: use fresh fruit, mind, and no bruised ones in the *tarte tatin*.

I wish you'd been there to enjoy it. Apples, butter and sugar never tasted so good.

X

9

I WILL ABSTAIN FROM WHATEVER IS DELETERIOUS
AND MISCHIEVOUS ...

MONTDEVERGUES ASYLUM
5 SEPTEMBER 1943
20H50

Freedom! Well, freedom once I'd got through a night of insane dreams featuring Head Nurse in an officer's cap, shouting the schedule from a podium: "Poitier! 06H00 patients' doors unlocked; patients washed, dressed; hair combed, skin examined, state of evacuations noted 06H30 lunatics to laundry 07H45 to chapel 08H15 breakfast 08H30 clean & open windows 09H00 patients outside/inside till 12H00 lunch 13H00 bed-rest 15H30 outdoor exercise (walk stumble strut stalk) 17H00 quiet time (hush) 18H00 chapel (hush) 19H00 supper: clean up, count, lock up forks knives spoons, not soon enough 19H45 bedtime (clothes removed from rooms, wrapped, placed outside wards; windows, doors locked; do not forget a single one or OUT GOES Y-O-U! 20H00 night nurse comes on. But don't think for a second that you've earned leisure time."

I woke up still wearing my uniform, and much too early — 05H20 — for a day off. That voice of hers was still echoing. A sign of my dedication that I felt more tired than rested? I managed another hour of shut-eye — much appreciated, I must say.

Mademoiselle's envelope was still in my pocket, but I wasn't about to waste a minute fretting over it or anything else. The day ahead was a sterile pack to be unfolded, contents fresh from the autoclave, hot and germ-free. Peeling off my uniform, I put on a sundress and some lipstick — just the cure for the piqued look staring from the mirror. The letter I popped into my purse, the better to safeguard it from the curious, prying eyes of Novice and any other dorm-mates looking to borrow a nail file or eyelash curler.

I was passing Admin when the secretary flagged me down, beckoning me inside. Being there on a Sunday, did she have no life? "I forgot to show you these," she said, waving a thick folder.

Fortified with twine, it was bursting with envelopes addressed in Mademoiselle's hand, each containing a letter, none of them postmarked. The secretary watched me rifle through them. It felt a little odd, awkward, browsing through the correspondence of someone all but dead. Addressed to various people in Paris, its dates were all over the map, some as far back as the '20s.

"Not that Monsieur Directeur's behind in his screening" — the secretary gave a breathy laugh — "it's just that we assumed most of these people were deceased." With a dismissive shrug she said, "You can add the latest to the pile or destroy it, your discretion." She tottered off to replace the file and return to her typing.

The gateman barely grunted as he buzzed me through. Straight ahead and all around me, the perfect morning yawned: soft sun, fields leavened with blue, and the snow-capped gold of Mont Ventoux in the distance. Blissfully quiet, the road was empty of cars and pedestrians — still, I looked both ways while crossing to the opposite shoulder. Deeply shaded, it hugged the tiny Canal Crillon, which watered the farms which raised the cows which gave the milk, cream and butter which went to the Nazis. Feeling rather like a soldier on leave, I was glad once more of the canal flowing greenly past the woods en route to the village. If its surroundings were parched from the heat they didn't show it, not this early. Ivy choked the trees. Birds tweeted. A fox darted from the underbrush, something in its mouth, and disappeared again.

It wasn't far to the train station. Its presence was signalled by the overpass where I'd sought shelter so recently — if time could be trusted, the weeks dissolving into a blur. This time I was glad of its dank shade, grateful, except for the motif splashed on it, the crushed black spider ringed with red and white. Best to ignore it, though as I emerged I was unable to.

The quiet was shattered by shouting, voices barking orders. *Achtung.* Of course it brought back the train ride, all of us passengers hauling out our IDs, not to mention Sister Ursula and the other nuns seeing me off, their odd, foolhardy fearlessness. "No one can steal your devotion," Sister had said, and no matter what shape or form it takes I believe this is true.

If not for devotion, or some such weakness, I might have turned and run from what appeared next on the little rise just below the station. Armed men in uniform — two wearing swastikas, the rest a team of our Maréchal's *Milice* — herded people into groups. Soldiers were forcing others aboard freight cars which stood at the platform. Southbound, were they? Since the bombings it was hard to think of anyone going to Marseille. Were these people being sent there to work?

I noticed a young couple and their three little girls, a middle-aged woman with what might have been her mongoloid son, and an elderly man with a cane. More remarkable were all the men, a restless, growing swarm of them. Just boys really, most of them hearty and hale-looking but for their gauntness, quite common now due to the shortages.

The *gendarmes* were forcing everyone into lines, jabbing at people with their rifles. A peculiar, icy feeling climbed my arms. I couldn't help thinking of the *rafles* we'd heard about in Lyon, the government rounding up the Jews wearing their yellow stars, sending them north — for their own safety, it was said. But there wasn't, or didn't seem to be, a yellow star to be seen anywhere among these people. Ordinary Frenchmen by the looks of it. The ones who hadn't yet been queued up huddled like cattle under trees.

I told myself to keep moving, but too late. A fellow caught my eye, a civilian, rather handsome in a shabby, meagre way. Noticing me as well, he almost smiled, and I remembered what Head Nurse had said about our boys working in Germany for "decent" wages: "How lucky for them!" Making guns to use against our own, the orderlies said.

At the end of one line was a baby-faced youth who couldn't have been sixteen. Never mind Vichy's laws of eligibility for "joining" work crews, Maréchal Pétain's term for mandatory labour. Spotting me, the boy gave me a look as desperate as a guest's, begging to be unshackled, as if I could help him. Desperate yet fresh-faced he was, except for a nasty gash near one eye, and able-bodied by the looks of him.

Almost clinically, I watched a woman cowering against the station's grimy wall. I didn't wish to stare, but a panicky feeling kept me riveted. Muscling and shoving others into place, the *gendarmes* seized a boy and were strong-arming him into one of the waiting cars. The woman — his mother, I knew instinctively — kept wailing.

For no good reason, images from *Obstetrics for Nurses* leapt to mind. Illustrations of breech and normal births. Buttocks and heads crowning. Babies' bloodied ankles and scalps. Snippets of text, too, on administering scopolamine — invented by a German, so Germans mustn't be all bad. The twilight sleep it induced geared to erase not the pain of birth, but pain's memory.

Bobbing in the crowd was a pretty green shape, a blouse I'd recognize anywhere; wearing it, the guest I'd come to know as Simone, the one who worked in the kitchen and laundry. Simone, a name that matched her pinched reticence. Now her shirt had a yellow star pinned to the front, the badge relegated only to Jews in the north, supposedly. Had there been some method, some purpose, behind Admin's placements, working her to the bone? Punishment, or an effort to make her useful? I'd heard of this from the sisters: placements made in order to garner individuals a different kind of asylum. Instead of its usual blankness, Simone's face had a stricken look.

"Wait!" I heard myself stammer, but it was routed by orders as two soldiers manhandled the guest, dragging her by the arms and legs and pushing her into the last waiting car. Barely a second later, the whistle blew, and with a grinding shriek the train jerked from the platform.

Behind me, a scuffle erupted. Officers shouted in German, which I understood enough of to guess that something unforeseen had happened. Had someone broken ranks and escaped? Two soldiers following a dog's lead disappeared into the woods. Heaven only knows who'd got away. It struck me that the fresh-faced teen who'd caught my earlier attention hadn't been among the final queues stumbling onto the train — at least, I hadn't seen him there.

Meanwhile, that poor mother slumped to her knees could've used attention, though her misery was of a type that few medicines could relieve. A shot of Veronal might've helped — hardly a drug I carried around in my purse! Before I could offer so much as a consoling word, a soldier who looked no older than those boys yelled at me to move on. Reluctantly, despite the sick feeling in my stomach, I did so.

—⚹—

THE EVENT ALL but sabotaged my morning's pleasure. What was to be done about it, though? Send a letter of complaint to the Maréchal? I told myself — I made myself trust — that our patient, Simone, was going somewhere she mightn't, wouldn't, have to work quite so hard. Pointless letting what I'd witnessed ruin the entire day. But as I continued toward the village, I felt as though I were walking underwater, waves lapping overhead, clogging my ears.

Not soon enough, signs of normalcy came in view. Little houses and shops, one selling dresses, another flowers, and a *pâtisserie*. All closed, sadly. If it hadn't been a day of rest, one could have almost forgotten the war. A man walked his small white dog. A woman hurried past with her children, gripping their hands.

Soon the church appeared, the church of *Bon Repos*. It was as ancient as the yellow dirt in the square surrounding it, where a monument to sons felled in the first war was draped with the Reich's flag. Bells tolled, marking the beginning or the end of Mass. Elderly people trickled out, blinking at the brightness. I considered going in and kneeling, simply to collect myself; instead I circled the building and found a bench in the spire's shade.

It was a day made for leisure, though Montfavet was no Lyon. In the church's dusty courtyard old men played *boules*, adjusting their straw hats against the pulsing sun. Across the square, under a café's awning, a waiter lifted chairs from tabletops, shoved them into place. I had a strange hankering for a treat and felt for my money.

Inside, men huddled at the bar reading newspapers on varnished poles. They barely glanced up when I placed my order. I found a quiet corner and picked at the croissant, nursing my *café crème*, feeling shy, even cagey, at being out in the world — its clumsy, glaring bigness, the café's dimness small consolation. It was impossible not to think about what I'd seen, about Simone being taken away. At the next table a tired-looking couple conversed, sort of, evidently steeling themselves to visit the hospital — no other reason to come here. A daughter, I gathered, they were here to see their daughter, who had younger siblings. Who would be minding them?

Such speculation occupied my imagination, but not for long. *Obstetrics for Nurses* reared itself again. The imagination has ways of making the unknown seem worse than it can prove to be, particularly in matters of the body, and the gruesome complications of childbirth are a prime example: 1) Placenta previa, 2) toxemia, 3) prolapsed cord, 4) puerperal fever, 5) puerperal insanity, 6) hemorrhage. Not to mention 7) stillbirth, 8) craniotomy, 9) fetal anoxia, asphyxia, malformations, the failure to thrive. It's a list that made me grateful for the crackling radio behind the bar, for the tinkling piano music — "Clair de Lune."

As the nuns say: despite the world's evils, grounds exist for keeping up the spirits. One has to marvel at the fact that everyone breathing has made it through the birth canal, when even in this day and age the owner of said canal sometimes does not live to tell the tale. Though some things that happen, good or bad, are a matter of choice or attitude, birth comes down to luck.

With more than enough change in my purse, I ordered a second *café crème* — an antidote for feeling restless — and asked to borrow a pencil. In my purse was a standard war issue card, purchased for Sister Ursula, to let her know I was settled. I scribbled my note to her, thanking her again for her recommendation, and found myself perspiring — with belated relief, maybe, a near overdose of wonder that I'd arrived in one piece, and that I was nursing mental and not maternity cases. I did, however, question why Sister had been so keen to let me go.

I refused to give the *rafle* — because that was what I'd stumbled upon — another thought. Really, what could I have done to stop it? I smiled encouragingly at the couple nearby, old enough to be my parents. The music broke off and a speech by the Maréchal came on, his keening old voice crackling over the airwaves to pitch his slogan, *Work, Family, Country.* As good a reason as any to go and pay the bill.

Wandering out into the brightness, I found a tobacconist's that happened to be open, wonder of wonders. I had enough for two stamps and a single cigarette, dear these days and in short supply, a treat to savour in my room. Wordlessly the shopkeeper counted out my change, a few centimes. I applied a stamp to Sister's postcard, and opened my purse to tuck the cigarette into the case nestled there.

The cigarette case. My souvenir, discovered all those years back in some grass under a tree. *Sure it's valuable,* its finder had said. Using blades of grass, he and I drew lots for it. His lot was the longer so in effect he won, but after he had his way he said I'd "earned" it. A treasure, he called it. Talk about naïve.

Mademoiselle's letter also blinked up at me from my purse. Was it also to be a kind of memento for its recipient? Except it carried only good wishes. What harm, mailing it? What possible harm? The directeur had given his blessing to dispose of it as I saw fit, more or less his go-ahead. What could possibly be wrong with an elderly patient sending her brother greetings? If I had a brother I'd do the same. Goodness, if I'd had any way of contacting the donor of the cigarette case, I might have tried at some point, just to know he walked the earth.

I found the post office kitty-corner to the square and slipped Sister's card into the outdoor box. What harm, I told myself. The banality of Mademoiselle's letter was quite laughable set against other matters I've been privy to. A patient once disclosed in detail how he'd contracted syphilis, and I, though obliged to inform the authorities, agreed not to tell his mother. But the situation with Mademoiselle was, is, hardly comparable. No threat to public health, certainly nothing underhanded. The only wrong, surely, is holding those letters in the file, allowing the patient to believe all had gone unanswered. To mail or not to mail it. A choice as simple as breathing.

I licked the stamp, pressed it on, and popped Mademoiselle's envelope into the slot. Pictured it sitting atop Sister's card. Somehow my purse felt lighter. Done. But I wondered a little about my remark to Sister about the Maréchal's likeness being everywhere, a bland enough comment, as his bust's sightless eyes peered down through the post office window. Perhaps he has more followers than we'd imagine — never mind the archbishop's criticisms coming from Lyon, falling on deaf ears in the Vaucluse. Head Nurse isn't alone in her adoration.

— ✺ —

HURRYING PAST THE station, deserted now with not a trace of the earlier goings-on, I tried not to think of Lyon crawling with Gestapo. But there were other things far less repugnant that still turned my stomach. Certain details in *The Essentials of Pediatrics* — please, let's leave behind *Obstetrics for Nurses* — another field I might've entered but had taken pains to avoid, given the slight fear or discomfort I feel around children, particularly infants and toddlers, a distaste not for the patients themselves but their needs. Or maybe it's the Maréchal's talk of mothers being France's salvation that continues to put me off. The way he places nursing second to motherhood in virtue.

When I passed the little canal, I was suffering slightly from sunburn. I'd have liked to splash my face, except its water, a greeny blue-black nothingness, had an oily tinge, its cement banks thick with algae. The gateman glanced up from his magazine, waving me through, then watched as I passed. Only 15H44, hours of freedom remaining. Back in my room, I rearranged my textbooks — weighing down my luggage, how they'd screamed to be left for the benefit of Sister's newbies — on the dresser. After, I took out the cigarette, but the heat and a wave of hunger — certainly not, heaven forbid, any fear of patients watching — kept me from lighting up. In the refectory they'd just be getting started on supper, today's version of cabbage-dressed-as-mutton. An hour or two on my hands were opportune for reading *Principles of Nursing*; nothing one knows by heart doesn't benefit from review.

Reminders: 1) The science and art of nursing = practising decent, normal conduct in expression of decent, normal character. 2) Discipline is key, and 3) the development of sound attitudes and habits stem from a sound understanding of oneself. 4) A nurse is to be of all things a good, upstanding woman.

It helped, of course, to imagine Sister Ursula's voice stressing all that, her soft but penetrating voice issuing from a shapeless birdlike body. Her tutelage, of course, had pulled me out from under what Florence Nightingale and Maman Bottard might consider my lapse. Luckily my mother, having died when I was twelve, had been spared the shame, the embarrassment.

My review complete, the cigarette beckoned. Fingering the dented, pitted silver of the case for the umpteenth time, I recalled the story the boy had concocted, quite shamelessly, about how the case had shielded its owner's heart from a bullet. *A soldier,* he'd said. A hero like our dear doddering Pétain, I imagined, dodging Boche bullets in the first war! Chances are the yarn-spinner was a soldier now himself, not that it matters. Anyway, it's a waste of time to speculate. Resisting the cigarette, I buried my nose in *Nutrition and Disease* till it was safe to visit the refectory without having to wait there.

—⁊⁊—

IN THE KITCHEN — the place where rickets and scurvy fight head to head with the Maréchal's rules, our Maréchal, who fought hand to hand at the Somme, don't we know? — the air was so thick you could barely see the steam curling up. The weekend cook was commanding the stove and a new girl diced turnips. The stool usually occupied by Simone held a sack of onions. A slew of women in hairnets, some from Pavilion 10, slopped food onto plates.

I was helping myself when a little commotion interrupted the dishing out. The farmer was at the delivery door, arriving as he did each day for the slops, slops for his animals. Where normally he was quiet, he seemed upset, his agitation catching, of course, and jumping germ-like along the queue of workers assembling trays. Despite the cook's shouts for quiet the place buzzed. The man kept throwing up his hands: "Not Simone!"

Looking warily in my direction, the cook tried consoling him. "Yes, yes, and we've lost a good pair of hands. I did my best, you know. But when the men from the *Milice* came there was nothing I could — nothing anyone could do." Eyeing me, she crowed at him, "You'll have to come back, I'm afraid, after we've fed ours."

I managed to muscle in, avoiding the farmer's eyes, his pained look. I wanted to tell them that I'd seen Simone being put on the train. I wanted to tell them, somehow, that she had looked calm, perhaps even glad to be leaving, embarking on a trip. A lie, of course, but I wanted to believe that she would be all right. I wanted them to believe it, wishing with all my heart to be able to come up with something — some comforting little story, that Simone's family had been waiting at the station, there to take her home.

Instead, I struck on a brainwave. Because people feel better when you distract them from their suffering, when you give them a purpose, however silly, I faced the man squarely and said, "Maybe you can help with one of my patients. A funny request. But seeing how you're situated — on the land, that is" — I admit, I felt idiotic — "what are the possibilities of bringing some mud? Clay, I mean."

"To make mud pies, is it?" The cook smirked, before snapping her head around. None other than Mademoiselle had appeared, stumping in and flagging in the heat, the hair escaping her hat stringy with sweat. "Oh look, here to eat one is *la duchesse*, who'd have us all poisoning her."

The farmer's reddened, beady eyes narrowed, and he found his voice — a voice shot with pity or nerves, who could tell? "I'll be back this evening for your scraps." And he promised to see what could be dredged up. "There's clay in the riverbank." The banks of the Rhône, he must've meant.

By then, of course, all eyes were on my patient. Like a home-less person foraging for food, she lifted the lids from this pot and that, not noticing me. I intercepted her at the vegetable bins, one of her hands curled around a potato. She reeled, catching her balance. In her other hand was a page torn from a magazine, the flimsy paper smelly and wet. Smoothing it out, she shook a carrot peeling from it and held it aloft. Whose eyes but Pétain's twin-kled back at us. A beardless Père Noël in a braided cap, his pale moustache gleaming through a grease stain. His cartoon bubble instructed citizens to go forth and multiply. Well, Mademoiselle wasn't having any of it.

"Who is this?" she demanded. "He thinks he's as famous as my famous rat, the scoundrel?" Clutching the potato to her bosom, she shook her head, amused. Then, before I could stop her, she reached into the flour bin and dusted her face. "Beauty knows no bounds, Polange Soitier. You agree?"

The cook was not impressed. "Remove her, please."

Replacing my unused plate, my appetite oddly sated, I escorted Mademoiselle back to the pavilion and to her room. Once there she clung to me, agitated about something, spooked even, yet stubbornly refusing to talk. 18H35, but it might as well have been the dorm's Lights Out. The evening was no longer mine.

"Did you mail it?" the patient finally blurted out, loudly

enough to be problematic. It's plain the walls have ears. But no point shushing someone who'll only ask again, louder.

"Yes, of course," I said, being sure to whisper, "and I hope you hear back soon."

LUNATIC ASYLUM

TUESDAY? AUTUMN? YEAR?

DEAR C,

It bears explaining. Manhood, womanhood — Monsieur unlocked the secrets behind each. In those days our work was joined at the hip, like Siamese twins. Mutual worship, sleight of hand. All we did together, a kind of alchemy — magic. Solid things giving shape to the invisible.

Posing poured insight into me. The body's secrets. It was an essential part of the practice, being splayed, displayed, cracked open. You recall Maman's saying, "It's a fine life if you don't weaken"? So I sat for him. Crouched, sprawled, cat-arched my back. I won't be coy. Posing for him, I spread my legs, the light covering my skin like a dusting of snow. His caresses pushed aside boredom. "Just a little longer," he'd beg, as he never had to the

Italians. Arranging me like fruit, though who wanted to be still life? Wooing me. "It's good for you."

Voilà! Cast in stone, my graven image appeared! Yet my spine was a kite-tail, soul jigging beyond his reach. Because I was young and he wasn't. As he worked me from the neck down, his adoration grew addictive. I am not making excuses. Who minds having her beauty shown? An ear a seashell, hair an ocean's wave. Under his gaze, his touch, I floated, soared.

But I swear, while he captured my face and the nub between my legs, he did not capture the me who smoked, whose hands chiselled hard truth, whose eyes held thoughts greener and livelier than the Seine, its current ruched with light.

Such a green and lovely chartreuse world out there!

"You leave me weak. I suffer, loving you. Have pity," he whined on paper. Never letting details interfere with his idea of me. Of us. "Cruel," he called me. What would he have called you? And how was I cruel? Twenty-two years old, and he more than twice that age, did my youth injure him? Yours would've separated him from his balls. Grotesque, any man who grovels.

His hands made me a monument to him and to myself. Perfected in marble, relieved of my fault — what Maman called my "impetuous, demanding nature." I hate to tell you this, but sitting still will cure that. Lying on your back, biting your tongue when you can do better.

Nobody, least of all Monsieur, could carve marble the way I learnt to. How sure was my chisel. The patience it took, polishing a surface day after day with a lamb's bone! Right and just to focus on bones, C. They don't yield the way softer parts do.

"Love makes people do frightful things," Monsieur said, behind his office door. His greatness shoehorned into his fireplug body, into that small, ugly part of him I gripped in my hand, a *boulette* skilfully kneaded then pulled, once I learnt to use my hands for more than sculpting, my tongue for more than talking.

His tiny, choking voice: "Do whatever ... you want."

I pulled the sheet over our heads. Covered his mouth with both hands, counted. I'm sure it shames you to hear this. You'd have been appalled. Or you'd have laughed. A piece of theatre, mine the role of a girl not from his beloved *Inferno* but from Pigalle. His flesh trembling as I kissed him there. The thumping, clanging and pounding around us of others minding their business, unaware.

"What if your heart gives out? Or you quit breathing?" As if these were my concern! Oh yes, like you, *ma petite*, I could be a tease.

"Your fault," he said. He quoted Nietzsche again, that syphilitic genius, about a person being no more than a body, the soul just "a word." To think I believed him.

—∿—

SOUL BROUGHT TO mind church, a source of bitterness. That Christmas, you'll recall, our brilliant brother succumbed to things we'd railed against. Remember. The mystery of Notre-Dame Cathedral, cobalt blue, cardinal red — the rose windows' colours obliterated by night. Wedged between our parents I dreamed of sex shaped in marble. You were in the moon. Our brother too, apparently, falling in love with Christ.

Later, Paul hummed Aquinas's hymn, *Pange lingua gloriosi*, translated the Latin for us:

Word made flesh, the bread of nature
By his word to flesh he turns;
Wine into his blood he changes:
What though sense no change discerns?

It was the death of our brother of reason, though not of the one I'd sculpted, the boy-poet seeking adventure. "Aren't you curious? You don't want to know what's out there?" he goaded me, about something larger, something beyond us, something that existed everywhere. He seemed to leave you out of it.

Who'd even mentioned God? To me, creation is clay's chemistry. I parted my lace, allowing a glimpse of bosom, thinking only of shuttered light, tangled limbs. "What is god but this, *mon petit*? Chasing God! What about your poet friends, chasing skirts?"

"What about them? No wonder Maman thinks the worst of you. Why can't you be like your friend? A nice girl, decent-seeming," he said.

My former friend, who now had a gentleman underfoot, an Englishman with a camera, who wanted nothing more than for her Englishness to move home and have babies. Purer, if less alluring, than a fairy-girl in some quaint photograph — which was how I deported myself, returning each night to my little bed.

She came to our flat to celebrate the engagement of our *petite* Louise. A lawyer, no less, the unlucky man looked askance sitting next to Maman, our Louise her understudy, Maman herself a sour weed yanked from its soil, while Papa, my friend (ingratiating as ever) and our oh-so-Catholic brother encircled me. Latin chants encircled Paul's thoughts of Rimbaud, no doubt, while Renan the heretic's words encircled mine.

My friend's Englishman came too, to snap a picture. When he yelped "Fromage" we all looked.

I missed you so much that day.

—ɷ—

AND WHILE I slept in my bed, someone stole about Monsieur's atelier, draping his figures to keep them from drying out — vital, because his practice was to accumulate. Building pieces by adding parts, grouping, regrouping. Mine the opposite, a matter of stripping down, stripping away. He sought permanence, and I, fluidity — so much more to it than making monuments! Stories brought to life, not just recounted. A Hindu legend of fragile love enraptured me, yielded a statue. A prince and nymph entwined, an eternal liquid embrace. Forgiveness and supplication. My man knelt, my woman, seated above him, gave in.

"But they look so tentative, unsure," went Monsieur's critique. "Wouldn't it be better if they rested on the same plane? Doing what they ought, kissing."

But that would be predictable — you would have agreed. I reminded Monsieur of his own advice, to not show what people know. Better to keep them guessing. "See how patient she is, this girl?" And I nudged him, and named my piece after her: *Sakountala.*

"Show me some patience," he said in his office. Such an appetite, Monsieur's. Taking his time while flames guttered in the pot-bellied stove, the divan's springs complaining. My skin sopping up his kisses, his promises. *I was the only one he could really love.*

Cathedrals have their charms, C, as do older men. As did his famous *Kiss.*

He'd take me places, introduce me to gallerists, collectors, journalists who could help. You'd have listened.

For a time, he did.

—⚬—

THAT YEAR, AT the Salon des Artistes Français, my work gained notice. *Sakountala* won honourable mention and enough of a write-up in the papers to turn Maman's head and delight our brother. What better praise than printed words! They softened Maman, made her a little kinder, more patient, more accepting of my quirks, perhaps. She minded her own business, attending to her petit-point and giving lunches, and showing appreciation for presents I brought.

I picked up oddments for her at Samaritaine after work, out of pity. The reason behind her misery? She was homesick! For our native soil, the Champagne's chalky dirt, vineyards and rolling patchwork fields. I missed the country too, the way I missed you. The roots of her longing ran deeper than mine, but not so deep that they weren't soothed with gifts. Sensible knickers, hose, the odd trinket to replace one you'd broken. "Yes Maman," "No Maman" were easily said in exchange for peace, peace to live and breathe work and Monsieur. I wanted only to please her, and Samaritaine was on my route home from the Louvre, which I'd begun to haunt again during moments stolen from his atelier.

I sketched there — studies, secret ones for the pair I would sculpt. Maman the gentle mother, and you the child, taking shape in my mind. Now was just the research phase, combing the galleries for Madonna-and-Infant paintings, Raphael's Virgins and da Vinci's Saint Anne looking at the Madonna looking at Jesus. Drawing after drawing I made, stepping over students from l'École des Beaux-Arts. Boys wrapped in scarves huddling over sketchbooks, too self-absorbed to hail the living artist in their midst. To think that once, like you, I too had been so unaware!

Then love crept up without my knowing it, gaining ground. Monsieur's attentions, his thirst for me grew unquenchable. He left notes full of pestering questions: What was keeping me? Surely all I needed was in his studio? Why hadn't I waited for him? Why wouldn't I wait? "I looked for you all over," he complained with his pen, "waited half an hour by the *Venus de Milo*, half an hour more by *Winged Victory*. Still you didn't come."

Finding someone in the Louvre was like finding a potsherd in a trash heap. "It's not that I'm avoiding you," I said, perfectly candid.

"How do you expect me to feel, when you're not where you say you'll be? Don't you see? I give all of myself, every ounce — must you take it so lightly?

"My love," he said.

Tears in his eyes, to my great embarrassment.

Because Maman loved me, as Papa did, and you do, and Paul, and maybe even Louise, in her way ...

"What am I, a priest stuck with your confession?" I joked — a mistake, touching on churches, which possessed him — albeit in a worldlier way than they did our brother.

His response was a riddle. "What's the one thing that rivals a woman for beauty?" A *petit four*, a salmon *terrine* from Stohrer's, you'd have said, but a cathedral was the answer. As if the spat hadn't arisen, he spoke of visiting Chartres. "A miracle of light and stone, its cathedral, a rival any day to Notre-Dame."

"My brother would know," I said.

—ɯ—

HE RAVED ABOUT its stained glass windows, their singular hue — the bluest blue — which made me think of the Madonna paintings. In them the Mother wears sky-blue robes, unlike the *mère* in my work-to-be, Maman in her unwidowed widow's weeds.

Cerulean. Cyan. Azure. Is there a name for that blue?

Then Monsieur had an idea, for a piece having to do with water — very odd, his work usually intent as it was on solids. He had me strip and fold myself over a mound of rubble, broken studies swept into a pile covered with a blanket. The fetal position, he wanted, a half-crawl, half-curled posture — weariness — and my hair spilling forth over my head. Left arm folded under, right one forward, cheek on wrist. Arch your right side. Stretch! Bend to the left, shoulder and hip pressed toward each other — that's it.

"As if you've carried the weight of the world on your back, Mademoiselle."

"A world of rock or water?"

"Please. Don't move!"

And he sculpted me, all of me, not as the busy, breathing being you know, but a slumbering silent one. Never mind that the story he used was Danaïd's, water-hauler of the Underworld forever condemned to filling leaking urns. A girl who couldn't, or wouldn't, lie down on the job.

Monsieur was a man who was expert at making the living look dead.

"Surely it would be more moving to see her labour?"

"But, Mademoiselle, why choose the infinite, when the finite has its logical ending? Everyone dies, my dear."

"Really? No!" Our Monsieur, so easily teased! Resisting his certainties was just one way to pique his desire; nobody likes a milquetoast. "All the more reason then," I said, "to show what it means to be alive."

—⁓—

HIS DANAÏD WON accolades: such anatomical correctness! It reminded me of a moth, beautiful and deceased, another monument to something unliving. Its success was toasted at a dinner in Palais Royal, a restaurant in one of its galleries. Yours truly not the party-going type, but he persuaded me to go, even bought me shoes.

"Ah! So you're his muse," said the old goats and gawkers introducing themselves. The ladies resembled pastries, dresses and hats sugary confections, the food itself too pretty to eat. Champagne flowed.

They were moths, and Monsieur was a stubby flame attracting them. Drifting about on his arm, I relished their stares. You'd have expected me to.

Afterwards I waited for him to propose a task requiring our joint attention: A riverside stroll (no one but lovers that hour on the quays, free to do as they pleased)? Drinks in a café? But we crossed the Pont des Arts without mention of these; too soon, I would find myself alone in my bed.

On St. Germain he hailed a hansom. He had someone waiting,

he said — his housekeeper, with petty matters to broach with him. I shouldn't mind, just this once, but he had to hurry home.

"Your wife, I suppose?" My flirtiest voice, loud enough to forestall the cabby's impatience. I'd heard rumours and had my guesses about the phantom that draped his figures — one that cooked his meals, too, and mended his socks and other garments. Such thrift in view of tonight's finery, his top hat and tails.

"Of course not," his answer indignant and stiff. "Mademoiselle, if she were my wife, my obligations would be plain — and, God knows, there'd be none of this business ... How would a married man keep up with you?"

We kissed, he paid the driver, we parted. Then, when Monsieur turned onto rue de Bellechasse, I asked the driver to loop around, let me off near rue de Bourgogne. You'd have done the same.

A velvet darkness. I walked as quickly as possible in party shoes, ducking past doorways. I caught sight of him and concealed myself in the shadows of a *crêperie*. Watched him hurry closer, my Monsieur. He disappeared into a building, a dismal, unadorned place like the rest on that block where, in an upstairs window, was a hag's face. The light burning there soon extinguished.

It was late. Because I had no money for a tram, I walked the two or three blocks to the atelier, his atelier, and slept on his couch.

—⁂—

"YOU DIDN'T COME home last night!"

Maman ripped into me at the first opportunity. Her concern was justified if her anger wasn't; I'm glad you weren't there. I'm glad you were spared the ranting. "Where on earth were you? Does it even occur to you that I worry? That you might call? For all I knew you could've been raped and left for dead, dumped in the river! My darling girl —" The way Maman spoke she couldn't have known of my posing, or of Monsieur's water-bearing nymph, though it was a matter of time before word leaked out. "Just when you start making a name for yourself — a good one — getting ahead in whatever it is you do," her concern a harangue, "you still haven't learnt common sense?"

Thankfully her anger didn't last. That night our brother had friends, a bunch who took pains to call themselves poets, holding forth in Maman's blue-and-yellow parlour. Paul recited Baudelaire till Maman was safely in bed. Then out came the brandy and sheaves of verse — theirs, a torture of rhyming couplets and plans to send them to Mallarmé and any other famous writer patient enough to read it.

"What do you think?" one asked my opinion, a pimply kid who, like others our brother brought home, had his eye on me. If not me, it would've been you.

Paul cornered me when they left. "Indeed. *Ma chère soeur*, what do you think? What goes on in your head while you're fucking that man?" His contempt for Monsieur was quite obvious for a while, it's true, but till then mostly kept to himself. Who knows what gossip his friends picked up and traded? "For such a grand place, Paris can be smaller than Villeneuve, you know." He wagged his finger at me.

"Then you'll excuse me, *mon petit*, for not being like you, a man of the world and a saint."

"Doesn't take a saint to respect Maman's feelings!"

"Please — you'll wake her."

"As if you cared." A hard glint in those eyes so like yours. "I'm afraid for you, is all. I've heard things, not too pleasant." His mouth looked hard, too, in the lamplight, his cheeks pale. "For one, your monsieur has more women than women have hats. More women, even, than France has churches."

"Ridiculous!"

Roused by our arguing, Maman appeared, a brass tack to a magnet. Her face was as long as the braids she did her hair in for bed. "Enough, bickering like children! Is it asking too much, a person getting her rest? You should be asleep, both of you — all those tomorrows ahead." A bitterness there; a touch of envy, you think? Only the slightest sarcasm.

I put aside the studies for her piece, the one that would include and incorporate you, that I was almost set to begin sculpting. Monsieur had allotted me time with one of his models, a crone who was standing in as one of his damned (it wouldn't do to have only males among them). It had taken some doing, finding an old woman hungry enough to pose without clothes, so my time with her was all the more precious — another perk of "being Monsieur's."

—ɯ—.

HE WAS WAITING the next morning, waving a piece of mail. On violet-scented paper was a polite invitation: Maman asking him to lunch with us in Villeneuve on our holiday that summer. *Please accept my best wishes,* I glimpsed, before he stuffed it back in its envelope. More important, Maman had extended *fond hopes* that his wife would come too. Seeing it in Maman's hand was a slap to the wrist, let me tell you. Or perhaps that's dishonest. A kick to the stomach was more like it. Rather unhinging.

"So there is a madame!" I batted at his shoulders. In the heat of the moment I picked up a head, hurled it, watched with a queer fascination as it exploded. Terracotta pieces everywhere.

"That woman is not my wife, she's my housekeeper." He very roughly twisted me towards him. "If she was my wife, wouldn't I take her to parties, openings — wouldn't I? My dear Mademoiselle, how could I be married when it's you I want, you I share anything of value with?" And on and on, how she rarely left the house, this helper of his. How kind of Maman to include her, because a visit to the country would do the poor wretch a world of good.

"Fine."

And following your example — who wanted peace more than you? — I picked up the mess I'd made. Sealed our truce with a kiss.

—ᴍ—

SPEAKING OF WHICH, I send you one. X

II

... AND WILL NOT TAKE OR KNOWINGLY
ADMINISTER ANY HARMFUL DRUG ...

MONTDEVERGUES ASYLUM

MONTFAVET, VAUCLUSE

11 SEPTEMBER 1943

"**D**octor says you've made nice things with clay," was how I broached it. *Be subtle, never too obvious*, Sister always said.

I set the pail in the middle of the floor, having hauled it up to Mademoiselle's room from where the farmer had deposited it in the refectory. Escorting Simone's replacement had provided the opportunity for me to collect it. When I had mentioned Simone to Head Nurse, I was told, "That poor creature? Don't give her another thought. She's gone to her family in Nice. Sometimes, if rarely, cures can happen, you know." She had spoken with such conviction — why, she'd signed the release herself! — which only added to my unease.

Mademoiselle eyed the bucket. She didn't make a peep as she watched me transfer her jottings to the bed, but when I spread the tabletop with newspaper she ground the stumps of her teeth. I found it impossible not to dwell on a note scribbled in her file, regarding a self-made remark about her *caprice and inconstancy*. The contents leaving the bucket made a disgusting plop.

The patient sat on her hands. "To think I modelled the most exquisite mother and child out of such shit."

No need for foul talk, I bit my tongue to keep from saying. The muck was dug and delivered that morning, the fellow had said. A greyish brown, it smelled of dung. I prodded it with the stick I'd used earlier depressing her tongue, a routine oral check. "Something to keep you busy, love. The merits of recreation can't be overstated."

She gave the mound a poke using her index finger. For one indelicate moment she looked about to taste it.

"It's not chocolate, dear."

But she seemed to have another beef. "You don't expect me to knead it, surely? Criteur! I need my assistant, Criteur." That small, plaintive voice suddenly haughty, insulted. "You can't expect me to work without a model."

Be kind, be patient. Be willing to play along. So I struck a pose: chin up, chest out, perfect posture if I do say so. But Mademoiselle glowered and stubbornly folded her arms.

"If you would be so good, give me my pencils. I prefer not to soil my hands."

After the trouble I'd gone to — not to mention that of my accomplice, who supposedly raised pigs but hedged, very conveniently, on the location of his or any farm. "Come now. So much brooding on paper, Mademoiselle!" I suppose I spoke from experience. "Making something nice will do you good and pass the time."

"Writing doesn't?"

For someone inconstant and capricious, my goodness, the guest was obtuse, constant in her self-absorption. More writing would produce more letters, more pressure to flout hospital policy. And Head had just reminded me at the start of shift that no matter what the directeur said — "his laxness notwithstanding," as she put it — the rules on sequestration were to be obeyed. Unswervingly.

Sighing, Mademoiselle timidly pinched off a bit of the stuff, rolled it between her trembling palms. The effort couldn't have been all bad: a faint smile curled her lip. Closing her eyes, she caressed the mud, stroking, squeezing it, pulling and stretching it. What she laid upon the newsprint made me blush, I must say. Quite a specimen — that aspect of male anatomy the nuns deemed unmentionable, but we'd all seen our share of, though in my case, only a couple of times intimately, truth be told. Textbook illustrations hardly count.

"From memory," the patient cackled, taking obvious delight in my reaction.

"Well. You have a good one, then. Memory, I mean. Though I'm not sure what the orderlies will make of this." My best attempt at humour.

Not that she noticed or was even listening. "Criteur?" she addressed nobody, or nobody visible, then eyed me squarely. "He had the patience to pose. But not the physique, alas. Though it's spiritual substance we look for. So you, Soitier Polange ... you needn't bother posing." Grimacing as if it pained her, she closed her fist around her handiwork. Greenish slime oozed from between her fingers. She let the thing fall to the floor, then, quite innocently, held out both palms stained that foul colour. "It's useless, don't you know? When one can't see properly — a torture, to lose one's gift. You have no idea, do you, do you, how desperate it feels being blind."

Patience, patience, I could almost hear Sister Ursula's voice. Deep breath in, deep breath out. "Now, now. That speck above your bed, Mademoiselle? You see it, yes? Tell me what it is."

"A fly. Of course." But her eyes had a dewy look.

If necessary, count. Slowly, while breathing. Running my tongue over my bottom molars, I counted these, while bending to scoop up the offending object. Its mud felt warmed by her touch. It felt vaguely improper, too, and I dropped it quickly into the pail, as if it were a real appendage that deserved a proper disposal.

Fortunately I'd had Novice drop off a supply of good hot water. I cleaned off our hands — the patient's, then mine — and set about straightening the bed. It meant tiptoeing around the guest, because once more she was engrossed. She had retrieved another blob of mud, prodding and pinching it into something like a face — recognizably human, with a nose so lifelike I blinked. What Mademoiselle accomplished was rather remarkable, really.

"The orderly will come to tidy things up. I asked him to, once you're done."

She barely glanced up.

This business was a lot messier than jigsaw puzzles or crocheting, but at least it didn't involve dangerous tools, thank my lucky stars. Not too much harm could be done by an *aliénée* using her bare fingers. "There, dear — see what you can do without fussing over anything sharp?" Like a nib, I meant — and better had kept to myself, I realized too late.

"Sharp!" she lit into me. "Lunatics screaming and laughing! Blades slicing up my heart, my mind. These aren't sharp?" Then her voice dipped. "Scrapers, rifflers, chisels ..." She continued rhyming something off, half under her breath.

Save for the racket from the hallway, the only other sound was the feline licking itself. An inspiration. "Maybe you could make a cat? No trouble getting it to pose, Mademoiselle. Seeing how it likes to sleep."

She gnawed her lip, weighing the pros and cons of divulging some dreadful secret? "Once, if you are at all interested ... if you care to know … I could sculpt the human form to make a man weep. My mother and child was every mother and child ever born in the world." She gave the mud a vicious shove.

Novice couldn't have picked a better moment to arrive. The patient three doors down, "the one whose fever didn't take last time," was prepped for a second treatment. Cadieu expected me to start it. As if I'd forgotten.

"Fever!" Mademoiselle was quaking. "Boiling a person like a lobster! You, Nurse" — those eyes bored into mine — "that someone who pretends to be so sweet could be a torturer!" Shaking her head, blocking her ears to any protests, she spat, "Isn't that what you are?"

—⚓︎—

IT IS A well-known fact that the success of fever therapy hinges on the nurse's skill. Novice had everything ready — pressure cuff, stethoscope, thermometer, washcloths. No fever cabinets available, unfortunately, so treatment had to be given the old-fashioned way. I was relieved that today's recipient wasn't Mademoiselle.

Steam rose from the tub; this in combination with the room temp soon accelerated my pulse rate, a sure sign the procedure would go off effectively. The guest, a girl suffering from hysteria, squirmed a little — "No one enjoys having this done, dear" — when we got her into the tub. It took both orderlies to apply the restraints. I pumped up the cuff — "Pay attention now, Novice" — and noted the pulse rate: steady and smooth. Testing the water temp, I admit I winced. It was hotter than hot, scalding. Within minutes — "Excellent, love" — sweat beaded the patient's face. She kept keening. One orderly helped hold her under while the other augmented the hot. The patient stopped shrieking enough to ask how long the treatment would take. "Only five or six hours," I said. Optimum results required up to twelve, but no point upsetting her.

It took Novice, plus an orderly borrowed from Men's, running back and forth to replenish the bath at optimum temp. One hour in, the patient's temp remained steady, despite her racing pulse. Her blood pressure dropped abruptly — very good, and critical for sending the body into its restorative state of shock. *Fever is gentler than coma therapy,* I repeatedly told myself, fighting the patient's thrashing. It would've been much easier, a lot more efficient, with a cabinet, designed to raise and maintain body temp significantly higher and equipped to spray hot or cold water as needed.

After two more hours, body temp at 40° Celsius, the treatment began to take effect. The patient stopped fighting and her eyes became filmy. Her skin, red earlier, now appeared colourless. It might've been cause for alarm, but the textbook and Dr. Cadieu agreed that a body temp of 41° is vital for success. *The duration of the febrile period depends on the disease, the patient's condition and the physician's judgment,* I recited to myself. *The utmost care must be taken to observe minute changes in vital signs.*

Then the pulse became almost non-existent and the eyes rolled insensibly. An orderly of all people had the presence to pull the plug and add ice, a bucketful of chipped ice hastily obtained from the refectory. Someone else, Novice perhaps, helped apply cold cloths to the wrists and temples. As the tub drained, a warning — *the excessive build-up of fever causes many fatalities* — pounded inside my head, as I grappled with the patient's to hold it up. The same orderly wrested the patient, dripping and unconscious, onto the tiles. Only Novice's quick action, covering her with towels soaked in ice water, revived her.

The individual's tolerance threshold must never be overstepped.

Aftercare indicated a cooling sponge bath, an alcohol rub, cold compresses for headache. Check. No such care, however, for rattled, distraught personnel. The only treatment available for us was the quick mental run-through of a checklist, our nurse's code of conduct:

1. Like it or not, a nurse is a teacher. Good, average or poor is not an option.
2. Listen attentively. Engage patients in diversionary conversation as needed. Dead silence frightens or depresses the sick and is especially bad for those requiring distraction.
3. Cultivate a confident, cheerful manner. A dead, expressionless voice is unattractive and to be avoided.
4. Never whisper. Never tiptoe. Whispering and tiptoeing are irritating to the healthy and fear-inducing in the sick, inviting anxiety in all but the imbecile who will think their condition has taken a turn for the worst.

The exercise hardly restored my nerve before I was called to treat another hysteric. I raced to administer Veronal by suppository. A shot of chloral hydrate would have done nicely but for the patient's automatism — rather violent head-banging — which would've snapped the hypodermic in two. It took both of our orderlies to restrain her. After that was a case of nervous exhaustion, which meant employing the crib; it took three of us to subdue this guest on her back in order to secure the lid. "Escape that, Houdini!" Novice said.

"All in a day's work," said Head Nurse.

The doctor appeared as I was helping myself to a sip of water. "You're interested in sine-wave therapy, aren't you? If you hurry, Nurse, they can use you over in Eight — behind Men's." Cadieu's calm, I might add, goes quite a long way, whether she means it to or not. "Head can spell you for an hour or two, I'm sure."

In Lyon I had, on a few occasions, assisted with electroencephalograms, at least: shaving patients' heads, helping the technician fix electrodes to grease-pencilled Xs on their scalps. The jumpy, scratchy noise of the EEG machine tracing their brainwaves had been rather relaxing.

I tracked down Cadieu's colleague in a small, windowless room, where the attending physician merely gave a nod. "Cadieu sent you? That's good." The sight of the thin, sallow patient strapped to the gurney made my stomach contract a little, and my throat go slightly dry. On cue I bandaged the guest's jaw shut. The air's staleness — yes, better ventilation would certainly help in such situations — made it hard to breathe deeply.

When I was told to help apply the paddles, I hoped the bandage was tight enough to keep things from breaking. Watching the convulsions, most violent through the extremities, was a bit distressing. The smell of scorched hair and skin, of burns to the patient's temples from the paddles, made me queasy. It also dispelled the questions I'd formulated, rehearsed even, while looking forward to the present procedure. The treatment was almost over before I could ask, strictly to clarify, "It's always given without anesthetic?"

Part of ECT's desired effect — also a slight drawback, I'd discovered in my reading — is that it mimics that of guzzling copious, near-toxic amounts of icy wine. A freezing effect, if you will, on memories, blotting them out. Could the therapy have a peripheral effect on those applying the shocks? It took my mind off the fever treatment, which I had, despite all precautions, clearly mismanaged.

"Can you stay for a couple more treatments?" the doctor asked, as soon as the patient was wheeled out.

I began explaining how short we were in Ten, when a nurse stepped in to relieve me — relief being the operative word.

—w—

RETURNING TO PAVILION 10 offered a certain reassurance, a sameness. The guests' automatisms, if not exactly predictable, were at least known.

Compared to the sine-wave therapy, tidying up from Mademoiselle's occupational therapy would be a piece of cake. Neither Novice nor the orderlies had thought to do so, I discovered, too hard-pressed to peek in on her till after Quiet Time. She'd shoved the whole mess, clay, newspaper and all, onto the floor, and in the process managed to get the wall, muddy spatters sticking to the plaster. It was enough to give me pause, I must say. Mud also decorated Mademoiselle's blanket, though her clothing had somehow escaped sullying, not that another layer of dirt would matter. The head and face she'd shaped was now an indeterminate lump.

"Oh dear. After you did such a lovely job —"

She turned on me then. "You say you are my friend. But you're like the others, and I refuse, do you hear, I refuse to help you!" Her voice trailed off, but she was only gathering steam. "That you would use me! Ah — and because my beautiful mother-and-child was stolen you would trick me into making another. All so the scoundrel and his cronies — my jailers! — can profit from this poor old woman's misfortunes." She hurled a last bit of mud; the cat, napping atop her papers till then, scurried for cover. "I expected more from you," she railed, sounding genuinely wounded. "I believed it too, that in your kindness, Miss Poitier, you were a friend. The only one I have in this place willing to help me."

A presence breathed behind us: my supervisor, who'd picked now of all times to do her rounds. "What is going on here, Poitier?" Head's tone would've curdled milk.

I took Mademoiselle's hands in mine and held them tightly, soothingly. In my steadiest voice, as if Head were far away doing paperwork, I asked about the statue of hers. "Tell me about it, dear — the one that's of a *maman*?" I helped the patient to the bed. "I wish I could see it — I'll bet it's every bit as nice as you say."

From the doorway Head gave a sympathetic cluck. "Clean up here, please, and see me downstairs," she ordered, went clicking off.

Now Mademoiselle was crying soundlessly, slumped against my arm. "You could see it — if only you could get it back for me. I mean no harm to anyone, you know, Solange Poitier."

"I mean no harm either, love." Flummoxed, I braced for the request sure to follow.

"You will find it for me, won't you." The patient's smile showed a strange resolve — perhaps even hope. Perspiration beaded her broad forehead. "Before I die, I would like it back. Then you could see for yourself. Everyone could see, everyone who doesn't believe that, once, my eyes were wide open ... saw what others' didn't. Couldn't."

Along with everything else, no one had thought to remove the washbasin. Wringing a cloth, I went to give her brow a quick wipe. She shrank away at first, then yielded — like camembert in my hands, Novice would say. It seemed opportune to ask, "Did they ever try coma therapy on you, Mademoiselle — or fever?" It was the only explanation — logical, maybe — for her aversion to water, but the information wasn't in her file.

Gloom filled her eyes. "Where water should be for drinking, Miss Poitier — fresh water and love all the sustenance I ever needed! — here they make it an instrument of torture."

"So they did treat you." I asked very quietly, "Did you feel the benefit?"

Mademoiselle just gazed back, all brazen and defiant. Her voice was agitated, querulous. "Find my work. Then perhaps you'll do one more thing? Bring paper, please — and don't bring more clay. Do not," she repeated, as if I were stupid or about to argue. "And promise you will not deceive me any more."

—ш—

DOWNSTAIRS, HEAD WASTED no time confronting me. "You have no business upsetting a guest. Any breaks with procedure must be cleared first with me — understood? I would've told you, Cadieu tried — and failed — years ago to interest Mademoiselle in that exercise. Sculpting," she snorted. "If you'd thought to check, we'd all have been spared grief, not to mention a fine mess and extra work. We're here not to befriend the guests, Poitier, only to care for them."

"Of course," I said, and hesitated. "Maybe I'm a touch confused. But if protocol's to be observed, shouldn't it be consistent? I thought patient release was up to Monsieur Directeur, that he signed ...? Granted, in Simone's case, if we'd all attended to her more closely —"

She cut me off. "Who?"

———

IN THE QUIET of my room, simply too pooped to undress, I stretched out in my uniform — *just till the feeling comes back in your feet*, I told myself. I didn't want varicose veins, a Nightingalian woe for sure, to which the best of us are prone. Then I sat up, with *Essentials of Medicine* braced against my knees and some graph paper — the back of an electroencephalogram salvaged from the pile on Head's desk marked "D" for deceased/destroy — for stationery. The peaks and valleys of someone's brain activity, the brain of a stranger safely dead, formed red zigzags over the blue-checked paper, mimicking some illegible hand. Bound for the dustbin, the paper was perfectly usable and better than nothing, though there's something slightly creepy about a brain being outlived by its recorded impulses.

Sister would approve of my resourcefulness. Waste not, want not. Putting aside my pilgrim's progress report, I wrote, *I don't mean to complain, or to criticize. All is well, but things can be difficult here.* I immediately regretted my tone and in a burst of guilty chumminess described things I'd neglected to on my last postcard: the train ride, the treatments, Novice, Head and Mademoiselle. In a quick postscript, I mentioned the Jewish patient, Simone, asking all too piously that the sisters *pray for her*. For once, just once, I wished Sister were here to dole out her brusque advice to keep calm and "E.T.B." — expect the best — or to quote the pigeon-loving St. Francis, who said it's better to be the consoler than the consoled.

Before signing off, I enquired whether she knew anything about statues, secular ones of course — or about finding needles in haystacks, needles that likely didn't exist, and even if they did, few couldn't care less about.

I sealed the envelope graciously provided by the secretary and dozed off with it in my hand, waking just long enough to finish this journal off. A comfort, as it turns out, given the stuff flitting through my head, dreams, in fits and starts, about arcing electrodes. Lights out.

12

DEAREST C,

You know me best. My playful heart — my country heart, fickle yet true. As I know yours, a trickster's. Was it you who egged me on? No. Simply the flirt in me, and the urge most women have to gain, then keep, the upper hand. Who doesn't want that? Nothing like competition to sharpen desire. A mere whiff of it, even. If Monsieur had his lonely *hausfrau* and I our long-suffering Maman, we could share our pain.

Ah, Villeneuve-sur-Fère in summer! Impossible to think of it without thinking of you. The smell of hay in the fields around the village. Grasses shifting in an unbroken breeze.

Cook spent a full morning preparing the lunch. *Coq au vin* and a *pommes purée* so creamy that to Maman's disgust I double-dipped

Cook's spoon. She had me lay the table with her mother's china. Papa was there. He and I had returned from a walk, were sitting in the cool of the garden, behind the wall latticed with vines, when, fashionably late, our guests arrived from the train.

The housekeeper, introduced as Rose, floated in on Monsieur's arm wearing a flowery concoction more suited to someone half her age, a debutante. Once upon a time, before pushing a broom and darning socks had taken their toll, perhaps she had been pretty. But with one look at her face, my faith in Monsieur (oh, I hear your laugh) was restored — faith that flourished as the wine flowed. The housekeeper, who pursed her lips at each large sip, had crooked teeth and a crooked nose, a coarseness that made Maman, for all her prudery, seem refined. The woman yap, yap, yapped in her bad grammar, barely looking at Monsieur as she complimented Maman on our country home and shared sewing tips. He, bent on ignoring her, drained his glass faster than Papa could fill it. Still, he seemed pleased, and as grateful as I, when Maman clapped her hands at the housekeeper's wit. No surprise that they hit it off. Like Maman, the woman had a flair for the obvious. "Madame," Maman kept calling her.

Our dear brother stayed away till the food was served. Seated across from me, he barely spoke, answering "yes" or "no" to Monsieur's polite queries. His eyes burned with distaste when he passed the butter to the housekeeper, who helped herself to more as she slurped up her *pommes purée*. After dessert, the last crumbs of Cook's prune tart devoured, Paul excused himself and disappeared while the rest of us repaired to the parlour.

It wasn't easy to sit in that dark little room making small talk, with the sun breaching the ivy at the windows. How many times can you coo over a crust's flakiness? I longed to be out in the fields, fields that I missed in the city, the Luxembourg Gardens and the Tuileries no match for the rolling hills and open spaces here.

Villeneuve, summer '88. Even then our small valley and village had a starkness that sang. The straightforwardness of bare slopes, the river winding between muddy banks. Wind bending the hay, the only sound. As surely as *Sakountala* described love, this place described freedom, unlike in Paris where every square inch bore the mark of someone's aspirations, good or bad.

"Why don't you show Monsieur the fountain?" said Maman, eager to have Madame to herself and show off her petit point. As if Monsieur cared to see this quaint fixture in the square outside. But it allowed our escape.

Behind the trunk of an ancient pine he covered me with kisses. "Stop!" I said, laughing. But a craving welled up inside. Of all things I'd have liked to lie with him in the garden, just us, to bend my ear to the dirt and the worms' tunnelling. I longed to share with him your ease, the ease possessed by children, the candour that his liberties led me to expect. But such ease was not to be with the family nearby. Slipping back into the sitting room, where Maman fielded Madame's gushings about her needlework and Papa hid behind his ledgers, I felt something shift, as if the vines at the window cast a deeper shade. The housekeeper lapsed into silence, signalling *time to go*.

Monsieur kissed Maman's hand and shook Papa's. "So nice to meet you," Maman told the housekeeper who, wincing a smile at me, thanked her coolly for lunch. I noticed how Maman looked askance, managing a bow. I noticed too the wispy curls at Madame's wrinkled nape, and it hit me again how, once, she might've been like me, vivacious if not nearly as pretty.

"Well that was an amusement," said Maman when they left, as she helped Cook tidy up, "an afternoon I'll never have back." Yet she seemed satisfied somehow, spooning up the last of the purplish gravy and picking thyme from her tongue. "It's a soft life, isn't it just, for those lucky enough to choose it," she clucked.

Funny she should say soft. That Sunday hinted at a shift in her softening towards me. So much for my gifts from Samaritaine, and the sculpture I was doing, albeit unbeknownst to Maman, to please her.

Our brother was waiting in the garden, writing in the shade of the cup-and-saucer vine. He dropped his pen, setting aside the play he was drafting, and made no bones of his hatred. "The man's a swine," he started in. "Don't you get it? Think with your head! Your Monsieur is no better than a snake crawling on its belly — the nerve of him coming here with that whore, and her making up to Maman like a chum. And who gets hurt?" he railed before I could unlatch the gate — remember the gate? — and flee. "The woman, always the woman," he shouted with pigheaded assurance.

"What makes you so certain, a boy your age?" I shouted back.

If it were not so pitiful, his look would've been amusing. "Do what you want, then, but don't come crying when he tires of you."

Such nonsense! I wish you'd been there to tell him, though I didn't really need you to stick up for me. "If anyone tires of anyone, it will be me growing sick of him, *mon petit*. Monsieur adores me! No artist tires of his muse."

"The muse between your legs. Don't think I haven't heard."

"Maman will hear — don't be crude," I hissed, a mistake because it baited the boy that was holier-than-thou. "If you acted your age you might understand."

"I only want to save you," he said.

"Me, and the rest of the world. You and your Church, a mission as big as your pride."

"Don't be mad," he spat, gathering up his work. But, seeing I was right, he kicked a stone, stormed inside without apology.

"Believing in God is mad," I yelled after him. A mad response to the world's evil, I'd have explained to you. But what would you know of madness or evil, besides the evil of our brother's arrogance?

—⁂—

TO HIS CREDIT, Paul had avoided the word *slut*. But others had ways of saying it for him, in company more refined but less polite than Maman's. Take the soirée I attended as Monsieur's guest, in the apartment of a countess near Parc Monceau. Monsieur bought me a gown for the occasion, red silk embroidered in the Japanese style, flowers of blue to set off my eyes. All the right people will be there, he said, as solid as a capstan in his top hat and cape, a figure to set off my litheness. Heads turned. We garnered flickering looks.

"As good as *foie gras*, this one — you have to admire his taste," someone said loudly enough to be heard above the music.

An old lecher from the Salon addressed my chest. "Ah, the mistress herself, the gifted Mademoiselle, our lady of nudity! My dear," the goat took it upon himself to say, "your Indian princess would have won first place if she'd been dressed."

Monsieur's elbow in my side, I gave a weak smile. "And who are you, sir?"

Breezing past him, a posse of tittering matrons waylaid Monsieur with a flurry of air-kisses. Monsieur eyed the edible delicacies being passed around. He never was able to pass up free food. Oysters on ice, *terrines* and platters of jellied chicken, *foie gras*, duck *confit*, *coquilles* St. Jacques — *pâtisseries* prettier than haute couture.

I'd have liked to be you, or a spider watching from a web — I was never one for crowds, crowds of beautiful people hardly an exception. Taking a glass of champagne, I found a spot by the piano. A man with wavy black hair and a very black beard attacked the keys. Eyes closed, fingers flying, had he thought the very night had ears only for his efforts? If you could call them efforts, C, so freely did the melodies mimic sounds of the countryside. Brooks sluicing over stones, wind rustling leaves shot with sunlight. Music with the colour and light of Monsieur Monet's water lilies.

Muted applause. The countess hailed the pianist, "the illustrious and soon-to-be-great Monsieur Debussy." Our Monsieur liked Monet well enough but thought little of this Claude's efforts, pulling me away as he bowed.

"Tuneless cacophony. I don't understand the fuss, do you. Ah, but the countess likes to be in the know, doesn't she." And he nodded to one of his friends, a government agent. Guiding me over. Piping, "Have you met my prodigy, the lovely Mademoiselle —?"

The balding man scrutinized my dress, adjusted his monocle. "I know of her."

Monsieur praised *Sakountala*. "A masterpiece — if I do say so." He invited the agent to see for himself, recommending that his ministry put a bid on it. The man looked worried.

"I'm afraid, Monsieur, my superiors frown on such … explorations by the fairer sex," he said, his small eyes undressing me.

"But you, my friend, aren't such a cretin. Tuesday, then? Mademoiselle will receive your visit, then you'll take me to lunch?" The fellow allowed himself a smile. Monsieur breathed into my ear, "*Fait accompli*, my dear."

Then, all rustling silk and dripping diamonds, a human chandelier, the countess bustled up to introduce us to Debussy. "I've heard about you, Mademoiselle," he said, barely acknowledging Monsieur, "timely, that we finally meet?"

—⁓—

THE URGE TO create was a siren call and a wolf at the door. Slowly I worked clay in the image of Maman, the model before me round-shouldered, her female parts sagging. Neither you nor I had a clue, of course, how Maman looked under her clothes — no doubt she'd have been appalled at this facsimile. Shape and bone structure I sought to replicate, less aging's peccadilloes.

I saved this work for when Monsieur was absent. My toils on his behalf continued apace, while his schmoozing — his daily toil if not his daily bread — increasingly kept him from his projects. The love of work, the feel of clay between my fingers, distracted me from Monsieur's comings and goings. He puttered and left, returned, departed.

I kept myself company by conversing with the fat little man Monsieur hired as one of the dead in his *Gate to Hell*, a casualty of sin destined to dangle from its tympanum. "Off visiting his concubine, is he," sneered the grotesque little model, eyes flat with boredom. He deserved to be damned for his presumption.

"Can't you read the sign?" I said. Tacked to Monsieur's office door in his absence was the note, *Visiting cathedrals. If you need help, see my assistants.* That Monsieur thought of great churches as womanly entities was nothing new or surprising. Neither was his delight in Christian angels and saints, apparent in his homage to John the Baptist — though not enough to win our brother's heart.

It was a relief, frankly, when the ugly put their clothes back on, all except for the crone posing as Maman, who bared more than withered dugs. "So, do I get to be in Monsieur's Gate?" she demanded.

I lied, saying I didn't know. I had other ideas, a brilliant plan: I'd use her to model a distaff, a statue representing fate staggering under the burden of its spinning, a nest of tangled hair like worms' castings. *Clotho*, I named her, this woman who turned Monsieur's hankering for womanly beauty on its head — Clotho, the woman who oversaw birth and drew from women's slaving the threads of life. A concession, maybe, to all the world's *hausfraus*, the Roses and Mamans.

Glorious grotesquerie — was Monsieur's fascination with gargoyles rubbing off on me?

Returning, always returning, he promised to take me to Reims to see its cathedral, a squatter, grimier version of Chartres' not far from our country home. Our family saw it whenever we holidayed there.

His hands were those of an angel, I let myself think, that strong and graceful. Our strength and a grace — call it what you want — burned into whatever we touched. His devotion took shape in his version of my *Sakountala*, a statue he called his *Eternal Idol*, sealing the truth of our romance. Difficult not to see myself in its woman, patient bearer of her worshipper's love. Its tenderness dripped with lust. What would you have thought of it? That the abandon it showed would feel much better in the arms of a younger man?

Playing on my good nature, Monsieur deflected the rancour of others. Slings and arrows. Rumours, innuendo. Unbuttoning each other, we took to leaving his note on the door while stealing fast, furtive *coïts* behind it. What can I say? All that existed was our mingled form.

"If we could lie like this forever," he crooned, hastily throwing on his pants, squinting — the way he viewed the closest objects with or without his glasses, not quite believing they were as hoped or expected — to do up his fly. Each evening, despite his longings, he said his tender goodnight out of respect for my obligations. Before heading home to Maman's, I had the day's efforts to wrap — as if for burial, it would cross my tired mind, the way women wrapped Christ's corpse with no thought or inkling of what might follow. Recalling Renan the heretic, I imagined my fingers as theirs, while Monsieur donned his hat and slipped off, his footsteps in the courtyard melding with the river's twilit sounds. A sharp rain cleansed me of his scent.

But in the afternoons, taking breaks, we promenaded publicly. Along the rue de Babylone and rue du Bac to Bon Marché, where he bought chocolates and perfume. Oh, the looks on the sales-ladies' faces when I doused myself from head to toe: "Don't I smell like a rose?"

"Doesn't she smell like a rose?"

They scowled, shaking their heads.

But what a pair we made, May and November strolling arm in arm past walls of tumbling jasmine, kissing under blooming chestnuts. Those days a season all its own, C, blossoms falling like snow. We talked, talked, talked — Monsieur comparing the body to a church, a piece of walking architecture, while I spoke of da Vinci's sketches of hearts and wombs, chalk the colour of dried blood. Other times, we ventured across the river to stroll the Grands Boulevards and Montmartre's seediest alleys. For he was always on the lookout for models bearing the features of characters in his head, assuming they existed somewhere, for his use. Such faith was precious. Despite my unbelief I thanked God for his favour. My affection for Monsieur bloomed along certain pathways. How to confine it to the studio's tattered divan?

"I'd give up heaven to share your bed each night, Mademoiselle."

A fine pickle, that; you'd have laughed aloud! Oh-la-la, my bed a stone's throw from Maman's!

But he muttered guiltily that in taking me on, he'd marooned me on some island, one with only dreams to look forward to. Clutching my arm like the wing of an uncaged canary, he proposed living together.

Oh, he'd raised it before — marriage, contracts, trips to Italy and Chile, of all places. Now he had a plan, whisking me into a café to divulge it. "Making love is thirsty work," he said, ordering champagne. "All you have to do is promise me you'll stay here in Paris, and work with no one else." My part of the bargain. And his? To take no other models and make his most useful friends mine also; I would have no rivals in the studio or in bed. This is what I asked, and what he promised, wooing me with talk of this commission and that. His latest, a monument to Calais's anti-quated townsmen.

And, do you know, to prove his devotion, he signed the lease on a love nest! An ancient hôtel in the south of the city, far but not too distant from Maman's. Lived in once by George Sand and her beautiful, tubercular Chopin, he said. A place to die for, though it needed a bit of work.

—⁓—

I SET ASIDE my mother-and-child piece to do a bust of Monsieur, a portrait for which the beloved man was happy to sit. Bourdelle executed one too, to our subject's vain delight. But it was mine that he and his patrons treasured. Before its bronze was cast, his bust took pride of place in a row of maquettes, flayed crouching men …

From these he chose the most tortured-looking. You see how even then he relished others' suffering? An assistant followed his grunted instructions on building the armature for his work. "An artist is only as good as his helpers, Mademoiselle." If only I'd listened.

One afternoon I went to his office. Through the door the usual pounding and clanging resounded. Monsieur took forever teasing me with his tongue, a luxurious torture. Just as my breathing matched his, the hammering was replaced by knocks. Sharp, rapacious ones.

"Auguste?" A shrill, shrewish voice penetrated the closeness. The doorknob rattled; against the pane the blind shook, Monsieur's visiting note whisking across the floor. Peering between the slats was a face, with steely hair and a scowl that in Villeneuve had made Maman's seem beneficent. "I know you're in there, and she's with you — your little strumpet! The filthy slut!"

Monsieur's cheeks matched the yellow-grey in his beard. He hiked up his trousers and slunk out like a man facing the guillotine, quietly shutting the door behind him. Their quarrelling pierced the air, the rest of the atelier stock-still. Her voice was a siren, the alarming kind. His, a mincing sputter. I made myself small, as small as you playing hide-and-seek behind a rock.

"Introduce us!" the housekeeper shrieked. "What, she isn't decent enough to meet me?"

"Of course she is, she already has … met you. Be sensible, Rose. We were discussing work."

"Work! You enjoy working each other to the bone."

Yes dear, I heard, *no dear,* then his simpering "Of course. Dinner at eight. As always. No later. I promise, I do."

The siren abated and the *clonk* of her buttoned-boot heels faded. Re-entering the office, he averted his gaze.

"My fault for keeping her on all these years," he said in that charming, shameless way of his. "Do you know, I've lost count of how many she's worked for me." Laughing, he swept aside his desktop sketches. I was to ignore her, to forgive her delusions, her self-importance — pathetic, he said, but understandable given her lowly position. "The poor thing, with her limited brains an employer's loyalty is bound to be misinterpreted."

He embraced me reassuringly.

"Ah, women. Why can't they all be like my Mademoiselle? My loyalty's to you, my dear — I'm in your debt for all you give me." And he mentioned my hands, the many, many pairs of hands which I had produced, single ones too, fragments. "The more gnarled and desperate, the more gorgeous. Their reach exceeding their grasp. The essence of our aspirations, of the plight that damns us all?" It was enough to put you to sleep, C. You'd have been in dreamland before he got to the point. "You capture the emotion of my *Gate* in a single gesture." He could've continued. We both know my creations were beautiful. But he sighed. "Such a process isn't for the weak or faint-hearted, is it."

He snapped his fingers and went to check on the armature, the half-size skeleton of wire and wood for his figure's next incarnation. If all went well, my modelling of his next maquette would be the design for another armature, only full-scale, and eventually, for the final plaster and bronze versions. "Instant fame for you, Mademoiselle." So I was happy enough to do it, though my own work beckoned. Perhaps Danaïd's water-hauling describes the sculptor's lot? You tell me.

—⚯—

AWAITING YOUR VERDICT, I am yours, always. X

13

I WILL DO ALL IN MY POWER ...

MONTDEVERGUES ASYLUM

MONTFAVET, VAUCLUSE

12 SEPTEMBER 1943

Mademoiselle's brush with occupational therapy necessitated serious bathing.

"I don't see why she resists," I let slip to Head while making conversation, a glib observation because of course I had a pretty good idea of the reason.

Our supervisor quit shuffling charts long enough to look up. "Wouldn't you?" Her voice was just a little abrasive. "I'm sure hydrotherapy helped at some point. But all these treatments take their toll, Poitier. No accounting — no denying either — how troubled minds see cure as culprit. Don't be too rigorous. You'll wash her properly when the reaper comes. Meantime, I don't need to remind you, it's her happiness that counts."

No argument there.

At least Mademoiselle is constant in her quirks and inconsistencies; it's those of the otherwise sane and reasonable in life that feel harder to negotiate. For all our supervisor's resolve, Head can flip-flop overnight on some matters. One never knows which matters they'll be. Novice frequently rolls her eyes behind her back; the trouble is, Head's own eyes are evidently in the back of her head.

"Before you two go on duty," she began today, "I'm reminding you both. No correspondence and no patient information leaves the building without written approval. Do I make myself clear?"

Dr. Cadieu emerged from a ward and asked if anything was amiss.

Head waved the *Dead and Delete* EEG folder — empty, of course. "It's come to my attention, Doc —"

"Discarded test results are to be destroyed, yes?" Cadieu eyed her strangely. "And?"

I anxiously raised my hand, I'm not sure why. It wasn't as if I were being quizzed, though it felt almost as awkward, discomfiting. "They're in Mademoiselle's room — for drawing on." I was perfectly matter-of-fact.

"Better that than letter-writing," Head exclaimed. "But since these tests — the hospital's property, I caution you — are highly confidential, the patients' families would scarcely approve —"

"Nonsense," Cadieu interrupted. "The tests are quite anonymous, none of the patients living. They were going to be destroyed anyway — correct? Good for you, Poitier, finding some use for them." Reaching into her pocket, she produced a grimy ball of string. "From our patient in 102 — like a little bird making a nest, isn't she just?" Cadieu deposited the twine in Head's palm.

"What are you waiting for?" Head gave me a nudge. "Doesn't your Mademoiselle need tending to?"

It's nearly impossible to speak around Head in her presence, but who knew when next I'd catch Cadieu? "Doctor. Do you know anything," — I felt a little ridiculous asking, as if party to a patient's delusions — "about a statue?"

Cadieu looked at me, bemused.

"One belonging to Mademoiselle, or someone. Who might have it? The patient's brother, perhaps? Do you suppose," I hesitated, wishing Head would give herself a tea break, or something, "suppose I might write and ask him?"

"For goodness' sake, Poitier! If by now you can't tell when you're being had, may I suggest —"

Dr. Cadieu silenced Head with her look. "As you see fit — with the directeur's approval, naturally. But I caution you, Nurse. Some of us have been down that path before." She gave me a tired wink, then scurried away, the spongy squeak of her soles receding with the comfort of her presence.

As if only just remembering it, Head tugged a postcard from her pile of charts, passed it over. Not war issue, it pictured Lyon Cathedral. According to the postmark, the card had taken almost four weeks to get here; it seemed much longer since I'd had contact with anyone beyond the village, or received more than Vichy-approved post, with its safe little statements and boxes ticked by the sender — *I am well. Oui √/ Non. The weather is fine. Oui/Non√* — missives that gave away nothing. At the instantly familiar handwriting on the back, the neatly crossed *t*'s, my heart goose-stepped.

—⁓—

TO MY ALARM, I found Mademoiselle still in bed. What showed of her hands and wrists below her sleeves were mud-stained despite all attempts to sponge them clean. I told her, maintaining a cool, collected tone, that I saw no reason why she couldn't get up and eat with the others. "Why not take breakfast in the dining room?" I tried to make it sound like a hotel's, if not three stars, two.

The blanket drawn to her chin, she gaped back sourly.

"It's only that a little walk would do you good, not to mention the change of scene. You must get up, Mademoiselle. We can't have you lying in."

The patient waved her hand as if conducting some small symphony. "The way they chew, Miss Poitier! Their table manners! To sit for two minutes with these lunatics is enough to send any sane person to an early grave."

"Well, yes," — diplomacy in all things, that cardinal rule — "maybe it's not the most pleasant pastime, watching others eat."

"I would rather starve."

"Yes, dear — now tell me something I haven't heard." I smiled gently. Encouragingly. "First off, let's get you to the bathing room, shall we?"

Complying, the guest pushed both legs over the bedside with the care of a stooped old bird, allowed me to guide her feet into her shoes. A case of corns on the left one, but of lesser concern than when she tried to stand and both knees buckled. I managed to catch her just in time.

"Spared, for now," I tried to make light of it. "The things you'll do, dear, to get out of having a bath!" But it was hardly a joking matter. She'd gone quite pale and needed assistance simply to lie down again. "That's it, now. Relax and stretch out."

Carefully tugging into place any clothing that had ridden up, I eased the patient's knees sideways to turn her, arranged the pillow to properly support the neck, and tucked her in nicely. This was the practice I was trained for. Of course we could've used more pillows, thin as they are; one for under the knees, one between them, an extra for the shoulders. It wasn't the first time I'd experienced the pang of missing Lyon's Hôtel-Dieu, and I felt for Sister's postcard in my apron.

Curled up, childlike, Mademoiselle had a look of gratitude that threw me off. She gestured to the graph paper on the table, with its red tracings. The sheet on top was crammed with sketches of skeletal hands and feet.

"You did these yourself, love?" There's nothing like a little wit offered kindly.

I slipped out just then to ring for a basin. While waiting for it I peeled back the covers, quickly lifted the patient's skirt and pulled down her drawers. Remarkably, she made no protest. Her condition was less of a surprise. The skin of her haunches was flaccid and sallow. There was the definite start of a pressure sore to the left of her tailbone, a nasty location when it comes to healing. When Novice finally appeared I sent her straight to the refectory for Mademoiselle's egg.

"You need to keep up your strength," I said, dabbing carefully at the sore. A weakened solution of potassium permanganate might do the trick. "As soon as you've eaten we'll get you up. No rest for the wicked," I said.

"You should know to let an old woman die in peace." For once there was hardly any bitterness in her voice; it was more a misplaced urgency. "Tell me, Miss Poitier — is there news?"

Feeling once more for Sister's card, I shook my head.

"You *did* do me that favour, Nurse? You've seen to it that my brother receives all I send?" Her voice lifted. "He will know where to find *Maman*," she said brightly. "You haven't forgotten your promise?" Reaching between the wall and the mattress, her trembling hand produced an envelope of sorts. Decorated with red zigzags and loosely folded, it was addressed in pencil to some woman in England, I saw, before it fell open and its contents glided under the bed. When I reached to retrieve whatever was there, a set of claws hooked my thumb.

"She might know where my statue is," the patient fussed, "my 'friend,' being one of his accomplices. Though perhaps she never meant to be." Then she snapped her fingers. "A pencil, please, and something to write on."

Feigning deafness — a selective deafness, important at times —
I held up the nailbrush. So much for Mademoiselle's request.
Forgetting it, or at least neglecting it, she gave her hands over to
some much-needed attention, suffered it. Such compliance left
her flagging against the pillow, though not enough to prevent her
querying, "What occupies your head all day, Solange Poitier?
Submitting the lunatics to your tortures?" She snatched the letter
from where I'd laid it, quivering fingers replacing it inside then
painstakingly refolding the envelope. "You will do me the favour
of mailing it, of course." She pushed it into my lap.

Don't argue; arguing is pointless. "When you're feeling stronger
we'll do a proper bath." What choice, but to slide the item into
my pocket?

"And, if it pleases you, will you do me one small favour? Will
you be so kind, and bring a poor, miserable friend the littlest bottle
of India ink?"

—∭—

FINALLY, WHILE EMPTYING the basin in the quiet of the utility
room, I got out Sister's post. It was dated August 23rd, more than
a week before I'd mailed my first to her.

My dear Nurse Poitier, she wrote, *One trusts that you are safe
in your position. Our work proceeds. Who knows how many
have been taken, or worse. We've lost a surgeon mysteriously —
Dr. Feinburg, you remember? — and fear for him. The Archbishop
begs the Lord's mercy. Yet we are told things remain worse farther
north. One prays without ceasing. Surrender not one's hope —
despair is of the devil. The peace of Christ be with you. Sister
Ursula Agathe,* she signed off, *Sisters of St. Charles.*

"So you're missed," Head cut in, jangling keys. She seemed
caught off guard, even more than I was at her intrusion, her look
the same as when Cadieu ordered ECT for guests who in her opinion
were better placed in cribs. Her chapped lips gave her plainness an

almost prissy look. In someone junior it might've hinted at sweetness, the self-denying kind, or a certain innocence at least. Maybe I'm just projecting here. "Your friends, the sisters — they should be more careful, if they think Lyon's being run by the Butcher."

Barbie, I knew she meant: Klaus Barbie, a name spat more than spoken the day it came up in the refectory. In the days after Simone's release, after Cook had remarked vaguely that I had a kind face — why wouldn't I, since I was always smiling or making every effort to? — I had overheard her whispering with some of the other staff. Klaus Barbie was the Gestapo agent supposedly behind the assassination of Jean Moulin, the hero of the resistance. Moulin's murder was a blow to the *maquisards*, those fighting for us where the Vichy cowards refused to — not that I was instantly sympathetic, given what I'd heard of their lawlessness — though one orderly said he was even more of a thorn in the Maréchal's side now that he was dead.

Now Head reminded me, "You're with us, Poitier." She made no bones about my "former loyalties" to other institutions being "just that — former. You see the need, surely, for a certain — how should I put it? — allegiance. To ours. If we're to do our best. The guests' well-being relies on this."

Her small eyes fixed on the spot on my chin where a patient had left a small scratch. "Feinburg — that's Jewish, isn't it?" She launched into a story, gossip as far as I could tell, about a fellow who might or mightn't have been "of that persuasion," but who either way preferred men to women and was rounded up. She said, with that waxy smile of hers, "So perhaps the enemy's not entirely evil."

One of her keys grazed my knuckle when she patted my wrist.

"And what I've said about Mademoiselle's delusions? It's just to save you a wild goose chase. Save you wasting time." She tapped her temple, smile replaced by a grin. "Don't let her get the best of you, is all. Don't worry, even I fell into that trap. The best you can do is pretend to listen. Let her talk, let her see some concern."

I busied myself counting *camisoles* — a freshly laundered stack ready to be hung up — but felt her still looking my way.

"I tell you for your own good, Poitier. Don't get drawn in to their dramas. Contravening hospital policy will get you dismissed" — she sucked her teeth, the sound like a syringe being stepped on — "like that."

—꩜—

WHEN I POPPED in to check on her, Mademoiselle's eyes were closed, mouth open in a snore. The heat in the wards was enough to cause hyperventilation and subdue hysterics. The guest's latest jottings had slid to the floor, where the cat stretched out on them. I stooped to pick them up, shooing away the pest, and couldn't help but read, *Oh,* mon petit, *why can't we be in Paris? Not an hour passes that I don't long to be in Quai de Bourbon, with Cléome and Algernon, Balzac, Napoleon and Josephine ...*

Pinned beneath her elbow was another improvised envelope, its flaps pasted down with a residue of flour and saliva. It was addressed to the brother. *Why don't you answer me?* the note went on. *It's not as though I'm begging you for money.*

Her eyes fluttered open and she smirked, having just pretended to doze. "My progeny, you see? My brood — my cats," she said, eyes fixing on mine. "Tell me about your little ones."

The way she looked at me — it was as if she knew.

What harm telling her? No one heeds what mental cases pass on; what difference, her knowing?

It rolled out like a rehearsed recitation: "I gave him up at birth, barely saw his face. I hope he's prospered, I hope he's loved."

There. I'd said it. The sky hadn't fallen. What could anyone do? What's past is past.

The guest blinked and a weak smile crept over her face. "That's all? And where is he now?"

By some small feat of determination a fly had got in. I swatted at it through the bars and tried with no luck to force it through the opened sash. Giving up, I began gathering up any unused stationery to restore it to the D&D folder, until Mademoiselle's croak stopped me.

"Where, might I ask, are you going with that? My friend would renege on a gift?"

I set the papers down again, all but a couple of blank ones, which I folded and slipped inside my apron. "Just the once, my dear, I'll ask that you share."

"You're writing to him, your son?" the patient persisted. Her slyness felt almost spiteful. "You must miss him. You must send him a kiss."

"No reason to be harsh. I've done nothing to hurt you," my words raced out before I could stop them, like very runny calamine lotion — overshooting the wound, and no returning it to the bottle.

"To hurt me!" Her laugh was indignant, her breathing a laboured wheeze. Was it new or was I too preoccupied to notice earlier, seeing how prone she was to babbling? "You think this talk of your child causes me no pain, Miss Poitier? If I had a son would I be here? Sons love their mothers best," she added cruelly — out of envy, perhaps, but still a test to my patience.

"You speak from experience, dear?" Notwithstanding Nightingale's every principle, it can be very difficult on occasion not to respond in kind.

"Pull up a chair, take a load off," Mademoiselle said, mimicking me. Yet her look, full of appeal, seemed sincere.

In spite of everything, I sat, fully aware of the error of sitting on the job. My ear was steadily cocked for sounds of Head in the corridor, because no part of a shift feels free of her watch. Laziness was not the least of the trespasses any one of us might be accused of.

"It must be hard, giving up something — someone — fully

formed," the patient said, squinting at the light passing through the bars.

"Harder, I wonder, than giving up something, a child, that's, ah, not had a chance to … thrive?" I felt compelled to raise, thinking of Sister Ursula and her touchy, towering contention that all life was precious, a gift from above. Sister had praised me, those years back: *You've given your son that much.*

A rustling just outside set me on my feet.

"I must check your legs," I said loudly, and maybe a bit too brusquely tugged the sheet away from Mademoiselle's shins. Her ankles were swollen, the skin tight and hot to the touch — a new development, as they'd been reasonably fine the day before. Such edema was a definite cause for alarm. "I don't like the look of that," I let slip. Rolling up her blanket, I wedged it under both heels, insisted she keep them elevated.

"I don't know why you're upset. They're mine, not yours." She eyed me with no more than suspicion now. "You should be more concerned with my request, Solange Poitier. If only you will help me to see my *Maman* once more, I'll leave you in peace. You will write to my friend, then." It was an order, not a request. "You'll mail my letter too, of course. Hearing from you directly, she and all the rest will have to listen."

Show little emotion. Be professional, not personal. But it was impossible to hold back a little laugh. "And who am I, Mademoiselle? I know next to nothing of your business."

"You know all you need to, Miss Solange," the patient sniffed, and let out a soft moan. "Why should I die so alone?"

Asking about it would be treading on eggshells, but regardless, where a patient's well-being rests, no nurse worth her salt minds the odd incident of having egg on her face. "When did your *maman* pass away, exactly?"

I braced for the answer. Was it her actual mother and not a statue that the patient was missing — hearing, who knows, some voice from the grave? Squelching any doubts of her delusions would let me off the hook. Enough already about this foolish statue, in all likelihood a fiction. With any luck I could confirm that the mother's still being alive, and the statue's existence, were figments of her illness, and I'd be spared the ridiculous task of chasing down her demand.

Without the glimmer of a tear, Mademoiselle's gaze was steady. "Years ago Maman died — almost too many to count," she said, not missing a beat, "which is why her statue means everything to me."

Of course.

—⁓—

A CHANGE OF *scene is as good as a rest*, Sister would say. Rather than amuse myself in my room after work this evening, I opted for a walk. When I cleared the gates it was already twilight, the night man shouting that he locked up at ten. That left little time for off-grounds recreation.

The village square was in darkness but for a light gleaming through the stained glass of *Bon Repos*. No sign of the old men or *boules* players, but a youngish couple strolled nearby, and along the gutter a couple of cars were parked. The café bustled, though, people spilling from it and crowding around the tables out front, their voices and the faint strains of a broadcast spicing up the air. Drawn to it, I walked closer, till shyness held me back. Leaving the hospital so infrequently makes me feel sometimes like an inmate carrying the whiff of sickness on my clothes. So I took a seat on an empty bench by the courtyard, content just to take in the air perfumed with more enticing things, cigarettes and beer.

Out of nowhere, a scuffling with muted but angry voices broke the quiet nearby. Two men in uniforms were hustling someone, an elderly priest in dark robes, through the church's shadowy side door.

I shrank into the bench; if I'd had half a second I'd have scurried away, but regardless, it was as though, sitting still, I were invisible.

They roughed the priest up and pulled him toward one of the vehicles. His sharp protests rang out in the balminess, his heels scuffing the pale dirt. No one else seemed to notice, not the passing couple or the café-goers — not even when the priest was noisily wrestled into the rear of the car. The last I saw was his head slumped against the window as they screeched off.

A shout erupted and the knot of people gathered outside the café grew, curses slicing through the lively hum. A man kicked something into the gutter and swore unrepeatable words against Pétain and his friends *les fritz*. Spotting me, he threw his hands in the air. He was a slight, surly individual. In the dimness of the streetlamps his face looked hollow, shadowed with several days' beard, and despite the evening's warmth he was wearing a leather jacket.

Sliding to my feet I tried to get away, but too late. A nurse's duty doesn't end with her shift.

"What did you see?" he shouted, as if I hadn't the right to be there — or if I did, could explain, or should have intervened. *What's your business here?* he might've demanded, his tone that hostile.

Shaken, I said I didn't know, I had no idea.

"Maybe you need a drink?" the fellow mocked me. Did I appear so dizzy, so ignorant, ineffectual and easily thrown off? Then he asked if I was all right.

I could only shrug, blurting out a lame joke about the asylum: try leaving for an evening and look what one saw!

"You are a patient?" His expression beyond wry. "What is your connection?"

Somehow I found myself being steered into the café and to the bar. Charles de Gaulle blared on the radio, lamenting Moulin's death but promising to free us all from the Nazi occupiers.

Our elbows bumping, the man motioned to the barkeep for drinks. I stole a look at him in the dingy brightness. His mouth had a winey tint; beside it a scar, perhaps an old laceration that hadn't been treated properly, interrupted his stubble. Something about him — the way he stood there, sticking close beside me — summoned an over wound watch, a tightness that seemed to seize the room. Somebody plunked a watery *café crème* before me.

Abruptly, the broadcast was interrupted by music all too familiar, that scratchy enemy anthem, "Deutschland Über Alles." The barman switched it off, and silence thickened over the room, each crowded table observing a sullen peace. Then someone at the back started to sing, quietly and slowly, the weak strains of another familiar song strengthening as another voice chimed in, then another cautious voice, then another. The fierce words — *To arms, citizens. Form your battalions. March, march. Let impure blood water our furrows* — made me think less of fighting than of lavender fields and a tiny canal irrigating them. Some of the voices sounded heavy, others rowdy with alcohol. A low, atonal hum came from my, ahem, companion's throat.

Faster than I could down my *café crème* a glass of something yellow appeared: apple brandy, its donor said, knocking back what I suppose was whiskey. He leaned close enough that I could smell its distinct resemblance to rubbing alcohol. Murmuring about a Father Girard, he shook his head in disgust. "Do you see such madmen at your work, who'd bully a useless old priest? A priest," he spat at its absurdity, "one of us they could snatch, just like that — but a priest! Shows how stupid they are." He laughed. Sweat beaded his thinning hairline. "My name is Jules," he said almost grudgingly, barely bothering to extend his hand.

Around us the singing swelled rather violently. One raw voice rose above the rest: *Tremble, tyrants and traitors, the shame of all good men!* There was something oddly, vacantly familiar about it and its owner sitting near the back. Spying me, he raised his glass, his uneasy smile nearly lost in the gloom. On the front of his jacket was a yellow star. It struck me that he was the thin, sharp-featured man who'd brought Mademoiselle's clay, who collected the patients' scraps. He was most certainly not a farmer. Too slight and genteel for that. Nor did he seem robust enough to do what Cook hinted at, which was feed and help hide others of his kind.

"Friend of yours?" said Jules, who gave his last name as the quite unlikely "Renard," as if I cared one way or the other.

"Not really. I've seen him around the hospital, perhaps." I left the yellow drink untouched — a small glass of red wine would've been harder to walk away from, though I imagined it staining my mouth like his even as it warmed my esophagus — and said goodnight.

—⁓—

I RAN MOST of the way back, sticking close by the canal. There was something reassuring about its engineered flow, the way it was so narrowly, uniformly enclosed; something comforting about its murky persistence, doing exactly what it was meant to so effortlessly.

"You're early," said the night man. Pity in his voice?

Hurrying to the dorm and to my room, I couldn't stop thinking of the priest seized by the *Milice*: where was he now? On a train to the north, or, like Simone and the young men, bound for Marseille? Who knew where they would end up after that.

To focus, I opened my medical dictionary and tried doing a spot quiz. What better place to start than with the *A*s? Eyes closed, walking my finger over the text, I picked words blindly, mining my memory for their meanings. *Athalposis*: inability to perceive warmth. *Ataraxia*: perfect peace or calmness of mind. It was more productive than drinking warm milk, if I'd had any, until my finger landed on *Ataxophobia*: the morbid dread of disorder.

Which sent me flipping back two pages, to one I'd skimmed. *Astraphobia*: a morbid fear of the sky. Nazi Stukas came to mind, dropping bombs, carpeting not just the north with them but everywhere.

Thou shalt not kill, the sisters preach, as does the rest of the Church — except, they say, when killing is just. Fine. But who, then, is qualified to decide just or unjust?

An effective nurse does not brood, but focuses energies on easing others' sufferings. Nothing for it but to switch tasks, to pick up my pen again and apply it — not quite yet to this insufferable progress report, but to the bit of good writing paper from Lyon I'd squirrelled away. You never know when you'll need decent paper for certain correspondence. I had thought, briefly, of using the graph paper I'd "pinched," Cadieu's blessing notwithstanding, but somehow it just didn't seem right to use it to contact a family member.

Despite how nervous this whole business made me, I knew the address, had it wired into my brain. *A nurse does not sidestep her duties or postpone what can be accomplished today.* I would be direct and to the point. On my very next trip to the village I'd mail it, along with Mademoiselle's letter to her friend. Ignore the fact that doing so would be tossing it to the wind, seeing which side up it landed. *A caring nurse places patients' interests above hers.*

Dear Monsieur, I began, apologizing if my query seemed in any way presumptuous, out of step or downright silly. *Writing on behalf of your sister, I am given to understand that you might know the whereabouts of some work* — yes, a word broad enough to cover numerous possibilities — *with which your sister wishes to be reacquainted. It is a piece* — that, too, just vague enough; the brother surely was able, one hopes, to guess what is meant! — *about which she expresses some attachment, and wishes to see before much longer. She has indicated that said object is in your possession. If so, please return at your earliest convenience. If not the case, please notify me, care of Monsieur Directeur, of any location where said item might be found. Sincerely, Solange Poitier, RN.*

There. For the record, the least effort is better than no effort at all.

—⁓—

OUR ANTHEM'S BLOODINESS echoes back even as I undertake the chore of getting all of this down. An annoying chore at the end of a long day, I'd give my eye teeth to have a radio, with a station playing only music, thanks, to lighten the exercise. But then I mightn't get down to it at all. No matter how devoted one may be, it's awfully easy to get distracted.

I must say, though it's become something of a habit — a habit borne of what, I'm not sure.

14

LUNATIC ASYLUM
AUTUMN? YEAR?

OH, C —
If I could've brought you there! Sleeping under the stars, in the
moon-shadow of leaves, you'd have thought you'd died and gone
to Villeneuve. That is, except for the stink of tanneries and dye-
shops, the filthy trickle of the Bièvre nearby.

On its edge, on the fringes of a ruined vineyard, was a lovenest
Monsieur had arranged. Back in '88, I believe it was — such a
grand year. Monsieur said that La Folie Neubourg, once the home
of Sand the writer and her sickly composer, had also sheltered
Robespierre and even Napoleon's doctor. Glory days past, its
rooms brimmed with neglect, its façade a tumble of headless statues and prying wisteria. The smell of wet wool and a dead-animal

stench drifted through its rooms, depending on which way the wind blew.

The perfect place to work! I fell in love with it. It was, of course, haunted. How could it not be, having housed figures who'd suffered such reversals of luck, and when its neighbourhood, Boulevard d'Italie, a bit on the seamy side, swarmed with others down on theirs?

But you'd have loved its banisters and balustrades! "It's beautiful — I am beautiful," I shouted from its crumbling staircase, not to flaunt myself or mock Monsieur's scalping of Baudelaire's line to title his work, but to enjoy its echo. Our Monsieur struggled to think up his own names, you see. As Maman struggled with me.

— ∞ —

IN THE WAKE of our sister's getting married off, I pitied the family poet, Paul, who was left to deal with Maman by himself. If you had come to visit, rest assured, she'd have accused me of bringing you to a slum. "Why would anyone frequent that part of town?"

When the truth about our luncheon guests had surfaced, she lit into me: "How dare you bring those creatures into my house — and knowingly? That man, your fine Monsieur and his mistress! Eating off my mother's plates, her carrying on like my long lost friend — and them not even properly married!" On and on she raved, accusing me of ruining her reputation and our family's, entertaining such rabble in "our great-uncle's rectory"! As if she cared about priestly piety. Had her face been terracotta, it would've cracked. Her voice did, gasping for air. "And you, I see what you're capable of! But it's worse, isn't it. Much worse. Your deception. The things you've been doing with him. I've heard. Don't think you can hide it. Don't think for a second you've pulled the wool over my eyes."

I braced for a hard slap, but she did not touch me. Out of my mouth came a rush of self-defence, about pieces I'd shown in the Champ de Mars, journalists' praise. "Just the beginning, Maman!

Be patient. My best is yet to come."

She regarded me with a dry calm, a blanched look about her eyes and mouth. "You have no business calling me *Maman*. No daughter of mine would behave like such a tart."

You're hearing it first; you're the first I've told about this.

Smoothing away her wrinkles, Maman's icy dryness left me no recourse: "If you're so in love with your art, my girl, sleep with it. Let him keep you."

—⁂—

I TRIED NOT to think of Monsieur's I-am-Beautiful *Woman*, raised in her man's eager arms, as I arranged my tools and unpacked my work. You could say Maman drove me to it, C, to exchanging the crisp, ironed sheets of our family's flat for the mussed, smelly ones at La Folie. Monsieur and I revelled in twin gods — love and art — all day long in its musty rooms. From morning to dusk the hôtel's sprites oversaw each chiselled mark. Unfettered, we celebrated our collaborations with kisses and vinegary wine, among the most rudimentary furnishings.

But at night, after drifting off in his arms, I would wake to find his place empty.

Dante's lovers, Paolo and Francesca, suffered eternal torments for their illicit love. So Monsieur enjoyed recounting: "Imagine, your greatest desire being thwarted. Another version of hell!"

But why the fixation on storybook passion, I grilled him. As if ours wasn't equally potent, whether hidden or revealed.

Watching light play on the water-stained ceiling, Monsieur scratched his beard, sat up. "Don't you see the truth in this beautiful pair's tragedy?"

"What about us? We have a few tales to tell."

"Oh, my dear, it's old stories people want."

"People? Like Rose?" My voice was fawning. I wound a strand of his beard round my finger. "Your government friends? Your friends in the Salon? Look at you. You're your own story. Today, Paris's gift from God. Tomorrow, the world's?"

"I won't argue with you." I could see the anger twisting there.

"Don't forget your promises!"

As if on cue, we were interrupted by a noise, a fumbling below. Rats in the walls? Some beggar seeking refuge? A homeless drunk? The neighbourhood teemed with them sleeping on sidewalks, bare soles tattooed with filth. The street was full of hovels where vagrants drank, the Bièvre one big urinal.

Shouts rose, violent shouts, a thumping to shake the dampness. Stumbling into his clothes and out to the landing, Monsieur shouted to someone downstairs, his words impatient and rote. When he returned to root through his wallet, I tiptoed out wrapped in the sheet. Peering up from the foyer was a man-boy in tatters.

Impossible, dear C, to guess the age of those who call the streets home.

The fellow's leer was obscene. "Papa?"

Monsieur's look was that of his most indignant, squirming damned. Without a word he sent a handful of coins skittering over the chipped, checkered marble. The fellow scrambled to retrieve them, his grin made ugly by its familiarity — the shadowy echoes of a face I knew.

Sweeping past me, Monsieur said God's curse had made him a father.

With a slurring laugh the fellow staggered off, leaving behind a scrap of paper that had fallen from his coat. A line drawing of birds in a tree. "Don't worry," said Monsieur, casting it into the stove, an act of shocking efficiency. "He only comes when he's looking for money, our Auguste."

Like father like son. His namesake.

Running a hand over his hair, our Monsieur then groomed himself to pay a late afternoon visit to Notre-Dame — the light at that hour lovely for viewing her rose windows, I do recall.

But I stayed behind to await the agent from *Beaux-Arts* who'd promised to come. My time was horribly wasted when he didn't show up — time that could have been spent applying finishing touches to Maman's gesturing hand, as I sought to capture her in a kindlier attitude. Hours lost to my agitation at such discourtesy, I could not pick up my tools again until night came. "They know your modelling is first-class!" Monsieur was always reminding me; I could've used those words of solace as the shadows fell. I could've used your company. La Folie was slightly forbidding with no one around.

Not that I've ever minded being alone.

Working by gaslight, it took some doing to finish Maman's fingers, especially since I was working from memory. Though the apartment was a mere tram-ride away, she might've lived in Japan, so removed was I. But the god of solitude let me visualize her body's presence, muscle by muscle, and, before I knew it, I'd captured it. Positively ghostly, her half life-size figure gazed from the worktable.

The insects chirring outside added their assurance. *Seek and ye shall find*, they said. Into the night I worked her figure. The sagging arms, the hollow chest, the place in her lap to accommodate the seated child. A simple matter now of assembling parts. *Mère et enfant* sharing some tender secret. By the wee hours — stillness, a rancidness wafting through the shutters — I'd worked her below the waist, done the modest drapery of her skirt.

Stepping back to view the work, after being lost to it, was like coming to after a long, peculiar dream.

Somehow, amid pigeons' rustling, the Bièvre's gurgle, and the zzzzz of sleeping mice, I missed Monsieur. At a different time, a different hour, I'd have caught a tram to rue de Bourgogne, watched for him in the window.

Now that I was free from our family's routine, part of me pitied him, this person held hostage by a crone and her spawn.

Still, turning my work this way and that, admiring its progress, I recited Maman's words: *As a person makes their bed, so they must lie in it.* Because part of me hated him also.

"You can't mean that, my dear?" said a visitor, whose sudden appearance took me by surprise. Criteur, of all people, the *praticien* from Monsieur's other atelier. Since our move to La Folie, the Master was less and less likely to be found at his old premises, having opened yet another atelier in rue de Vaugirard to meet demands for his work. The one near the Seine was now so busy I was glad of this separate space.

Perhaps I seemed less enthused than I felt. "Oh, it's you."

"What a relief to find you," Criteur gushed. A gleam in his eyes — was he unwell? Not the most robust, he sometimes begged off work, feeling ill. "Monsieur has more studios these days than ladies do silks." A joke with a sickly bent.

Before I could throw a wet shawl over my creation, he ran a palm over its planes. "Nice work — commissioned?" Surely he teased. "Your subject, I'm sure, will be happy."

"Will you take some wine? Tea?" I rummaged around our excuse for a kitchen, a coal fire rigged for boiling water. Who had time for such mindless chores as cooking? Monsieur and I — oh-la-la — love kept us fed.

"No, *merci*." Criteur's answer was curt, his gaze vacant, features blurring in the darkness.

"Any message to give Monsieur? You could leave a note." I pushed paper towards him. On the back was a study, one of a series: a child's little portrait. I needed only to picture you, your eyes opened wide, lips parted as if you'd been startled from some reverie. Perhaps it was how I would sculpt myself. The enquiring child that inhabited us, the one who'd just discovered mud from the river behind our house. Fingers star-fished in delight, the moment between her first touch and delving in for more.

"Nice." Criteur eyed me playfully — playfully for him. I half imagined calipers measuring my skull, his probing and prodding, but he held off. "I only came to make sure you're all right. Not the best place in the city to be alone." He joked about the famously guillotined coming to taunt me, his nonchalance maddening. "You must see them, these headless ones — the way you and Monsieur see, through nerves in your skin? The way earthworms do." He laughed. "You should get a cat. Something to keep you company while Monsieur" — he looked furtively about — "is on his jaunts. Strays prowl outside. Why not feed one and bring it in?"

Then he said what I'd been thinking: that a change of scene, a trip, might do me good. You know how it is, the power of suggestion.

—〰—

MY FRIEND, MY old friend, invited me on a jaunt to England and the Isle of Wight. (Who knows what, if any, grand designs she included in this?) Wanting fresh air and a bit of distance from Paris (don't ask), I agreed — against all better judgment and only because Paul would come too. I missed him, frankly, the willing playmate of our childhood.

Away from Maman, he was a different person. On the beach, he recited his poems while, unfettered as the fuchsia blooming along the shore, I was just another girl again, whiling away the hours sketching. My friend and I beachcombed and found the sun-bleached skull of a seal, which she drew. She too was easier company away from the city's grind — she and another friend, in whose stupid notebook, *An Album of Confessions to Record Thoughts, Feelings, etc.*, I wrote fitting answers to stupid questions.

YOUR FAVOURITE VIRTUE.	IF NOT YOURSELF, WHO WOULD YOU BE?
I don't have any: they are all boring.	A hackney horse in Paris.

YOUR FAVOURITE QUALITIES IN MAN.	**YOUR FAVOURITE POETS.**
To obey his wife.	One who does not write verses.
YOUR FAVOURITE QUALITIES IN WOMAN.	**YOUR FAVOURITE PAINTERS AND COMPOSERS.**
To make her husband fret.	Myself.
YOUR FAVOURITE OCCUPATION.	**YOUR FAVOURITE FOOD AND DRINK.**
To do nothing.	Love and fresh water.
YOUR CHIEF CHARACTERISTIC.	**WHAT IS YOUR PRESENT STATE OF MIND?**
Caprice and inconstancy.	It is too difficult to tell.
YOUR IDEA OF MISERY.	**FOR WHAT FAULTS DO YOU HAVE MOST TOLERANCE?**
To be the mother of many children.	I tolerate all my faults but not at all other people's.
YOUR FAVOURITE COLOUR AND FLOWER.	**YOUR FAVOURITE MOTTO.**
The most changing colour and the flower which does not change.	A bird in the hand is worth two in the bush.

My true confidences were kept for Paul. We shared a lemonade, he and I, passing the jar like toddlers, I the sophisticated elder.

"There's nothing between Monsieur and me, besides the fact that we're friends."

Away from his church's judgment and Maman's, he listened.

Brushed sand from his knees, kissed my cheek. "I don't believe you," he said, "but, if Monsieur makes you happy …"

What made me happy was sculpting. Being away from it left me homesick — work-sick — and jittery, as fear does. Fear that a neglected muse will one day desert you. The sea made it worse. All that restless blue and too much sun and sand made the weeks a carousel, spinning, spinning. Eating, drinking, suffering others' pleasures, was a too-giddy, dizzying ride. The sky's glowering haze made me crave the studio, a stick of charcoal no substitute for a chisel. Work's pull caught in an undertow sparkling with grit; frothy champagne or seawater, it mattered not.

The sense of being becalmed is a torture, *languish* a word that gives *anguish* a despair all its own, C. The queer thing is that only one would understand: Monsieur. Despite his lies, his flightiness, I longed to stroke his bristly nape, the fold of skin above his collar. Such a dogged little man.

—m—

MONSIEUR WAS WAITING when I returned in September, tanned and sick of moonlit strolls on rocky strands. I was unnerved to find that he and my friend exchanged letters. Little did I know, he had enlisted my friend, for all her discretion, as a spy to monitor my comings and goings. As if I had the guiles to escape an island! A seagull's wits, maybe.

Yet his kisses were like *chocolat*. He placed a rose on my pillow. Why a red one? He fancied me in silk that colour, not the grey pinstripe I wore, also courtesy of him, for the photograph he arranged. "Let's cultivate a more polished image, let's appeal to patrons." Yet after the shoot, as we lay in each other's arms, he spoke of the ancients and of Donatello, Michelangelo, et cetera et cetera, something something "in the heaven of their dreams": a man's need to strive despite the world's oblivion. "What are we, if not our dreams? Windmills tilting at gusts?"

How I despised the luxuries he took, going off on these long, fanciful flights. "And you have grounds to complain."

Lifting my sun-bleached hair from my nape, he kissed its paleness. "I ask only that you be more patient, my dear."

"With your government wags and cronies?"

"With my charlady," he said.

So, you'll perceive, no matter how much of himself he poured out, more than a little was held back. A reserve of something dark, dull and a little oily.

One evening the pair of us left to stroll the Bièvre and happened upon a vagrant taking a piss, which inspired me to ask, "So, what about your son?"

"His life has nothing to do with mine. Neither does his mother's."

But he went home to more than a charlady's *boeuf bourguignon*. More to her appeal than adeptness at mending and sweeping. He cared for her, however pitifully.

Picturing my body under his, I said, "Leave her."

He didn't seem to be listening. He explained how the woman's sewing had kept them while he'd struggled to sculpt in Brussels. "But I can't talk to her." His voice was so loud the drunk turned, shaking himself off. "How can I talk to someone with nothing to say?"

This was my problem? "You must have loved her, once."

"At the time. Perhaps. A long time ago."

"Your cleaning lady!"

Be wise as a serpent and simple as a dove is wisdom our Paul imparted, cribbed from his bible — advice I was starting to heed, though my finger traced his palm, the blind reading Braille. My feelings for Monsieur shifted with the light through La Folie's windows. His shadow covering mine.

—⊀w—

LA FOLIE — MY folly, you will think, staying on as I did. But work filled in where doubts tunnelled. And do you know how I picture doubt? Like hunched little men wielding pickaxes, the ones boring caves in Épernay's chalk to rack a thousand years' supply of Mumm's. To every challenge, dear, a purpose. The year Eiffel's tower rose to fuck the sky (pardon, but that's how it seemed), I strove to give the world tranquility. *Psalm, Young Girl with a Hood, Prayer:* variously I titled a bust, a woman's face, her eyes closed, lips parted. Acceptance, repudiation. Grief, praise. Her look was of trusting uncertainty, peaceful worry — the state known as gratitude — for I'd earned a small commission to do the bust of Monsieur's friend's son. Practice for my much more pressing depiction of a child.

Yet peace eluded me. One day the door blew in. A flounce, a fever of frills, and there she was: the steely-haired hag, Rose herself, with her jeering poker face. She flew at me, a rasp in one hand, Monsieur's chisel in the other, her cesspool mouth unleashing insults. "Bitch, bitch!" she screamed, completely berserk. I wrestled her weapons away, held her wrists. Still she clawed at me, savage old fingernails scraping and gouging fit to take out my eyes, both of them. I waved the rasp, only to show her who was who, as one would a snarling cur.

"It's not my fault Monsieur loves me. Not my fault you're a dried-up twat."

As gentle as a dove, I was, and she a harpy, with switchblade eyes and tongue. Dove-gentle, to her serpent's rant — and dare I say? Dare I think it? Her preachiness like the worst of Maman's. "Get your head out of your arse, slut! You're *fou*! Think for a second. Where does he go at night?"

"Go home to your broom." I threw the rasp. We both watched it stick in the blackened parquet and wobble. "Rose." That poisoned name summoned every slight, every injury to me, every shortcoming, past, present and future, caused by her existence.

You will appreciate what I mean, C.

"'Madame' to you. You little whore."

Dovelike I held my tongue. Her nose, all but touching mine, grew longer, I swear. Face as puckered as feet steeped in the bath, the dog bared her teeth.

Monsieur, off lunching with friends, was due back at any moment. You'd have been impressed at the charity I showed. "Best to leave, I think, before he comes and throws you out."

"Monsieur!" she taunted, snivelling. "Stay the hell away from him."

Looking her up and down, trembling, perhaps, ever so slightly, I expressed only pity. "Poor thing. As if Monsieur would want to be seen in public with mutton dressed as lamb." Such honesty simply meant to be helpful.

"Don't fool yourself, my pet. He's no different from other men. Wherever there's a warm pussy ... his heart only has room for me."

"Age before beauty."

Then, I confess, I acted as you might in such a situation. I picked up a fragment — an imperfect but perfectly useful fist, its finger cocked in the way of a pistol — and brought it down hard on Monsieur's worktable. The pieces flying after her made me think of arrows. Maybe there was no need to yell, "Next time, 'Madame,' that will be your head."

—⁊⁊⁊—

"CALL HER OFF," I ordered at the first opportunity, which was some time in coming.

The World Exposition had opened in the Champ de Mars, featuring our Master's work and Eiffel's marvel, or monstrosity, of engineering. How can iron resemble lace? To be fair, not just Monsieur had his nose in the air. "The grand *asperge*" was a darning needle stitching the clouds, casting its massive shadow over the Seine and the Trocadéro, not just the fairgrounds. Calling it a vegetable now seems unkind.

"Climb it with me," he said.

I said I didn't like heights, and repeated my order.

"Rose isn't well — she gets hysterical. You know what it's like to be female. You're even prettier," — he sweetened it with a kiss — "when you're pissed off."

"Forget her." Can it be our country roots, C? I've never been too proud to plead.

"But Mademoiselle. Do I ask you to forget your *maman?*" With this, his oldness grew loud and noisy.

—‧‧‧—

I HOPE I don't offend your virgin ears. If such is the case, I send two kisses. xx

15

... TO MAINTAIN AND ELEVATE THE STANDARD
OF MY PROFESSION ...

MONTDEVERGUES ASYLUM
18 SEPTEMBER 1943
23H57

Observation 1: It helps to designate a regular time slot in one's
off hours for a program of self-evaluation. Unfortunately, free
moments counted upon with regularity, when one isn't battling
fatigue, are a luxury few of us enjoy. A good nurse, however,
makes do.

Observation 2: The primipara has two distinct lives, one preceding
the delivery table, and one following it. The cutting of the cord
is decisive.

Observation 3: Personally speaking, there is life before the passing
of one's mother and life after it. These separate lives can feel
completely unrelated.

Observation 4: Maternal separation affects each of us differently.

Many patients appear to be too far gone to show its effects. It's unclear how Observations 2 and 3 connect, though they seem to. Neither has much bearing on my professional day-to-day.

—᠁—

THE SECRETARY HAD provided a half-full bottle of ink and a pen whose rusty nib still worked. I made a show of arranging these on Mademoiselle's table.

Rather than thanking me, us, she asked, right out of the blue: "Wouldn't you like to find your son, the one you gave away?"

Perhaps she meant to be kind by showing an interest. Such "kindness," however, is not appreciated. "Water under the bridge, long past. I wouldn't know him, wouldn't wish to." Maybe I was overly brusque stating this. *In taking full responsibility, the nurse buffers her patients from strains and burdens not theirs.* "I don't like the look of that sore," I told the patient. Even if my voice carried a note of apology, it was abrupt. Purposeful. I explained that to keep it from festering she would need to remain a little mobile.

"Like being a little pregnant? You'd have me run a race? Dash off into the sunset, I suppose? Once, I would've — gladly. How tiresome, being on my back," she complained to the wall while I swabbed the wound. *Decubitus ulcer, right sacrum.* Another was forming above the left buttock.

"If I could get you to sleep on your right side," I advised. Despite the worrisome bedsores, having the patient lie prone provided relief to her ankles. And the edema was abating, like the summer's heat.

But it's well known that the geriatric body plays tricks. Sometimes patients rally even as their vitals suggest sending for the priest to administer last rites. *Where there's life there's hope*, Sister Ursula says, and Dr. Cadieu as well. Viability upheld to the point of becoming burdensome in some cases; the worst pressure wounds commonly result from patients lingering far past the point at which death should spare them.

A certain starched presence announced itself. I was vaguely aware of Head scowling at the ink bottle. "A word with you, please."

Duty kept me from looking up. I continued to apply the dressing, Mademoiselle wincing. "Certainly. Can it wait?"

"Wait?"

My supervisor breathed in time to the scissors' wheezing through the adhesive tape. Piece by piece I tamped it over the gauze. Gently drawing up the patient's undergarment, I smoothed its threadbare cotton over the bandage. Then I took the pillow I'd managed to wangle from Men's and wedged it carefully between Mademoiselle's bony knees. Heaven forbid they'd rub together and break their skin. Recalling Sister's adage, *a job done well takes time*, I drew up then carefully folded back the sheet. There was still the sponge bath to be managed.

Tapping her foot, Head sighed with impatience.

"An emergency?" I said. I'm not sure what overcame me. "If not, perhaps it doesn't need fixing quite this second."

The look she gave me was doubtless deserved. Without a word, and in an obvious huff, she slipped out.

When I emerged, she was parading up and down the corridor as if guarding a cell block. The soiled gauze in my kidney basin had a faint but unmistakable odour that, of all things, reminded me of the cat, which I suspect has an abscess, the result of some injury from fighting with toms on its forays outdoors.

No such forays or escapes for *moi*. Tailing me downstairs, Head wasted no time getting to the point. "It seems, Poitier, that Mademoiselle's letters are getting out, without being screened." She waved an envelope, the pale blue check of its graph paper and red zigzags starkly recognizable, and allowed the note inside to flutter out. "You realize how distressing this is for the family. You understand the light this puts us in, puts you in ..."

Her look was cauterizing as she pushed both pieces at me. Scrawled across the name of Mademoiselle's friend and her address in England was *Return to Sender. Recipient unknown.*

"Deceased," my supervisor said, her certainty quite rattling. She clearly had something else on her mind. "I never accuse anyone falsely, but it's come to my attention that you've been seen. In the village. Drinking." She peered at me.

As if sipping coffee in a café was a crime! As if this were a hundred years ago, and Florence Nightingale and Maman Marguerite had no sway, and all nurses were, if not nuns, drunks and whores. Novice, passing with a cart piled with supplies, stopped, eagle-eyed.

Head raised her voice. "You of all people, Poitier, should remember: virtue isn't just a word, it's a practice. A nurse's is reflected by the company she keeps."

Shooting me a sympathetic look, Novice tugged a small paper sack from her cargo and, wincing a smile, passed it to Head. Impatiently — stiff with irritation, actually — Head opened it, looking befuddled. It was a present from a guest on the first floor, explained Novice, pushing off. Head thrust the bag at me. Inside was a tangle of greyish hair, nail clippings, bits of grass and toilet paper.

I'm afraid I couldn't help myself. "Useful, if you're building a nest."

Head gave a chilly nod. "I strongly suggest, Poitier, that you mind your lip."

"SO MY FRIEND IS too busy to accept mail from her poor forgotten chum," Mademoiselle said. "This is why you must write to her, Miss Solange, and demand to know what they've done with my statue! Very likely she knows."

"Whatever you wish." It's no great hardship, being agreeable.

"Have you seen the bridge, the one people sing about?" Saint

Benezet's bridge, the business end of which had washed away, rendering the thing useless. Hundreds of years, modern equipment, and nobody fool or genius enough to rebuild what he'd supposedly constructed single-handedly, stone by stone — go figure. A safe change of subject.

"The only bridges that matter are the ones across the Seine," said Mademoiselle, and closed her eyes. "What's the point of a bridge going nowhere? Write to her, will you."

—⚓—

BY THE END of my shift I was resigned to spend what remained of this evening doing some reading, but my best efforts to ignore Mademoiselle's request ended up driving me to the village and the café. Let Head think what she wants about her girls' after-hours activities.

I nursed a cup of tea sitting as far as possible from the bar, keeping to myself. The mystery of who'd seen me and, worse, had reported back to her, was baffling, not to mention troubling. Was it someone from Admin or another pavilion? An orderly, another nurse? Personnel from kitchen or laundry? Except the refectory has no use for Head, it's obvious, from the way they ridicule her devotion to the Maréchal — meaning no disrespect, the one cook is quick to add.

Tonight the only familiar faces were the barman's and Renard's, leaning over a beer. I took pains to avoid Renard's gaze, but he came over.

"They let you out again," he said — his idea of a joke?

I eyed him as Head might, but with a touch of Sister's quiet reserve. It was and is more than a bit unsettling and unseemly, this perfect stranger knowing what I do and where I do it, when the most I know of him is a name — the one he gave me. I figured I'd return his interest, just to be polite. "What line are you in, do I dare ask?"

"Designing things, building them — things like bridges," can you believe he actually said, the odds suggesting he was talking through his hat.

"You're kidding." I was thoroughly unimpressed.

"Not really," he insisted. "I follow their engineering — you understand me?"

"Oh? Well. I'm afraid I don't."

"Afraid? Oh, but it seems to me you're brave, Mademoiselle. Quite brave, doing what you do. Some might say fearless, or cra —" He was teasing me, and testing my patience.

And yet I didn't mind the company, not so much — its novelty, perhaps, its unlikeliness, and maybe, just a little, the feeling of thumbing my nose at Head's wackiness. Yes, definitely a bit of that. Whatever. I heard myself babble, a little inanely, about Benezet's miraculous — crazy — construction. A blunder, because Renard eyed me as if I were an *aliénée* and belonged where I work.

"You don't look religious," I think he said. It was hard to hear, our voices competing with the radio, Pétain's hogging the airwaves yet again — *Travaille, Famille, Patrie* — an old speech being looped and re-looped.

I made the mistake of wondering aloud, "Do they think we haven't heard it? At work we'd call it 'echolalia.' Well, some of us would."

"Who wouldn't?" Though his smile was friendly enough, encouraging even, it was also as wary as it was baiting, begging more.

"A love of babies and motherhood and unleashed patrimony is quite darling — if you're an eighty-year-old with a functioning penis," I couldn't help blurting out, hardly seeking his or anyone's approval.

Looking a little surprised, Renard studied me and laughed. "Pétain's days are numbered, you know." A daring comment — but possible, I gathered, if what the orderlies say is true, that with *les fritz* pushing deeper and deeper into the free zone, there's less news of the Maréchal on air aside from the regurgitated speeches.

"Busy taking the waters in Vichy, is he?" I said. "And Monsieur de Gaulle urging the rest of us to reclaim 'our France.'"

"From the safety of England, easy for him." Renard snorted unpleasantly. Far be it for me to be critical, but not only could he have used a hot shave, the hair in both his nostrils needed clipping.

"Better that, I guess, than a geriatric kissing Hitler's derrière." I punctuated this with a snicker, not wishing to sound obtuse or ingratiating.

Renard barely cracked a smile. "Using us to wipe the Nazis' boots and their shitty arses — I guess you'd know about that, wiping arses." His look was indulgent, or rapacious — in either case, eager enough to make my skin crawl slightly, although, if he were better groomed and dressed, he'd have been halfway attractive for someone short and rather lizard-like.

But what was I thinking? Under the circumstances — being virtually under a microscope, subject to who knows what scrutiny and for whatever reason — entertaining any such notion amounts to willingly swallowing a scalpel. Never mind that most share his and my contempt for Vichy, the government no more than a poultice, as far as I can tell, on a dreaded contagion.

Don't say anything else, I thought, yet heard myself pontificate, "Evil is rather pustular, when you think about it." Good heavens, and I hadn't had a trace of anything remotely alcoholic.

Renard eyed me quite earnestly, respectfully even. "The only one we could trust, you know, was Moulin. Resisting *les fritz* from the ditches and upwards. There's no running away for a true son of France. Even in death."

And a true daughter? I might've asked. But he was clearly high-minded and meant well. *Though good intentions pave the road to hell*, Sister sometimes said. Alternatively, a straight road could get tedious.

"It's all the same, politics," I said. "One bunch as bad as the other, and no worse time to show for it than war."

"You'd feel different, I'll bet, if you had a son."

At that I stood up, such rankling presumption suddenly eating my patience. "As you must, I take it, in order to be so sure."

"Flesh and blood, no." He laughed, self-conscious. "Plenty of young fellows in my line, though. I see them all the time. Nice fellows. There's a few you should meet — one I know of could use your attention right now. Your help, actually. Smart enough to dodge the *rafle*, but not enough to escape getting hurt."

"If you're thinking you'll enlist me" — being forthright, direct, is something I continue to work on — "I'm sorry, you're mistaken. Sixty need me to do slightly more than dress a few wounds and wipe their bottoms."

"Miss Poitier," he said, a poor listener, apparently, or a poor learner, "in this war if you're not for us, you're against us. You're saying you won't help?"

"Not won't. Can't."

"Suit yourself — if your conscience is your guide." He waved down the barman to pick up my tab. I left enough to cover my tea and escaped outside, a little the poorer but free of him.

—⁂—

AT THE GATES — a welcome sight — the attendant nodded vaguely as he let me in. Lights blazed from the directeur's villa. Was he hosting a party, perhaps, to wine and dine real guests? Several vehicles flying Vichy's colours were parked along the curving drive. I hastened past, acting as if they weren't there. But in the backseat of a large black one a couple caught my eye. A couple, I assumed — why else would they be sitting like that?

It took a few seconds to recognize her: Head Nurse! She looked different out of uniform, almost glamorous, at least in the dark and shadowy depths of the car. She was leaning in close, speaking to the man, who was wearing an officer's cap, a member of the *Milice* by the looks of it. They stopped talking, peering out as I passed.

Don't borrow trouble, I thought, striding off, then slinking past a stretch of shrubbery. It isn't out of the ordinary to feel jumpy when crossing the grounds at night, even while exercising caution and vigilance. Certain secluded footpaths are well shaded and in some cases poorly lit.

I was aware of someone behind me but maintained an even pace, mindful not to show any bodily indications of fear. I'd almost made it to the dorm's entrance when her voice rang out.

"Nice to see you out and about, Poitier. It's important, isn't it, that we keep up with the world." Head smiled half pleas- antly, catching up. Missing was the officious tone that precedes a "strike," as Novice dubs her fault-finding. She sounded out of breath. "I must tell you, that wasn't what it looked like, back there. You needn't think it was anything untoward."

Then what was it, it was all I could do not to ask, restraint being, of course, character-building. "Dinner at the directeur's? I hope he fed you well," I quipped at his expense, recalling his stale croissant, and not even a speck of jam with it.

I was instantly corrected: "Now, Nurse, we must think beyond our stomachs." Yet she said it with a smile, and continued smiling as she, completely without warning, invited me up for tea.

To what do I owe this audience? was on the tip of my tongue, excuses winging through me. A deaf mute, honestly, would've heard my dismay when I said, "Right now?"

"No time like the present, Poitier." She adjusted the sparkly clip in her hair — rhinestones, not diamonds — and her bodice, which only emphasized the broadness and boniness of her chest. Yet she almost beamed with unusual kindness. "A nightcap will do us good. Tea and a chat — you look like you could use some company? Lately you've seemed, well, somewhat morose."

Eyeing me, she produced her key from the depths of her little beaded clutch, nudging mine away, and lowered her voice.

"What you saw outside the directeur's, I trust, stays between us. I'm not in the habit, you know," she actually chuckled, "of fraternizing with strangers, particularly men."

She led the way upstairs, her dusty-rose dress swishing against her stringy calves. Her stockings bagged at the ankles, their seams twisted and a ladder starting at one heel. The stairwell's brightness perked up the grey, though, in her blondish spit curls.

Head's quarters are one floor above mine, off-limits to all but her favourite colleagues. Formerly the Mother Superior's, they are twice the size of mine, but seemed gloomier and no less cramped, owing to a hotplate and two shabby wing chairs flanking an electric fire. Its fake logs gathered dust, the walls too, loaded with scenes of puppies and children done in needlepoint. Crochet adorned every other surface, the radio cabinet graced with a runner.

"Just finished," Head said. "It relaxes me, my handiwork." She cleared a spot for me to sit, then fussed with the radio's knobs. A rousing march leapt out and she hurriedly lowered the volume. "Some girls will be trying to sleep. But there's a program I think you'll enjoy. If you're not in a hurry. Make yourself at home." She rushed to fill a kettle.

I had to say something. "Nice digs." A cup of tea, a few well-picked words, then I'd make my excuses. Switching to some silly old ragtime, the music lent the scene a certain giddiness that pushed Renard from my mind and made it slightly easier to overlook Head's oddness, if not deny it altogether. *Be consistent in your treatment of others; cut a clear path*, Sister's words echoed.

Head doled out our tea like medication, half-filling two dainty cups. "Everything all right with you, Poitier? You're liking the work? More used to it now? Getting ample rest?"

The word rest triggered in us both a yawning fest, contagious. I struggled to contain mine — as well as the urge to ask, as strong as the need to urinate: *Why did you invite me?* Was she lonely after her tête-à-tête, needing amusement?

She put both feet up, working off her stubby-heeled pumps and finally noting the run. She rummaged for a bottle of nail varnish, clear, and painted some on it. "These do's at the directeur's — he means well, perhaps." She looked at me, almost sympathetically. "It would help if he were more ... competent. Co-operative, perhaps, is a better word."

"Oh?"

"Attuned. To how things work. For everyone's benefit. We are, after all, wheels in a cog." Her voice was so chummy, as if our being on staff forged some unseverable bond. Did she want a confidante? A good nurse is a good listener. But being a good listener gets old, and feeling trapped into being one can be unsettling. "So, Poitier. I'm dying to know. What drove you to nursing?"

It was not what I was expecting. "I really ... couldn't, can't, say." As if I'd tell her the truth.

"Oh, come on — false modesty? It doesn't suit you."

"Charity. The sisters' charity."

"Ah."

"So — you're seeing someone?" I asked, perhaps more pointedly than was wise. "Your ... escort this evening, your friend, I mean. He's nice? A nice fellow?" *In the Milice?* I was thinking.

She gazed at me intently, a little smile on her lips. Seeing it made me leery, if I wasn't leery enough already. Then she closed her eyes, seemed to drift off. Had she been drinking? I'd have smelled it, though.

In the lamplight the corns on her toes showed through her stockings. She looked thinner and more worn out than she did by day — something gentle, gentler, almost winsome about her "letting down her hair" like this, save for how awkward it made me feel. Horribly awkward.

It seemed the perfect moment to escape. Except her eyes fluttered open, fixing on me — forcing all my attention to a doily on the little table before me. The music changed to someone's warbling in German.

"What'll we discuss?" she said, quite amicably.

I raised the topic of phobias, heard myself babble on about how there must have been some reason for the directeur's get-together besides socializing, some more serious, pragmatic one. Perspiration tickled my sides. As long as I kept talking she couldn't raise the issue of Mademoiselle's letters. I talked through the singing and after it ended.

When the Maréchal's speech came on, Head turned up the volume, cutting me off. Perched on the edge of her wing chair, cradling cup and saucer in her lap, she listened as if he were the great Piaf. I didn't dare interrupt.

France is sick, Pétain wheedled. *She will take a long time to recover ... the worst lies ahead ... Never doubt her survival, which will continue long after we're dead ... Every nation at some point suffers defeat. Think of our occupiers.*

The same old same old, it was enough to put anyone to sleep or worse.

If we maintain our unity ... our faith, France will emerge victorious!

Not soon enough it was over. Another march filled the airwaves, its jaunty notes emphasizing the brewing silence which only deepened and swelled when Head switched the radio off. Sitting back, she eyed me accusingly.

"What more does anyone need, to be convinced? The Maréchal has our best interests at heart and merits only reverence." Her tone suggested that I aligned myself with imbeciles.

I found it hard to keep my lip buttoned. "I can't see how this helps with our job." I carefully set down my cup.

Head leaned so close I could see the spidery blood vessels in her nose and cheeks — perhaps she had a mild case of rosacea?

"Respecting our duty to those properly in authority is how we advance, Nurse Poitier. Despite what you think, Monsieur Directeur is far too lax in his policies — especially those meant for guests that don't belong here."

"Like Simone, I wonder?"

"You've noticed, surely" — her gaze was half pitying — "how it's a disservice, a misappropriation if you like — considering our current problems with need, overcrowding — to make this place a holding pen. For the incurable, I mean. There are better places for them."

"But ... you found her — Simone — well enough to let go." What tea I'd managed to down had curdled in my upper gut.

"Indeed. But you're missing the point. I'm saying the directeur has little grasp of things. I mean, foisting his responsibilities on us — vetting correspondence, for instance. Judging what's acceptable for a guest and her family to be told or not told." Her voice sounded thin, and beyond tired. Bored. "Having Simone removed was in everyone's interests. Especially her people's. I'm sure she's much better off where she is."

With appalling familiarity, a familiarity that frankly gagged me and made it impossible to speak, she reached under her skirt, undid her garters and rolled down her stockings. If Novice had been there she'd have called it a striptease — the one thought that kept me afloat.

Head wasn't finished. "You'll find, Miss Poitier, as I have, that a girl sleeps better on a clear conscience. And what's conscience but the fruits of obedience — wouldn't your sisters say?" Her raised brow signalled, at long last, my visit's end. My release.

—⟋⟍—

I COULDN'T GET out of there fast enough.

Once in my room, I found thoughts of Head, Renard, and Mademoiselle tangled in my head, so many balls of wool, a cat inside clawing and unrolling them. But it was Mademoiselle's demand, its absurdity, that kicked and scratched and wouldn't let go.

I tried drafting another inquiry about the blasted statue — tried, then gave up. That a letter like Mademoiselle's to her dead friend had got through at all, posted on such markedly non-war issue paper, was stunning. What difference, anyway, as long as Mademoiselle thinks I've tried? Head's earlier advice — tainted as it was, all the more so now — came back: *Let her think you take her delusions seriously enough to act on them.*

Sister's voice, too, pestered and begged. *What might I do in your place?* What would Sister do? Not just regarding Mademoiselle, but Renard, and the escapee he'd mentioned, the boy in the *rafle* who'd somehow managed to get away.

Faced with Renard's request, doubtless Sister would've rushed to treat the boy, or whoever needed help, regardless of character or stripe. Sister, who'd catch someone's vomit in both hands before she'd utter the slang for their privates. She'd have seen any inconvenience or obstacle as opportunity. *It's in giving that we receive, in pardoning that we're pardoned.*

At least two weeks had passed since Sister's card came and I had yet to reply. Instead of sleeping, I found myself scribbling: *Dear Sister.*

I began wringing my fingers. Wringing out their foolishness?

All's well, save the usual, expected ups and downs. You have more than enough on your plate. Forgive me if this is amiss — it's a queer thing to ask after so long. Please be sure that I mean no impropriety and no harm —

I stopped again to shake out any stiffness.

— but I would like to know. I need to know. Please consider my curiosity nothing more than that. It's a little late to be asking, I admit —

My hand moving the pen had a mind of its own. A lump was

lodged between my stomach and esophagus. — *but do you, would you, have any ~~idea~~ recollection of who ~~took~~ adopted my baby?*

I watched the ink set.

I think of you often and with admiration, seemed the only way to end. But after my name I added a P.S., a proverbial dab of zinc oxide on my conscience:

What do you know about statues?

A silly question whose answer didn't take an expert to anticipate. *Statues of Jesus? Of Our Blessed Mother? Or the two together, mother and son, like the Pietà?* I scratched it out and sealed the letter inside the envelope.

Though writing had a sedative effect, the dreams that ensued — annoyingly vivid snippets of Head scolding us all for this and that, consulting her military beau on the methods of our punishment — did not.

But my dreams weren't all of Head. In one of them, a doll made of mud was ripped from the arms of a woman sporting a yellow star. The mother could've been Simone, all in green, except that when she flashed her ID card, whose picture did it bear but mine, my name typed below it, *Mademoiselle Solange Poitier, RN.*

16

DEAR C,
I need you to know I was forthright. "Don't deceive me anymore," I put in a note to Monsieur — had to. But instead of leaving his *hausfrau*'s in Paris, he spirited me off to the Loire. To his favourite château, if you please.

At his little rented castle there was nothing to do but swim and watch bullfrogs. The place surrounded by lily ponds, an island in a stream, and I all alone, Rapunzel in a turret, not a soul to see if I let down my hair or not.

"Buy me a bathing costume," I wrote him, "the one I like at Bon Marché: navy blue, size medium, top and bottom." Might this bring a soupçon of shame to the shameless? The tiniest taste of embarrassment? What glee, picturing him ganged up on by a gaggle of salesladies. The big man making his girly purchase. Their stuck-up titters and giggles. Worse than sneaking around a pharmacy seeking French safes. If they'd been available.

I did try to work, mind you, in a room the landlady set aside for its light. She cooked dishes like Maman's, taking me back to our childhood at Villeneuve — when we were one, I suppose — and I was a little girl crouching on the doorstep, skirt tucked over her knees, wanting lunch. I was frightfully hungry. I missed my cat, and my lover. I missed his body, stubby as it was. Sex easily as addictive as salt.

As my appetites grew, the days became a mirage. The scene beneath my window was like one of Monet's beautiful paintings, a prettiness that tempted me to take up a brush. After all, people bought paintings. There was nothing I couldn't render.

But the test and temper of stone held me.

Once, I dreamt the château slipped its moorings. Glided down-river all the way to the sea and washed up on Guernsey, giving me over to my old friend and her man. Asleep on the sand, I was awakened by kisses. The kisses of a svelte Monsieur with eyes only for me, the tide scouring away all blights: the *hausfrau*, the drunken son. Maman's scandalized hurt, Paul's piety.

In the dream I paid my own way and Monsieur had no other women.

Then he arrived one morning, on the early train, with studies in hand for another commission. And the bathing suit — he brought it! I enticed him on a stroll upstream to a willow-shaded pool. Spreading a blanket over the grass I stripped to my costume, unbuttoned his shirt. Sun haloed the leaves, its warmth moving to those female places he liked describing in pencil. The smell of trees, mud and manure was soothing, but the river's calliope dizzying. Before I could wade to my knees it all soured.

The suit felt a little too tight.

He waded in after me. The river sucked at his pant legs, tinting his feet. "Are you all right?" Such a stupid question, his hand on my shoulder while I vomited. And just as quickly as loveliness soured, so did his mood. So much for his happy plans.

"You're not," he said, disgusted. "You can't be."

"Oh can't I?" The sick in my throat, *ma petite*! And a feeling more raw, of a power mightier than if I'd gained an army's faithfulness. How else to explain it to one who'll never know it?

"A child! A woman like you — a mother?" he spat. "A woman with your gifts. And me, a father?" As if fatherhood were a new invention. His face was perfectly bloodless as he climbed the bank, grabbed the blanket, shook it out. Strange, his not expecting me to do it.

At lunch I could barely eat his landlady's duck *confit*. Refusing to talk, he doodled — a sketch of a woman's torso, which I longed to rip in half. When he finally spoke, his was the voice of a milksop. "Mademoiselle. If it's a family you want, I'm just not equipped —"

Who is, I ask you, darling C?

"Oh, but isn't it you who thinks anything's possible? If we imagine it — if we let ourselves. 'Our great gift, the imagination.' '*I think, therefore I am.*' If you wanted, you would be."

"Ah. But that's a choice. Assuming a person's able to make it — which is different. Another thing altogether. If I were able, for chrissake, my duty would be clear."

To whom — me?

The landlady hovered, coming to take the plates, and her little daughter brought dessert.

"Don't I deserve a kiss?" he said, unctuous and hateful.

"The idea of one," I hissed, raising my fork.

Snatching his sketch, he scrunched it up and shook his fist. I feared he'd strike me. "Can't you stop? Can't you just shut up! Such bitterness!" Then he lowered his voice. "Take care of it. It's yours to deal with. My dear — you know I've always done all I can for you. Yet it's never enough."

With the gentlest flick of my wrist, the wine I swirled in my glass — its taste strangely un-stomachable — went flying. Little drops of red in his beard, red seeping into Madame's creamy linen.

He gaped at me as Madame hurried in with a cloth. "Get rid of it." The cruellest smile was on his face, and any hint of apology was aimed at her, not me. "Be reasonable, Mademoiselle." As if he was. "A child would make short work of you. A waste, to throw everything away, and for that."

Then he had the crudeness, the arrogance, to stroke the wetness from my cheeks with his thumbs.

"And if I don't?" For it was crystal clear now, C, how selfish he was, how greedy for his own success.

And still he minced: "It would ruin me to see you give up your art."

"And stop feeding yours."

"Mademoiselle? You need reminding, who feeds whom — and foots the bills? You've never paid for a thing in your life." His eyes were as shallow as the pond outside the window, as shallow as the light reflecting up. And I floated leagues above him, do you see? As if he were a dragonfly on a pin, to be twirled between my thumb and forefinger. Because I was alive and he was dead to me. "You inspire me — fine. But your condition makes you confused. You forget: who taught you? Every fucking thing you know."

When my hand hit the table the lid danced in Madame's pretty sugar bowl. But the ghost of a flutter fluttering inside made me hold my tongue — until at its heels a sick wonder demanded to know, "Since when, Monsieur, did you or anyone have a claim on what I do?"

—⁂—

ON LEAVING FOR Paris, his parting words were, "There's a lady in rue Gabrielle who'll help you. Some of the others have gone there."

You've had your fun, now pay for it. Could you have freed

yourself from Maman's voice, her judgment, had she imagined you in this situation?

A heart beat inside me no bigger than a tadpole's. Was it something I'd picked up in the river, a parasite, an infection? I told Madame, had her bring gin and draw a scalding bath, two liquid priests to exorcise a demon. Alone in bed, dizzy-drunk, I pictured and cracked open a kind of door to it. In my mind its gleaming eyes were two black pearls, the thing itself a barnacle, its grip fortified by Madame's remedies.

By dawn, dear C, I was hopelessly in love with it. For three days I gloried in its weightlessness, swimming in the river while it swam inside me. It acquired a sex, this presence only the landlady and I and Monsieur knew of, so secret it might've been a mere figment, triggering fantasies and other flights. Pegasus, hiding in Medusa's neck unbeknownst to everyone, the winged horse of inspiration waiting to leap.

I'd never wanted children. Loving you is quite enough, and my idea of hell being mother to many. But in my hot, troubled dreams voices sparred: mine, yours, Monsieur's, and common sense.

— Get rid of it.

— But it is a child!

— The sins of the father loosed on the world ...

— That's the son you know about ...

— He is his mother's son, not mine!

In the dead of night these words were knives; my belly a hard, ripe squash, though despite the bathing suit's tightness I barely showed.

My voice screamed the loudest:

— She is a girl and she is mine.

The latter I knew to be true, the former a gut feeling.

But debate dissolved when, in the dream, my heart-doors slammed shut. Double doors as imposing as those of a grand hôtel — one in the Marais, say — each carved with Medusa's screaming face.

Barring me from Monsieur, yes — but also, much more concern-
ing, from the Salon, the papers, the government and all his cronies
who thought with nothing more than what was in their pants.

I don't need to tell you it's always been so. Penis-heads guarding advancement's ladder, claiming the light reflected by women.
Look what they did to Medusa! More to her than snake pit hair,
that gaze turning the bastards to stone before Perseus arrived
waving his sword, his mirrored shield. Did you know, once, she
was tongue-tyingly heart-stoppingly lovely?

—◦◦—

A DISCREET LITTLE notice advertising Madame Lajeune's "female
renovation" ran in the paper, listing the street in Montmartre
that Monsieur had named. I took myself to her narrow shuttered house, where the woman — wearing too many frills to
be a doctor — dropped tablets into a bottle marked *Madame's
Renovating Pills, take as directed*. "No luck in a few days' time,
come back," I was told. Lacking the heart to peek inside it first,
I slipped her the envelope Monsieur left for me.

The pills tasted of turpentine and caused only a bad case of trots,
which was problematic, as I was moving out of La Folie and into
a little studio down the street, which Monsieur had graciously —
I choke on the word — set up for me.

By now, alas, the pearl-eyed barnacle was a nub of coal.

When after three days still nothing happened, I found myself
behind a curtain off Madame's parlour, in a room marked by its
coldness and the smell of boiled turnips. A woman moaned nearby. I was told to lie still, shut my eyes, lift my skirt. Not so very
different, maybe, from when we would play doctor.

The pain was a piercing, tearing scream.

"Quiet now," rasped Madame's assistant, stuffing something
between my legs, getting me onto my feet.

"Put her in a hansom cab," said Madame, who promised to

send the bill to Monsieur and that in a day or two I would pass any remnants. "Any troubles, see a doctor. Say you've miscarried." The only doctor I could think of was our Maman's papa, long gone but once the doctor in Villeneuve. Explaining to him would have equalled explaining to God.

For days I lay in a kind of dusk. Pain in all its shades moved in and out, an ocean current carrying off this unborn one but not my thoughts of her. A petal drifting towards the dim horizon.

Monsieur brought freesia from the market on Île de la Cité. Was he inspired after visiting Sainte-Chapelle, that dusty jewel of a church, a marvel of stained glass he called it?

"Regret is a useless emotion," he said, spooning soup into my mouth.

The fever abated.

"You only love what's useful. Only what you can touch. You love women only for their cunts." In his lexicon, Lajeune's pills were pills. The twist of a wire, wire — no more. "It's a cruel world, Mademoiselle. One gets used to it. You'll get over this in time."

I'd stopped listening to what he said. His words had no more weight than floating lilies — though he was right in saying he'd be a terrible papa.

It's strange, isn't it, how the briefest taste of the forbidden spawns a craving for it. A craving I squelched by diving into what was familiar and therefore safer. Perhaps my pearl-eyed one would give way to other, living children?

In work I found comfort, though for many months I was dreadfully low.

"What ails you?" our brother demanded, coming around now that I had a place, of my own no longer shared with the Master.

When, out of stupid honesty and seeking absolution, I confessed to my renovation, and that if not for that, he would be an uncle, Paul said, "To his bastard? I can't imagine. But you! Is there nothing you won't do for him? You would even be a murderer!" A certain marvel to his righteousness, his bitterness.

I'm telling you, until the day I was ripped from my life, I never felt lonelier. You know I never liked suffering alone.

"God might strike you dead, then, *mon petit*, for talking to me. So maybe you should leave."

—◦◦◦—

CONSOLATION LAY IN work, and in sex, I found. Obtusely? I permitted Monsieur to visit once a week on Tuesdays, afternoons spread into evenings. I was jealous of my time.

He squandered his on dinners, openings, parties. But sometimes I let him drag me along. At one such an event I again encountered Monsieur Debussy.

"Still going around with that maker of gamey art, I see."

I took this as a musician's teasing, tamed by his attacking the ivories. The rills and trills he drew from them were rushing, sun-flecked water. I had a tin ear but who cares? His movements moved me: his hands were butterflies barely lighting, the notes they summoned summoning a leafy greenness, while Monsieur limped about kissing old ladies' jewelled, spotted hands, banknotes dancing in his eyes.

Neither of us was groomed for the occasion, the pianist and I. The pinstripe silk Monsieur had bought for me was shiny with wear, and Debussy's frock coat was lumpy-hemmed, as if he'd worn it too often in the rain.

"But you have doting patrons," I said. "Tell me your secret?" My question was only half-hearted, at least some of my blazing interest having burned away. "Forgive me — not that you shouldn't be their darling."

"If you think I can fill Opéra Garnier, excuse me, think again. I compose. Performing? Bread and butter. I'd sooner play with no one watching."

"Everything's better with no one watching," I agreed, thinking of you dressing your dolls. I raised my brow at Monsieur's hobnobbing, as another Tuesday of his grunts and his rubbery lovemaking and his leaving me alone again began to unfold in my mind. Except, touched by the pianist's playing, I instead pictured a last dance: young lovers waltzing into that eternity that exists only in dreams.

X

17

... AND WILL HOLD IN CONFIDENCE ALL PERSONAL
MATTERS ...

MONTDEVERGUES ASYLUM
21 SEPTEMBER 1943

At the start of shift I found Mademoiselle barely able to sit up in bed. Hardly an optimal start to the day, one's adrenalin charging. For one very long moment she appeared to stop breathing. Had she taken a turn overnight? Was it too late to call the priest?

When I moved the cat to feel for a pulse, the guest's eyelids fluttered and, almost imperceptibly it seemed, under the sheet her chest rose and fell. "Mary, Joseph and all the angels, thank you," I might've said, forgetting myself. The bedside is no place for superstitious outbursts.

I noted the sheaf of papers at her side, the cause of Mademoiselle's exhaustion. A splotch of ink sullied the blanket, the secretary's bottle almost empty. The spill could've been much worse.

"Mail them to Paris," she said, barely opening her eyes. She drew a shallow breath and shut her mouth as if loath to exhale.

"Up all night, were you, dear? Cat got your tongue, or your efforts got you tongue-tied?"

"I've said enough to those who don't listen. I'm saving my words for those willing to hear." Her tone was wistful, begrudging. She put her hand to her chest quite dramatically, then breathed deeply. "If I'm soon to get out of here, I've arrangements to make. Even" — she eyed me — "the odd goodbye to be said."

Helping myself to the letters — "May I?" — I saw that some addressed her *Dear Sister*, several to *Dear Monsieurs* including one named Blot and another Dayot, and still another without a first or last name. "Writing to old flames, are you? Old *beaux*?" I shouted, a little, when she seemed not to hear.

"Friend and foe," Mademoiselle sniffed — no effort there to hide any sarcasm. "They say one must make peace. The last thing I intend is to send anyone into a flap."

"No flap there, asking after dead people's health." A bit of humour, but it drew a glare. "I'll take these off your hands, then have a peek at your bottom, when you're ready."

"You'll do no such thing, Polange Soitier, without my brother's consent."

"Your brother's?"

It often helps to allow oneself a deep calming breath.

"They're keeping his reply from me, aren't they. Up to their old tricks hiding things, stealing what isn't theirs. Don't tell me otherwise."

"I'm — I'm afraid he simply hasn't answered — yet."

Eyes full of disgust, she sank against the pillow. "Then you must write him again. Remind him, I beg you, if he hopes to see me free of this vale of tears ... If he doesn't come for me soon, Miss Poitier, I might never get out of here. Aren't you afraid of dying in this place? Oh, but you're not so old, yet — younger than

I was coming here," she said archly. "Aren't you terrified of dying without seeing him?"

"Your brother. I'm sure he's a very nice man, but —"

"You know who I mean."

"I'm sure I have no idea," I said. "There there. We all have to go sometime, don't we, dear. If we've said our prayers there's nothing to be scared of."

Yes, Sister Ursula. Thank you, Sister Ursula. If only it were true.

—⚶—

I WAS DRESSING an abrasion on a first floor patient when Head called from the corridor. Though she had been slightly more cordial since our little *soirée*, by the sound of it she had returned to her usual self. I fought a very human urge to turn a deaf ear, but after securing the guest's restraints I succumbed to reflex.

I smelled Head's scent of carbolic soap before I saw her frozen to the desk. A guest — a patient of Novice's who routinely shredded her clothing with her teeth — crouched before her, brandishing a fork, ready to spring. Her expression made me think of barbed wire.

"Help, please." The look in Head's eyes completely belied her chilly calm. The corridor drained of all sound besides her respiration, the measured breathing you might expect of someone stepping around a live grenade.

My eyes glued, certain muscles flinching, it was rather like watching a newsreel. From somewhere deep within a chain of reflexes, I mustered a soothing tone, issued an order from a place outside myself: "Shhh, now." I felt like a car on an incline gaining momentum, poised to intervene.

Unfortunately I was not quick enough. The guest lunged. Though Head managed to seize her attacker's wrist, the fork sank into her forearm, her *extensor carpi radialis brevis* by my estimation.

Juddering to her knees, the guest rocked back on her heels and squatted, hugging herself, before an orderly wrestled her onto her back. Her spine made a crunching sound, vertebrae being pushed into the floor — a sound I could feel in my molars.

Head kept panting, that slow, deliberate breathing recommended for transition and delivery. I had to tell her to keep still while I pushed up her sleeve. There wasn't that much blood, the four small punctures resembling a bite. When Head spoke — "I can manage from here, thank you" — her voice was pure adhesive being ripped from skin.

—⁂—

"DID YOU MEET your maker? Is that what took you so long?" Mademoiselle clucked at bedtime, when I finally managed to collect the letters.

"Hardly."

I was famished and my feet hurt. What to do with these missives, anyway? I could just as soon file them in my suitcase as post them, or even turn them over to the secretary — it amounted to the same thing.

Once again Mademoiselle had exhausted herself by crafting and addressing envelopes in that meticulous if shaky hand of hers. "Since I belong on my back," she said almost gleefully, "you must act as my legs. Of course I would be your messenger in a blink."

It is, and was, the heart the patient appealed to. Aching shins and arches: if I'd listened to them instead. But a good nurse cannot.

—⁂—

"YEA, SOLANGE POITIER, though I walk through the valley of the shadow of death," the old woman intoned mawkishly — joking, I was sure, until she grimaced. "Stay with me. Just for a while. Please."

—⁂—

BEFORE MADEMOISELLE DRIFTED off, she regaled me with stories, fibs and fabrications about her exploits in Paris, clearly more fiction than fact. What choice was there but to listen? When I finally got to leave, it was long after the end of shift. Night Nurse barely glanced up from her nap as I slipped past the desk, the letters forming a bulky shield under my bib. No point checking in or out. Our hours are regulated by other than clocks.

In the safety of my room, I spread out the envelopes on my bed and had a change of heart. Instead of stuffing Mademoiselle's busywork into my suitcase, to be forgotten about, I applied what postage was in my purse. I slipped the letters left unstamped into a drawer; the brother could take them when the time came, if he cared to.

Against all better judgment, I used the last of my good stationery and, managing a hand that mimicked Head's — upright, purposeful, my fingers pressing firmly — wrote:

Dear Monsieur, Your sister's days, I regret to inform you, are becoming shorter. Your visit would be appreciated. If you wish to see her I would recommend that you come without further delay. Sincerely.

I swatted at a fly. Its buzzing reminded me of patients being strapped down, ETC pads applied to their temples. It seemed incumbent upon me, now, to wonder what went through their minds on seeing that grey metal box, its wires and switches.

So there would be no confusion or mistaking my position, I jotted *Room 232, Nurses' Residence* beneath my signature. I also added a postscript: *If it's no trouble, please bring food items, a warm nightgown, and Mademoiselle's statue if it isn't too unwieldy.*

I exercised considerable restraint — a credit to Florence Nightingale — by not adding more; it seemed enough to say it aloud: "You'll hurry your arse, Monsieur. If you know what's good for you."

18

LUNATIC ASYLUM

? ? ?

My dear c,

Is it possible to live two lives at once? I think so. By day I sculpted my waltzing couple. By night I abandoned them to walk the streets, appeasing my heartsickness. You don't believe me? Such heartsickness was all too real.

"Will you ever make good on your promises?" I asked Monsieur each Tuesday, already knowing his answer (Rose is sick, she's unwell; a cad couldn't leave her just now; yes yes yes, government pals would soon commission your work if you waited just a little bit longer).

Walking helped. Under the lacy shadows of Eiffel's edifice, I strolled past buildings being razed for the next World's Fair.

ONE WET NIGHT I had just enough for a drink in a bright café. Sitting wedged between two strangers was Criteur, who, like Paul, made himself a little less scarce now. He waved.

A more steadfast lover he'd have made than what I was used to. He could be impetuous but he was more than an opportunist. I could've fallen in love. But Criteur was a lover of neither women nor men, seemed immune to charms besides his own. A bit too sure of himself.

The place was packed with Americans, women in bright hats only a little droopy from the rain, men swigging bourbon. As gaunt and undernourished as ever, Criteur lit a cigarette, passed it to me.

"Lonely, are we? I don't see anything wrong with your pianist friend." Nudge, nudge, omitting the "a" in the word. Winking.

Thinking of you, I said, "Don't be juvenile." Too loudly, though I wasn't unused to having strangers, men, look at me.

"So the Muse has flown, has she."

"You sit around naked. I'd rather not."

"What would Monsieur think of you, saying that to him?"

"Don't be small-minded." I wiped away a tear of laughter. Whiskey burned my throat.

Feeling for his watch, he found he'd misplaced it; things get lost when you walk the streets. The café all but emptied, the stragglers grinned wolfishly, and my friend, excusing himself, was gone.

—∞—

YOU COULD'VE LOST yourself with me in the Louvre, in a happy way. Miles and miles of antiquities.

I was kneeling before a caryatid when a strangely familiar voice boomed, "What is it you see?" It was my new acquaintance, Debussy. "A woman bearing up under unbearable weight."

All around us, a gaggle of students were watching. More admirers of Monsieur's? As populous as houseflies — and oh, my —

maybe they fancied themselves as such. Blending in with the statues, gilded walls and ceilings.

"A strong woman, then. Does her strength have grace?" my interrogator persisted. "Is there gentleness in it?"

Out of exhaustion — weariness at the hands of art — I rested my palm on his lapel, gave him a little push. Playfully, as you would've, not to encourage him. You — whom I itched to sculpt to complete the statue of Maman — would never have behaved in that way.

"Let's get out of here," he said.

—◦◦◦—

RAIN TRACED THE windows of his room. The piano stood under a hail of staff paper; the jar of daffodils was a far cry from the sickly potted jades Monsieur kept.

My host served tea in chipped cups, his dark hair falling across his eye.

"With all respect, you're wasted on that boor. What do you see in him?"

I loosed the smile Maman hated, all the wily impatience and inconstancy I could muster. "Play for me!"

When he didn't I rose and put my arms around him. Who doesn't seek to be appreciated?

"It's not so simple for me," he said. Which even you would've taken to mean there were other women. "You deserve someone who cherishes you."

That word, like cherries dipped in chocolate. In his reserve was a longing, and the potential to rub away my pain. Did you know pain has its own patina?

"The only thing Monsieur will make you is old." When Debussy played for me, his fingers chiselled away any lies. "He'll make you old. And slowly but surely he'll make your art his. If he hasn't already. He's only out there to make everyone's style bolster his."

We're not used to such frankness, C. It can hurt. We have our pride.

Even when defending myself, I defended the "defender" of my work. "What you don't understand. Is how … dependent. How he's put me … providing a certain. In this position …"

My friend could be as exacting, as unforgiving, as you. "But a true artist makes do. Always. No funds for travelling? You travel in the imagination. And so on."

Easy for him, of course, after winning at least one Prix de Rome and escaping there. "Ah yes, the imagination, friend to all!"

"Without it, my friend, the best dreams never touch ground."

"You trust in destiny?" An odd thing to wonder aloud.

"You don't?"

One glimpse of his hands at birth, he said, and his mother knew she'd borne a performer. Safe to say, *ma petite*, one glance at ours and Maman should've known she'd given the world a — but she'd only noted the lack of a male appendage. "So the flesh determines fate? When one is partnerless, one dances in solitude?"

I watched the rain destroy the blossoms in the street.

"Unless you count the partners in your head. Then you're never truly alone," he said. When I wound up in his bed, the pianist was all courtesy. His youth was a marvel to me: leanness, blue-black hair instead of grey, washboard ribs instead of a spare tire. A wiriness that begged the question why Monsieur had such luck with women — not that Debussy was a slouch himself.

I was quite eager, but when his kisses progressed there was something amiss. Was it knowing he had other lovers? Try finding a man in Paris who didn't, or doesn't! Except Criteur, poor Criteur — hardly a man at all.

The pianist's touch was wrong, all wrong. Too quick, too delicate — I hesitate to say, too unconvincing.

Leading him to water, I couldn't let him drink. He was much

too polite to accuse me of being a tease, and too much a man to feel that some failing on his part put me off.

The light was draining from his room. Crumbs in the sheets. We lay barely touching: two keys, one sharp, one flat. More tea, and the consolation of more piano playing, a looping rondelle. Yet he wasn't about to give up. "If you'll excuse my presumption. If you could just detach from him ... I'm prepared to wait." He kissed my knuckles, his youth both pitfall and advantage.

I agreed to see him again — as a friend.

Like wind and rain, wildflowers and weeds springing up in knot gardens, his notes leapt from silence with a liquid quality the opposite of Monsieur's suffocating thunder. Debussy was air and sunlight on faceted water, Monsieur a little volcano spewing rocks and dirt. Given my tin ear I was earthbound, rockbound. But my Waltzing Lovers found breath in the pianist's music. As long as his fingers didn't stray from the keys I liked the flattery of his performance.

He enticed me to climb Eiffel's tower, finally, months and months after its rowdy opening. The needle of a massive gaudy dragonfly, it cast its massive shadow over the crowds it still drew, long after the Fair closed and the hoopla waned, despite the pleas and promises to tear it down.

I despise crowds, as you know. But on Debussy's dare I overcame this and the hatred of heights you and I share. Too poor to take the elevator, we took the stairs. Sunlight flickered through tons and tons of filigreed iron. An acid fear blinked and grabbed at me, burning as my brain floated and bobbed ahead of my body. My gaze locked on my friend's heels, the hems of his pant legs. Up we climbed, up and up and up, the people below becoming pinheads, sticks, then tiny, tiny dots. The dead pavilions on the Champ de Mars were ever-shrinking anthills, the barges crawling up the Seine mere slugs. My heartbeat was a snare drum's, though the higher we went the more bodiless, heartless, I grew.

At the *premièr étage*, stopping to rest, my companion stood wobbly-kneed.

That we'd ever disparaged Eiffel, mocked the ego behind his erection's thrust! Debussy's face was a balloon bouncing before me — drifting, for I had eyes only for the spectacle: the Invalides' gilt dome, the Taj Mahal white of Sacré-Coeur on her hill, Notre-Dame's bulk, Père Lachaise's green hump on the horizon; the panorama all topsy-turvy with cupolas, spires and chimney pots, the pea-green river winding in and out a snake's glittering coils. Amidst the jumble, I tried pinpointing where Monsieur might be, until Debussy urged me to the *deuxième étage* — the better to touch the sky. From there we watched the clouds stream by as if, turned liquid, the sky stood on its head. A strange inversion I highly recommend. We had left earth and no longer climbed or flew, but swam.

Spreading my arms, I could have leapt into its depths, never touching bottom — until I nudged my companion toward the rail. Though we artists were acrobats, made to swing from trapezes, it was a mistake to look down. We descended, one stiff, cautious step at a time. Hands gripping railings. Solid earth looming, looming, as did roof- and treetops, some in bloom, explosions of white growing larger, larger. My eyes were pinned to the piston-chug of Debussy's shoulders, not the faces below sprouting eyes, mouths, noses.

If it'd been Monsieur, we'd have ridden the elevator, dined in the restaurant near the top.

Back on terra firma, the pianist saw my exhilaration and expected a kiss. Instead I shook his hand. "I prefer to do my soaring on notes," he said.

When you've had strong wine, how can grape juice satisfy? Or plain bread after buttered?

I watched him disappear into a sea of hats and parasols, then raced to find Paul, who had his own place by now, away from Maman. I needed to tell him what I've told you, how it felt, all but touching heaven without having to die first. But when I reached his apartment, his glazed look turned me away. He was writing a play. It was his everything, his firstborn he called it, as much in its thrall as in the Church's, and not to be interrupted.

Through the window I shouted how the tower was a true cathedral. Then he invited me in, to set me straight.

"It's all human engineering, hardly divine." His eyes were full of suspicion, for he wanted to know who'd accompanied me. Surely I hadn't climbed on my own?

"Monsieur Debussy, you've heard of him, of course."

His whole face changed.

"At long last. Someone worthy of you."

"Hardly." For something else had come to me — a recollection of the pianist kicking a cat from his doorway that first, rainy afternoon.

—⁓—

THAT WEEK, IN spite of myself, I welcomed Monsieur's visit, hungry for love though love had long fled. Though he repelled me, a certain *je ne sais quoi* held me captive.

But what was it? you keep asking, badgering, in fact. Quite simply, *ma petite*? The pull of a shared passion for the work. Plus I longed to have my waltzing couple cast in bronze and didn't have half a centime to pay the founder. But Monsieur did.

With that throaty, disgusting chuckle of his he applauded my sculpted lovers, his own rotund form toga'd in a sheet. "They look ready to waltz to bed! If their bodies were any closer, Mademoiselle, you'd show the man planting his ... Well. You've outdone yourself."

A compliment I'd hoped for. Still it dredged up pain, less over lost love than of giving up my little one, my chance at having a little one, the one with black-pearl eyes. Unable to speak of it, I said, "Planting? A seed, Monsieur?"

Of destruction, you understand. The ruin in everything, there all along and only waiting to grow.

But he babbled about Michelangelo, the ruin embedded in perfection. "We keep our optimistic spirit, Mademoiselle."

"Without that," — impossible not to roll my eyes — "we'd walk into the Seine, a bronze in each hand?"

"Now, now!" He balanced my plaster in his palms — an offering to some god, himself perhaps. No doubt he saw himself in it, the male a figure of grace leaning into eternity. Never mind that his dance partner was more than his equal; a pair of nudes made to fit together. Ever my teacher, he offered his critique. "The only problem, the only flaw … their pose isn't … set. They look so precarious. Like they'll wash away."

"That, stupid, is their strength."

He struck his pose, the one reserved for parties, kissing cheeks as well as arses. "But they're too beautiful to be real. If you added a blemish …"

"So they looked like us? How sad. How boring — copying life."

The prig — the prick — persisted. "But … it looks like you've done water."

"Not frozen like ice, the way some would do it?"

Did he know he was being mocked, or did it fly over his head, unnoticed? Such was his arrogance. I leave it to you to decide. Ever the chameleon's, his face paled. "My dear. To make bad art takes a ham fist — and a fucking frozen heart."

And yet, helping himself to my paper, he wrote a note to his best friend in the government, giving me full assurance that the agent would be by — immediately — to offer a fat commission.

Not to make excuses, my dear C, but you can see how I was caught.

Yours truly. X

19

... COMMITTED TO MY KEEPING ...

MONTDEVERGUES ASYLUM
27 SEPTEMBER 1943

Attacking another's vanity has no place in a report of this nature. But, what a sight, the secretary, with her frilly blouse and freshly permed hair! Her face bloomed behind the double doors' glass — she must've had a key to the downstairs entry. Novice had no choice but to let her in, and unable to contain herself, she clomped towards us, stopping Head in her tracks.

"Imagine," she said. Word had arrived. The brother is planning to visit! Who knew buttercup-yellow frills and candy-floss curls could be harbingers of disaster?

Seeing the note in her hand, I took myself directly to the supply room. I was busily counting *camisoles* when Head stormed in. She tailed me to the desk, practically stepping on my heels. The secretary was gone, as was the note — one small mercy, not that it spared me.

"So you took it upon yourself to summon him? Mademoiselle's poor, unsuspecting relative! Who do you think you are, Poitier? It's your responsibility to keep loved ones apprised? Have you no care for rules? The heart of France is being eaten away by traitors — and you think it's fine to flout all respect! For the hospital's integrity and the family's! You can expect to be terminated for this."

She yanked a chart — Mademoiselle's — from its peg and scanned it, pale with anger.

Patient C, 19/09/43, 10H17. Decubitus ulcers, sacrum right &
left, buttocks right & left, salve, dressings appl'd. Complains of
noises, chills. Temp normal. Hands warm to touch. Dehydration.
No trouble communicating. Head of unit informed.

—⁊⁊—

ITS LAST ENTRY was more than a week old. I was about to update it, until she clasped it to her bib so I could hardly pry it away.

"Make yourself useful, Nurse, till we hear what discipline comes down. Be prepared."

—⁊⁊—

IN ORDER TO peacefully sponge-bathe Mademoiselle, I chose to hold off giving her the news. One maintains calm, particularly when physical needs must first be met. Focusing on the patient helped displace Head's anger somewhat. To keep up Mademoiselle's humour I teased, "What have you got against water, anyway?"

Her response caught me off guard.

"My *maman* would ask the same thing. You fancy yourself as her? She abandoned me."

"Now, now. Of course she —"

"Oh, but she did."

"Now, dear. It serves no purpose ..."

There are days when one's best intentions can serve to create a small hell.

"But my brother didn't, you see. Abandon me. No, he never did." From what I gathered, he pretty much had. Regardless, this made it harder to keep his plans to myself. Of course I'd tell her, at the right moment. But what if something happened and he was unable to come, was somehow prevented? He was old himself and travelling anywhere these days could be problematic. The poor thing had suffered more than enough disappointment, I'm willing to bet.

"I would bathe in milk, no, champagne, if he had his way," she rambled, eyeing me, "the waters of Villeneuve. Not this! I'd rather roll in cat's piss." She flailed her wrist and I caught it, held it. "Poitier Solange, your fingers are like bisqued clay."

Beyond the bars, on the other side of the windowpane, a faint brownish yellow shape flickered past, and another.

Mademoiselle gave a rough laugh. "I'll be a leaf, that's what I'll ... Whose pages will I get pressed between, do you suppose?"

"There, there." Best to avoid gloomy talk of the eventual and the inevitable, and to train attention on the present. "That friend of yours — the one you've been writing to ... She's unable to vis —?"

Her silence indicated that talk be avoided, period. But talk is part of a healthy disposition, as long as difficult topics are avoided. If a patient goes into cardiac arrest over something, better it be joyful than grievous.

"You can expect your brother within the week," I divulged.

When the patient finally spoke, she sounded positively childlike. "Will he bring *chocolat*, do you think, when he comes for me?"

"*Bien sûr*. Champagne perhaps, and roses?" I was being playful, not glib.

Mademoiselle shuddered, suddenly covering her face. Instead of the expected tears, a pinkish red oozed between her fingers. Nosebleed.

"Tilt your head back, there's a dear." Her shoulders were trembling. I put my arm around them.

"If he were really good, as good as you, he'd bring me mud," she laughed. I didn't like the sound of her chest. Clamping her hand around my arm, she dug in her ragged nails; a manicure was in order, if any of us had a moment to burn. "Did I tell you how we used to play? In the mud in Maman's garden. I tell you, Soitier, with mud in my fists, I felt God's pulse."

Was my timing an error in judgment?

She shivered, eyes squeezed shut, complaining of being "so cold. The mistral, this time of year. When I first came here ... It will be warmer in Villeneuve, won't it?" She drew a slow, deliberate breath, appearing to collect herself. "Good clay, Miss Soitier? It feels silky and chalky on the palms, drying ... Mud between my fingers and toes. I wasn't a boy or a girl, but a cipher, you see? I was God's seeing eye, his eardrums ..."

The nosebleed, at least, had abated. I managed to wipe off her upper lip.

"I made mud-cakes for Maman, which my brother tried to eat! Taste and see ..." She was sobbing again, but allowed me to clean up her nose. "The doctor, the one whose name is a gift but who looks like snow — she wanted me to work again. To sculpt again. The devil himself, the rodent, I know was behind it. The one I've told you about, who put me here. His friends still try to poison me, as you're aware."

"Oh, now. Enough excitement for one afternoon, I think. Let's get you something to help you rest."

There was nothing for it but to tear downstairs to fetch a dose of Veronal. So much for my outside efforts, my attempt to bring light into her days. By soliciting her relative's attention. I'd very likely fleeced myself of a job — not just a job but a bed and a roof over my head.

—⁂—

NOVICE SPELLED ME for a short break during Quiet Time. I raced to the dorm, collected whatever letters I hadn't posted, hurried down to Admin, and set them on the counter for the secretary, who wasn't at her desk.

An unfamiliar voice, a man's, was barking instructions from the directeur's office. Secretary emerged looking flustered, even a bit unnerved. "I'm sure our new directeur will know just what to do," she told me, straightening the little pile of correspondence.

Not wanting to appear too curious, I asked what had happened to our old one. I didn't dare mention the note, which she seemed to have forgotten about.

"He's been replaced." She gave me a wan smile and ducked to retrieve a familiar-looking folder, which she pushed towards me. "When they cleared out his files, a few things appeared. A couple of bits and pieces I stuck in here — nothing too important. I don't suppose you're interested." A tiny muscle in her chin, the mandible's *mentalis*, twitched. Her eyes were dulled by a certain resignation — or by her blouse, not the best shade for sallow skin.

New to the file was a carbon copy of the papers signed by Mademoiselle's family, her mother and brother: the original order to commit her. There was something else I hadn't seen before, a photograph with *1929* pencilled on the back. It appeared to have been taken in early spring. Two old women sat together in the bleak sunshine outside what must be Pavilion 10. Both looked bundled up, Mademoiselle in the same old glad rags, only slightly less shabby. The white-haired lady beside her was wearing a ruffled blouse and a corduroy suit, and was reaching across Mademoiselle's lap for her hand. But Mademoiselle was having none of it. Arms folded, hollow-eyed, she gazed straight ahead as if the other weren't there. A caged bird and a thwarted feline, she and her visitor looked like. Because the woman had to be a visitor, looking so proper. Could it have been the mother? Not likely. Stapled to a page of Mademoiselle's doodling was a letter

dated the same year and signed by the brother, requesting *Whom-
ever It May Concern* to inform his sister of the parent's death.

I asked to borrow the photo, giving my solemn promise to
return it at shift change. Secretary simply shrugged. "Be my guest.
Not like anyone's screaming for it."

The subject of the brother's reply to my note still hadn't
come up, but thinking of it — and Head's vexation, as well as
Mademoiselle's excitability — made the picture seem sudenly
burdensome, scarcely worth any further grief or grievance. Anything was liable to happen under Head's hawkish attention.

I nudged the pile of Mademoiselle's handmade envelopes forward and set the photo on top of it. "You'll give these to the
directeur?" I paused, fishing for something, anything to do with
the note, and steeling myself. When Secretary said nothing I asked
if he wished to see me.

She eyed me strangely, shaking her head, then swept everything
into the folder, and the folder into its drawer.

—⚹—

THE REST OF the shift was no less eventful. At 19H52, with a doctor
unavailable, a catatonic threw a fit, perhaps from some irritation
of the brain's motor centres. Hysteric convulsions, tonic contrac-
tions — causing rigidity — as well as screaming, laughing, frothing
at the mouth. Eyes rolling but pupils reacting to light. Two fingers
down the throat just in time to prevent swallowing the tongue,
Veronal administered successfully. Patient cribbed, the best means
of holding her in a recumbent position.

20H22. With malnutrition already a worry, three cases of dysen-
tery today alone. A walking recipe for beriberi wet or dry, pernicious anemia, pellagra, rickets, scurvy, et cetera. Where it couldn't
be injected, Veronal was doled out like bonbons, inserted, shoved.

At such times it helps, it truly does, while breathing deeply, to
inwardly recite physiological terms — in this case, the muscles of

the human mouth and lips: *Orbicularis oris, buccinators, quadratus labii superioris, quadratus labii inferioris, caninus, mentalis, zygomaticus, triangularis, risorius.* A Latin hymn to the god of speech who'd have us eating starch.

Sometimes, though, stronger meds than recitation are required.

—॰॰—

I DO NOT consider nicotine a harmful drug. Back in Lyon, Sister and I would savour the occasional *clope*, which worked wonders in calming the nerves. A girl in the refectory here will trade cigarettes for lipstick not too obviously used. Under the circumstances, such barter seems more than fair. *Une clope* in hand helps one commit one's honest thoughts to paper.

Ready to light up in my room, I stashed the rest of my bounty in the silver case, the better to be rationed and thus less likely to become habit-forming. Out of sight, out of mind. I did worry, though, about the smell drifting upstairs and under Head's door, a scented trail to draw her here, and putting on a sweater I hurried outside. Best not to smoke in the entryway — a nurse upholds at all times the habits of good health, hygiene and behaviour — so I stood well out of the light.

I was about to strike the match when Novice and two girls from Men's ambled up. Their presence — "Look who it is!" — cheered me at first, better company than that of some prowling guest's without an orderly as backup. But I didn't feel like sharing just then. My desire for a fag only increased by their idle chit-chat, until one of them said, "Oh, did you hear Head's got it in for someone?"

Who? I almost said. Excusing myself, I let the urge pull me toward and beyond the gates to the road, and in the wall's shadow I lit up. Cool for this early in autumn, the night was chilly and clear. The stars beamed down, so many icy grits up there only egging on my agitation, as though bracing me for something — the humiliation of being let go, or the deepening of fall?

Pulling smoke into my lungs, I coughed even as it buoyed me, and found myself sputtering when a shape emerged from the thoroughfare's darkness. I felt his grip on my shoulder almost before I recognized him.

Renard peered at me from under his shrunken beret. His eyes were oily-dark in the gates' distant light, his reedy face glistening with sweat. His overbearing grin seemed almost febrile, it was that nervous, and filled with a smarmy charm, as if just by being there I had asked for, arranged for this!

"I'd hoped to see you again — doubted I would, actually."

His breath came in spurts, its sourness piquing concern for his gums. He'd clearly been running, from someone or something. Or had he been lying in wait, waiting a very long time, watching from the woods, stalking me? No. I was letting Head's hawkish supervision take over and colour everything.

More unkempt and even less appealing than he'd been in the café, Renard brushed bits of dead leaves from his clothes. He must've seen my confusion and gave me little chance to pull away, though I might've shouted to the gateman when his hand closed, a bit too smugly, around my wrist. He had a calculating look of desperation and relief. No attempts at pleasantries.

"The boy I told you about — the kid I mentioned, that night at the bar? He's not in any grave danger, I hope. But he needs to be seen," he said, his breath rasping unpleasantly close to my ear. His voice made me think of patients, strictly medical ones, making the most banal requests while suffering grievous pain. I felt my diaphragm press my lungs, was about to drop and stamp out my cigarette when he snatched it for himself and dragged away as though his life depended on it. He gestured at the gatehouse. "I'd have looked for you inside, if not for that bastard — Peter guarding the pearly ones, is he? The nearest doctor's in Avignon —"

I voiced my doubts of that — enough, I hoped, to be discouraging.

"Look," he said, "the one in the village can't be trusted."

I am noting this for the record, since Head's vigilance, her dislike, makes an accurate reflection of my activities all the more prudent, pressing even.

Renard was only too persistent. "Have a look, is what I'm asking. He just needs reassurance, to be told that his wound will probably heal. *Bien sûr*, if you'd seen him earlier —" His look was gloomier, more put-upon and guilt-inducing than Head's and Night's combined. He held the cigarette the way one would an insect, loath perhaps to crush it out. In the dark his surliness seemed lightened by how pathetic he appeared, whether he was lying or not. It was enough to arouse my natural curiosity. "Look. It's a small thing I'm asking. He's a kid. If you have any kindness, Mademoiselle Poitier ..."

If you have a gift and don't use it, watch it turn against you, Mademoiselle liked to say. Sister's words came to me also: *Oh Lord* this, *oh Lord* that. *Spare me no opportunity to serve.*

"You have no business coming here," I said succinctly. The last thing I wanted was a scene. I wished the gateman would doze off.

Renard's grip tightened, his sweaty paw melded to my wrist, and he stepped into the roadway. I resisted, for a second almost wishing that Head's policeman friend might come barrelling along. Let someone else deal with this however they would.

Simply by being here, certainly not by choice, I'd been knocked from my perch atop an invisible fence, the line of non-allegiance I called fairness and true professionalism. I couldn't stop thinking: no job, no place to sleep, how will I feed myself? This is what comes of overstepping, overextending one's duty.

I finally shook Renard off and watched him sprint to the

opposite shoulder, where he waited. Dry leaves skittered along the verge, the cigarette's tip a firefly against the trees' blackness. Then he leapt the width of the canal.

If only I'd pocketed another for courage.

Miss Nightingale's example made me dart after him. I ate my pride all the way across the cracked asphalt and onto the raised embankment, soles skidding on its slippery cement. I managed to easily jump the stream, and in doing so felt something inside me lunge too. Perhaps it's how a guest used to restraints feels having tethers loosened, or, heaven forbid, slip and slide away. Perhaps — and this scares me — it's how one has to feel to undertake our job, and to do it well. A queer mix of fortitude, determination and feeling utterly helpless.

Once I was in the rustling woods, I gave myself an enervating shake, as Sister advised after an especially difficult shift. I then followed with her calming technique of pushing both arms straight and taut, fingers pointing downwards, and uttering *vexed*.

Vexed, vexed, vexed.

An awfully silly exercise, yet I swear it helped.

20

LUNATIC ASYLUM

WHENEVER ...

DEAR C,

You come to me sometimes, still, in my dreams. Does it please you to know this?

When you do your voice fends off the terrible shrieking. You would think after all this time I'd be used to it. But the lunatics' noises are chisels working my brain. Fine-tooth, three-point and flat ones. My brain jailed in my head, jailed in this place where ...

If it mattered to you, wouldn't you have sprung me from here by now?

People lay their own traps, you say. In some cases, true. Like Monsieur popping on his silly hat, swinging his walking stick and returning to Our Lady, saying he was off to visit Notre-Dame when it was Rose he was seeing.

"Oh yes, and her light will be glorious. Here Fido, Fido!"
I shouted to his back. "Go home to your bitch." An overblown
poodle, his whore — that snout of hers, those ruffles and frills,
and old enough to be Maman.

Without turning, he told me to shut up.

As his footsteps died away I picked up a fresh maquette and
dropped it, its wet thud like something dead hitting the floor.
Then I took up my latest addition to his oeuvre, a woman's hands
modelled as if to cradle a tiny infant's weight, all self-love abandoned for a love without conditions. The hands wobbled on their
board as I held them to the window — the weight of your ambition, chirred a cricket inside me. Do it. One of the hands fell and
broke. Each perfect finger snapped off at the knuckle. *Do it.* I
raised the other to toss at the wall but something stopped me —
was it you?

—ɯ—

"WHAT ARE YOU most afraid of?" our brother asked one summer
a very, very long time ago, before he had religion or I had Monsieur.
We lay on our backs in the garden at Villeneuve watching the
clouds. You remember.

"Afraid of? Pfff. You joke. And you, *mon petit*?"

"Of looking stupid. You haven't answered me."

"All right. Of everything. Of nothing. Of denying myself."

Even at his tender age, our little Paul quoted the English Bard:
"'When our actions do not, our fears make us traitors.'"

—ɯ—

"YOU'RE EVEN LOVELIER angry," Monsieur would say.

I was angry — furious, who wouldn't be — when his officious
evil friend — never trust those in government — told me, speaking
in a voice like *blanc mange*, to dress my waltzers — dress them,
as if they were a cancan girl and her let's-rent-a-room lover — if

I hoped for any kind of commission. Because women didn't do nudes, he said. God forbid.

"Don't take everything so personally," Monsieur said as we walked along the rue Jacob, defending this baboon, as if any man would bow to such a demand! He gave a hacking laugh as though it was just a dirty little joke. "Women aren't privy to such ... sensual feelings."

"If I grew testicles, would my lovers be pleasing? Less scandalous? What would Rose think?"

He seized my arm roughly and spat into his handkerchief, years' worth of dust in his lungs even with the *praticiens* doing all his work. "You play along. Don't think I haven't suffered too, the same stupidity. Idiots holding the purse strings ..."

Monsieur stopped to buy wine to fortify me. He opened the bottle at my atelier and, behind my back, filled a glass, which I gratefully drained without thinking twice. A dark if slightly watery red, it didn't taste off. He watched me take another glassful, not touching a drop himself.

"Cut out the smut. Drape them," he said of my figures.

As soon as he left I realized my folly. Knew I should've been more careful. I paid for it, let me tell you. I was up all the night with vomiting and trots. The room spun so badly I had to lie there keeping one foot on the floor.

I knew for certain I'd been drugged. Drugged and all but poisoned to death! Under the poison's influence, I gowned my woman from the waist down, gowned her with vines. Roots bound her to the ground as she leaned into her man's arms. My waltzers were no longer whirling, but suspended, the second before a striptease. On the edge, the promise of an elegant fuck.

—⁂—

THE MINISTRY OF *Beaux-Arts* never did purchase my piece, though it won enough praise from critic-cronies — crickets — that I was able to have plaster and bronze castings made. Ooohs and aaahs. "It's so *Nouveau.*"

Alas, you can't dine on the chirps of reviewers, on old men eyeing your cleavage while raising toasts "to Mademoiselle — such a pretty thing." Monsieur — my teacher, mentor, benefactor, friend, you name it — took all the credit.

— ⚬ —

NO ONE ANSWERED my knock when I went to Debussy's apartment. He was well over me, so it was safe to go. The door was ajar and voices came from within, his and a woman's. A wife's? I left his present — a token of our friendship, a little bronze of *La Valse* — on the threshold. No need for a note, for regards or regrets. He would know the giver by her gift. Fleeing down the stairs and into the street, I knew very well I wouldn't see him again.

His name did crop up in the papers, though. For some, C, persistence and perseverance pay off.

I didn't give another thought to him. You kept calling out to me, more charming and unattainable than any man. Even the mad know what's dead can't be raised, except by Christ. How cheered Paul would be to hear me say that. The closest I've come to seeing you, your likeness, was in the Loire, when oh so briefly that fetus swam inside me.

— ⚬ —

I DID GO back there, you know. Once or twice. The landlady welcomed me though her small daughter was the one I wished to see. Her cheeks' smoothness, her innocent eyes, everything about this child said: Don't grieve!

I helped the little girl bathe her dollies among the lilies, play that reminded me of you, of us. Did it wash away my guilt? My sorrow? Not really. My unborn child's laugh echoed down a corridor composed of water-mirrors. What she might have looked like, what she might have been. A smaller version of you? She begged to be given a body, a face.

With crayons, manila, and *macarons*, I paid Madame's daughter to sit. She wriggled and twitched. Her modelling took months. It was a good thing the dreaded Monsieur persisted in footing my bills — I give him that. Alas, his way of keeping me in his clutches.

But when the child smiled and the sun lit her pale braided hair it chiselled fine memories. Memories more of the body's than of the mind's.

Yes, yes — she might have been you.

But like any labouring mother I had to push. Her marble head crowned. Mouth, nose and eyes appeared.

A heavy braid fell upon her shoulder, the curve of her neck pure grace. Her ears were seashells, her lips parted in wonder. Her expression a perfect question mark. The little *châtelaine*, I christened her, and might've wept watching the landlady caress her cheek, then bat away the real girl whining for cake.

"The easy part, Mademoiselle, is giving birth."

The getting of wisdom, the hardening of a childish heart — all these things a mother sees. Our *maman* no different, C. Childless, I would be spared? Hardly. I'd put myself in Maman's shoes, watching you.

Back in Paris I itched to show off my achievement. To show Monsieur what parenting meant. To deliver something into the world without another's interference, left to its own devices to weigh good with bad.

But sense steered me clear of him and his new digs on rue de Vaugirard. From Pont Marie I watched the river, swells pocked with rain. In my mind the child to complete my *Maman* piece grew. Her prototype was my little *châtelaine*. You.

The finished sculpture of Madame's daughter caused a stir at that year's Salon. *An expert execution of Innocence on the cusp of being corrupted*, was one happy cricket's chirp. Others were less kind. *The*

*sculptress is the eager recipient of her Master's gifts, which begs
the question why such gifts are devoted to the banal — a child as
subject! Don't we know the domestic has no place in Art?*

Monsieur, predictably, naturally, suggested a Tuesday rendez-
vous. And I agreed — though at the appointed time I neglected
him, to make up with Criteur at the Rotonde. Lingering over
coffee, making it last, I wrote a letter to our brother who, riding
the coattails of his friend Mallarmé and the wings of his diplomatic
career, moved now in America's circles. La-de-da-de-da.

When Monsieur arrived only my cat Cléome was there to
receive him.

Though money was tight — the bastard was never all that
generous; I had to pick the gutters to feed my cats — I commenced
work before visions of you could fizzle. You sprang from my imagination with the pertness of a flower, shaped to fit the mother's
arms but refusing to be coddled. Wiry and unyielding, your figure
had a life all its own. A fiery girl who favoured rocks and mud
over dolls. And yet ... there, hidden, were seeds of the distaff:
Maman and me, each of us in you, spinning our separate fates.

Your neck was a tender stalk supporting a head of wild hair.
Serpentine ringlets, writhing locks. A woman's hair is her crowning glory — didn't Maman always say? Spun from your head as
a *maman* spider spins its web, your coif signalled the start of a
lifetime, a career of spinning that, yes, grows burdensome.

But in your face would be what I loved about you: something
defiant, rebellious and fleeting in that sullen attitude.

I bolted the door and devoted myself to you, unavailable if
anyone called. Welcome visitors were rare. The odd cricket would
come to pester me with questions: *What drives you to do a man's
work? Who feeds you your ideas? In doing what you love, surely
you don't expect to be paid too — isn't that a little rich?*

"How much will you make printing this?" I would say. Journalists
don't pay for artists' time, of course. I had a good idea Monsieur

sent these ones to waste mine. At night birds with voices like theirs crowded my dreams. Nattering gossips, they hatched eggs of all doubt's possibilities.

"Sink or swim. Rejection is rejection," said Criteur, ever helpful. "But maybe you should change your line. If a painting doesn't sell it's no huge loss. Spare us the horseshit about destiny. You don't even believe in God."

But I did, I do, when it's convenient.

Unfolding his penknife, he took an apple from my table, pared away bruises. "You say yourself, many are called but few ... if you can't be one of the chosen, there's nothing wrong with painting. So what'll it be, starve or —? It's just a matter of time before your belly forces your hand." The knife piercing the skin made a pulpy sound. Cléome leapt from her perch. I gnawed on the peelings. "It doesn't hurt to please people. People besides yourself."

I covered my ears. "Don't lecture me!"

And he was gone.

But then Monsieur came along, offering more kindness. Stupid to change course in midstream, he said. He inspected the works in my atelier and kinder than ever — oh, he could've killed with kindness! — invited me, on this perfect day, on a stroll.

—◆—

THE AIR WAS laced with lilacs, the river its echo. Crossing Pont Saint-Michel, my grip on his arm was wary, unwilling. The Palais de Justice, the spire of Sainte-Chapelle, the Hôtel-Dieu, and the yellow-grey of Notre-Dame — that fortress for Christ and such footsoldiers as Paul — loomed before us. Dressed for work, I wore no hat. Could've used the silly wedding bonnet in which Monsieur had adorned me in one of his effigies, or the cowl my model wore for *Le Psaume*. As if God cared whether my head was covered when we passed the cripples begging alms. Outstretched palms, sightless eyes — eyes like statues'.

Monsieur squinted up at the portals, the pair of us tiny as beetles. The scene of the Last Judgment towered there, depicted in stone: the trumpet blast raising the dead, a stalwart saint holding the balance. The weighing of souls: heaven or hell-bound? You'd have thought of Monsieur's infamous *Porte*, maybe pictured him at the weigh scale. I'm sure he did.

In the echoing nave, light glowered through the transepts, a red and blue bruise on the checkerboard floor. All that worn-down marble reminded me of our Paul's Damascus. Candles flickered. Our footsteps echoed. Gazing up into the heavenly vaults, I felt everything foreshorten. Your life, mine, and oh so much glory, we who worshipped stars, contained by these brutish walls. *Lord, I am not worthy* stuck to my churlish tongue like a hair. Far above, the rustling wings of pigeons. An invisible bird came to roost on my shoulder, Maman's spirit digging in its talons.

Monsieur tugged my sleeve, whispering hoarsely, praising the divinity of this and the divinity of that. Ceiling braces, buttresses, quatrefoil, rosette. His ears were cocked, you could tell, for trumpets blaring his greatness. A woman in widow's weeds praying over the poor box failed to glance up as he rambled about heaven this, heaven that, the heaven of people's fondest imaginings. Birth, love, suffering, death — life's spectrum was represented here. On and on.

Profane, Paul would've called it. I was sick of this slavish routine. "You're full of it," I said.

The sun lighting the vast rose window cast a watery purple wheel over us. The cosmic rose. The Catherine wheel — instrument of punishment and torture.

"As if we belong here. Sinners. Fornicators." Made so very, very small, I wanted only to disappear.

"Speak for yourself, my dear. You might try thinking first."

"You might try thinking before fucking —"

"So prudish all of a sudden. There's the confessional. Tell the priest, if you're feeling guilty," he said.

Sinners little better than dogs fouling God's nest.

The widow rummaged for coins for the box.

"Ah! Charity." Monsieur's grip on my arm was shrewish.

Truthfully? I could have separated each of his fingers from their sockets.

"And doesn't charity begin at home?" For I was thinking, honestly, of his grand *collage* with Rose. His kindness to me a choke chain while he and his bitch were locked in the act. Two grey-snouted dogs going at it.

"Leave her," I mocked him, before a priest came and told us to quiet down.

Leave her. It was a lament for what might've been, for a lifetime's grief outreaching anything. The last thing it was, a plea.

—◊—

ONCE, COMPLETELY OUT of the blue, our papa appeared. A stranger, he had aged since I'd last seen him at Paul's, at a small reception *mon petit* gave himself before embarking on his first trip abroad.

Papa smelled the same as always: pipe tobacco and ink, as if it seeped from his bookkeeper's pores. He kissed my cheeks, asked how I was, petted Cléome's head, all without once mentioning Maman. Departing, he left behind an envelope. I watched him totter down the sidewalk as quickly as possible with the aid of his walking stick. Briefly he turned and waved, the way he used to leaving us on Monday mornings.

"Come back anytime, please, Papa!" I shouted so that I swear everyone on the Boulevard d'Italie heard.

So happy to have seen him, astonished at how painfully I missed him, I almost overlooked his envelope. To my shamed delight a pauper's fortune was inside. It enabled me to complete the clay version of my *Maman et Enfant,* as much of your figures as I could. Both faces I left blank though, the better to arrive at, eventually, the exact expressions for each, once our differences were put to rest. Maman's and mine, once we were reconciled, of course we would be; and to a lesser degree, mine and yours. I had to be true to both of you, you see, and wasn't yet ready. Until I was, any expressions given you were bound to be sentimental and false — falsely sentimental.

Good things come to those who wait, our brother says. Truth in art takes lifetimes to convey.

—⁂—

PAPA'S IMPROMPTU VISIT softened my resolve about locking doors. Exhausted by work, I witnessed things that should've kept me alert. The flash, for instance, of a cloaked shoulder glimpsed in a grackle's blue-black head. A pickpocket seen in a dog disappearing under a hedge during a late-night stroll through a park. My imagination, of course. I was working all hours. But in such a state my guard was let down. In such a state you become a target.

I'd barely lifted your maquette to its shelf when Monsieur the meddler appeared unannounced, a stubby gnome in his twee black cap. As if the altercation in Notre-Dame had never happened. Lacking the decency to knock, he ogled my masterpiece. My mistresspiece.

Standing much too close, he fingered the bone at the top of my spine. Eyes full of crocodile tears narrowed in his trademark squint. Was he too vain for spectacles? That prying gaze! For once he was speechless.

To protect my mother-and-child, I confess I threw myself at him. Set myself between him and you. A quaint reversal: a womanly Perseus fending off the monster's stare with kisses. I succumbed to his, steering him away.

"Come to dinner, Mademoiselle."

I did, because I was hungry and had spent the last of Papa's money. But dining in the grotty rue Mouffetard wasn't what I'd expected. He was ashamed of my attire, so unsuited to the chic cafés he favoured. The dingy place he took me to was warm, though, and served large portions. I refused the wine, of course, careful to keep an eye on his every move. He'd grown up nearby, I knew, so despite all his airs this was his turf.

Then he hit me with another invitation. The *hausfrau* was off visiting friends in Saint-Cloud. I know as well as you, curiosity kills the cat. I rode with him in a cab to rue de Bourgogne.

It felt cheap and distasteful to enter his apartment, but even you couldn't have resisted. The rooms were less opulent than I'd imagined, and showed a woman's touch. The bric-a-brac! Trinkets and knick-knacks Maman would shun.

A painting stood out, one in a cluster of bourgeois works. Done in a palette of muted pastels, it showed a mother tenderly cradling a child, and was signed by one of Monsieur's pals.

"Carrière, the Symbolist — know him? '*Mère et Enfant*,'" he said, so lightly it was sickening.

I'm not as quick as you, but I immediately guessed what he was up to.

In the habit of collecting others' sentimental portraits, he wanted to outdo his friend. He needed something far superior to show as his own. His designs on my piece couldn't have been clearer.

"So, you hope to embarrass Carrière, 'proving' how much better you can do."

Our master of deceit, our clever chameleon, was appalled! "Mademoiselle. That is the last thing on my mind. If you're wondering why I invited you, there's something I should say. Rose and I are moving to the country. Which means I won't always be near. But I'm always with you, certainly in my dreams — in the heaven of them."

Laughing in his face — "In the hell of mine" — I didn't waste a second getting out of there.

In the peace of my atelier, I wondered if his words weren't an attempt to bully me. A fresh kind of manipulation, for he was set on getting his way.

—⁓—

NOT A MONTH later his despicable friend from the government, the one who'd insulted my *Waltz*, turned up, apologizing for being out of touch and asking how things had progressed. It was "the maternal piece" he was after — the work I had underway when we first met. "By now I trust it's completed?"

"You, sir, can kiss my maternal arse." You'll be happy to know I shut the door on his fingers.

With Monsieur's meddling now a conspiracy, it was worse than folly to stay where he'd installed me — where my every move could be tracked — in my little place near La Folie. I crisscrossed Montparnasse in search of a new home, often circling L'Hôpital Sainte-Anne. Round and round its imprisoning wall I went, as lunatics peered out through its barred windows. Ghostly faces. Muffled screams. Never in my wildest imaginings did I dream that Monsieur's evil would land me in a place far worse.

Increasingly my all-nighters took me across the river, through the Marais' shadowy maze, twisting streets and alleys as good as an enchanted wood for getting lost in. There, the most persistent followers could easily be given the slip. The Master couldn't have tracked me with a search party. In the gaslight I admired Medusa's shocked scream adorning that hôtel's huge doors on the rue Vieille du Temple. Dodging drunks and loose dogs, I would peer through the windows of a foundry at rue Rambuteau and rue des Archives.

One night a well-dressed man came out and, instead of telling me to move on, offered a drink. I declined till he held out the bottle and I saw what it was. Moët & Chandon. Like bubbling spring water from Épernay, in the countryside our parents had at last escaped to — this I knew through Paul. Several genteel sips loosened my tongue and quenched my thirst.

In answer to my question, the stranger said the foundry was owned by a dealer named Blot, one of the few dealers in Paris whom Monsieur seldom favoured with his business. "So the Great One and his mistress are trading Paris to lie around the suburbs," the fellow said, setting down the empty bottle.

"Good for him."

And before my acquaintance could ask anything in return for his kindness, I hurried on. Much as I needed it, the soothing darkness could be daunting, but wasn't so deep as to blot out signs. One, in a window not five blocks away on the rue de Turenne, said *Studio to let, terms negotiable.*

Given the stranger's way of speaking and what he knew, I wondered if he himself weren't the dealer, Monsieur Eugène Blot — a person adept, it struck me, at fighting fire with fire.

━━

I FOUND SOME peace when I moved to the rue de Turenne. But I'm afraid it was short-lived.

Though I was desperate for cash — oh, to have sold a slip-shod version of *Maman et Enfant* to the first bidder! — I was less willing than ever to part with the piece till its perfection was mine and its ideal patron secured. I know the Meddler was determined to give both of your faces his personal stamp, the soft yielding doormat loveliness he adored in us women. He was not above out-and-out sabotage, and his meddling exceeded his physical reach.

I was saving it for Maman, a gift to mark our reunion. Futile, perhaps.

I kept up my walking, in search of someone who looked like her, or who looked like you — because isn't it said we each have a double, a doppelganger? And knowing Monsieur Blot had a gallery near the Madeleine, I took to wandering such glamorous areas, scurrying past the Opéra and once even ducking into the Café de la Paix.

A mistake, a very bad mistake. Amid the yackety-yack and air-kissing of dolled-up ladies and the mincing men with them, a waiter demanded to know if I was meeting someone or had a reservation. He asked me to leave, but not before I heard one tart tell another, "Do you know Monsieur the great man hasn't just one but four brats by her, the pitiful thing?"

Do you know what it's like to be gossiped about? To be made to feel like bruised fruit? Lies heaped on lies. And here I was being treated lower than some swarthy immigrant, some Algerian ... Worse than a pack of dogs chasing me, this drove me to take up palette and brush. Though I rarely thought of my unborn girl now, at Criteur's urging I set her down on canvas, if only to let her rest out of harm's way. The sins of the mother bound and loosed, I painted her sleeping on death's dusky shore, a flock of doves guarding her. Their wings' flapping sufficient to drown out the father's bluster.

Such is the power of art — even painting, which concedes defeat to a world that's flat.

—⁂—

ONE NIGHT I spotted Monsieur's son, the drunkard, asleep by the fountain at Place des Vosges. Just blocks from my place. Where a bad odour rises, you know its source can't be far off. An omen, you see — a sign that Monsieur was exactly as he'd said he wouldn't be: near.

"Pose for me," he had begged the final time. Without each other, he'd said, we were as good as a walnut cracked in two. One half without the other could never be as fine as the whole. As if, once, we had been of a single mind. As if, once, he had cared for symmetry, though he refused marriage's balance and spared me the drudgery of a charlady's life.

But he continued to send money. A pittance, of course, just

enough to keep his hooks dug in. Long after any love was buried — more rubble than the cribs of ancient ruins under the Île de la Cité — I seem fated to waltz with him, like it or not, beyond the grave and back!

Sometimes it seems the hard clay under loam is being packed around me, its coldness seeping through my veins. As though he lies here too — the rankness of his scent, the scent of other women — and try as they might to keep our bodies from touching, my muscles fail. His breath turns me to onyx, no, coal.

X

21

... AND FAMILY AFFAIRS COMING
TO MY KNOWLEDGE ...

MONTDEVERGUES ASYLUM
28 SEPTEMBER 1943
02H10

"A girl's got to live," I told myself in the woods. If not for the
trees' spookiness — the moon throwing more shadows
than light, fungus in the branches resembling carrion nests — I
might've laughed at myself. Better than being appalled, held back
by usual caution and sense.

Trust your gut, Sister would say. By now I had little doubt that
Renard worked for the Maquis, though I suppose I'd suspected
it all along. Was he hiding from the police? The Gestapo? Aiding
the resistance, resisting Vichy and all its collaborators, balking at
nothing to defend what he believed in, what many if not most of us
believed in — an end to the occupation, the *rafles*, the war?

He kept one hand in his pocket as I caught up. *Good God,*

concealing a gun, was my first thought. Somewhere above us a bird hooted. I could have lied, made some excuse other than the fact that in another hour the guard locked up. I could've said I was doing nights and due for work. Would that I had been! I could've turned back — how would he stop me?

In the moonlight his face was grim and his hair a greasy thatch. He grabbed my wrist again, and for one truly awful moment I decided his wounded friend was a ruse. Did I look like the kind of woman he'd help himself to?

Renard grinned in my face. "You'd make a fine *maquisard*, I think." And instead of pulling me closer — *those gums*, I was thinking, *that mouth* — he brought the dorsum of my hand — think of where it had been, that hand, wiping and scouring — to his lips. Their scratchy warmth oozed to my palm and carpus.

When he let go, I stumbled on a tree root. It would've been awkward, unseemly at that point to bolt — perhaps he'd think I was disappointed — so I fell in behind him, following a crooked path through the underbrush, at a safe distance of course.

Soon the glow of a small fire — the embers of one, that is — broke the darkness at the edge of a clearing. Someone huddled beside it, a boy or a very young man — it was hard to tell exactly, the way he sank into himself, nursing on a flask while he slouched against some toppled stones, what appeared to be the remnants of a little wall.

"How old is he?" I asked, having put from my mind whatever details Renard had divulged.

"Sixteen, seventeen."

Peering up from his flask, the boy's eyes roamed mine. Dark and fearful, their colour was indistinguishable. Something about his face seemed remotely familiar, enough that the feeling it gave me made it a little difficult to breathe. He'd been among the crowd that morning at the station, those young men being prodded and coerced with Gestapo rifles. My memory faltered. Was he the one

I'd thought of, whose mother had behaved fit to be tied? Looking away, flinching, the boy let out a curse. He scanned the trees. Was he on the lookout for something? Who knows what was lurking. His alertness, his unease — what a strange thing, youth, its innocence so easily spent, squandered.

Only then did I recognize that Renard had brought me, not exactly in a circle, but in a meandering loop that ended near the hospital's cemetery. Through a scant border of trees, the field stretched seemingly forever under the chilly moonlight. Only a few of its stony mounds were marked with wooden crosses; most were left bare. I'd stumbled on it once during a walk and, struck by some of Head's choicer wisdom — "Sometimes, Poitier, the body knows what the mind can't, or refuses to" — had taken pains since to avoid it. Barren of names and dates, it has nothing to recommend it, nothing of interest beyond its occupants' anonymity. As if they all died by their own hand.

The boy's eyes had an unpleasant sheen. A sign of fever? The metal flask clicked against his teeth.

"He took a bullet. To his shoulder. Just a graze, the lucky little son of a bitch." Renard sounded half gleeful yet shy, appealing to my know-how, or perhaps what he took as professional vanity. He was sweating rather heavily — perhaps he bordered panic. They say you can smell it on people. Up till now, in my experience it's been true.

All the more reason for proper bedside manners. They hadn't failed me yet.

"It's all right. Now that I'm here, let's have a look."

Glowering, the boy looked away as he peeled off his jacket and shirt, both crusty with blood. An odour wafted up of ammonia, the bodily variety — the sweetish, peaty smell of poverty, of unwashed clothing, of some hovel having served as bomb shelter or foxhole. It's a smell that doesn't leave you. I recognized it from doing home visits while studying a unit in public health.

Renard stirred the fire's coals with a stick and held it out, its burning tip providing the only light for an examination. Better than nothing, though it hardly helped matters.

Sister's words came back: *By touch, Nurse, sometimes we see what otherwise might get missed.* I don't know why, but I felt clumsy and awkward touching him, probing his skin. It was like giving my first needle, or shaving my first surgical patient, or the first time I shouted "ten," the code for an emergency in Lyon, a cardiac arrest.

Predictably surrounded by contusions, the wound had suppurated, but as far as I could tell it was fairly superficial and showed no damage to the muscle. It was too late for sutures, and I said so, but with some antiseptic it would perhaps heal all right on its own. Still I felt oddly helpless.

"I've nothing to clean it with. Without supplies there's not much I can do." I held my hands out, surrendering. The boy's eyes followed them to my pockets, where I found a couple of centimes, which I pressed on Renard, instructing him to get his friend something to eat.

The boy's expression was more worrisome than his wound, his wary smile full of mistrust.

"I'll be back," I promised against all good sense.

Renard eyed me with surprise, even satisfaction. "My brother's boy, a nephew, sort of. His father would thank you, if he could. Raised the kid as his own, him and his wife. Like their own little Moulin, a proper hero." He smiled grimly. "They had some kind of arrangement. She wanted a kid, see. My brother's wife, a Jew — she was."

"Where are they now, the parents?" It pained me to ask.

Renard shook his head, gaping at me as if I were stupid, then gazed at the woods. "You might guess."

"Bear with me," I said, words no different maybe from Sister's *Wait on the Lord* or *We'll see.*

—∿—

IF I HURRIED, I might make it through the gates in time to fetch the requisite supplies. I slipped past the gateman with easily fifteen minutes to spare. With any luck at all, Night would be napping, and sure enough, she was snoring away in the near dark, sitting up at the desk but otherwise dead to the world. Getting past her was no problem, though I did encounter something unusual. The door to the supplies room was ajar, which of course made getting inside that much quicker.

The autoclave needed emptying and tweezers and bandage scissors were in extremely short supply. A quick search turned up not a single clean pair, which was odd but not completely unusual. When things get hectic on the wards at night there's no one to pick up the slack; one felt, feels, a certain amount of sympathy for Night, who does her best, or claims to.

Aware of the clock's ticking, I was forced to pillage a sterile pack for its instruments as well as adhesive tape and gauze. The large bottle of rubbing alcohol on the shelf was almost empty. Rather than searching for a smaller container to take the remainder in, I found a vial of potassium permanganate, a worthwhile antiseptic in a pinch, and wrapped everything in a clean hand towel which fit nicely under my sweater. Of course I'd take the cost of these items out of my pay, "for furnishing first aid to the dorm," perhaps, and at the first opportunity settle with Secretary.

The snoring out at the desk ceased. There was the sound of a little commotion, the rustle of Night getting up from her chair — and then, oh my nerves, the sound of her screaming. I dropped the supplies as if they were scalding. I was no longer thinking of excuses, there were no excuses, not for my being there.

But Night didn't ask. Her screams were hard to distinguish from those of the various guests' who, awakened, may never go back to sleep. She was kneeling at the utility closet — normally empty — where something red was spilled on the floor. *Nazi red*, was all I could think, the red of those flags we keep seeing everywhere, red with black in the shape of an amputee spider —

Then I saw inside the closet. Saw the pooling blood, and the patient — blessed God, a girl we'd all thought was doing so well, the one with the funny sayings about living — slumped there. Both her carpal regions were sliced open.

—൜—

NEEDLESS TO SAY I only got out of there now.

Nobody asked what I'd been doing on the floor after my shift. Head, summoned from her room, even commended me for being there and promptly calling the orderlies to remove the body.

Now that I've finally got this all down on paper, I'm going to take a good long soak; but before that, a drink of the wine that the orderlies, good as they were, left on the desk for us. Night has sworn off all alcohol, or so she said, pushing the bottle at me. So here it is on my dresser. I have to be up in a few hours but don't care.

My improvised sterile pack is here too — a lot of good it will do now. In the chaos of Head storming onto the floor in her nightdress, I didn't know what else to do but slip it under my waistband. It escaped her notice — I suppose I've got so thin it hardly looked like padding.

"You," she said. "I suppose we can give you a half-hour's grace to sleep in. Don't worry if you're a minute or two late coming back in the morning."

It is more than a little alarming, though, how one small slip, one transgression — one tiny breaching of rules — leads to another, and another. It is a slippery slope. So, despite the hour, I will not take Head up on her concession, and make every effort to be there on time.

22

A PLACE FOR LUNATICS

WHEN AND WHERE —

DEAR C,

Do you give a shit where I am? Where I've been? There's some-
place you'd rather hear of? Try this. A stone-and-mortar paradise,
Île Saint-Louis. Like a squat little fortress in the middle of the Seine,
strands of river for a moat. Forget lily pads and the Loire, forget
the rue de Turenne — this was the best place left to manage my
affairs when affairs with Monsieur turned dangerous. The cobbled
shade of Quai de Bourbon, piss in the gutters. A shuttered flat with
two rooms at street level, by the seedy embankment. This was my
château, in the heart of Paris. Cheap rent, the river's rushing all the
music a woman needed. And cats, a pride of them. Two scraggly
toms, Cléome and Josephine, and a batch of kittens named after

poets (a nod to Paul), Rimbaud, Rossetti, Baudelaire, Verlaine ... Sentinels. All mine.

And you thought I couldn't be happy?

Fishermen's leavings fed my brood. Fish guts. In spring the scent of poplar and lime, a melody to the nose drifting in, a welcome interloper interloping with the scent of my familiars.

The stink of cat, Paul called it, touching down on visits between global flittings to and fro. Did he bring souvenirs for you? I thought not. But for me, hearing of Monsieur's antics — his latest, pulling strings to cancel support for the lovers' triangle I was making — our brother pulled strings of his own. A champion for my work!

Toiling in secrecy I'd perfected a three-figure group, showing mortal man in the clutches of a hag while a nymph in youth's prime reached for him. As you see, *ma petite,* youth is sometimes wasted on the young, and beauty reduced to begging. My nymph watched the man turn his back on her, death's harpy swooping in to claim what was rightfully hers. Life's way. The piece was all the more gripping for being true.

My only jibe at its culprit was to render it with grace; but, catching wind of this — did even the birds act as spies? — the evil one, ever the narcissist, took the piece as a slur and short-circuited plans of its purchase as fast as his hateful agent friend proposed them. Needless to say this made me all the more wary and vigilant about protecting the work closest to my heart.

Paul convinced the government, the very ones who refused to hear my complaints against their bumbling agent, to give me another chance. How I wish that our brother had gone the extra mile and permitted himself to sit for me.

By then I was embroiled with Perseus, carving my hero wielding his shield and his gruesome trophy, Medusa's head. A motif that Monsieur, with his penchant for bodiless noggins — for carving my head on a block and calling it *Thought* — would have loved.

No money for models, so for Medusa's face I modelled the mirror's flash of myself. In carving this nightmare, was my motive pre-emptive? Was I lopping off my own head before the enemy could, denying him the pleasure?

If only Criteur had been up to posing as my warrior son-of-a-god. I tried to coerce him but he refused. Just as well. Time is money and money is time. Both eluded me.

Living on *pommes purée* without butter or cream, I slaved at a new version of my threesome-gone-wrong. Showed Age herself, the winged grim reaper, severing Man's grip on Youth. The *hausfrau*, the little ball of hate that was Monsieur, and beautiful me cut adrift. Its urgency was everything. It aired our dirty laundry.

A different agent sent to consider purchase had demanded that its plaster be warehoused — on Monsieur's premises! How transparent! A gift of a chance for the evil one to destroy it.

"Maturity," I called the piece. *L'Âge Mûr*. Which means what, my dear? Knowing better. Knowing better than to let those who would bury you win. That's what.

Oddly, the agent relented. When the money came I threw a party for our brother, home from his posting in China, and a few of his friends. Stringing up paper lanterns, I bought a good Bourgogne and a red silk dress embroidered with flowers à la *japonisme*. I wore it with my face powdered white, white as a geisha's. Vanity, you say — to impress a bunch of writers?

Of those invited only a few appeared. I'd even asked Papa and Maman, but do you think they came? Even Criteur stayed away, and you, *ma petite,* you … But Paul was undaunted, raising his mustard-pot-for-a-glass, toasting my *coup d'état*. "You shouldn't be surprised by good fortune. Now that the government supports you, others will." He denied his own influence, whispering, "Don't thank me, thank God. My dear sister, to everything is a purpose, all part of His plan."

Beaming at the faces round the table, all three of them, I said, "Let's hope Monsieur's not included in it."

"That which doesn't kill us makes us stronger, *ma soeur*."

After downing my wine, all too soon the others threw on their coats. Writers as faint- and fickle-hearted as painters — what a breed! My earnings gobbled up in one fell swoop.

And our brother? "We know you like your solitude," he said, excusing them.

—m—

IF THE REST of the world had been so obliging and left me to my work ... But the evil one's cricket friends kept interrupting, always interrupting. Using my poverty to make themselves look good. They broadcast my hardship all across Paris, as dignifying as lifting a woman's skirt to show her goodics! It wasn't pity I wanted but the pay any worker deserves.

Their "charity" attracted the further attentions of Monsieur Sylvestre, the government toad who'd rejected my *Waltz*. He kept pestering to see *Maman et Enfant,* no doubt working on the enemy's behalf since Monsieur had first spied it.

Inspired by you, I chose a bold tact. During Sylvestre's visit I whisked off the dustsheet. Your figures were achingly incomplete yet so close to being finished, the blankness of your faces gaping back.

"Look! Can't you see I've lost interest? Are you deaf or just stupid? The way things are going I'm afraid the piece will stay this way." I hoped, seeing this, he would give up and go away till the work had found its true home or I could demand its figureless price.

But his eyes brightened. His cheeks bulged with greed, his porcine grin flush with naked opportunism. "Brilliant, brilliant!" He bowed and scraped, oily enough to slip through the floorboards, blathering. "The possibilities! Fill in the blanks. Imagine the features you could add! Personalized! One size fits all. What mother, grandmother, sister, auntie wouldn't love a statue of herself with a tyke? Though you might make the *maman* more appealing — a bit of a hard-looking stick she is." Nerve heaped on nerve, the gall to crown it: "Once you've got the prototype, I'll be most honoured to market your efforts."

Why did you keep quiet? Because you were there, somewhere, lurking — being shy? I could've used your help, your defence, as I could've used Criteur's.

He had a huge laugh about it later. "The ass! And how does the man propose to cast these confections? With interchangeable faces! Genius. Such genius puts to shame the integrity of a Eugène Blot, say. A decent man like that."

I found his sarcasm contagious. "Sylvestre would have me painting souvenir plates!"

At least Criteur saw it my way. But he was cannier than either of us. "Just a matter of time before Monsieur's dealers strong-arm the piece from you. You know the man wants what he wants."

—m—

THE EVIL ONE might have left Paris but the Paris papers still trumpeted his triumphs. The review that hooked my attention, bait to a hungry trout, was enough to turn my stomach. *The Hand of God,* my tormentor's work was entitled. How apropos. The fawning crickets, doubtless part of his gang, chirred with glee at the Great One's modelling of an oversized hand "in perfect proportion." ("Such delicacy! Such strength! So lifelike!")

I didn't need Criteur to remind me of the hands I'd made for Monsieur, countless ones swallowed up in his great inventory.

Held in its "sensitive, all-encompassing palm," one cricket rambled, was a "clod of earth" containing a "fully formed yet embryonic Adam and Eve, less in their nascent state than in the throes of their Fall." Enough to make your skin crawl, this word-picture — to such a degree, alas, that the piece screamed to be seen.

Lead us not into temptation but deliver us from evil. Perhaps if I'd listened better to our brother's prayer ...

I picked a time when Bing's gallery, that elegant little place not too far from Blot's, was likely to be empty. Anyone who was anyone showed there. Not that I was overly worried about my dress; you wouldn't have cared, so why would I?

There, there, just inside doors of bevelled glass, stood the *Hand* itself on a breast-high plinth. In its palm cavorted The First Couple after sharing the forbidden fruit, entangled in an after-sex tumble. The smarmiest thing I have ever seen, bar none — all the gamier, as Debussy might've put it, for its scale. The hand's huge gleaming fingers, the figures' overripeness. Exhibitionism at its finest. As steamy and lurid as the guts my cats helped themselves to on the quay, if marble can be either. Who knows what man my persecutor had in mind shaping Adam? Eve's resemblance to his Danaïd — to me — made me heartsick, queasy.

Its profanity didn't end there. I recognized the overblown, oversized hand subbing for the Creator's. It was more than obvious. So obscenely sure of itself, it was a replica of the fleshy one that had touched, stroked and brought me to and away from myself, and wrought such misery. In his head the Master had replaced God, stooping to the depths and rising to the heights of smugness! A grasping, thieving smugness — revealed in a hand whose maquette I'd likely modelled and he'd usurped to mock me. Paul would've called it blasphemous.

It was too much to stomach, forcing me out into the street where I hurled up whatever food I'd managed to scrounge that day.

—⁂—

THE EGO THAT thinks itself omnipotent, C, threatens all in its path. The innocent victim and enabler of evil-at-large, I saw myself under siege, caught in a war. What could I do but watch my back?

Even an incomplete work was unsafe. I swaddled the statue of you and Maman in a rug, hid it under some rags in my wardrobe. Luckily I hadn't made it life-size.

Sylvestre returned by the week. "All you néed to do is sign it over. Once you have, I'll do everything in my power to see other pieces bought." Appealing to my vanity, as if I had any, he suggested the perfect home for Perseus was the government's Luxembourg Palace — naturally — where the rodent Monsieur placed his work.

I'll credit you this, C. Even at your most defiant you were never so devious or transparent.

"Don't believe a word he says," counselled Criteur. My devoted *praticien*. If only he'd had a model's physique and could've sat! But a diet of starch puts dough on the bones.

Watching Cléome and the other cats gorge themselves, we eyed their treats like children eyeing a *chocolatier*'s. In broad daylight I ventured down the steep stone steps to the quay and cast a line, a length of twine and a hook. My catch? A shoe — a cumbersome man's size forty-two.

"What good is that," Criteur complained, "unless I lost a foot?"

"Stop it!" I had far less patience with him than with you, and greater worries than filling my belly or finding footwear. No matter how secure a sanctuary, evil can creep in. It has ways. Nowhere is quite safe, even with shutters bolted, furniture shoved against doors.

My rooms backed onto a courtyard, one where children played. Dangling strings, they teased my pride, my little lions. Think of my feelings for you, growing up! I would never suspect innocent tykes of evil, of being accomplices. Certainly not accomplices to our Monsieur.

But then Cléome disappeared. Lured by these children — how else to explain it?

Night after night I combed the streets, calling her name. Not one to mince words, Criteur said, "What's one cat when you've got eight?" The last thing I'd expected, or needed, was being blind-sided by another "friend"! Preferring their company to his, I ordered him out.

That other treacherous one — who knows what gods were at play? — unveiled a work of his, years in the making, and had it rejected! Teach me to resist temptation! Wanting, needing to twist the knife, I sent congratulations "on his fine accomplishment." The stupidest thing I could've done, for he wrote back, snivelling, "grieving" my absence — a grief that was larded with insults: "Perhaps Mademoiselle's imagination plays tricks? Maybe she could try being nicer to those nice to her?"

I found Cléome's body underneath Pont Marie, a stone's throw from the flat. She'd been in the river for some time, her splendid coat eaten away. A wizened eyeless stare, jaw in a horrid grimace. Only a moron wouldn't guess she'd been poisoned.

Now I'm not saying a child did it. Of course not, not at all. Only one creature capable of such a deed — you'd have agreed, if you'd cared enough to be there when I buried her. Such evil doesn't just grow overnight, C. You know all too well how it feels losing a pet. Because of that I remain, in spite of everything, yours.

XX

23

... IN THE PRACTICE OF MY CALLING ...

DORM LAVATORY
MONTDEVERGUES ASYLUM
03H30

Finding no solace in smoking, I hid the uncorked wine in my towel and scurried down the corridor. No taste for it, however, as I half-filled the tub and locked the door. Tepid water was better than none at all. I scoured myself, as if this might clear away my slippage. Lying back I let my ear canals fill, the lovely hardness of porcelain at my occiput. A person can drown in an inch of water — the slight twist of my head is all it would take, God forbid.

Someone banged on the door, would I be much longer? The loo was hardly a spa such as at Vichy, a place to soothe away worries; it was more what you'd expect to find in the basement of some old gym.

"The one upstairs is free!" I yelled. Whoever she was went away. *A warm bath replicates the womb's comforts*, the gentlest hydrotherapy. But the bath only made me think of things I'd rather forget. Adolescence. The village where I grew up. A family that hid their retarded daughter, who'd get loose and swing on the swing in their garden, pumping her legs fit to shoot through the sky.

When I'd found myself out of sorts, my worst fear — besides what would happen to me — was that the baby would be like her, or mongoloid, or harelipped, or missing parts. Deformity almost *de rigueur*, one might think, glossing an obstetrics text. A relief, such as it was, when the nuns said the child was normal.

Then I thought of a poster pasted up all over Lyon of a little girl playing with dolls. On it was the government's slogan, *Maintenant un jeu, plus tard une mission*. All that poster sought was free brawn for the Boche's factories — in order to save whose skin? Our Pétain would have everyone be a walking uterus, loving babies as he does — as long as they aren't Jewish or over sixteen or have minds of their own.

Well, I'd done my part before turning seventeen. The sisters arranged the adoption. I never held the baby, saw its face no longer than it took to notice that it was slightly bluish. Infant cyanosis, I suspect. The nuns insisted it was healthy and even saved a wisp of its hair. His hair. A boy, but at the time mostly a weight I was glad to be free of, the worst that could befall a girl — worse in some eyes, like my father's, than getting lues. His silence was just one of my punishments, compounded by the consolation he found in the bottle after losing my mother.

The boy — the donor of the cigarette case and more — said he was sorry I had no mother. He wasn't completely unappealing. I remember his eyes, their watery green in the light under the trees. He'd brought cheese from his mother's pantry. Tiny black ants crawled over the rind and wasps circled; while swatting them away his hand fell where it shouldn't've. "Your papa's not a bad man. But

I see where you'd find it hard." The kindest thing he had to say.

"Will you teach or nurse the sick?" people asked, some time after, but before the Maréchal declared nursing second only to motherhood in virtue and value. I hadn't minded a bit giving my life to giving needles, dressing wounds, draining incisions. "You have a gift for it," the nuns said, Sister Ursula the loudest of all.

Someone tapped at the door. The tapping became a pummelling. "Really — really, whoever's in there, I have to go!"

In a couple of hours, all will start up again. Shut-eye for the lucky.

"Won't be a second," I yelled. "Just drying off."

—⁂—

20H05. AN UNEVENTFUL day. Head was surprised but clearly relieved to have me turn up on the dot as usual. "No rest for the wicked, Poitier?" But she wasn't letting me off the hook, her gaze as penetrating as a proctologist's headlamp's. "The problem remains, Mademoiselle's letters getting out. With the change in Admin you can be sure there'll be action taken. You realize the light you've put yourself in — put us in. After last night, we're all under scrutiny."

No mention of the deceased's name, the bloodied scissors at her feet. Her file's transfer to Admin was expedited and that, sadly, was that.

I consulted my patient's chart, was about to go and examine her. Bedsores, I thought. Decubitus ulcers, yes yes yes, pressure wounds.

"This breach of trust, of security," Head continued. "How dare you make anything more difficult in such times?"

Malnutrition, I thought. Dehydration, poor hygiene, topped off by immobility.

Head looked at me strangely. "What happens happens, Nurse. We may be their keepers, but we can't watch them every second. The place would fall down around our ears." Her tone was almost warm, not unsympathetic. A gentler way of saying that it was tempting fate to interfere. To intervene. Almost but not quite as brutal as telling someone, *Talk to Cadieu, take an Aspirin and try not to hang yourself in the morning.*

Sleep deprivation no doubt had me confused.

"Poitier?" Head said. But I was thinking: Stage I, intact skin with localized redness warm to the touch.

"Do I make myself clear?"

Stage II: shallow ulcer with pinkish-red wound, intact or ruptured blister.

"Are you listening?"

Sores that aren't skin tears, adhesive tape burns, macerations or excoriations.

"Nurse!"

Stage III: full-thickness tissue loss, subcutaneous fat visible, but bone, tendon, muscle unexposed.

"If Monsieur Directeur knows of your insubordination, you will be subject to instant dismissal."

Stage IV: full-thickness tissue loss with exposed bone, tendon or muscle visible or directly palpable. The skeleton as poles propping up a leaky tent.

"Yes. I mean — I'm sorry," I said. "If having Mademoiselle's best interests at heart means I've done something wrong, what choice have I but to pay the price?"

—⁂—

"YOU NEVER TOLD me about your friend." I nudged Mademoiselle, getting her to shift slightly so she'd be easier to turn. I half wished I'd hung on to the photograph from her file. "The lady who visited, a long time ago now. Someone snapped a picture. Maybe you don't remember."

She eyed me curiously, her look turning fierce. "Did she have white hair? An English lady? We studied together. When we were young. One of us was pretty. You're right: I don't want to

remember her. A turncoat like the rest. Her husband the shutter-
bug, he was her accomplice. An informant, she was. Keeping the
rodent up to date."

I took extra care to be agreeable. "Right. The one behind your
being here."

She had clearly weakened overnight. Her skin had a pallor I
didn't like and she moaned while being moved.

"You never have told me how you came to be here." I didn't
mean to pry; asking was a way of priming the pump, so to speak,
in case she had anything to get off her chest. At this stage in a
patient's care it behooves us all to allow him or her to unbur-
den. *Keeping things bottled up diminishes the sum of a life*, Sister
always said. Should the brother's upcoming visit be a final one,
there might be things the patient needed to say in advance.

"You don't want to know. They came one Monday morning,
two policemen, and dragged me out the window. Don't think I
didn't put up a fight. Not that it did any good."

What Sister overlooked is that listening often entails hearing
things one would rather not. While they tended to be true in Lyon,
here they're often to be taken with salt.

The poor woman winced as I dabbed as carefully as possible
at the spreading sores on her backside.

"But they helped you to feel better, yes? The people at the
hospital, after a while?"

Her eyes glittered. Her laugh erupted into a coughing fit, and
she screwed her eyes and mouth tightly shut — oh dear, not
another nosebleed? "You're like the snow-headed doctor. 'Fresh
air, hot baths, decent food.' You see that it worked. Better they'd
tied me to a statue as big as one of Bourdelle's awful ones and
thrown me in the Seine." She started to hum softly, some unrec-
ognizable tune, as if to hum herself to sleep, then suddenly piped,
"Does a cat know its kittens, do you think, once they're grown

up? This child of yours — the boy you had — would you know him if you saw him?"

"Your friend," I said firmly, "the one who came to see you. Did she keep in touch?"

The patient's eyes opened, the torment there replaced with tolerance, perhaps a degree of affection. With effort she rolled them in the direction of the table, a frail hand pointing to the drawer. "In there, Soitier Polange — almost finished. This work has saved me, you know. It's the last time I'm writing to her, though. Another needs my attention. When my brother comes, give him the letter. He'll know how to find her."

I held my peace at that. "Your mother, did she visit?"

"What a friend you are, asking. To put your mind at ease, I'll tell you: No. After they took me away I never saw my mother again."

"Your statue" — it might've been a boulder rolling off my tongue — "I've asked him to bring it." An open invitation to further provoke Head, if she was anywhere in the vicinity.

I asked Mademoiselle if she had received hydrotherapy. Not that I meant to cause trouble — no end to the ways of being irksome, even when surely I've exhausted them — and certainly not to upset her, but in the absence of certain records, how else was I to find out?

"Hydra — isn't that a kind of monster? One with three heads?" Laughter sputtered from her, then her voice went tiny. "Even the monsters abandoned me. Everyone I loved, you see. Including my friend. She was jealous, that's all."

More pointless than ever to argue. "Well. If it pleases you to think."

"It does indeed. She failed, Miss Polange. She had a husband and children and money, and squandered her gift. A squandered gift, as you know, is a gift thrown back at God."

"Now, now, I doubt God would fret. A family's a fine gift, the finest." A change of subject, please. "Your other friend, Monsieur Criteur? The one you've written — didn't you see him again?"

She covered her eyes. In her sigh I could almost picture nerves charging, cells oxygenating themselves.

"Do you have one clue, Nurse — how it is to see by touch, then have this talent ripped away?"

—⁂—

SISTER'S POSTCARD WAS waiting at the desk, delivered by the boy Admin had recently hired. Expressionless, checking her watch, Head slid the card towards me.

You must serve as you see fit, Solange, its brief note read. A postscript wound around the margins, tiny script all but illegible. *Your son was raised by people in Lyon. Not so long ago the wife contacted me. The husband was killed and the boy disappeared; she sought information to trace him. With great reluctance I told her about you, forgive me. One must not carry too much regret — good comes of the crosses we bear.*

Head eyed me frostily, and I couldn't help imagining the man in the *Milice* touching her cheek. "You'll have Mademoiselle ready first thing, then," she said. "The brother's car arrives at ten. He has a driver and not too far to come, though far enough — two hundred kilometres!" As if this excused his absence. His negligence, really. "He'll be in the visitors' lounge. You invited him, he's all yours."

"When had he last seen her?" A casual question. I suspected never.

Head's reply, uncalled for: "Who's testing whom? You think I don't remember?" But then, to butter me up or perhaps to apologize, she said, "You couldn't have got much sleep. And since things are under control — well, as much as we can hope — I don't suppose it would hurt if you left a little early."

—⚭—

A TREAT, A very rare one, to be spared doing supper — an even rarer treat to get off work while it was still light. I didn't bother changing into civvies, and slipped the improvised pack under my cape. Waving to the gateman, I headed in a different direction from my usual one, waiting till he was out of sight before veering into the woods near the cemetery.

It was as I expected. No sign whatsoever of Renard or the boy, besides some charred stones, the stick he'd used as a poker lying there. As if I'd dreamed most of it. When dusk fell I tried to retrace our path, but having little sense of direction it seemed futile. Leaving the woods the way I'd come, I hurried past the gateman at his duty, and toward the village.

In the square, the leaves were pale rags against the purpling sky. They jigged and swirled, the mistral tearing them from the branches as it pushed me toward the café. The place was full of old men, and neither Renard nor his young friend were anywhere to be seen. The voice of de Gaulle, our saviour, our self-appointed Liberator, crackled over the airwaves. All the way from England, it sounded close enough to be next door. When his speech ended, that familiar tune came on, "Clair de Lune," following me to the street and across to the square again, acting as Veronal might've: sedating, if not soothing, and unlike anything of this world.

The bench where I huddled, in so public a place, was hardly a spot for passing out — more to the point, to be seen passing out, even as tiredness wrapped itself around each muscle and nerve, a kind of person-eating weed. There was, however, the church, the Church of *Bon Repos*, which struck, strikes, a funny chord, if that's not too irreverent. The repose, the consolation, of spit and polish. Stand up, sit down, kneel.

A stooped, solitary nun, her black habit melding with the gathering night, swished past and disappeared inside. Behind dark stained glass, lights flickered and leapt. I suppose it was the thought of candles, of flickering warmth, that made me go in. That and the need for quiet after de Gaulle's rallying cries.

Ignoring me, the nun shuffled about dusting and straightening things, painstakingly tidying the pews. The only sounds were of the little straw chairs being scraped and jerked over scuffed stone, each squeak and squeal echoing sharply. She didn't so much as look over when I sat, reluctantly, laying down my small bundle on the adjacent seat.

Unlike the chapel, *Bon Repos* had no kneelers, and it was hard not to imagine arthritic knees pressed against dingy marble, stiff necks, white heads bent in prayer. Old people were the only ones who frequent these places with regularity. The elderly, the dying. *Un bon repos* of last resort. The silence put me in its pocket, shored itself around me, a soothing, echoing gulf of nothing. It comforted me.

The quality of light, however, left something to be desired if, for instance, I had wanted to read the battered hymnal on the seat ahead. The dimness around me was an obtuse reminder of light's therapeutic value, particularly in sickrooms. *What's a nurse, really, but the opener of windows and shutters, waving in Mother Nature to do her work?* So I told myself as the stained glass went from coloured to black and the darkness outside deepened.

By now the nun had progressed to the altar, slowly and method-ically picking dead blooms from withered bouquets, arranging and rearranging what flowers remained in their vases and baskets. Impervious to me, she bowed, knelt and blessed herself before the blazing red light of the tabernacle — a red that made me think of bombings, infernos, blood, as well as some strange eye glaring down. Thinking this, I rose and slipped out.

—⁂—

ALL THE WAY home it seemed the roadside woods were watching, though not the slightest flicker of movement came from them. I felt much the way one does when seeing the amputation of a foot to save a leg, and considered venturing in to leave the sterile pack on a rock or under a tree. *If only you'd come in sooner.*

A slim moon appeared above the mount of virgins. As opposed to a mount of Venus. Hardly a joke, summoning, as it does, bath days. P for pubes and psychoses. *Wash out my mind and pen with carbolic soap and water*, I'm telling myself as I write this. A nurse must be free at all times of dark and unclean thoughts.

And on that note, Dear Record of Professional Failings (Failure?), lights out.

24

NO PLACE FOR AN ARTIST
WHO CARES WHAT DAY, WHAT YEAR?

TO WHOM IT May Concern,
People can surprise us. I speak not just of you, C. Reappearing from wherever he'd hidden away — no questions asked, no explanations given — Criteur came to my aid. Brutal but true, he encouraged me.

"You're on the front lines now."

He expected me to track the evil one's comings and goings. Useless to rely on gossip sheets — *ppfftt*, newspapers! — to keep abreast of the enemy, to keep ahead of him. "It means spying. What choice is there? Hasn't the good Lord given you eyes, ears and feet?"

I was supposed to fly to the wilds the Great One called home?

"Go by boat. You're not so poor — yet — that you haven't the fare."

I was loath to travel a river tainted with Cléome's blood — and seeing as Monsieur had tried to poison me, his tainted wine as proof, why wouldn't he try to drown me? He would do anything, anything, to get his grasping hands on my work.

Out of coin, I wrote asking Paul could he, would he front me fifty francs? Which he did, with no hope of compensation. Perhaps I overstepped myself, now that he had a wife and children to pay for. "One comes to the Lord no other way but emptied," he wrote back to me.

His visits had grown rare but when he came he came bearing gifts of money and food. "The humble of heart shall inherit the earth." He never missed a chance to profess, press, his faith.

"Good, because I'm nothing but." I elbowed him robustly, no longer a sylph, sylph-hood sent packing by potatoes and cheap brandy. Poverty's diet. The doughy woman who peered back from my cloudy scrap of mirror was a stranger as pale as one afraid of the sun.

"You should get out more," our brother nagged. Was he in cahoots with Criteur?

But, you see, C, my soul if not my heart had been robbed by an evil Perseus. The soul lives in the mind which lives in the head. His trophy. Yet I fancied myself a Marie Antoinette in better days, sculpting away in my velvet robe, hem gathering hairballs, not blood.

"Let your brother eat cake," Criteur said, miffed that I balked at "our" plan, and doled out his advice, that it might be better to learn how to fail than succeed — that learning to fail is success. He stroked my Perseus's thigh, beheld the statue's sightless eyes, and conceded that Paul's nagging was apt. "There's no such thing as a poor loser," he said. "You could take a train."

Far be it for me to stoop so low. But stoop I did. How pride
bows to self-preservation, my feline pride as testimony. How it felt
hurrying under evening's cover to Montparnasse station, riding
the westbound milk run past the city's edge.

Criteur was correct. Finding the Monster's villa was no problem. It stood atop a bluff, naturally, the city's lights twinkling
beyond Saint-Cloud's woodsy hills. We'd read all about it in the
journalists' rags. Perfect sense, its name: *bien sûr,* Brillante a haven
for the Brilliant and His Art.

You think I'd lost my nerve? Dressed in shadows, I strolled its
allée of chestnuts like an honoured guest, the first time under their
snowy blooms. Vicious barking nearly turned me back, a baying
like that of Anubis guarding Pharaoh's tomb. Would that Criteur
had come instead. But I darted fearlessly across lawns and out from
under hedges. Quite deafening, the barking wasn't that of one
dog but a pack. I thought of Cléome. Without human meddling,
feline wiles foil curs' any old time.

The breeze scattered my scent, and the racket ceased. I bur-
rowed through jasmine, braved a rose-bed wilderness till the
moon paled behind the clouds. A light burned in a window, bright
above the pricking thorns nurtured by her, the evil queen. Hardly
so stupid or sick with purpose to forget that one twig cracking
would set off the hellhounds, I waited. If she were there, the
charlady would unchain and sic them on me: *Find her scent, go
for blood.* The Master having rolled in both.

When I made it to the window, the scene within was a bit of a
shock. The room was austere but for a gnarled jade on the dining
table, a miniature Greek torso on a plinth. The plant's pot was
rimed with mould like the rind of a ripe brie. My belly rumbled,
hollow under my thumping heart.

The *hausfrau* sat at her sewing, a teacup beside her. A more
forlorn face I hadn't seen, until I came here. But it was her age, not
her general grimness, that struck me. The exact opposite of you,

she was an old, old woman, stooped and wasted. In her house-dress, she looked worse than mutton dressed as lamb — she was mutton fit for the abattoir. Perhaps the evil one hadn't lied calling her sickly. Not that she aroused pity. Who pities anyone who's let the devil use her up?

The devil, on this occasion, was nowhere in sight, so I hastened back to the safe haven of Île Saint-Louis.

A few more forays into his suburb revealed little worth seeing, nothing worth getting mauled by dogs or squandering what centimes I had on train fare, until my last visit, when a sight for sore eyes met mine. The antique couple, the *hausfrau* and her rat, were enjoying each other's company. The length of their bare table separated them, no more than a bowl of gruel at either end, the *hausfrau* shivering in her shawl. Even at a distance she looked ghostly, her sunken lips addressing him. He shoved away his bowl and lifted a small terrier into his lap, stroked it. His queen coughing into a hankie till he yelled at her to stop.

It was then she turned to the window. I ducked, but not fast enough.

Her whole face was a muttonly grimace, her bald eyes staring.

I tripped free of her bushes, the thorns ripping at me painfully, but nothing near as bad as being in his clutches.

They were made for each other, these two.

"Make your bed with a dog, Monsieur. Have fun lying in it!" I sang out, and chortled all the way home to my cats.

—ᴧᴧ—

NOT LONG AFTER, I had visitors: a writer known to our brother (another of the Master's cricket-shills?) and a man I didn't recognize at first. Neither of them would I let in. Only the stranger lingered, allowing me a decent look at his face through the shutters. A lucky thing, too. It was the fellow who'd treated me to champagne in the darkness of the Marais. He called out his name; sure enough it was Eugène Blot. And yes, besides owning the foundry, he had a gallery in the Grands Boulevards, right across from the Madeleine. A church that looks more like a stock exchange, but who am I to criticize?

You won't believe it. I didn't, at first. He was looking for works for a show. Would I consider his space?

"What's in it for you?" I shouted out.

Blot was pleasantly handsome, neither handsome nor ugly enough to be a rogue or a liar. His broad, high forehead was the opposite of Monsieur's low one, and he was slender, courteous, unassuming. His manner eased my fears enough that I unbolted the door to size him up, and his gentle eyes convinced me to let him in. Taking care not to touch anything, he admired my pieces, promising to have a few of them cast. Most important of all, he put his money where his mouth was, and paid up front for two small statues — enough to cover several months' rent! I'd have sent him packing otherwise. We know not just our enemies but our saviours by their actions.

Blot's only fault, I believe to this day, was that he'd made Monsieur's acquaintance. Who wasn't tainted by it? When he brought me to his gallery I glimpsed myself in the window. A forty-year-old debutante, a fat Cinderella in tattered clothes. You, C, couldn't have been more remote, or removed. But my work would redeem me, redeem us. The other pieces on display would be worthwhile company, exquisite little statues set on polished stands, the room positively alive with swishing palms in pretty pots, and bamboo. So Blot too hankered after the Orient, sharing the passion I shared with our brother, if vicariously.

Suspended from the ceiling were tiny sculpted angels, porcelain-white. They danced a little in the draft rustling the palms. "Seek out signs of goodness, signs of light," our brother had said, after one pilgrimage or another — a trip, I think, to Lourdes. "Expect the best and tides will swing in your favour." Angels, if you know a thing about the Bible — why we have Paul — are monstrous, scary things. Did pretty, sweet ones measure up? Were they the sign I needed, C, to somehow "qualify"?

—∽—

BLOT INSTALLED THIRTEEN of my pieces. Ever kind and generous, he fronted funds for the opening, for my proper attire. More flaming crimson to accentuate my face powdered a perfect white, one way of hiding my age. Alas, none of this compensated for my upstaging by a German — a German! Kitschy painters of sublime mountains and waterfalls! — whose sculpture sucked up to "the great" Monsieur's.

Hardly the show's anchor, I was a tugboat towing a barge.

Called away on business, our brother couldn't come. The *hoi polloi* attended, though. Champagne flowed. The rich riff-raff, Monsieur's circle, milled about ignoring me. Dripping with furs, ladies in lavender and mole-coloured silk dangled from the arms of men cowed by cows, ogling the German's overripe nymphs. You'd think they'd never seen tits before! Such stagey sentimentality surrounding the swirling grace of my *Waltz*. And so like men — well, men like this — to see no farther than the eyes of their trouser-snakes. Even Paul, for all his piety, is guilty of this.

The one exception, perhaps, is Blot. When the last of the air-kissers left, Blot, kind Blot, tried to put me in a cab. It was December, you see, and cold and raining, and in such rainy cold and darkness Paris cannot be crueller.

I chose to walk, though, and walked and walked till the powder streaked from my face.

After two weeks not a single piece of mine had sold. At such times, let me tell you, a thick white masque is useful, leaving just the eyes to bare your feelings.

As usual, Criteur was right. I needed to mix and mingle with

people who spoke with their pocketbooks, and to steer clear of
tyre-kickers, those who gawked but never bought. He was good
at plucking up my courage with his humour. Maybe he got it from
you. But humour only goes so far.

The crickets kept chirping, notice after notice in the papers
linking my work with Monsieur's, write-up after write-up calling
me his pupil. Would I never graduate? The right circles orbited him
like the Earth orbited the sun, and unless I did too, their favour
couldn't be curried.

All this while he dumped more and more of his kitsch on the
world, blinding the public to all efforts but his. He had them
hoodwinked, all right. His reach was as noxious, no, deadly, as
sewer gas.

Fighting this battle, I listened to you. Think small, you said.
On a child's scale. A child's level. All right, then. I would change
my style, give the world what I thought it wanted. The intricate
charm of tiny details. Small things, playful things, in a way. Table
decorations. I worked these pieces in onyx and coloured marble,
using little blocks I could afford. Not that they didn't demand full
attention. It takes an eternity of days, weeks, to work in such perspective. As exacting as doing surgery on a squirrel, or a mouse.

Perhaps I had our Maman more in mind than you, as I carved
a little woman dreaming by a hearth, lost in thought. A clutch of
gossips, monkey faces all agog, sitting in the curl of a wave ready
to swamp them.

Blot showed the pieces in his gallery. Admiring them, the odd
old bat would come up and say, "Someday I'm going to take up
sculpting, or painting, or writing," and I would say, "Yes, and I'll
build a tower twice Eiffel's height," which made Blot smile.

Yet the crickets harangued: "Parlour ornaments! The pupil is
making parlour ornaments!"

"Answer them with what you do," urged Blot, so curiously loyal.
A gift unused becomes a torment, he said. Hope against hope,

he succeeded in winning commissions for me, and even the nasty government agent was finally persuaded to make a purchase. Not of your piece, which was the one he had his eye on.

Of course Blot wanted to know, "What is this work that Sylvestre's so fixed on?"

I shrugged off his question, sure that my break with Monsieur made Maman's forgiveness forthcoming. It had to be — only a matter of time before she would see the foolishness of the rift between us and want it mended.

It's all about that, isn't it? The elder forgiving the younger. Though in fairness, sometimes it must be the other way around.

"Good things come to those who wait," wrote Paul in a letter from China.

But by then I was tired, so tired.

My *praticien* nagged, "You're letting your guard down! You'll regret it! Just because Monsieur is out of sight doesn't mean he's out of your hair. Better be safe than sorry. Keep your eyes open. Don't think his evil desists."

And, no word of a lie, a note ran in the papers that the Master had returned — was he bored with country life and hungry for the city? He'd found himself a mansion, formerly a convent, not far from the golden dome of Invalides — Napoleon's tomb, how fitting. Soon, too soon, he had a show, and at Criteur's urging, against every intuition, every ounce of my own better judgment, I went to see it.

Better the devil you know than the one you don't. I wasn't afraid to face him.

The Great One's secretary, a tubercular-looking youth, let me in. Dressed in my finery, I stole across the foyer's creaky parquet and was directed upstairs. I barely knew myself in the gilded mirrors, one above each of the green marble mantelpieces in three huge drafty rooms. Rooms filled with statues thrown up onto worktables, travesties all, but for my bronze bust of him.

How I wish I could've fit it under my coat, or heaved it through a window!

But this was just the warm-up to the ugliest riff on religion imaginable — the hideous proof of his thievery, all the more grotesque because it was beautiful. Alas, C, it was. Bathed in the pure light of the window, a sacrament made sacrilegious, it comprised two hands. Two right hands, my hands, carved of white marble, with a delicacy that I alone, in this time, in this place, could have wrought. Reaching upwards, they were poised as dancers, a cathedral's stillness contained between them.

How many ways, C, can the heart break? And broken, how is it ever repaired?

The Ark of the Covenant, the entitled had entitled it. Boasting the length, depth and breadth of my betrayal, it proclaimed the extent of his deceit. A covenant exalting one at the ruin of another.

You'd have gone down kicking and screaming, and thrown a tantrum fit to rattle windowpanes and shake dust from the ceilings above and below.

I tried to control my distress.

Milling about below, the secretary offered small talk. He said he was a poet — had our brother heard of him? And was I quite all right?

"No, and no."

He trailed me to the threshold, held the door. Gathering my wits, I asked him to find his Master. "If you would be so kind, I wish to speak to Monsieur."

"He's not here."

A lie, I'm quite certain.

"You say your name is Rilke? Well. I'll remember you to my brother."

The one and only thing I'll say for maturity, C, is that it brings composure.

—ɯ—

I SAW MORE plainly Monsieur took any chance to steal my
work — and in his grasping pursuit, what was to stop him from
going farther? What was to stop him if my life got in the way? You
didn't have to warn me. I saw the threats, now, in shadows passing by the shutters. In strangers lurking outside in the street. My
flat became my fortress. It wasn't safe to go out. I barred windows
and doors, blocking them with whatever furniture I hadn't bartered
for materials.

Twice Sylvestre came knocking. I yelled till he went away,
"Give me 10,000 francs. Twenty thousand! Then we'll talk." Our
beautiful, unfinished *Maman et Enfant* was tucked safely in the
wardrobe, or so I thought.

Blot came by, shouting through the window, proposing more
shows. You might have let him in. I wanted to, desperately, but
couldn't. "If Monsieur's circle sees that one can slip inside, who
knows but they'll find a way, too," I whispered to you, wherever
you were, and to Blot, too, through the keyhole.

Good man that he is, or was, he paid a small boy in the courtyard to bring me food. I heard him arranging it. The boy left bread
on the doorstep, which I retrieved in the dark of night, heaving
aside my heaviest work to open the door wide enough to thrust
out my hand. Who knew but the evil one and his gang weren't
waiting with an axe!

Stepping outside was risking life and limb.

You of all people cannot imagine the terror of being under
such surveillance. Knowing your every move — each blink of
an eye! — is being noted, recorded. You have no idea how fear
reduces hunger to a twinge and makes the smell of cat pee pleasant.
The smell of safety, it is, in the closeness of two small rooms. A
queendom.

If only my cats had been lions, or Dobermans. But never did I love them more, C. In your absence, in this house-arrest-for-my-own-protection, they alone were solid company.

Don't be a stranger. Why don't you visit? I wrote our brother, knowing perfectly well that he was far away and couldn't.

Finally, sick of waiting, sick of hanging on forever to our conciliatory piece, which, stored as it was, might any day crumble — victim of dryness, dampness, cramping and dirt, if the government agent didn't seize it first — I wrote to Maman herself. A kindly note on a scrap of wallpaper, from a ready supply peeling from the walls. I mentioned none of my trials, said how I missed her, how her silence pained me. Circumstances meant I couldn't get out — my cats needed me here at home — but I would be more than happy to entertain her.

Such is the life of a prisoner, practice for later, I guess.

If only the police could've been called to help. But it was useless, useless, seeking their aid. With everyone in his thrall, Monsieur had these other authorities under his thumb too.

When Maman did not reply, I glimpsed the fullness of it: Monsieur had bamboozled her too. All but Papa and our brother were swayed by the lies he spread to turn Paris against me, and the world. And you.

Besides my cats, the sounds of the river beyond my shutters kept me company. When spring's restless glimmer crept through the slats, I heard Debussy in thawing notes, ice melting in the gutters. Then summer's hazy bird-tones, and fall's rustling ones. But all too soon winter came creaking back, hunger holding me in its grip.

And then the river betrayed me.

I knew something was afoot when the shearing roar of barges ceased and a rushing, shushing noise replaced it, forcing me to peek outside. Sludgy water geysered and roiled from grates, rubbing the bridges' underbellies, one vast swollen surface boiling over the embankment and shortening trees. Apocalyptic, it was. A flood with the power to tear my island from its footings and sweep it downstream, like the château in my old dream being washed away in a tangle of lilies.

Another tribulation sent to plague me: the work of Monsieur? It was tempting to think so. The smell of shit was the only sign of anyone else alive, living. The lights died, left me to huddle in darkness, the days and nights a dingy stream mimicking the floodwaters. Higher and higher they crept, till they lapped at the doorsill. When the water slid in and pooled round my bed, stranding me there, the cats clawed their way to the top of the wardrobe, where, inside, our precious, faceless mother-and-child was only barely spared its reach. I waded through the mess to retrieve it, a rigid spectre wrapped in its rug. Brought it into my bed — and none too soon.

There came the shouts of paddlers, the sound of knocking oars, laughter. Fists pounded the door and hideous shouts poured in. "Open up! We need to take you to safety!"

We know of the evil that follows disasters. Looting, pillaging. Criminals robbing the stricken. Monsieur's powers fell short of visiting catastrophe on a city. But there was no catastrophe he wouldn't exploit to his benefit. Doubtless the rescuers were Monsieur's thugs, probably aided by Sylvestre, come to rob me. My only possessions worth stealing were my works.

Alone, friendless, I hid under the covers, playing dead, with your statue in my arms. Have patience, our brother once said. And so I did. Eventually the thugs went away, and the waters receded.

Criteur appeared. He mentioned the folly of living in dread, said I was foolish to think I could keep on resisting. There remained only one way to keep thieves from my work. "'The Lord giveth and the Lord taketh away,'" he mimicked Paul. "Too bad it's come to this. But you must take matters into your own hands. What recourse have you? If God the father could destroy his son."

His shrug left me baffled, then, frankly, aghast. But he was right. So much for my brilliant career. Our brilliant career.

"Brilliant, yes," he agreed, "but on whose terms?" Testing me, always testing me — the way you did and keep doing. "Nature's way," he called it: the creator creates, the destroyer destroys. "The power's in her hands, or should be."

Did I hear you somewhere, cheering?

—⟊—

PAUL APPEARED, TO drive the point home. He'd been posted to Frankfurt, considerably closer than China. His visit was a complete surprise, and only his dogged knocking verified his identity. I greeted him with bouquets of kisses, but he didn't seem pleased to see me, and avoided my eyes as if I were someone other than myself.

"Look at you, how fat you've grown," he said, out of sorts. "Your dress, your hair. *Mon Dieu.*" His criticisms could've been Maman's. Did he mean to be cruel and insulting? His eyes were blank as he swatted Baudelaire from the table. He glanced about, maybe in search of the broken mirror I'd discarded, no longer needing it after *Perseus.* "Can you not see yourself? You can't afford soap?"

To soothe him I tried to stroke his forehead, his ebbing hair. He caught my hand, gripped it too tightly.

"Are you so unhappy, *mon petit?* Your life is full, yet you have time to fuss and primp?" How to explain that letting go was my shield, my cross, my sword — armour and armament against interlopers? "How do you know this isn't my penance? For dancing with the devil?" Laughing, I attempted a pirouette. "I wear them, you see? The sins of his kisses, his touch." It was a concession to Paul's rightness, purely to amuse him.

Yet he seemed incensed. "You live like an animal. How can you stand yourself?" In a trembling voice he accused me of self-sabotage — a term that conjures intrigue, showing how deeply he'd fallen, too deep for his own good, into the diplomatic corps. "No wonder Maman refuses to come. Seeing how you've let yourself go."

"Not for a lack of eating, you think? Hugeness of body, hugeness of name, what difference." He'd wounded me, mentioning Maman this way, and I quietly suggested he leave.

He mocked my "devotion to filth."

"Think of it as a reverse baptism, *mon petit*. Rather than washing away sins I'm accumulating them. Layers of protection."

But his words had torn a strip off, if not torn away the top one. Was I called to be a snake shedding its skin, losing innards along with it? The only proof that I wasn't loosed from Medusa's coiffure were the dusty footprints I made across the floor after he left, when I thought I heard you knocking.

Ever yours.

X

25

WITH LOYALTY WILL I ENDEAVOUR

TO AID THE PHYSICIAN ...

Good god, once again I'm wide awake. The nonsense that takes over the mind in the dark! I am or should be grateful it's just in the wee hours these ideas come knocking. How's a sane person to treat and dispose of them? *A Report on Obsessive Speculative Thinking, to be burned at first light*? Worth a try, maybe.

Speculation #1: Once upon a time, a baby boy was adopted by Jews, a lovely young Hasidic couple. No debate over circumcision, but they fought over a name — David? Micah? Aaron? — and finally picked Moses. The child liked to tug on the husband's beard and sideburns. When he cried, though the wife had no milk she held him to her breast anyway.

Speculation #2: When the boy started school, he learned the Hebrew alphabet. He grew up preferring numbers to letters.

Speculation #3: A huge, happy family with many cousins, aunts and uncles attended his bar mitzvah. The rite of passage made for a good party.

Speculation #4: When he was snatched from his desk at school, the boy's eyes looked very much like mine when I was sixteen. Unlike me, he was told he was useful for things more important than studying and was loaded into a cattle car with his classmates.

A complete dead end, this line of thinking.

Here's a better one, perhaps.

Speculation #5: The boy died hours after birth and was buried in a tiny coffin, forget-me-nots growing on his grave. A tidier ending, far less troubling. Though it doesn't hurt to imagine things, does it, as long as one keeps both feet on the ground?

Speculation #6: The boy was raised by a wealthy Parisian couple with three other sons and three daughters, say — enough siblings that he always had company — and was loved and schooled as their own. He excelled in mathematics and science, and aced the Sorbonne's entrance exams, where he planned to study medicine or law or engineering. His brilliant future was assured, until he was shot at in the street and put on a train — a Gentile, his foreskin intact, at least, but —

Speculation #7: A handsome, strapping young man, the boy kissed his mother goodbye at the train station — with more affection than I kissed the nuns, but this goes without saying — and promised to send a telegram the instant his ship docked in North America. An unsinkable ship protected by a convoy of unsinkable ships, as far the mother knew.

If not for writing all of this down, my head would explode, especially with the day ahead promising to be a little out of the ordinary. As if I need it. The distance from speculation to wishful thinking isn't always wide enough.

Speculation #8: A healthy sixteen-year-old heart pumps well-oxygenated blood with optimal hemoglobin. The perfectly balanced functioning of a healthy, inquisitive brain exudes intelligence — and a natural, perhaps inescapable question, which arises repeatedly, of whether or not its owner is well-loved, well-schooled, well on the road to whatever brilliant future imaginable. Because something is missing, something as important, say, as a cardiac valve faulty since infancy and creating a kind of hole, no matter what nuns, peace-loving Jews, or rich Parisians have or haven't told him about the person who conceived and gave birth to him.

If I have the urge to know about him, is it illogical to think he might feel a similar urge about me?

It strikes me, Dear Record of All My Past Failings, of What I Am, Have Been and Hope to Be, that when we're small we are each very much one person, before our worlds-to-be collide and shatter us into several people, at least two — the one before and the one after. Before we lose our *mamans*, and before all the rest of the things happen that we choose or don't choose. I think this when I remove my clothes and every time I take a bath, actually. A foolish enterprise, navel-gazing; still, the wink of mine is often enough to make me want to slide underwater and count and count until I can't count anymore. Like nothing else in this world, the umbilicus shows how one is attached to the dead, to the lost, whether one wants to be or thinks about it or not — a circular, fleshly reminder of things continuing, of eternity, Heaven even, if such a thing exists. That they've been, and that we carry

their mark, and that in a certain way they're still out there somewhere or might be — the lost — and if so, somehow, perhaps, is it
such a stretch to think that we'll meet again?

Which brings me to

Speculation #9: He has smooth, almost baby-soft skin, healthy
except for an infected flesh wound, peripheral swelling and
bruising. Likely has a washboard abdomen like other boys his
age, a slender ribcage, a thin, dark line of hair above and below
a belly button like an eye that can see and a mouth that can
talk. The parts of the son like the father's.

Oh, my. That the body speaks and can be spoken for! How presumptuous we are, dealing with Nature.

—⁓—

21H45

WELL, HE PICKED a fine day to come, I'll give him that. Mademoiselle's guest. When I hurried to work this morning the sun
was just coming up, everything in a burnished mist. Birds squabbled over the berries ripening on the yews. A few sprigs with their
dots of red would've spruced up the room, certainly, except those
berries are toxic. Not really an issue for my patient, though. One
knows all too well that no matter how much care is taken, for
those so disposed to dispatch themselves, like our scissors victim,
where there's a will there's a way. Mademoiselle's had thirty years
to do it, and not a single mention of such tendencies in her file.

She was still dozing when I went in. I reached under the blanket
and felt for a pulse.

Her eyes flew open. "*Mon petit?*" The dullness clouding them
lifted only slightly when I helped her sit, placed an Aspirin on her
tongue and held the water for her to sip. No cure for bedsores, but
it eases the pain. "You're the perfect *maman* picking my poison!"

Her voice was weaker than usual, and she squinted at the bars. "*Mon petit* is here to take me? You'll help me pack."

When I patted her cheek the skin was stiffened with dried mucus.

"Don't just stand there, Poitier Solange. Help me up."

Try as she might, her legs wouldn't co-operate. She slumped against the pillow.

"It's all right, dear. No need to worry. He'll come to you."

"But how will he find me? How will he know where to come?" Then her voice brightened a little. "He's a writer, you see, my brother." As if this made some sort of difference, as if it mattered to me. Was it an excuse on his behalf? "He has no idea what I've suffered."

"Now, Mademoiselle, you'll want to look your best." The occasion was an opportunity to put comb to head and wash what parts showed, face, hands and neck. "It's been some time since he's seen you, yes?"

"Time means nothing in jail, you should know." She pointed to the drawer and whispered, "Don't forget, in case I do. *Mon petit* is to deliver what's in there. He's able to go, Miss Polange, where you can't." She laughed, her trembling fingers closing around the letters I handed to her; clumsily she stuffed them under the blanket. "My legs will be more use to me in Villeneuve, of course," she rambled, "though I don't expect to get around too much. Poor you, having to stay here." Beckoning me closer, she gave my cheek a feathery poke. "I'll write you, that's a promise."

"Promise accepted," I said.

—⁂—

IT WAS AGREED that I would meet the visitor in the visitors' lounge, a yellow and brown room furnished with straight-backed chairs, in a wing just off Admin. The sharpness of disinfectant and lemon oil greeted me, as it must everyone arriving here — that, and cautious voices breaking the silence. An elderly couple were disentangling themselves from a pimply youth, possibly a grandson. A nicely turned-out woman with two tiny children on her lap held hands with a man who stared into space. Two matronly ladies tried interesting a third — a grown daughter, sister or possibly a niece — with a jigsaw puzzle.

In the middle of the room, redeemed by its bouquet of chrysanthemums, was a round table with initials — so-and-so was here, and various dates — carved in the top. Various attempts at varnishing over them had failed. Seated there, reading a newspaper, was an elderly gent wearing a good, if old-fashioned, woolen suit. A paper sack and something wrapped in tissue took up the chair beside him, the only free one. The woman with toddlers could've used it; perhaps if asked nicely he'd have obliged? Glancing up, he grimaced at my approach. He made me think of an owl, or maybe a hawk, his mouth tightening with obvious displeasure. Of course it was him; it couldn't have been anyone else. His forehead was as broad and pale as Mademoiselle's and his eyes were a similar blue, with the same haughty, hunted-so-as-to-be-indignant sort of look.

Someone had brought in tea for everyone. Amid the symphony of slurping he cleared his throat. "So we finally meet, Miss Poitier." His tone couldn't have been chillier, his chin puckering in an effort to be polite. Mercifully he didn't extend his hand, a gesture that would've been as welcome just then as squeezing fouled gauze. He gathered up his things and pressed them on me. "The kinds of treats our mother would faithfully send my sister," he seemed anxious to explain, nodding curtly at the paper bag, which contained confections. I saw the parcel was from a shop in the village. "And the nightdress you requested."

"That's everything?" I didn't mean to be snide but couldn't help feeling a little prickly, disappointed. "You didn't bring her work? You received my note, of course. The statue?"

He smiled primly, as if to spare me embarrassment. "*Mon Dieu.* What has she been telling you?"

He followed me outside, past the chapel and up the hill to Number 10, and remarked on the day, the sunshine's chilly warmth. Impossible to tell if he was being appreciative or sardonic. "Ah, the light of Provence!"

"Enough to boil your snot, is he?" Novice said under her breath, meeting us at the desk.

"Travel disagrees with him," I whispered back, my eyes on the tiles.

Head practically curtsied — a gnarled vein bulging in one calf — as though the visitor were her beloved Maréchal, and immediately sent Novice off in search of refreshments. *A lump of sugar or shit for his tea?* I could imagine her joking.

I showed him upstairs, wishing I'd had time, at the very least, to dust and do some tidying first. He walked with a stoop, afflicted either with some geriatric ailment or a bad case of nerves, his shoulders hunched to his ears as if he were ducking something, the cacophony maybe. He hadn't been here before, he said, not inside this building. On a previous visit he had met his sister in the directeur's villa.

"Oh yes, and when was that?" I was just being polite.

"Why does it concern you?" he said.

Dr. Cadieu was waiting outside Mademoiselle's room, looking drawn but still gracious. She touched his sleeve lightly and accepted his cool greeting. His pursed, quivering lips grazed the air near her cheeks. "Your timing couldn't be better, sir," Cadieu smiled. She nodded pleasantly, my cue to allow brother and sister their privacy, and escorted our guest's guest inside. "And how are we feeling today, Mademoiselle?" I heard her say, before she explained about relapses and rallies, what we like to regard as patients' second childhoods, and whether the phenomena occur as dreams or figments of dementia. Small respites from the ravages of aging.

When the doctor emerged, shutting the door behind her,

Mademoiselle cried out, "Nurse? I want my nurse. Miss Solange! Please, please, don't let her leave me!"

Quite gracelessly, Cadieu pushed me forward.

Mademoiselle peered up with a look of relief and turned to her guest — our guest. "But is it really you, *mon petit*? Or am I in heaven," she gave a choking laugh, "the heaven of our dreams?"

The visitor stooped over the bedside, clasped her hand. A decrepit greying bird in his fine dark suit, that's what he was, the wispy hair on his shiny pate as fine as feathers. There was something sad and pathetic and touching about him, all the same, for all his crankiness, for his airs. He had come, at least.

Nudging the chair closer, I gestured for him to sit. "You don't want to strain your back."

Not a word in return. But his face was waxen, and Mademoiselle's shiny with tears. She was going on about a garden — their mother's, I'm guessing — and about tulips and lilacs and chestnuts blooming. It was extremely awkward standing there, not knowing if I should stay or go, so I tried to make myself invisible, especially when her smile clouded.

"Come closer," she said suspiciously. For a second I thought she meant me. "*Mon petit*. Let me feel your face to make sure it is you."

"Could you give us a moment?" he said gruffly, avoiding my eyes.

But the instant I turned my back Mademoiselle began whimpering, "Where are you going, Polange Soitier? Please, please, sit, stay."

Well, I wasn't about to sit, but I positioned myself just close enough for her to keep an eye on me. Not that I would have or could have left her; but I'd have deeply preferred to be a fly on the wall.

Fortunately, such situations aren't without humour. Beaming, the patient called out, "My shoes, *mon petit*! Fetch my shoes ... I don't want to shame you. You can't expect me to go home barefoot!"

The visitor was forced to behave as if I weren't there. He ignored her demand and bent low — to kiss her, I thought, but no, to say something. "Maman and I, we did what we had to, you do know that," he murmured, hesitating.

I busied myself with arranging his presents on her table. There were packets of sugar, some excellent chocolate, butter, an orange, two pink *macarons*, and a small, very ripe wedge of cheese whose smell would no doubt attract the cat. Loudly folding their paper sack, I pretended not to hear.

"It wasn't all Maman's doing, keeping you here. I should have —" He broke off and covered his face with his pale, age-spotted hands. Some writer, no better than the rest of us at finding words Mademoiselle might want to hear! "I should never have left you in this place the way I did. Perhaps you blamed Maman." His voice trailed off again.

The patient's gaze flickered. Its blueness fixed briefly on me and darkened. Her lips drew tight and her jaw sagged a little. Her paleness had grown quite sallow. Was the room's ventilation adequate? Should I have forced her to eat, earlier? For a moment the involuntary effort of her breathing was the only immediately audible sound, her inhalations and exhalations rather shallow and slow. Should I summon Head, or Cadieu? Where had Novice got to, anyway, with her tea tray, and, I hoped, at least a few goodies?

"My dear sister, may God forgive me." The visitor reached over her, seeming to bless his loved one with the limpid movement of his hand. The sign of the cross! The patient was in no near or grave danger of passing, and he was not even a priest — not as far as one could tell, anyway, though men of the cloth, like the rest of the world, can be full of surprises. When he leaned down to kiss Mademoiselle's cheek, she batted him away. He stood up, a bit rough on his pins I have to say, enough to merit concern, and turned his back to us both.

Only then did I remember the letters she'd squirrelled away

under the blanket. Pointing to the little mound there, I gave a tiny cough.

Eyeing me, Mademoiselle rubbed her head to and fro against the pillow before finally gazing at the wall. "I thank you from the bottom of my heart, *mon petit*, for all you've brought — for all the things you've ever given me." She spoke in a monotone, a tired kind of recitation. Out of stubborn necessity, perhaps, she made no move to watch him go.

He stalked stiffly out into the corridor, ending the visit abruptly. It was now or never. Someone had to speak up.

"Monsieur? Your sister's statue," I almost had to shout. "If it's in your possession, please, before she ... She would very much appreciate having it back."

Something glinted in his eyes' fiery blue. Perhaps it was the hallway's reflected sheen, or perhaps it was the hint of tears, I told myself — tears and not just the glaze or glare of an icy demeanour. I could be mistaken.

"My dear Miss Poitier. I thank you for your interest." The visitor's voice was weary, brutally humble or humbly brutal, and accusing. Hardly a surprise. "For your involvement, I mean. How gullible you are, believing everything she says. If you must know, my poor sister took a sledgehammer to anything she didn't sell or blame someone for stealing. Oh, she had her enemies." Sighing, he volunteered a pained smile. "You see how she talks through her hat."

Mademoiselle's guest left before Novice's little mission could be intercepted. When I met her on the refectory steps, she was bearing a plate of stale-looking *tartines*.

"The more for us then," she shrugged. "Oh, Cook's got something to tell you — catch her, quick, before she puts on the soup. You know how she gets."

—⁓—

COOK WAS DUMPING carrot coins into a pot. "Renard is dead," she wasted no time informing me, speaking in a hushed, cautious way. "He was taken by the *Milice* as far as anyone knows, and shot. Our farmer's the one that found him — he said you'd want to know."

It was on the tip of my tongue to ask about his friend, when Novice came back and asked what I was doing. "Head'll be after both of ours if we don't get back."

—◠◠—

BACK UPSTAIRS, I held the new blue nightie to my patient's cheek. "My, the colour suits you," I found it in me to say. I placed a sliver of chocolate in Mademoiselle's palm.

Sucking on it, the guest, my guest, rooted under the covers for her papers, pushed them into my hands. "You'll have to tend to them now. It's the last I'll ask of you." Brusquely, all in, the old woman pushed away a tear.

But I was thinking about Renard, remembering the dryness of his lips touching my hand, as off-putting as it had been. Even more off-putting was Cook's assuming that what had happened to him affected me. It did, no denying — any loss of life is troubling — and yet it didn't, not deeply or personally, not enough for me to need or want or expect details.

The grisly facts of war made one thing clear: maybe all we can trust in is the body, vulnerable as it is. Few other things make sense, it struck me then, and strikes me now. People — and the Lord, if one's able and willing to go that far — rarely behave as you expect. Expecting them to is, if not crazy, then a little unwise.

Mademoiselle gave me a nudge. "Why so glum, Solange Poitier?"

It was all I could do not to will her to drape a lank arm around me.

"You have no right to be sad, Polange. But me? I won't be leaving, after all." She touched my key on its little ring, and then the one from her coat that she'd finally, finally given over, given up. She touched them both as if they were live wires and the relics of some saint. "My girl," she said, and its softness made her familiarity even more numbing, "why do you stay, when they've no claim on you?"

"Oh, Mademoiselle." I steeled myself, which only made me picture Renard — not just him but the boy, the boy sitting by the fire, and his ugly wound. "I suppose, I suppose it's because a girl's duty is never done. Yes, that must be it, I'm afraid. One always has more work to do."

26

NO DAY NO YEAR

DEAR C,

Remember what I said about seeing? Is it possible we see only as
we ought? This explains our blindness, that of creatures burrow-
ing under dirt. I think you saw with your eyes wide open, so why
you stopped speaking is a mystery. You would betray me? Make
a fool of me? Allow me to make a fool of myself? You were much
too sweet for that, I longed to think.

But we think without thinking and see without seeing, stumbling over things we shouldn't. Knowing this, how do I show
your face, reveal the smooth, unburdened version of mine — my
younger, freer self, the child that felt all things were possible?

I'm afraid I never got around to sculpting it. There wasn't the
time, or the money.

Years now since I've looked into a mirror. No mirrors in this place. No reflections allowed. One jagged piece of glass + one wrist = a shout to the angel of mercy. But why not? you ask, you've always asked, if you hate it so much, if you want your freedom. A reasonable choice, when the only logic is caprice. But why rush this angel when she's coming anyway? Let her come when she wants, in her own sweet time. One thing we know: she will.

The Lord giveth and the Lord taketh. The creator creates. The destroyer destroys. The light behind the one reveals the light behind the other. So it is with urges and impulses more alike than you think. Which isn't to say you're entirely off the hook, that I don't blame you for what happened, at least a little. I can't put all the blame on Criteur. If you hadn't deserted me you'd have stopped him.

"Are you quite sure about this?" I asked him, my solitary honoured guest at our *soirée*, our opening of openings shuttered from the world.

Criteur raised his imaginary glass, toasting the show. If successful, we'd have more of these each time I had fresh work to offer. And if I was surly and wept for missing you, for missing all things lost, he'd understand. Monsieur's treachery had pushed us to this.

"You have to start somewhere," my *praticien* spoke, stripped down to nothing to execute his end of the bargain, finally agreeing to pose — to show what he was made of.

"For God's sake, put on some clothes." To think I'd once preferred a man with a full set of luggage. Poor Criteur, a pale, reckless eunuch.

Whatever we lacked in refreshments I made up for in dress. The red one from Blot's opening was ragged but no less resplendent. A grand occasion, this. A celebration of sorts — an inauguration, if slightly funereal.

I toasted Criteur by raising my hammer. All of my pride scattered at the first blow.

"You're certain about this? Certain you know what you're doing?" So like him to turn fickle, the briefest protest before he cheered me on. "Never again will Monsieur and his gang dare torment you!"

My hammer clawed and bit into dried, brittle flesh. The heads of statues cracked open and toppled from necks. Limbs fell from torsos. Clay and plaster pinging against walls and shutters were a hail of stinging insects. Swarming. Their dust, a greyish-pink cloud, left a bloody taste in my mouth. Metallic. When it settled, only a pile of parts remained, faintly human.

"Dust to dust, ashes to ashes," crooned Criteur, morose if not remorseful. "You know what they say about relics." He went on, once upon a time, about the fearless heretic in Florence, Savonarola, and his Bonfire of Vanities — Savonarola, who fought fire with fire and was burned at the stake, his ashes pulverized and tossed in the Arno. "Not a crumb remained to be bought, sold or stolen." My *praticien*'s smile was brave. Nudging a plaster finger with his toe, he kicked rubble into the tiny fireplace. We had just enough coal to start a blaze. "Let there be nothing left," he said, warming his hands. "Nothing the world's evildoers can salvage and reassemble — not a scrap to boast about and pass off as theirs. Ridding ourselves of what Monsieur covets is the price of peace — a hefty one."

Harder than agreeing was luring my lovelies, my pride, from under what furniture we hadn't burnt for warmth. The last tidbits left by Blot's boy did the trick. Slowly, slowly they came out, purring, rubbing at my shins.

When it was dark, very dark, I swept up the ashes and dumped them in a cart standing derelict in the street. A tinker's or traveller's, it was still there in the morning. We watched through the shutters. When the owner appeared, Criteur paid a franc to have him empty it into the river.

"Are you insane, stepping outside in broad daylight?"

My *praticien* grinned. "What's your problem? You're free now — who cares who's watching? If our tinker-traveller-carter was sent by the Rat himself, all the better, don't you see?"

But Criteur had either forgotten or gone blind. A few works remained, spared the hammer — not the least of which was yours, my mistresspiece, to be guarded with my life until such time as Maman forgave me. Forgave us.

And, maybe, just maybe, until I forgave you.

When Blot came seeking works for another gallery show, Criteur huddled below the sill. Speaking through the shutters, I was forced to tell a certain truth, that my oeuvre — what remained after Monsieur's helping himself to it — had been pillaged and plundered. Blot went away, but to his eternal credit, left bread and a hunk of cheese.

—⁊⁊⁊—

PAPA PAID ANOTHER visit, one so brief it barely allowed me the chance to cling to his hand. His grip was frail and his eyes were rheumy. His gaze lingered on the ashes strewn over my carpet, a scattering of rags, the one luxury in my cloister. Ice was on the insides of the windowpanes and our breath formed clouds. The fingers were worn clean out of my gloves. My poverty assaulted him. "Look at you," he said. "My girl, you're freezing. You're starving!"

"Where is Maman? Why won't she come?"

Looking away, he suggested that if I cleaned myself up he would take me for a meal.

"Does she think I'm made of air?" I persisted. "That I've left Paris, the planet — disappeared?"

He covered his mouth with his hand and tapped the floor with his cane, a rhythm prodding enough to summon Criteur, who thankfully kept out of view, slouching behind the wardrobe. Papa's tapping provoked tears; through their blur I saw the sum of things.

How Monsieur and his gang had turned the family against me. How no amount of thievery had satisfied his quest to destroy every last bit of what I valued.

I peered into our father's face, his breath warming my cheek. "Will you bring her to see me? Will you do that for me, Papa — this *maman* who gave birth to me, to my brother and my sister," there was no point even mentioning you, "who may as well be dead for all I hear from her? If I could just see Maman, I could show her — I've done my penance, whatever she expects. Paid for my mistakes, dearly. Papa," I begged, "if you would just bring her, I could prove ... prove that I'm still, still, the daughter she loves."

"*Ma petite*, you know I can't." He watched Baudelaire and Rossetti preening, then wrestling each other on the bed. "You've made your place, and it's not one, I think, that your *maman* can stomach. You can't expect ... surely you see? You know it's not a question, a matter of ... atonement."

Had he ripped a page from Paul's good book?

Flouncing my hem, I shooed Verlaine from rubbing her chin on his shoe — had Papa stepped in something bad? His eyes lit on my shins, their pale, bluish streaks. Chilblains. "But you love me, don't you Papa? You, at least, forgive me? The evil one and his friends haven't turned you completely against me?"

A sigh came from his throat — a sigh of weariness. It couldn't have been easy being married to Maman all these years. *Till death do us part.*

His eyes mirrored mine. "Your poor *maman*. She never showed it, but once, she had only love for you."

The room and even the cats seemed to recede — all of it but my pride cried to be swept into a bin and disposed of, somehow. I spat at a bit of charred clay. "Papa," I barely heard myself speak, "you would deny me? This small, small favour —"

"You deny yourself, *ma petite*."

Then he embraced me, his old man's arms enfolding me in what felt like a phantom's hug. My ear to his chest, only his heartbeat proved it wasn't a dream, its strange rhythm in my pulse. Wordlessly he pressed an envelope into my hand and vanished.

That, C, was the last I would see of him in this earthly vale. Whether or not we meet again, a taunt or a promise, I'm soon to find out, in that place where prophet Paul says everything broken is made whole again — where, when push comes to shove, most would hope to go, though I hear the way into it is tinier than the eye of Maman's finest needle.

Consolation lies in the fact these years have made me thin.

—⟋⟍—

THE ART OF destroying took what remained of you, as addictive as sculpting had been when you were still near.

One day, Monsieur's cohort — Sylvestre, who had all but thwarted that other agent's purchase of *L'Âge Mûr*, in who knows what two-step of deviance and deceit — rapped at my shutters. He had come to wrench away what my hammer and Criteur's flames hadn't claimed.

"Go away!" I hissed, but half-heartedly, for Maman's oblivion, and yours, had consigned my mistresspiece to a final limbo that neither it nor I could see a way out of. With my muse — my hope — all but run out, I could no more finish than trash what I had begun. It's hope that lets us keep breathing, hope that makes us act. Without it the only course is suicide.

Wait for death or bring it on — what difference, if we fear no judgment? Should life be like you and simply abscond, like puddles lifting from pavement when the sun comes out, lifting soundless into nothing?

Which, in the end, is what Criteur did.

That he would betray me, to act of his own accord! At the end of a long, long winter, near the beginning of March, I caught him one day before dawn, moments before darkness entertained daylight's creep. He had wrested your piece from the wardrobe and set it on the hearth. Its faceless figures, yours and Maman's, were turned toward the grate, your closeness, your togetherness an embarrassment, a sham no more to be. Worse than wishful thinking, worse than forgery, it was a patent falsehood. Maman and the child I'd been held tightly, warmly, lovingly in her arms. A lie.

A blessing, I now see, that I hadn't fully captured you. Seeing your graven face would've shattered my heart and the warmth of anyone's illusions.

And yet I tried to stop him. Seized his hand, gripped the hammer in my fist. I did everything in my power to deflect the blows.

I'm sorry to say, your figure took the worst, bludgeoned beyond repair or recognition. Though pieces of the mother endured, my idea — the grand idea of this work to outshine all works, to bring together all that had been broken and severed — succumbed.

I don't suppose you remember what the evil one once said? "If there's anything more beautiful than a beautiful thing it is its ruin."

Criteur's rebel act, though, was fortuitous, and perhaps one of mercy. I couldn't have safeguarded the statue any longer, lacked the heart to.

A letter from a long-lost cousin from the Champagne was the cudgel landing a final blow. I knew it was bad news, just seeing his name on the envelope. You can guess the rest — to me it was a shock, the kind that stops time and sense. Papa was dead. He had died many days earlier. Not a peep from Maman or either of my siblings. No one had even thought to tell me he was sick, let alone to offer the chance to say my goodbyes. I was worse than an orphan, cut adrift with no family at all. Monsieur had fully succeeded in poisoning against me those I cherished most.

All but my faithful *praticien*, I had let myself believe.

Somewhere in the gloom, I heard Blot come and be turned away. "Shall I finish her off for you, now that your *maman*'s heart is truly stone?" Criteur offered when I took to my bed.

"Be my guest," is what he said I said.

In darkness we stumble as far from lies as we do from the truth.

Hiding under the covers, I did not, could not, watch him strike the final blow or light the fire to reduce Maman's effigy to ash. Perhaps I even slept?

Possibly, instead of destroying her, he spirited her off to Sylvestre's warehouse. A thieving traitor like the rest. Nothing would surprise me, least of all his move to the enemy camp. Was the writing on the wall?

I've not seen hide nor hair of him since. To live is to see and be seen. Friendless and without talisman or taliswoman to guide me I entered a sightless state, a blind death. Worse than having both eyes put out, it has amounted to having the nerves stripped from my fingers. Deprived of touch, of sight, what remains?

—⁂—

FOR ALL I know, it was Criteur who called Monsieur's henchmen, the helmeted goons who came one Monday morning to abduct me. Two burly men in riot gear, they were. They ambushed me, forced their way into the flat. It was an act of outright war. A small miracle they didn't shoot or toss grenades through the window. Oh, but I put up a hell of a fight, gave them everything I had at first. Flailing, thrashing, kicking and scratching to fend them off, as tough as a cat being pulled from a mouse's nest.

It was Eastertime and the walls were papered with pictures of Christ I'd cut from the paper. Lent's fourteen Stations of the Cross, the Saviour's stumble towards death — his torments and persecutions not so different from what Monsieur's mob was inflicting on me. Except, unlike Pilate, they knew what they were doing, they weren't just blindly, dumbly, following their god's plan.

"Help me!" I screamed to the stricken thorny-crowned image, screamed and screamed in vain. "Call them off!"

Wrestling me into the devil's lingerie, their *camisole,* the invaders harpooned me feet-first through the window and into their waiting *camion*, a wailing flashing ambulance.

This, oh my dear dead younger self, was my breech birth into the long dark night that's been my life ever since. So I was borne into internment — an endless nothing, a nothing without end — as innocent, as dumb, as clotted cells scraped from the womb.

"Where are you taking me? What is my crime?" I screamed, friendless, till my voice, my senses, all but abandoned me too. But don't waste your tears on me, C — God, no. Who knows but we might see each other soon, if you have the guts to come and visit and allow your face to shine upon mine. You know where to find me. Your older, wiser Camille.

27

... AND DEVOTE MYSELF TO THE WELFARE ...

MONTDEVERGUES ASYLUM
19 OCTOBER 1943

Today a fresh list of directives came down from Admin, basically ripped from the pages of *Essentials of Medicine*. Head was only too happy to share them. They were nothing new, but it gave her a charge to impress them on Novice and me. She recommended that we girls take up crocheting and pass it on to those who could benefit, with no mention of its hazardous need for a hook. She was positively gleeful — till she read out the final point, her smile withering.

"'Psychiatric nursing places an extra strain on workers' patience and imagination, as recovery is often slow and the reward of a healthy patient delayed. THEREFORE, it is incumbent upon ALL SUPERVISORS to treat staff with understanding and respect.'"

"Amen to that," said Novice.

Head quickly flipped pages to a memo, with more of what we already knew. "Consider it a refresher, Nurse," she said pointedly, clearing her throat, and went on with a list of doctors' obligations.

Novice interrupted. "If that's it, I've got fifty sponge baths waiting."

If only sponge baths were all I'd had ahead of me. The shift started off with "artwork" on the wall — someone's finger-painting, more or less. Dear God, the things that can be accomplished with feces. With no orderly available to remove it, I found a scrub brush and applied my own elbow grease.

Having just mentioned occupational therapy, Head saw an opportunity. "You, Poitier. Since you have an obvious appreciation for guests expressing themselves," she smiled, "and the need to ingratiate yourself to Admin, you might consider volunteering. Extracurricular activities do help, you know. Keep guests and staff out of mischief. It's not too early to start considering Christmas."

A pageant, she meant. Novice had filled me in. The dreaded pageant was a yearly entertainment staged by the guests for the hospital's holiday enjoyment. I'd seen a few handbills from last year's event lying around.

"I'm sure you can organize something. Maybe your scribe, Mademoiselle, could help you write a play. Pity we didn't ask her brother for tips when he was here." Presumptuous as can be, her tone actually made me smile. "Think about it, Nurse. You could have some fun. And in the meantime, when our new directeur takes action —"

"But I thought —"

"That by now he would've? Yes. Well. He has things well in hand, I'm sure. Don't think for a moment you're off the hook for what you did. A little advice: I wouldn't second-guess Admin. The pageant looks very good on a resumé —"

"A play? You expect me to do a play —"

"You have a problem with that, Poitier? Oh, I see — it would cut into your off-hours."

I couldn't help thinking of Head's role model, the famous *surveillante* at the Salpêtrière, Maman Bottard, who did not leave her workplace once in three solid years — or was it six? Did she figure in some drama of our supervisor's making?

I said I'd think about the pageant, and I did, for the ten minutes it took to thoroughly scrub my hands. Even then a dead meat smell clung to them.

A play, for pity's sake. I could barely wrap my head around it. Something based on an Aesop's fable, some story featuring a tortoise and a hare, a tale about the nature of success? Or a fox and a rabbit, plus a cat — we could use Mademoiselle's — and a mole, a part made for Head. The moral of the story: *Keep your eyes on the prize, even if doing so is fairly pointless.* Something Sister might say, something which could seem vaguely uplifting for all but the most afflicted?

No play. A play is above and beyond the call of a Bottard and Nightingale, and where I draw the line.

—⁂—

ATTENDING AT DEATH is a necessary part of the job. "Think of the body as a house being vacated. Being objective helps," Sister Ursula told me the first time. "You're ushering the occupant to freedom. That's it." Never mind that she also said a camel would sooner squeeze through a needle's eye than the rich enter glory's gates.

Am I wrong in thinking helping a patient die is midwifery in reverse? Though it's easier for a baby's crowning head to exit the cervix, I suspect, than for a sane goner to wish the world goodbye.

I cannot help but compare everything to labour and delivery, to memories of mine. That day only the sisters' capable hands kept me from going completely off my nut. The pain of transition,

I've read, is like sustaining twenty bone fractures at once. A mercy I didn't know that at the time. I was too green to ask for anything for it. No nitrous oxide, morphine or "twilight drug," scopolamine. Was suffering enough to make me a martyr, make my resumé like Mademoiselle Bottard's?

"You don't want to forget," my midwife-sister had said. One doesn't forget, certainly not the pain. Oh, I remembered well enough to never put myself back in the position of repeating it. Maybe in that respect I am more like Florence and Marguerite, who stayed single all their lives.

I thought of Renard with a vague, rather generalized regret. Now that he was dead, I could almost call it a longing.

During delivery it helps greatly to dim the room. Different with the dying, though. As their sight fades it helps if they have good light. One wants to keep things bright to the end. If I could have, I'd have prised the bars one by one from Mademoiselle's window.

From the moment I stepped into her room, it unnerved me how her soft cries, tiny complaints, almost mimicked a newborn's. Not just those of any newborn, but of mine. As Sister said, it was — it is — a blessing that new babies can't talk. Nobody holds their hands through the ordeal.

I held Mademoiselle's hand continuously, massaged each burled knuckle. Her cries strengthened at times, as if she were rallying. "Soon I'll be there, won't I, Nurse? He's waiting, you see. In Villeneuve. Papa," she murmured feverishly. "*Coq au vin* for lunch. In the garden. Papa and I. We will draw lines, he and I ... in the dirt. I'll listen ... listen for insects, worms ..."

Her face was greyish. Her nightie was damp with sweat, her dressings too, despite her skin being cool to the touch. Her feet were cold, a mottled blue. Try as I might to keep the blanket on them, she repeatedly worked it off. A dreadful pity I hadn't gotten to her sooner. Morphine would've helped, though if the patient was hallucinating on her own — seeing bugs? — it wouldn't've been so good. But a moderate dose earlier on, staggered with small ones of scopolamine, would've helped keep things hazy, or hazier.

She moaned for her pen. "Before lunch ... please, Polange Soitier ... a few things I must say." Giving the patient that leaky implement was out of the question, but there was a pencil. I curled her fingers around it, clamping them with mine as gently as if they were a baby's, yet as firmly as when the midwife held my knees together to prevent untimely pushing and tearing.

It was hopeless. By now poor Mademoiselle had lost much of her grip. I offered to take dictation. "You didn't know I could be a secretary, did you, dear?" No holds barred when it came to keeping my voice bright. As if telegraphed from Lyon, Sister's words clicked through my head. *Be alert but calm. Nowhere are poise and optimism required as urgently as with the dying.*

Mademoiselle eyed me with a sudden sharpness. "Why so glum, Solange Poitier? Afraid we'll miss lunch? Not much time, you know, before the train comes. The train, it's coming. No criminals aboard this time ... no one suffering from dersecution pelirium." She choked on a laugh. Her mouth open, she was struggling to get her breath. "As they said I did." Slowly she rolled her eyes, which were already filmy. "As if they didn't fear the worst like the rest of us."

"Who shall we address it to, honey?" I cushioned everything with gentleness, as much gentleness as I had in me, wishing for more. In that moment I saw only my shortcomings. The weeks of tending Mademoiselle flooded back, the things she'd told me, fibs and white lies, word salad or not. If only there were a way of avoiding or skipping beyond the rest, the rest to come. Death has a way of setting even the most seasoned of us on edge. If only someone less familiar, less partial could take over from here, I thought, relieve me at least until it was over.

The nurse remains with the patient as long as there are signs of life, except during visits from family.

An urgency overtook Mademoiselle. "'To Monsieur.' *C'est ça*. But hurry. They're holding lunch." She fussed, twisting the bedclothes feebly in her fists. "Bring my shoes! My shoes, if you please."

A little Veronal would have helped, but like morphine, it is now in short supply, reserved for more active cases.

The patient's breath came in slow, shallow puffs. "'Monsieur,' that will do," she repeated, more agitated, and gave a name that rang a bell, a name the world had heard of, not that it was especially meaningful to me. A sculptor who'd died during the last war, I seemed to recall, setting down the pencil.

"It would make you feel better — and be of more use — if you'd let me change those dressings."

But she'd begun to ramble again, a dreary recitation. It took a second to sink in that I was meant to jot all of this down. "'You never saw them cut off my hair, strip me naked and toss me into a scalding tub, a roomful of lunatics watching. You were spared. I should've let you drown me like you did Cléome, poor Cléome. What you committed was worse than ... Yet I was punished like a murderer,'" she spat, struggling to sit up as if the recipient, this lucky Monsieur, had come to face her. "'My crime? Liking cats more than people — is that so bad? Yet all these years I've been locked away with lunatics. Lunatics who shape things from shit. Be glad I never wrote you in blood.'"

Just then it struck me. Where was the cat? I hadn't seen it in a while. Had it got lost outside, run over, or eaten by some other creature? God help me, I thought of the pageant, of guests dressed as hounds, their enthusiastic barking, Novice as the baby, me as myself, Head playing the wolf. But no cat. I didn't dare mention it; I could barely scribble Mademoiselle's words down fast enough. My hand started to cramp. "Are you finished?" I asked very softly.

My patient was beyond listening. "'May you rot in hell, Rodin,'" she continued to rant, though her voice wasn't more than a rasp, "'even if hell is the price I'll pay for my hatred. Sincerely,'" she sighed, "'Your Mademoiselle.'"

Flexing my fingers, I steadied myself. "While we're at it," — I made my voice as pleasant, as disengaged as could be — "shall I take one down for Mr. Criteur, too? You've written him before."

But Mademoiselle lay back against the pillow, exhausted. Her eyes were hollow, her lips parched from breathing through her mouth. I was so caught up in her dictation I'd somehow forgotten to keep them moistened.

At precisely this moment, Head decided to pop in. I fully expected to be called away. A fresh influx of guests were expected this afternoon, and extra beds from Men's already clogged the downstairs corridor.

"We could use you on first, in fact we need you. But," — she went silent, sizing things up — "since you're occupied, Novice will simply have to cope. Damn this war anyway, and all that comes with it."

Was I hearing correctly?

Not entirely to my surprise, she complained how the new directeur was already proving to be quite lame in finding a remedy for overcrowding. No doubt his failure so far to act on my "meddling and disobedience," and whatever Head might've said about the company I kept, wasn't winning him any favour.

The patient began moaning again. "They punished *me* for thinking the worst! Death is the worst, isn't it?" She almost seemed to gloat, gazing at Head. Mocking her?

"I'll call the chaplain," Head volunteered, escaping.

There's nothing to fear, nothing that's too painful to bear when you're in good hands, so the midwife-sister had assured me. Yet fear had muscled in, of course, in the greyness of my lying strapped to a gurney. *Never forget the pain, though; remembering it might keep you out of trouble, might even help you.* It did, too, making it easier, maybe, to imagine myself being inside the skins of some patients.

It's odd how, to the professional observer, the dying become nothing more than the bodies they are shedding, the leaky vessels less and less able to contain them. There's no fooling it. The body knows best.

The patient laughed feebly once we were alone again. "All their finery, all their *accoutrements*, all the things these jailers use ... but my age saved me from a chastity belt."

All I could think to say was, "Where, dear, should I send your note?"

The patient shifted restlessly, struggling again to work the covers from her feet. "Water. Please, Maman. I'm thirsty."

I held the glass to her lips and she managed a sip. Dipping a cotton ball, I dribbled water on her tongue.

Mademoiselle's toenails were blue, very blue, and the skin almost bruised-looking from the blood congesting in the veins. Gently I massaged the joints of each toe, the balls of each foot, the heels, as if readying an athlete's for a competitive sprint. A marathon. It almost amused me to think this. Whose toes had hers stepped on? Whose had they prodded, nudged and stroked? What lanes and alleyways had they tramped, the feet of a *flâneur*? What paths had they buffed in the same tired linoleum? It hurt to think.

Dr. Cadieu slipped in silently, touched Mademoiselle's hand then stood at the foot of the bed. "Mademoiselle made beautiful things, once," she said quietly. "I tried to encourage her, you see, hoped she'd continue. Therapy. She thought we were using her. Exploiting her, you know." She smiled wanly and patted my shoulder. "Sad, I realize, when they go. A relief, though, in many ways."

Then Novice peeked in, bringing rubbing alcohol. "All that doodling, letters to nowhere — you think they helped her?" Maybe the most observant thing anybody thought to say during the patient's stay and her active dying.

"Helped him, certainly — the brother." Cadieu's words had a tinge of sarcasm.

"How much longer, do you think?" Novice asked, as only a novice could.

It scratched at my resolve, arousing stubbornness in me. As surely as a fighter plane falling from the sky, Sister Ursula's convictions came to roost. "What are hours, do you suppose, compared to thirty years?"

The patient's eyelids fluttered. A flash of darkness seemed to cross her gaze. "Papa? You forgive me, don't you? ... It's hot ... so hot. Open the windows ... please, please ... Where is my friend the mistral?"

Novice began to rub the patient's wrists and shins, but the spirits she'd brought were bracing flesh already slackened and chilled. One shake of my head and off she scurried, just in time to make way for the chaplain.

He nodded, his gaunt smile lending the dimness a certain ... eminence?

"Don't leave," Mademoiselle cried out. So of course I stayed, lingering by the window as if I weren't there.

"Bless me, Father. It's been a ... thousand years ... since my last confession."

I tried, I really did, not to listen. Not that there was much to hear.

He pardoned her sins, whatever they might be, and after anointing her gave his blessing, his hand slicing the air into four neat blocks. "Go in peace," he said, as if sending the guest on an errand. With a stab of regret I thought again of Renard.

"My shoes — where are my shoes?" the patient wept.

And there was Head again, suddenly offering to relieve me. "You've been here all day. Get some tea, have a nap. I don't mind staying."

To call this a change of attitude would be like calling transition a painless shift, or whiplash a minor jolt. Given our new charges and dreading the extra work, had Head realized she could do worse in a subordinate?

A break would've been welcome, but I waved her off.

"Try to rest," I told my patient, this patient that despite all my pledges of fairness and impartiality, despite her intransigence and unpredictability, I'd grown fond of. "You want to be in good shape for that train, when it comes."

She seemed to sleep then, a little.

The light at the window went from gold to grey — the same dull pewter as the delivery room's half of my lifetime ago. The shaming, mysterious colour of secrecy, I couldn't keep from thinking. "What did you name him?" I'd asked Sister Ursula, the only one I could ask, because despite her penchant for quoting scripture, she was reliably frank.

"The priest christened him. The parents chose the name."

"But can't you tell me what it is? Please?"

"You're not privy to this, Nurse, remember: Leo. Short and sweet. That's what they called him, I believe."

In the weakening sunlight of Mademoiselle's room — the bars a solid black against thickening grey — I pictured an infant with reddish-gold hair and I pictured the boy with the gunshot wound, his features oddly melded, in my memory, with Renard's. From what little I'd seen in the firelight, his dark hair had darts of auburn, like that other boy's, the one who had fathered my boy.

The patient stirred, sending my thoughts packing. "Cat?" she cried succinctly. Her face was the same sallow grey as the room, but with a strange illumination. In a queer burst of strength she tried to raise herself, clutching at my wrists with the fierceness of someone delivering — and I pictured myself gripping the midwife's hands, growling with pain, pushing.

I've seen it often enough, this desperate last-ditch clinging to life. As useful as clinging to a sapling in a flood, hoping to outlast the torrent.

Beyond the dove-grey pane, birds squabbled. Nightingales? Of course not. It was barely evening, though one loses track of time. Death scrubs all meaning from it.

I freed myself from the patient's grip and gently eased her down onto the mattress. Sighing, she offered a fleeting smile.

I'd been at the bedside how many days, hours?

Somebody was weeping. It could only have been me. No one else was in the room besides the patient, her mouth open, a gateway.

Pressing my face to hers, I felt for a pulse. "Run," I told the wetness on her cooling cheek. "The train is there. Hurry, and you'll just make it."

Only then did the cat reappear. Reflecting the corridor's light, its gaze had an alien glow. Perhaps it had been there all along, hiding under the bed.

—✴—

CADIEU SIGNED THE certificate. Head was quite emotional. Apparently when she's upset, her nose reddens as if she's breathed in something caustic. "You've done your duty, Nurse. Well done," she said, an unusual blankness to her tone.

Following protocol, I closed the eyes and mouth, straightened the arms at the sides, elevated the head, placed a rolled-up towel under the neck. *Think of the body as a house.* Working from the attic to the cellar, I washed it, replacing the dressings and removing adhesive marks with benzine. I jotted the name, date and *Pavilion 10* on the tag and attached it to a wrist. Let the morgue worry about assigning a number. I placed the top sheet on the diagonal and used it to wrap the body, which was shockingly light. *Naked I came forth from my mother's womb, and naked shall I go back again* — the words of Sister's long-suffering prophet Job, as I recall. Then came the itemized list, clothing and other belongings, what few there were, tallied, bundled, tagged. I was careful to include the brother's gifts — all but the nightie untouched.

Next were the letters to deal with, the note to "Monsieur," and several to some equally mysterious friends or relatives. I tucked the wad of papers and Novice's bottle of rubbing alcohol into my apron bib, and took both list and bundle down to the desk.

Then I remembered there was one item I'd neglected. I hurried back upstairs. The orderlies hadn't yet removed the body. Careful not to look at the shrouded form, I peered beneath the bed. Mademoiselle's pet, its hostile eyes quite fearful. A bucking live-wire, it gave me a nasty scratch when I hauled it out, its heart pounding against mine as I clutched it, all four of its paws gripped in my fist.

Downstairs, Cadieu happened to be there, issuing instructions for someone's meds. She ignored my burden and held something out to me. Wrapped in newspaper was a leaden object, irregularly shaped. A large stone? "For you," the doctor said. "A friend let me have it years ago; actually, Mademoiselle's friend in Paris. I bought it from him. A pleasant old man — a Monsieur Blot. He tried keeping in touch with her till he died. He wanted us all to know what she was capable of." Her arms folded tightly, she looked brittle and old, almost as hawkish as Mademoiselle's brother, yet her smile was shy. "You should have it, Nurse."

Still clasping the cat, I loosened the paper and saw that it was a head — a head made of dull metal, bronze maybe, with what resembled a delicate tree trunk for a neck. Its face was a child's, the expression on it half-sorrowful, half-hopeful. *Soulful,* Sister might call it, facetious or not. Its eyes were opened wide and its lips parted as if to pose a question — a childish, hopeful one, the kind of question my father had usually answered with *We'll see.* Its hair was made to look shorn, a modest adornment, not flatter-ing, a little like a nun's. A girl's hair, I decided, but no, it could as easily have been a boy's. At the bottom was engraved that signa-ture so often and doggedly scrawled, Mademoiselle's initial and last name.

"If only it could speak." Cadieu's eyes were wistful, her shoulders stooped under her ragged white coat. "Take it, Miss Poitier," she said. There was no pushing it back at her; before I could try to she shuffled away.

My supervisor emerged out of nowhere and laughed too loudly when she saw me juggling the letters, the cat, and now the head. "Oh, for heaven's sake. Put your feet up, I'll have someone from Men's cover the rest of your shift." She reached to take the cat off my hands, but the thing hissed and swiped at her. "Well, maybe between here and the dorm you'll find a hole for it to disappear into. Believe me, it won't be missed."

IN MY ROOM, I dragged my suitcase from under the bed and abandoned the creature to the dust bunnies there. I removed my cache of notes, rewrapped the head, and laid it inside the suitcase. Fortunately I'm no clothes horse, otherwise it wouldn't have fit.

While I was at it I took out my silver cigarette case, hopeful, though of course the last cigarette had been made short work of. Its real treasure was still inside, though — the thing I'd stored and avoided, that I'd hardly been able to touch, loath to really, all these years. A wisp of pale reddish cornsilk, a curl of baby hair. *You mustn't let on*, Sister had said. *But I saved this for you.*

The cat yowled from its hideout. I'd have to find it some food, let it outside to do its business. But just now I had more pressing concerns. Uncorking the wine left after the suicide, I sipped some from the bottle in a sort of toast.

I laid out Mademoiselle's letters and unfolded them one by one. First, the note to "Monsieur." Somebody might want a note to a real, if dead, artist. I didn't feel I could just rip it up. I rolled it into a tiny tube and tucked it beside the baby hair, then slipped the case inside the secret lining of my purse.

I began reading the next letter, which crackled in my hands. It felt like an odd thing to do. Disloyal. It felt like prying. But then I thought of what Sister had said, back in training, about listening, and listening, and listening some more, and how we serve by assuming others' burdens. *For my yoke is easy and my burden is light.*

The letter began, *Dear Friend*, and pride spurred me to think it was for me. Mademoiselle's voice lifted from the page, hovering.

I always thought you were jealous: I was the one who turned Monsieur's head, the more gifted, prettier. You made me look bad to Maman, encouraged Monsieur to take advantage of me. You were not so good or deserving as I. Having a husband, a family, was so bourgeois — beneath me. I would never envy you. Pffft!

But I did. I do.

By the time you came to see me here it was too late to make up for my own jealousy, meanness. You were good to come after so long, you and your husband. He did like taking pictures, didn't he.

You were kind not to forget your poor friend in an insane asylum, you were kind to visit her. I wish I had been kinder to you, Jessie. If I take any regret to my grave, I wish I'd been a better friend.

I took up some other missives, a whole raft of them addressed to "C," her mysterious genderless penpal. Sipping wine — and eventually polishing off the bottle — I read with some interest, in fits and starts, as much as I could stick with them anyway. Mostly I skimmed. They were largely word salad, but aspects of them made me feel like a snoop, trading sound observation for prurient fascination, no better than happening by a patient's door and lingering to watch them masturbate. Not that her musings were titillating. Far from it, bits and pieces of them were dead familiar, recalling more than a few of the little rants and phobias that Mademoiselle had used to distract us from the task at hand. Especially bathing, I thought with a smile.

Not knowing quite what to do with them, I set the letters aside. Turning them over to Admin would feel disrespectful and only waste Secretary's time, not to mention the new directeur's. It would also be a betrayal, not just of the patient, but of the old directeur — the one whose only fault, as far as I could tell, was the laxness that sometimes accompanies kindness. The letter to the friend I folded into a triangle. A paper hat for the head inside my suitcase? Or a paper boat, that was more like it, one that fit nicely into my purse.

Finally, using the last of my stationery — the backs of two discarded electroencephalograms — I wrote to the new man, then copied it out for Head. If I'd had more paper I'd have written a copy for Lyon, too. It took no time to find the words, no fuss no muss. The extremely short notice was something I sincerely regretted. But I had more urgent work to attend to, more pressing duties, and they should have no trouble finding a more qualified replacement — of that I was confident, I wrote, signing my name under *Respectfully submitted.*

Mademoiselle's pet leapt to the sill, then scrambled from there to the bed, eyeing the tarnished crucifix positioned like a large gnat on the wall. These busy weeks I'd come to barely see it, except when it reminded me of Sister.

How would she have handled the letters?

I took them to the loo and tore them up very carefully, being sure to flush away all the pieces.

The cat was right at home when I came back, nestled on my psych notes. Though I was a little afraid it might pee on them — whoever inherited the room might find them useful — I resisted the urge to push it off. After a while, it traded them for my lap, and then my chest, purring and kneading with its claws. There was something about its prodding — a kitten rooting for the mother cat's teat? — that drew out what I'd largely succeeded in avoiding all day.

It's stupid to cry. It's stupid to cry. *Buck up*, I told myself. There might well be a better place.

I blew my nose. Still a couple more details to attend to, there always are: some sort of wrap-up to this conscientious examination, and then a tiny flask of water from Lourdes to dispose of. Not as useful as Veronal, but unlike Veronal it has no best-before date. A gift for Sister, perhaps — water in exchange for hair, the gift that had broken a thousand rules and directives. Had she known all along that the boy — if the boy in my mind could possibly be the same one — was here in the Vaucluse, in Montfavet? Hair in exchange for water. Except I'd need a river of miracle water to find Renard's young friend.

As for said wrap-up, I suspect that my reportage has been largely fruitless — a failure, in fact. The heart wants what the heart wants. Juggling what one is given with what one hopes for reveals only that one tries one's best. What's best for one often contravenes what's best for another. Yet one perseveres. *C'est fini.*

28

... OF THOSE COMMITTED TO MY CARE.

MONTFAVET STATION,
ABOARD MARSEILLES-LYON-PARIS EXPRESS
ETA LYON 16:00 HEURES
AWAITING DEPARTURE: 11H12
21 OCTOBER 1943

Sister says we're called to be God's hands. Does writing qualify? I have my doubts, but it has become a habit I'm not quite ready to give up just yet, at least while idle. Idling gives rise to loose-cannon thoughts.

When I handed in my notice, Head was aghast. "Is there nothing we can do to change your mind?" *And after I've bent over backwards for you,* her eyes said while she shook my hand, likely about as easy for her as shaking de Gaulle's.

Novice cried and the burliest orderly hugged me. Patting Novice's arm, I told her she'd do just fine. Isn't it what we're put on Earth for, to build others up? Even when there's no telling what happens, whether badness prevails or good.

The soldiers inspecting our papers have come and gone, and despite finding all in order, they saw fit to search and then confiscate my suitcase — due to its weight! The books at least can be replaced, and my uniform, but not, regretfully, Cadieu's *cadeau*.

Writing takes my mind off it. So let's start where I ended, bidding Montdevergues goodbye.

—m—

JUST COME FROM the chapel, the coffin waited on a wagon, raw wood and metal numbers glinting in the autumn sun. The new priest, the old nun from *Bon Repos*, and the chaplain, gathered at the gates — a prim-looking company, except for the nervous pastor robed in white. A tall, dark-haired, drop-dead handsome young man, he waited as I came struggling up juggling my purse, suitcase, and the cat wrapped in a sweater. The front of my cape was already plastered in orange hairs, no thanks owed to the sweater. "So God numbers the ones on our heads," the young priest murmured. Equally anxious to get a move on, the horse pawed the ground and dropped a load of dung.

The gateman, keeper of keys, nodded as if I'd soon be back.

When we started walking, it was a small ordeal to keep up. I could barely contain the animal in my arms. No luck finding anyone to take it off my hands, aside from Cook, who proffered a potato sack and a boy to throw it into the canal. That and a word of condolence. "You must miss Renard," she said.

I brought up the rear, not looking back. I couldn't. Everything I owned was piled inside my suitcase, including Cadieu's ungainly present — everything except this notebook, and what was in my purse, and what I had in mind: one could call it a mission, though ambition's a better word. Whatever a person needs to move on in this life.

The planes' leaves had turned a khaki green, dead ones sifting down. The climbing sun felt brilliant if remote, the air sharp enough that steam rose from the *merde* on the pavement. Thank goodness it wasn't too far to the graveyard, that barren field near the road, with its little smattering of crosses arranged as in a war cemetery, a proper one, row on row. Our party barely spoke and no one new joined in. The whole world was busy, I suppose, peeling potatoes, wiping bottoms, posting mail, milking cows, minding lunatics, whatever people get up to at 08H30 on a crisp Thursday morning. Not that it affected me. The rest of my day — my life — stretched like the woods and fields around us.

It was so quiet, I noticed. Apart from Cat's scrabbling and the horse's clopping, the only sound was of leaves shuffling along the ground. So quiet one could almost believe in peace.

Hanging on to Cat for dear life, purse slung over one shoulder, I propped my suitcase against the cemetery's little wall to collect myself. Some pink roses clung to a bush nearby. I broke one off, hooking myself on a thorn and losing Cat in the bargain. Gone, just like that, in a mad tussle of claws and teeth. Before I could even think to catch her, she scooted into the bushes by the canal, her coat a camouflage against the rust-coloured brush. The others kept going; those men taking down the coffin weren't wasting time.

Beside the open grave — a common one, of course — the religious caught their breath. The comb lines in the pastor's hair were pleasantly undisturbed though his chasuble fluttered in the breeze. Its gilt embroidery caught the sun, which was busily warming fresh-turned earth and the crawl of worms. He stretched out his arms as if welcoming us all to a feast. I couldn't help studying his shoes and his lacy hem as we prayed along — well, as I mouthed the words, sending Mademoiselle on her way to heaven, one only hopes. Or purgatory, or wherever one goes first. I like to think there is a beforehand, some place where people hover for a while, before judgment swoops in and snaps them up. *If there's any fairness*, I wanted to shout, *this woman's had her hell and won't wind up there*. In much the same way, I think of Renard and even my mother. We each of us are our own little balls of hell at times.

When a fistful of dirt hit the coffin, I threw in the rose, a confetti of petals shadowed by birds circling overhead. Swallows or magpies, they made quite a racket squawking their hellos and goodbyes.

"Good to see you — and bless you," the chaplain said over a handshake, eyeing my overstuffed purse.

"Souvenirs," I said. And severance pay, travelling papers, and dreams, my dreams.

"Should I wish you bon voyage?"

No sign whatsoever of Cat. It was as if she were a figment or an imaginary friend, a mostly hostile one I'd accommodated briefly. Plenty of mice in the fields, birds too, I told myself — and doorsteps bearing saucers of milk, God willing. In the name of Mademoiselle, Cat and all her other fur persons, real or imagined, I blessed myself, and stumbled off. My journey would be less complicated and lighter with one less creature to tend.

Speaking of lighter, I remembered the crinkled paper boat in my purse — a swan, I decided, nearing the petite canal. Its narrow bed hugged the roadside, its pea-green current slipping underground every so often. Moving as steadily as any God-made stream, possibly with less effort, it quenched the countryside's thirst even as it fed the Rhône. Who remembered what hands had built it? Nobody, I'll bet, its builders long gone.

Mademoiselle's swan-boat floated and spun there, soaking up the wet. Her writing, and those faint pink zigzags — lightning, mountain peaks and valleys — instantly leached away. When it snagged on a leaf, it wasn't a swan or a boat but a guest strapped to a bed, frozen. The leaf, curled and coloured like a cigar, reminded me of the paper tube in my silver cigarette case, so I pulled it out and threw it in too. In her right mind, Mademoiselle might have approved. What's the point of hating?

And now the first note, the one to her friend, was free. Off they both raced, sliding through a grate and down into the earth and, just like Cat, gone. Through the village, under the square, past the church and the dusty courtyard where men — men too old and too tired of war to fight over anything, I suspect — smoke and shoot *boules*. Then on to the river both would go, and with the river south, like the mistral.

You have to be open to God's will, Sister says. Whatever that means. Like the other winds, Cat and my boy — wherever he is — I guess we go where we will. Maybe I'll ride through to Paris to see statues and rip down Nazi flags in the streets, or get off in Lyon and join the convent or the Maquis. See where the northbound wind takes me, though Lyon is a good place to begin. My purpose is like the wind; my ambitions, our country's, and my son. A proper thing, too. Wherever he is, he is, whether I search and never find him, or whether I search and do.

ACKNOWLEDGEMENTS

Camille Claudel's art is at last widely celebrated, but until very recently — to North Americans — her accomplishment was entirely overshadowed by her fame as Rodin's mistress, his "tragic muse" who spent thirty years in an asylum for the insane. I first heard of Claudel a decade ago, when her story was mentioned in passing by two of my students. I was instantly hooked by her tragedy and then compelled to seek out her sculpture. I soon learned that she's legendary in France, for her work as much as her biography, coloured as both are by her mental illness. What I was to discover, travelling several times to France and experiencing her work first-hand, is how brilliantly it outshines the limits of its creation — circumstances driven by the rampant misogyny of her day. She lived for her art in a time when a woman's doing so was in itself a certain madness, especially a woman working in a medium known for its difficulty. The world was kinder to her teacher Rodin, who began an affair with her in the 1880s, when he was in his early 40s and Camille was still a teenager — a situation numerous biographers have glossed as being *de rigueur,* a part of artistic collaboration.

Plus ça change?

Time can be a bit of a healer, art too, though not always on its maker's terms or in her lifetime. As much now as in Camille's day, progress requires an army of supporters.

Too many to name have made this book possible. Thanks go to the students who first tipped me off to Camille's story, and to my late mother, Marion Bruneau, RN, valedictorian of her 1951 nursing class. Without her stories, the inspiration of her textbooks, the notes she took in training and the hospital scenarios she exposed me to, Nurse Poitier never would've reached the page. Also helpful were friends who shared professional expertise in mental health care, Dr. Mary Lynch, Nora Askew, and Pamela Donoghue. Many others helped nurse the manuscript through various stages, reading and offering feedback: Cindy Handren, Dawn Rae Downton, Sheree Fitch, Valerie Compton, Shaun Bradley, Catherine Marjoribanks, Bruce Erskine, and Michael Mirolla. Special thanks go to my publisher, Marc Côté, for seeing the true potential in the work, and to Bryan Jay Ibeas, editor extraordinaire whose brilliance helped me realize it. Still others provided encouragement when the project itself seemed terminal, as in lacking viability: Shawn Brown; the late Elizabeth Williams, whose creative spirit continues to inspire me; my inimitable writers' group, Lorri Neilsen Glenn, Binnie Brennan and Ramona Lumpkin; my sons Andrew, Seamus and Angus Erskine, and my dear travellin' partner, Bruce, who willingly retraced Camille's steps with me in some peculiar places.

For its support of the early research and writing of this book I'm grateful to the Canada Council for the Arts, and to Dorothy Sedgwick for her list of reference texts. I'm indebted to Claudel's biographers, especially Odile Ayral-Clause for *Camille Claudel: A Life*, and Reine-Marie Paris, whose *Camille: The Life of Camille Claudel*, translated from the French by Liliane Emery Tuck, includes the artist's correspondence held by the Bibliothèque Nationale in Paris. Numerous Rodin biographers have touched on Claudel, but most helpful were Ruth Butler and Rodin's contemporaries, Judith Cladel and Paul Gsell, whose writings contextualize and, whether or not intentionally, confirm the breadth of her achievement.

The headings for Nurse's chapters are from "The Nightingale Pledge," widely available online. The epigram is from *Rilke's Book of Hours: Love Poems to God*, translated by Anita Barrows and Joanna Macy, New York: Riverhead Books, 2005.

Mademoiselle's answers, on page 171 to questions in a friend's "Album of Confessions" — a popular form of amusement at the time — are based on a document in Musée Rodin Archives, dated May 16, 1888. The complete list of Claudel's original answers are in French and their translation appears in Odile Ayral-Clause's *Camille Claudel: A Life*, pp. 67–68.

NSCAD University and my colleagues there deserve ongoing thanks for nurturing artists and art students including Dorothy Skutezky, who graciously walked me through the old sculpture studio at Fountain Campus, and for the school's library and its wonderful staff. Thanks, too, go to Dalhousie University for its Writer-in-Residence program, which supported this project. Numerous other institutions helped sustain my interest, and visits to all of these were inspiring: the Centre Hospitalier in Montfavet, Vaucluse, France; the Nova Scotia Hospital's Mount Hope Library; Musée Sainte-Croix in Poitiers, France; Musée Rodin, Musée d'Orsay, Musée Bourdelle and Musée Jean Moulin in Paris; and the Art Gallery of Nova Scotia in Halifax. Most fortuitous of all were the 2008 Fundación Mapfre exhibition, *Camille Claudel*, which opened at Musée Rodin on the first day of my first trip to

Paris, and the permanent exhibition of Claudel's work in Poitiers, the city of my ancestors.

A SELECTED BIBLIOGRAPHY OF HELPFUL TEXTS

TEXTS ON CLAUDEL

Ayral-Clause, Odile. *Camille Claudel: A Life*. New York: Harry N. Abrams, 2002.

Bond, Alma. *Camille Claudel, a novel*. Baltimore: PublishAmerica, 2006.

Caranfa, Angelo. *Camille Claudel: A Sculpture of Interior Solitude*. London: Associated University Presses, 1999.

Claudel, Camille. *Camille Claudel: 1864–1943*. Madrid, Paris: Fundación Mapfre/Museé Rodin/Gallimard, 2008.

Delbée, Anne, translated by Carol Cosman. *Camille Claudel: Une Femme*. San Francisco: Mercury House, 1992.

Paris, Reine-Marie, translated by Liliane Emery Tuck. *Camille: The Life of Camille Claudel, Rodin's Muse and Mistress*. New York: Arcade Publishing, 1984.

Paris, Reine-Marie. *Camille Claudel*. Washington, D.C.: National Museum of Women in the Arts, 1988.

TEXTS ON RODIN

Butler, Ruth, ed. *Rodin in Perspective*. Englewood Cliffs, New Jersey: Prentice-Hall, 1980.

Butler, Ruth. *Rodin: The Shape of Genius*. New Haven and London: Yale University Press, 1993.

Crone, Rainer and Salzmann, Siegfried, eds. *Rodin: Eros and Creativity*. Munich: Prestel-Verlag, 1992.

Descharnes, Robert and Chabrun, Jean-Francois. *Auguste Rodin*. Secaucus, New Jersey: Chartwell Books, 1967.

Elsen, Albert E. *In Rodin's Studio: A Photographic Record of Sculpture in The Making*. Ithaca, New York: Cornell University Press, 1980.

Grunfeld, Frederic V. *Rodin: A Biography*. New York: Henry Holt, 1987.

Geffroy, Gustave. "The Sculptor Rodin." *Arts and Letters*. London, 1889, 289–304, quoted in Butler, *Rodin in Perspective*.

Gsell, Paul, translated by Mrs. Romilly Fedden. *Art by Auguste Rodin*. New York: Hodder and Stoughton, 1912.

Hale, William Harlan. *The World of Rodin: 1840–1917*. New York: Time-Life Books, 1969.

Rodin, Auguste. *Rodin*. London: Phaidon Press, 1951.

NURSING-RELATED TEXTS

Bostridge, Mark. *Florence Nightingale: The Making of an Icon*. New York: Farrar, Straus and Giroux, 2008.

Cooper, Lenna F. and Barber, Edith M., and Mitchell, Helen S. *Nutrition in Health and Disease*. 9th edition. Philadelphia: J.B. Lippincott Company, 1943.

Dorland, W.A. Newman, ed. *American Pocket Medical Dictionary*. 17th edition. Philadelphia: W.B. Saunders Company, 1943.

Emerson, Charles Phillips MD and Taylor, Jane Elizabeth RN. *Essentials of Medicine*. 14th edition. Philadelphia: J.B. Lippincott Company, 1940.

Gill, Gillian. *Nightingales: The Extraordinary Upbringing and Curious Life of Miss Florence Nightingale.* New York: Ballantine Books, 2004.

Harmer, Bertha, RN, and Henderson, Virginia, RN. *Textbook of the Principles and Practices of Nursing.* 4th edition. New York: The MacMillan Company, 1939.

Schultheiss, Katrin. *Bodies and Souls: Politics and the Professionalization of Nursing in France, 1880–1922.* Cambridge, Mass.: Harvard University Press, 2001.

BOOKS ON PSYCHIATRY & MENTAL HEALTH CARE

Alexander, Franz G. and Selesnick, Sheldon T. *The History of Psychiatry.* New York: The New American Library, 1966.

Goffman, Erving. *Asylums.* Garden City, New York: Doubleday, 1961.

Goss, David. *150 Years of Caring: The Continuing History of Canada's Oldest Mental Health Facility.* Saint John, New Brunswick: Mindcare New Brunswick, 1998.

McKenna, P.J. *Schizophrenia and Related Syndromes, Second Edition.* London & New York: Routledge, 2007.

BOOKS ON RELIGION

Bernstein, Marcelle. *Nuns.* London: Collins, 1976.